Eva's Gift

A.L. Walsh

Copyright © 2023, A.L. Walsh

All rights reserved. No part of this publication may be reproduced, stored in a retrieval system, transmitted in any form, or by any means, electronic, mechanical, photocopying, recording or otherwise, without the prior permission of the copyright holder.

ISBN: 978-1-913275-76-1

This book was published in cooperation with

Choice Publishing, Drogheda, Co. Louth,

Republic of Ireland.

www.choicepublishing.ie

Cover photograph courtesy of Last_firstborn from Pixabay.

Acknowledgements

This story started with a photograph, a picture on the News about a little boy who had drowned in the Mediterranean. A migrant child who hadn't made it. The first acknowledgement must be for him and for all the lost children. I would also like to acknowledge the many groups and associations who work to empower migrants every day. Some of those mentioned here are real though the individuals described, and all the characters who appear in this story, are figments of my imagination and not based on any specific people. Mary Elmes, the Irish Oskar Schindler, however, is real and I thank Clodagh Flynn, through her excellent book, *A Time to Risk All*, for bringing her to my attention.

It takes many people to turn a story into a physical book. *Eva's Gift* has benefited from the excellent advice of several, particularly the teams at Authors Publish, The Inkwell Group and Choice Publishing. I am grateful to you all.

On a more personal note, I would like to thank my first readers, Mairéad and Chloë, who have given their time, insight, and support. Their keen eyes have spotted errors and gaps but, of course, any that remain are due to my own oversight. Finally, thank you, as ever, to my family and friends and especially to you, for spending your precious time reading this story.

ALW

For all the lost children.

Go mbuailfidh tú le cineáltas ar do bhealach
May each of you meet kindness on your way

Preface

Mama! Baba! Where are you? Where did you go?

In the confusion, the girl had felt her mother's hand slip from hers. There were so many people, all trying to get on the boats. It was dark, hot, clammy. She didn't like it. She just wanted to go home, home to where her warm bed was. She wished she were there right now, with Mama telling her a goodnight story. That was her favourite time of the day, all tucked up, warm and safe, listening to her mother's voice tell of adventures in faraway lands, princes and princesses or just ordinary girls and boys doing incredible things and, most important, living happily ever after.

Mama! Baba!

Not here, not in this horrible place with strangers whispering instructions: Get on! Hurry! There's plenty of room! Move up!

Suddenly, she was lifted up and placed unceremoniously into a creaking boat. The floor was damp, cold. She was sitting beside two other children, a boy and a girl. They looked scared too and, without thinking, the girl took each by the hand and the threesome clung together silently as the boat was cast off, out into the deep, stormy seas.

Up and down. Up and down. Crash! Up again and down again. The journey went on for what seemed forever. She couldn't see anything but she felt sick and not just from the waves that bobbed them along in the darkness. No. The tightness in her gut was from fear. Fear that she would never find her family, her parents. Fear, too, that they would be afraid without her. She could not imagine how they would fare alone. She was their world and, though very little, she knew that they would never stop looking for her. With that thought, she fell asleep, exhausted from all the walking she had done in the previous days. She dreamt of safety. Soon, she would be safe. In her dreams, her trust was unwavering. The grown-ups would take care of her. That was their job, their only task. Why should she think they would fail her?

Chapter 1

'Good morning, Doctor, or should I call you Mr Neilson? I'm never sure of the correct formalities in these situations, you know, you being a surgeon and all that.'

'Good morning, Ms Murphy, isn't it? Just call me Chris. I'm not very impressed with formality, in any case.'

'Okay, Chris and do call me Jane.'

'Right, Jane it is. What can I do for you, Jane?'

What a mundane conversation! Did the man not know the effort it had taken her to get this far? Jane swallowed and took a deep breath before launching into her rehearsed speech.

'Well, I'm wondering if there's a procedure that would freshen up my face? You know, take a few years off it? I know I'm not old exactly but...' Jane trailed off and looked hopefully at the man seated across from her, expecting him to agree with her but to explain that it was fine, that such a procedure existed, was, in fact, run of the mill, routine, nothing to worry about. However, so far, the stilted introductions had done nothing to calm her nerves nor had the lack of empathy she sensed from the man behind the desk given her any encouragement. She'd never been in a surgeon's rooms before and was finding the whole process disconcerting. Still, she'd got here, that was the main thing. She'd get this expert's advice and all would be well. He'd know what to do.

Chris raised his eyes from the file he had been reading, his pen poised to make the usual professional notes that would add up to his client's profile and expectations but, contrary to his usual practice, and contrary to years of set behaviour, today something inside him snapped, like an overstretched elastic band.

After an uncomfortable silence that seemed to last forever, while Chris stared at his would-be patient – or rather his client as was the preferred term in these enlightened times – he felt his eyebrows raise up, his fists tighten and his jaw clench. And then, to his horror, out of his mouth there issued the most unprofessional stream of insults that shocked him as much as poor Ms Jane Murphy.

'I cannot believe the shallowness of women of your age, Ms Murphy – Jane. Why are you even contemplating spending what I expect is your hard-earned money on fixing a perfectly fine face that has served you reasonably well for, what, forty years? I'm not a miracle worker, Jane. And I am sick and tired of trying to accomplish the impossible for women, particularly, of a certain age who are suffering from First-World problems.' On and on the anger burst forth, words pouring out long before his brain engaged with what he was saying, every filter failing him. He would have carried on regardless if faithful Katie, his right-hand woman, hadn't rushed in to interrupt his tirade. She, and anyone unfortunate enough to be in the waiting room, had heard every word and she could only think that the best thing to do was to stop Chris from saying any more. She had never heard him speak in such a way to anyone, least of all to a client and she was horrified, not just at his breach of professionalism but at the possible reasons behind it. What had caused him suddenly to explode in such a way? Was it still to do with Sally, his wife, and the pain her death had caused him so many years ago? Surely he had recovered from that tragedy. Something else must have come to the surface for him to act this way, but, what exactly?

Chapter 2

Chris had thought all was going reasonably well in his life until yesterday, the 27th May, his forty-fifth birthday, or as well as could be expected given his circumstances. He had arrived home only to be greeted in the usual monosyllabic way by his son, Andy, and his daughter, Sophie. The only surprise had been that they were both at home for once.

'Hello, Andy. How was your day, son?'

'Fine.'

'What about you, Sophie? Anything interesting happen today?'

Sophie looked up from her phone, almost as if she were surprised to hear a voice in the real world.

'Hi, Dad. Nah, same old, same old.'

Chris had stood waiting for one of them to return the favour and ask about his day but no, their bowed heads proved they had returned to their virtual reality almost instantly. He hesitated, wondering if he should remind them that, actually, today was his birthday. He was the grand old age of forty five. After a moment, though, he decided to retreat to his own room and leave them to it. He was in no mood to celebrate in any case.

Upstairs, Chris had looked at himself in the mirror with the professional eye of a plastic surgeon and admitted he still had reasonably acceptable features: crows' feet that could pass for laughter lines, slight greying at the temples which his mother would have said made him look 'distinguished' though slightly weather beaten from cycling to work most days, an activity that also gave him his lean, sporty look. All in all, not too bad *for his age*. However, it was not his looks that were bothering him this fine autumn day. Instead, he was what was commonly known as 'taking stock'. He had built up an excellent reputation for himself in the area of plastic surgery. His name featured in most of the notable journals on the topic and he could list many a celebrity among his clients. All of which meant he was financially secure; more than that, he was what his siblings would teasingly call 'filthy rich'. Yet, what was he doing with all that cash? He rarely had time to spend any of it and he hadn't even taken a real holiday in years, not since Sally had died in a boating accident seven years back. 'Fun' was not a word that existed in his vocabulary. Not anymore.

The tragedy of his wife's death had turned him, overnight, into a single parent to two feisty teenagers, Sophie and Andy, now in their early twenties and determined to find their own way in the world with a little help from Dad's cheque book. They both still lived in the comfortable four-bedroom house on Sydney's Northern Beaches that had been their home for the whole of their lives, with Dad, of course, paying for all the amenities. Why wouldn't he? He certainly didn't begrudge them that. Yet, it was rare for the three of them to sit down to a meal together these days. One or other was always rushing out (or in), busy getting ready for the next adventure. Chris wondered when he had stopped thinking about his own adventures. Actually, he could remember the very hour and day: 11:05 am on the 6th November 2012, the day Sally had died and life as he had known it had ended.

Sally and the kids had been his reason for getting up in the morning, his source of laughter, the centre of his universe. Since his wife's death, he had been working more or less on autopilot, making sure Sophie and Andy were okay, at least financially. This particular morning, however, something had shifted in his mood. One more birthday and very little to show for it, he had to admit. Suddenly, he was wondering if there were more to do, more than fixing other people's perceptions of themselves, nipping and tucking his way through the weeks, the months, the years that were making up his rapidly passing life.

His career as a cosmetic surgeon had occurred almost without a plan. He had chosen medicine (or had it chosen him?) because his father was a GP, a general practitioner who had emigrated from Ireland in the late 1960s and had settled quickly into the heart of a small community in outback New South Wales. They had lived a simple life which Chris remembered with nostalgia - no frills, his father was fond of saying, almost with pride. Though the truth was they couldn't afford many frills. They lived in a rambling, plaster-board house, where the floors creaked and the plumbing moaned. Yet, what Chris remembered most now was how the Kookaburras sang in the morning and the cockatoos screeched in their gangs, acting like the bullies of the treetops. He could also remember the smell of eucalyptus, the smoky air in the summer that told of distant fires, some not so distant that, sometimes, crept too close for comfort. He remembered the vast night skies, where stars beckoned him to dream of far-off adventures and sun-drenched days that seemed endless.

People often paid their Doc, as his father was referred to, in kind: a chicken here, a few loaves of bread there, pots of jam, boxes of apples, pears or even a box or two of juicy mangoes at Christmas, if the season had been a good one. There were times when their house looked more like a grocery store than a home. Cash, however, was always in short supply. Outback living was always precarious, at the mercy of the climate - some summers too dry and hot, some winters too wet and cold, with either floods or bush fires a constant threat. Looking back, his parents must have lived with so many worries but they had protected their children from those adult stresses. It must have been a great relief to them when Christopher won a prestigious scholarship to Medical school. He had always been the studious one of the family but, still, his parents had been surprised at his achievement. He had a quiet way about him that often meant he was overlooked in the hurly burly of their noisy family where three boys and two girls were constantly competing for parental attention.

Years of study had followed and it had seemed at first that Chris would join his father as GP, perhaps taking over the practice when his father would retire. However, the city of Sydney had cast a certain spell over the young country lad who loved the hustle and bustle, the sense of being at the centre of things, the buzz of adrenaline the city-living provided. So, when the time came, Chris, once again, surprised all who knew him by choosing as his specialism the discipline of facial reconstructive surgery. His father had tried to hide his disappointment when he heard the news. It seemed frivolous to dedicate one's life to improving on 'God's work', as the Doc was given to repeat. Chris saw it differently, though. He had a keen eye and, it turned out, an even keener skill with a scalpel, and, under his care, many of his patients regained a sense of self-worth, of confidence and courage that soon won him a reputation among his peers.

All had gone remarkably well in the early years of Chris's career. At the start, most of his patients were children. Birthmarks and defects soon vanished when he applied his talents; smiles were restored, faces repaired and countless were the grateful parents. In those early days, he used to enjoy coming home and telling Sally about his day. They'd not been long married, but they'd been blessed with two healthy children. They used to hug those children tightly, relieved that no scalpel would touch their young faces. Soon, however, it was his patient's parents who sought him out. Perhaps he could do for them what he had done for their children. No worries! He was keen to branch out, to push his skills and develop as a surgeon. He hardly noticed when adults became his main focus, oblivious still to the day it became just the wealthy ones, when his skills were required to stem the tide of time rather than improve on nature: wrinkles banished, sagging jawlines restored to chiselled profiles, eyelids lifted, even whole faces lifted and enhanced. All in a day's work. Chris did not notice his financial success but his bank manager certainly did, as did Chris's lifestyle. He and Sally bought a nice house in a desirable location and set about creating and educating the ideal family in suburbia. All was going perfectly to plan, wasn't it?

As Chris stood looking at his own reflection that was the question he was asking of it: 'Had his life gone to plan?' He had always thought so. He had loved Sally and they had had two perfect children. From the outside, he had all the trappings of a successful life, a life well lived. Yet... If Sally had lived, he felt sure they would have continued living 'the life', enjoying two holidays a year, attending banquets and balls, premières of the latest 'must-see' film, wining and dining in all the right places. And, most importantly, watching their children grow and find their places in the world. Now, however, he was alone to do that watching and, if truth be told, he didn't much like what he was seeing. He was proud of his children, of course he was. Yet, the deepest conversations they had lately were about how much things cost and: 'Dad? I *need* a new phone!' or 'Dad? I just *have to* go to X's party this weekend and I have to buy a new outfit' ... just replace X with the latest girl/boyfriend's name and that same conversation seemed to repeat on a weekly basis. When had he just become the source of financial support? Had it always been so? When had his kids become so... well... shallow was the only word for it? From his perspective, at least, they seemed very self-centred, superficial, uncaring. Or maybe they just took after him. Communication wasn't his best strength, that was for sure. Would Sally have done better? He had to admit he was certain she would have. He, on the other hand, had taken his eye off the ball. In his grief, he had become an absent parent when the kids had needed him most. He had buried his grief in his work, sure that that was the only way forward. Today, however, that grief seemed to have come back to bite him, causing him to question the very foundations of his life.

Was it too late to change? Having spent the night tossing and turning, mulling over his life, that was the question Chris was left with, next morning. He hadn't slept at all, his mind still churning with the sense that things just had to change. He was now, officially, middle aged. 45 years old! Yesterday had been the beginning of the second half of his life. If he didn't do something drastic, he could see his life continuing in a bland, unremarkable way for years to come. So, what could he do? *Could* he change? Did he really want to? With a shrug, he decided he'd have to give that more thought. Now, it was back on the merry-go-round: Breakfast, cycle to work, work, lunch (perhaps), work some more, cycle home, dinner, bed... Oh, the excitement! Yes, things would have to change unless he wanted to spend the next decade of his life caught in a loop of a monotonous existence.

A couple of hours later, Chris was settling into his normal routine, sitting in his consultancy rooms. His mood hadn't lifted on the journey in. The traffic had been appalling on the Spit Bridge. He'd left the house a bit later than usual due to his earlier ponderings and had got caught in the backlog as the bridge was raised to let the sailboats pass under. How he'd have liked to be on board one of those and sail out into the Harbour. He wasn't the best sailor but liked the freedom of the open sea on a still day, the sun glistening on the ripples as the boat bobbed gently. He could just imagine how the water must be sparkling in the autumn sunshine. There would be a light breeze, perfect for ambling along through the Heads. He might even see some dolphins or whales breaching playfully on their way to feed. With a sigh, Chris turned his attention to the job at hand, his next patient, a woman who hadn't been to see him before but seemed to fit his usual profile: Her face was betraying her age and she wanted to do something about it. Usually, he had an excellent 'bed-side manner' in such cases, reassuring, confident of realistic improvement, giving full and detailed information about the risks and the pain involved. A thorough professional was the general consensus.

This morning, however, Chris was not his usual self. Far from it! His receptionist and right-hand woman, Katie, who had been with him for fifteen years, had noticed it the minute he had come in. His usual cheery good morning was just a bit gruffer, his humorous banter non-existent. In response, Katie resorted to her high professionalism, guessing he would confide in her in due course. After all, he always did. Whenever anything was getting him down, she had been his first port of call since Sally had died. Even before then, she had been indispensable. Katie wasn't much older than him but he viewed her almost as a mother substitute, his own Mum being up north in the old homestead, far removed from his daily life, though always ringing him to find out how he was. *Fine, Mum. All is fine. The kids? Yes, they're fine too.* Being one of the few people who could, at times, break through his outer shell of self-reliance was a position Katie valued and, while not exactly viewing Chris as the son she'd never had, she felt comfortable in the role of wise advisor, whenever necessary.

Today, however, something about Chris's demeanour warned Katie not to engage in idle small talk. He seemed tenser than usual, surly even, something that, in hindsight, she wished she had asked him about. It might have prevented what was about to occur but, instead, Katie just dropped the patient notes (at this stage, just name, address, and details about previous health issues) on Chris's desk and made a hasty retreat, telling the new patient to go in, which she did. And so it was that Ms Jane Murphy met Mr Christopher Nielson for the very first time.

Chapter 3

Curiously, what had led Ms Jane Murphy to the surgery had been a similar sense of dissatisfaction with her own life. She'd blamed it squarely on the passing of the years and how those years were becoming noticeable on her face. Wrinkles, where before there had been none, Crow's feet, laughter lines. Call them what you may, they were causing her to reassess, to shudder whenever she looked in the mirror. *Since when hadn't she liked the image that looked back at her?* She had always taken a certain pride in her appearance but, lately, those frown lines were all she saw as she carefully removed her make-up. She was reasonably fit, given that she loved to swim and loved nothing more than spending her weekends diving in some part of the Australian coastline but, lately, she was growing increasingly dissatisfied with her appearance. Perhaps it was that when any compliments came her way these days, they were always followed by 'for your age' or some such phrase: *Nice hair, for your age; Great stamina, considering; Fine figure, given your time of life*! Or maybe it was just the coming of the Aussie winter that was making her so uneasy but she'd really have to do something drastic one of these days. After all, lots of her friends were years into *Botox* injections and other such facial remedies. So far her fear of needles had precluded that particular pathway. Now, she supposed it was too late for superficial remedies. She'd have to find herself a surgeon, a good one, of course. She could just about afford to treat herself but was she brave enough? Without thinking any further about it, a few weeks before, she'd dialled the number she had been given by one of her fresh-faced friends and she'd been in luck: there was a cancellation. The great man could see her on the 28th May. Now, as she contemplated how that appointment had gone, she wished she hadn't been so lucky. *What a rude man!*

Why hadn't she said something suitably scathing in reply? Something like:

Have you looked in the mirror lately, Mr Nielson? No spring chicken yourself, are you?

No! That wouldn't have done the job. What about:

How dare you speak to me in that way, Mr Nielson. I'll have your licence! I'll sue you for everything you've got!

No! An idle threat. Jane was not about to sue anyone and, anyway, it wasn't as if he had actually done her any harm. In fact, his tirade might have saved her thousands of dollars for, in his unforgivable way, he had shaken her out of her self-pity. She wouldn't be returning to his rooms or any others but would make do with her face just as it was ...

She still wished she had said something - *anything* - rather than just let herself be steered out of the room like a sheep. *Can a sheep be steered?* That was just like her, though, a compliant sheep. Someone who never stood up for herself. At least, that's how she often felt. Others probably thought of her as capable. Yes, that's the word they'd use. But that's because she rarely expressed exactly what she was thinking. She'd just get on with the job and keep her opinions to herself. Well, all that would have to change. Perhaps instead of changing her face, she could change her personality. Jane wondered if there were any surgeons around skilled in doing just that. Not likely, she conceded, wryly.

To calm herself down, for she had spent at least forty minutes pacing around her living room, she turned on the SBS news. Pouring herself a cup of tea, she settled down to watch the latest world events. That, surely, would help put her own troubles into perspective. Nothing like daft politicians, crazy financial feuds, house prices going up or down to make her see how her life fitted into the bigger picture.

One news story, however, caught her eye and caused her to sit up and take notice. Migrant children rescued somewhere along Spain's Mediterranean coast. No parents, no adults, just three of the most beautiful, sad, terrified little people. One still image grabbed Jane's attention. It was of a little girl, no older than three or four, sucking her thumb as if her life depended on it with her eyes wide in wonder and panic. Staring straight at the camera, she seemed to appeal directly to Jane. *Who is going to look after you, little one?*

Across the Harbour Bridge, another viewer was watching the very same news story. Christopher Nielson had been feeling beyond ashamed of himself. He had no explanation for his unforgiveable behaviour, no excuse. He was grateful that Katie had made such a timely entrance for he had no idea what more he might have said. He could still see the look of horror on that woman's face. He would have to phone her or send her a letter in the morning, apologise, or try to, at least.

He switched on the news to distract himself from his feelings of self-loathing, just in time to see the image of a little girl appear on the screen. She was around four years of age, sucking her thumb with a little difficulty. To his trained eye, he could see that she had a problem with her lip, a cleft more than likely, he thought. Her confused and panic-stricken eyes seemed to look directly at him and he found himself wondering: *Will anyone fix that smile for you one day, little one?*

Sleep evaded both Chris and Jane that night. Each had reached a turning point in their lives and each tossed and turned for hours, trying to come to a decision about their new direction. Dawn saw them sit up in bed, mirror images of each other, with a resolute expression on their faces. Today was the first day of the rest of their lives and they were going to make it count.

Chris went about starting this red-letter day in the usual way following one unusual phone call. Then it was coffee, toast, cycle to work, greeting to loyal Katie. However, that greeting marked the end of normality.

'Katie, Good Morning to you. I must apologise for my behaviour yesterday. I know I went way beyond acceptable, professional conduct. I don't know what would have happened if you hadn't had the foresight to intervene. I'm very grateful to you, Katie.'

'Don't mention it, Chris – happy to help but it's not me you need to apologise to, you know. That poor woman. You should count yourself lucky if she doesn't report you for medical malpractice... or at least for professional misconduct. Whatever possessed you, Chris? In all these years, I've never heard you say one word out of place to anyone, least of all to a client.'

'To be honest, Katie, I've no idea what came over me. I felt like a man possessed. I couldn't control anything that came out of my mouth. And, yes, you're absolutely right. I must contact Ms Murphy immediately to apologise. Do you think a phone call or a letter would be best?'

'Oh I think a letter, don't you? Too risky to let you loose on the poor woman without a script. And I've taken the liberty of writing a draft for you to sign if you approve.'

At that, Katie handed over a beautifully typed letter: short, to the point and just the right balance of apologetic contrition:

Dear Ms Murphy,

I regret that our meeting yesterday did not come to a satisfactory conclusion. I would very much appreciate the opportunity to reschedule at your convenience.

Kind regards

Dr Chris Nielson

Chris read the words a couple of times. Though he agreed that poor woman did deserve some explanation, he also realised that the time had come to share with Katie his recent, night-time decision.

'A great letter, Katie. Just one thing to change. Ms Murphy will need to reschedule with one of my colleagues. I've decided to take a sabbatical. As soon as I can, I'm going to take time out of the practice.'

'Really? That's a great idea, Chris. You should have taken more time for yourself when Sally died. I said it at the time, remember? You came back to work far too soon and you really haven't taken any holidays since except for a few days here and there with the kids. A few weeks off will do you the power of good, no doubt about that.'

'You're probably right, Katie, but I'll be taking more than a few weeks. I've decided to join *Doctors without Borders*. You know, that group of doctors who volunteer around the world in crisis areas. I'm off to the Mediterranean to help out with the migrant crisis there. I rang them earlier today and it turns out my skills are in high demand ... or at least the skills I began with. Children's surgery. I'm going to go back to basics.'

'What? Chris! I don't know what to say! I thought you meant you were going to taking time out, to relax, recharge the batteries. Don't you realise that will be just more stress, more pressure? You need a break. If your outburst yesterday showed anything, it's that. You need to take time to recharge the batteries, Chris, not drain them even more!'

'Perhaps you're right but, you know, since I made the decision last night, I've started to feel an excitement that's been missing from my life since even before Sally died. A sense of anticipation, of exhilaration. Oh, don't get me wrong, Katie, I know it won't be easy. It'll be darned hard. But I need to do something so, at the end of the day, I can fall into bed at night with a sense of having done something worthwhile again. I haven't really felt that in a long while.'

'Is there nothing I can say to talk you out of this, Chris? Maybe you could talk with one of your colleagues, Charles or Julie perhaps? They may be able to talk some sense into you. You know you're not a young man any more or, at least, not as young as you were. And you have responsibilities. What about Sophie and Andy? What do they think of all this?'

'Ah, yes, well, I haven't actually told them yet. And Katie, please keep this under your hat, so to speak, until I've finished making arrangements. I'll let everyone know in due course but I'm determined not to have long, protracted conversations about my plans. I'm going, and that's final.'

'Well, if your mind is made up, I'll say no more.' Katie sniffed back a tear, realising that, in her heart of hearts, her reasons for not wanting him to go were more to do with her own feelings of affection towards the doctor than fear he wouldn't cope. She would miss him dearly. She really would.

Chapter 4

The next two weeks were a blur when Chris looked back on them, filled with rushed preparations, hurried farewells, and a tear or two. Once his children had verified that their lives wouldn't change substantially in his absence, they threw themselves into preparing a goodbye party, inviting all his, and, more accurately, their friends. It was only in the last few days that they began to understand the enormity of what was about to happen. They accepted his assurances that all bills would be paid as usual so they were happy enough about that. They also gave their own assurances that they would act responsibly and take care of the house and, of course, each other. His attempts to broach a deeper conversation about his need to do what he was about to do were met with embarrassed shrugs (Andy) and *Oh Dad!* (Sophie). Neither child, he had to admit, was given to effusion or demonstrations of affection. Not in itself a problem but Chris did feel a little upset that neither seemed to be worried about missing him from their daily lives. Not for the first time did he wonder where he had gone wrong. The answer always came back to being absent too much after their mum had died. Before then too, he had to admit. And now he was going to be absent again. Perhaps he was making the biggest mistake of his life? Perhaps he should stay and try to repair his relationship with his children? Perhaps.

Though his thoughts did cause him to pause in his preparations, they didn't dent his determination to take time out and to try to discover if he still had it in him to make a difference in the life of at least one child. If that child were a stranger rather than one of his own, well, so be it. He had skills and talents he had neglected. Surely it was time to do something about that.

And so, he found himself at Kingsford Smith International airport one rainy June morning, ticket in hand for Spain, or more exactly Barcelona where he was to report to the operational centre of *Doctors without Borders* or *Médicos sin fronteras* as it was called there. During his early medical studies, Chris had done some volunteering work in Colombia and had picked up enough Spanish to get by. He had continued to study it on his return to University so it felt a natural choice for him to head in the general direction of a Spanish-speaking country. He had done some further research over the last few weeks and had found out quite a lot about the organisation. It was better known as either *Médecins sans Frontières* or *MSF* and had been founded in 1971. A non-profit group of doctors with more than 36,000 members working in seventy-two countries. If there were an outbreak of disease like Typhus or Ebola, Sars or Mers, or any other yet-to-be named virus with pandemic possibilities, they were among the first to be there. If there were a cyclone or earthquake or hurricane, they would arrive within hours to treat the victims. In war zones, in famine areas, and what had caught Chris's attention in that news report, in migrant crises, there were doctors from *MSF* working on the front line, keeping faith with their organisation's principles of 'impartiality, independence and neutrality'. No easy task, given the instability of the present world, Chris thought, and he hoped that he too could remain faithful to such principles in the coming months.

Having landed in *El Prat* airport in Barcelona, three whole days after his departure from Australia, Chris made his way to his hotel, checked in and, once in his non-descript room, fell straight into bed, exhausted more from the emotional drain of the last few days than from the flight itself. The following morning, after a hearty breakfast, hunger brought on from jetlag, he made his way to his meeting with Doctor Arturo Méndez, his contact at *MSF*. He had been instructed to arrive at 11 am and to be ready to be deployed once all paperwork was completed. At the time, he hadn't considered how ambiguous those instructions were: how long would the paperwork take? What, exactly, did 'being deployed' mean? Would he have any control of where he was sent? He now wondered if he would be kicking his heels for weeks in Barcelona, not something he would relish as, now that he had arrived, he was eager to get his new life started.

He made his way along the *Rambla*, taking in the atmosphere. Barcelona was certainly a beautiful city, all the more so in late spring. Its status as capital of Catalonia gave it a lively atmosphere, even at this relatively early hour. The Mediterranean climate helped contribute to the festive mood and Chris found there was an unfamiliar lightness to his step as he turned right into *Carrer Nou de la Rambla* and found, on his left, the building that was home to his new employers, that was *if* all worked out well. Taking a few deep breaths, he opened the glass door, thinking how unimposing this building was. He had been expecting a high-rise, modern office block but this was anything but that: five storeys at most and a traditional building with wrought-iron balconies, and classic stonework. All the better, Chris thought, for he was tired of glamour and transient beauty. This area had character, history, a deeper sense of self-worth.

Chris had to interrupt his philosophising as he was approached by a young girl who was speaking to him in a language he did not recognise at first:

'*Hola, sóc Maria, ¿puc ajudar?*'

Chris understood the gist but didn't quite know how to respond so he just smiled and answered in English:

'Oh hi, Maria, I'm Chris, that is Christopher Nielson. I'm here to see Dr Méndez.'

Maria responded in perfect English:

'Ah, Chris, yes, you are expected. Follow me, Arturo is in the back office.'

Chris followed as instructed and soon found himself facing a pleasant, middle-aged man with a rugged face that spoke of an outdoor existence, far removed from his present surroundings: a desk piled high with paperwork, coffee cups on every available surface, floor strewn with the clutter of a busy, medical administration.

'*Benvingut*, Mr Nielson. Chris, if I may? Welcome. Take a seat, that's if you can find one. I'm afraid things are a little chaotic around here – or rather, I like to think it is organised chaos. A well-oiled machine!' This last phrase was said with a chuckle, as if it were something Arturo was fond of repeating and far removed from the actual truth.

'I'm delighted to be here, Arturo, delighted. I'm really looking forward to getting stuck in. I'm sure I can add my fair share of chaos to the machine.'

'Well said! Well said, Chris. We are all parts of that machine, it is true. It is good you are here but let us get out of this office and go for a coffee across the road. It will be quieter and we can have a proper talk.'

At that, Arturo led them back out to the front office and out to the street, shouting a cheery farewell to Maria, telling her to man the fort, or at least that's what Chris imagined he said for he was finding Catalan, the language he realised they were speaking to each other, a bit of a challenge, nothing like his basic Spanish.

Once they had ordered their coffees, *dos cortados*, and had sat at the metal table in a corner of the small café, Arturo got straight down to business.

'Chris, as I said to you before when you rang, we are very pleased you contacted us and want to volunteer your services. You can imagine how very much needed your skills are. However, I must voice a word of caution. From what you said in your telephone call, you are going through something of a personal crisis, ¿no? You want to change direction in your career. May I ask why, exactly?'

Chris was slightly taken aback at the directness of his companion. He had expected a few superficial exchanges on the weather or questions about how well his journey had gone. He didn't quite know how to respond to this turn of events.

Arturo continued his line of questioning, without waiting for the other man to speak.

'We at *MSF* are very careful about who we accept into our ranks, as I explained already in our phone chat. The work is arduous, as you will understand, and the focus is on the people we help, not on our own issues. We work as a team so each member of the team must be strong. In other words, Chris, we are not the Foreign Legion, so to speak, a place for people to escape from their problems, a safe hiding place. Do you understand what I am saying? I am sorry to be so blunt but, rather that now than later, *¿m'entens?*

It was now Chris's turn to put his thoughts into words. He appreciated the informal setting and the opportunity to speak to Arturo in private of his own reasons for being there.

'I certainly do understand your qualms, Arturo. If I were you, I too would question my motivations. An Australian suddenly showing up at your door, asking to be allowed into your fold. It certainly does look like I'm seeking a safe harbour, running from the storm of my own life ... if I'm not mixing too many metaphors.'

He heard his companion chuckle, a sound that he found strangely comforting and encouraging.

'It is true.' Chris continued, 'my life is not a bed of roses (silently he cursed himself for continuing the metaphors ... it must be the location that was making him feel quite poetic) ... it has been very difficult these last few years. However, I am not under any illusion. I am not running away from difficulty but, rather, hoping that I will rediscover the satisfaction I once had as a young surgeon when I could make a difference in my patients' lives. I am not running away, Arturo, but running toward ... I do not wish to sound arrogant but I do think I can make a difference here.'

'I suppose that is my second question. Why here? You could join *MSF* in Australia or in just about any country. Why come to Barcelona, Chris? What made you choose us?'

Chris hesitated, not sure if he should be totally honest with his companion but he found that he could not lie to this man whose gaze was so direct and open. So he explained his reason, the moment that had convinced him to take a leap of faith.

'To be honest, Arturo, I'm not 100% sure about that myself. Simply put, I saw the face of a little child who had been rescued from the Mediterranean near here. She must have been only three or four. It was hard to tell but her eyes seemed to plead with me. I was hoping I could find her for she clearly needed surgery on her mouth. I realise it's a long shot but she was the spur that pushed me into coming here. Does that sound strange? Crazy even?' Though Chris hadn't intended to be so forthright about his reasons there was something about Arturo that forced him to be honest; he was not a man to be fooled, that was for sure.

'Yes, it does sound a little crazy but who am I to question how the universe gets us to where we must be? You are here, you have skills we badly need. Whether you find that *nena*, that child you saw on the television, who knows? A needle in a very large haystack, I fear, but we will see. For now, I must return to the office and put things in motion. If you ring me tomorrow morning, I may have some news as to your application. There may be a need for further details. You understand it is not up to me but there is a procedure which must be followed, even for special surgeons like yourself.'

'Of course. I will ring you tomorrow. Thank you, Arturo, for your candour and I do hope we can proceed.'

'Yes, meanwhile, do take time to enjoy our beautiful city. Barcelona has many delights for the tourist. It may be a long while before you will have time to partake of them again.'

'Good idea. I'll do that and thanks again.'

'*Adiós*, Chris. *Nos vemos mañana* or, as we say hereabouts: *Adéu, Ens veiem demà.*'

Chapter 5

Chris did as instructed and headed back towards the *Rambla*, intending to play tourist for the rest of the day. His first thought was to follow the well-worn tourist trail: perhaps visit the famous *Sagrada Familia* Basilica (still unfinished since Antoni Gaudí had taken over the project in 1883) or go to the Güell Park or even take a cable car to Montjuic. As he walked away from his meeting with Arturo, he realised that none of these locations really appealed to him just now. He was feeling a little deflated. He wasn't quite sure what he had expected. Logically, he couldn't have been ready to start his new life there and then even if he had been asked to do so. There would have been some training to do, some preparation. Yet, now that he was in Barcelona with nothing to do but wait for the powers-that-be to give him instructions, he wasn't at all certain what to do with himself. He realised it had been a long time since he had had time on his hands. His strategy of keeping himself busy had worked so well that, now that he wasn't busy at all, he didn't really know how to fill in his time or what interested him. In fact, he felt he didn't know anything about himself outside of being a surgeon: what did he like to do? What made him happy? What, besides healing, gave him any satisfaction at all? He wondered if this is what people meant when they went 'in search of themselves' or came back from trips around the world 'having found themselves'. He had always scoffed at such phrases in the past but he now discovered he was hoping dearly that this trip would help him find some essential part of himself that he had lost a long time ago. He really hoped it would.

He continued to walk in the general direction of *La Rambla*, thinking that he might find inspiration along the way. When he got to the end of *Carrer Nou de la Rambla*, he turned left without thinking too much about it and found himself in what many consider to be the heart of Barcelona: the long, shady walkway along which pedestrians, especially tourists, ramble aimlessly. It was very peaceful now though Chris remembered seeing images on TV of that horrid night in 2017 when this had been the scene of a terror attack. He shuddered to think of the hatred that had led to that event. It seemed incredible to think of it when surrounded now by such peace and tranquillity. It was a funny old world, a funny peculiar one, that was for sure, a world where horrors were hidden just beneath the surface, waiting to erupt when least expected.

Chris set off to join the other tourists as they strolled along only to have another sudden thought, a memory really, that came to him, this time from his student days. He had taken an elective unit in Spanish Culture, mainly to fill out his CV; it had seemed a good idea at the time as he had just returned from Colombia and had been thinking of doing more volunteer work in Latin America when he graduated. The only course that fitted in with his crammed timetable had been one on the Spanish novel. He had cursed his fate in the beginning as he didn't see how he'd have time to read the list the lecturer provided on the first day of class. Begrudgingly, he had made his way to the library to find a novel he could specialise in (short and easy to read being his main criteria): the main task of the course involved choosing a novel and writing a report about it to present to the rest of the group. Armed with suggestions given in class, Chris found one that seemed interesting; it was called *Offside* and was written by a man called Manuel Vázquez Montalbán. The main character was a guy called Pepe Carvalho, a detective, whose task it was to discover who was sending death threats to Barça's, as the Barcelona Soccer team was known, newest centre forward. Chris remembered thinking that he could handle a book about football and so he checked it out of the library. Against his expectations, he actually enjoyed reading it (helped greatly by the translated version that he had also taken the trouble to check out) and, if his memory served him well, he hadn't done too badly at all in the assignment. As he walked along the *Rambla*, other memories of the course and his student life returned to him: his first girlfriend, Lucy, their short but intense relationship marked all his memories of student life, a bitter-sweet time where he learnt to love and learnt to recover from love's hard lessons. On a less profound level, he also seemed to remember that his Spanish lecturer had talked about how fond 'his' author had been of Barcelona's culinary scene, a trait shared with his protagonist. Chris found he was quite peckish and did a quick search on his phone: Montalbán, Barcelona, Food. Lo and behold he, Chris, discovered he was right, smack in the middle of Montalbán territory. There was even a 'route' to follow with one of the stops being a café, the *Glaciar*, which, happy days, was just a short stroll from where Chris was standing. Picking up the pace, he headed off the *Rambla*, via the *Carrer de Colom*, turning left into the *Plaça Reial* and, there on the corner was the very café, the *Glaciar*.

Chris couldn't help but hold his breath as he entered the premises, feeling as if he were stepping through a portal from real life into fiction. It was often how he felt when, having read of a place or person, he finally encountered them. Somehow, reading about something or someone created a picture in his mind that often clashed with reality. In this case, however, the *Glaciar* was exactly as expected: marble-top tables; wooden beams; an assortment of bottles lining the walls behind the counter; various appetising *tapas* on display; mood lighting reflecting off the selection of artistic photographs placed at intervals and, outside, tables lined up under the arches of the Royal Plaza. In some ways, a typical Bar/Café/Restaurant but, for Chris, it was a whole new world.

Finding he was standing foolishly in the doorway, Chris gave himself a mental shake and moved to the counter. Once he had ordered a beer with a variety of *tapas* (*pan con tomate; patatas bravas; croquetas* – those being all he could manage with his rusty Spanish), he chose to sit at one of the indoor tables, all the better to absorb the atmosphere of the locale. He wasn't the only guest seated there, with most of the other tables occupied by a motley crowd of tourists and locals, all in the act of enjoying either the vast selection of beers or nibbling on the snacks or, truth be told, in the majority of cases, doing both. Chris's eyes moved around the scene, imagining it in the good old days (it had been in existence since 1929) when Montalbán himself, at a somewhat later date, could be found seated at one of the tables or, perhaps it was Carvalho Chris imagined sitting there ...

again reality and fiction were merging in his mind, the edges blurring as he thought back to his studies.

Perhaps that was why he took so long to react when he saw her. He couldn't drag himself back to the reality of seeing someone from his life in Sydney, least of all *that* someone, the very catalyst for his present change of circumstances. For, there, seated at another of the tables, surrounded by quite a boisterous crowd it must be said, was Jane Murphy, the very Ms Murphy who embodied the straw that broke his proverbial back. Chris blinked once, twice, in an effort to rid his eyes of the incredible sight. How, in this very large world, could this have happened? How could two people, mere acquaintances if that, from thousands of kilometres away, suddenly find themselves in the very same bar in Barcelona? Chris didn't believe in providence but mere coincidence also seemed so unlikely. Was there someone *up there* who didn't like him? Someone who thought he needed to suffer just a bit more? Well, if so, they were going to be very disappointed. Chris stood up, intending to make his way discretely to the door and vanish into the crowds and erase this awkward moment from his memory as quickly as possible.

Alas, a smooth exit was not to be. In his efforts to be discrete, Chris had completely forgotten to pay the bill for the untouched food that now lay unclaimed at his table. All hell broke out as he reached the doorway. A voice was heard to shout in his direction:

'*Señor, la cuenta.* Sir, your bill. You have not paid. You cannot leave. *¿Cómo es que siempre hay un turista* (the Asturian waiter almost spat out this last word - '*turista*) *que piensa que somos tontos aquí? Hay que pagar como en cualquier otro sitio del mundo ¿no? ¡Imbécil! ¡Qué cara más dura! ...*'

And so, the waiter's tirade continued as he followed Chris to the door. Chris understood the gist and made to pay but discovered that his wallet was not in his pocket. He couldn't believe it. Where had it gone? He was sure he had picked it up from the bedside table in his hotel room, hadn't he? As he searched, feeling more and more embarrassed, he noticed that he had become the centre of attention of everyone in the café, all eyes now staring at him including *hers*. Any possibility of leaving unnoticed was gone. And, worse, *she* was now making her way slowly over in his direction, with an enigmatic smile on her face.

'Mr Nielson! We meet again! How very extraordinary to see you here in Barcelona.'

'Ms Murphy! Yes, indeed, very extraordinary. I...' Chris found he didn't actually know what to say to this woman. In any case, she had turned to the irate waiter, waving a couple of Euro notes in his face, and saying something Chris couldn't quite catch. It seemed as if she had waved a magic wand for the waiter backed away, almost bowing to her:

'*Muchas gracias, señora. Entiendo todo ahora. Es usted muy amable y espero que todo le vaya bien.*'

When they were left alone (or as alone as the crowded location would allow, with all eyes of that crowd firmly fixed on them), Chris asked her what she had said.

'Oh, nothing really, just that you were an Australian friend of mine who suffered from bouts of amnesia. That you were in Barcelona to see a specialist and that we were very worried about you as you kept wandering off!' Jane couldn't contain her mirth any longer and returned to her table, laughing loudly. The rest of her group soon joined in as, no doubt, she filled them in on events and Chris was left standing alone, wishing he were anywhere else in the world. He gathered himself together and made as dignified an exit as was possible under the circumstances, with the laughter of what seemed the whole of Barcelona ringing in his ears for the rest of the evening.

Jane simply couldn't believe what had just happened; When she had seen *that* man enter the *Glaciar*, it had seemed beyond incredible. How could fate, or whatever was in charge of us mere mortals, be so cruel? Here she was in beautiful Barcelona with her new-found friends, enjoying a coffee and chat and, suddenly, she had been transported back to that horrid day in Sydney when she had asked Mr Nielson for help. His response: anger and ridicule.

As she tried to ignore him, she slowly realised that he was in a bit of a pickle. She weighed up the choices: leave him to it or help him out. Oh the temptation just to leave him cope on his own! However, she could see he was struggling, both with his search for his wallet and with the tirade launched at him by the waiter. Her better nature took over and she found herself placating the waiter and paying the bill. She couldn't help adding that story about him suffering from memory-loss ... just a little joke at his expense. After all, he did deserve a taste of his own medicine. His face *was* a picture. She was still chuckling about it all, hours later, alone in her hotel room. It had, in fact, made her day.

And a very difficult day in a very difficult few weeks it had been up to that point in many ways. Jane had watched the news on that fateful night, exactly three and a half weeks ago, and had come to a decision. She wanted, had always planned, to travel but life had got in the way and the humdrum had taken over. She had been working in a legal firm for just over twenty years since she had left school and had trained in office administration or secretarial studies, as it was called in those days. She was highly regarded by her colleagues but she had always felt unessential. After all, she had no legal qualification, though she sometimes thought that she knew the intricacies of the law better than even the firm's partners: ask her any question about conveyancing, statutes, codes etc, and she'd have the information at the tip of her fingers. And the odd time she didn't, she'd know where to look to verify the facts. But she wasn't the one to present those facts in the courts, or enjoy the accolades when big cases were won. She felt she was just a very small cog in a very big wheel, important for the smooth running of the office but not irreplaceable.

When she had seen that little migrant girl, the refugee, on the TV, something in her heart just broke. Here she was, in her early forties, no children of her own, no partner either. What had she done with her life? She had never viewed her worth in terms of being married or not married though she was acutely aware of the horror she sometimes glimpsed in the faces of new staff, the young professional girls particularly, who thought that being alone must be the worst fate *ever*. No! She had wanted a career, independence, security. What cold words they now seemed as she lay alone in her bed. She often thought that she was driven by those words because she had lost her father at a young age. She knew what it was not to have security, not to know where the rent would come from, or the money for the next grocery bill. She *knew*. Those young ones never had experienced such hardship, or not economic hardship at least, for they were what were called by some the snowflake generation!

Snowflakes! What a silly term, she thought. So unkind to those young people who would face their own demons. They might have had a privileged childhood but no one escapes challenge. And, anyway, all snowflakes are different, right? All are individual, unique, beautiful, deserving of love and compassion. Her ponderings brought her back to that little girl. She was no snowflake in the modern term, but she was beautiful. And all alone.

With a determined shake of her head, Jane made up her mind that she was going to find that little girl and she was going to make a difference in her life, no matter what the challenges. She turned on her side in her bed and finally fell into a deep, refreshing sleep. She had a purpose now and she was content.

Chapter 6

The morning after her first encounter with Chris, on that fateful day back in Sydney, Jane had set about organising her travels. She had also researched all she could about that story about the migrant child. There wasn't much to go on but the rescue boat had landed on Spain's Mediterranean coast. That, from Jane's point of view, was a stroke of luck. Her name was Jane Murphy so everyone assumed she was of Irish heritage, which was partly true. But her mother's name was Ángela Hernández, whose parents had left Murcia in Spain for Australia in the 1950s in search of a better life. Their choice was a bit unusual as many Spaniards had headed for either a European destination such as France or Germany or else one of the Latin American countries during those dark days in Spain. But Jane's grandfather had big dreams and saw himself helping to construct a new country as he considered Australia to be. His wife often pointed out that it was not all that new, considering it had been there just as long as all the other lands on earth with a population and a culture older than many others including his own, but he would just shake his head and dismiss the very idea. *Mujer,* he would say, *such strange ideas you have sometimes, such very strange ideas!* And, to keep the peace, she would stay silent, knowing she was right and, more importantly, knowing that he knew it too.

Whatever the reason, the upshot was that Jane was a bilingual speaker of English and Spanish, since her grandmother had always spoken to her in Spanish while her parents, especially her father, whose background was Irish, had spoken in English though her mother did lapse into Spanish every now and then. At first, during her early school days, Jane had felt foolish as she often got a bit confused and would say things that sounded funny to her classmates. When they laughed, she would run home and hide in her room where her *Mamá* would find her and try to console her:

'*No llores, nena.* Don't cry, my little one. You must not worry about other people. They are just jealous that they do not speak two languages like you. You will see. They will not always laugh.'

At the time, Jane didn't find much comfort in those words but, as the years went by, her mother was proven right. Her ability to cross between two cultures was one of the talents that had got her work, and made her some very good friends. And now, it would help her find a child, a very tiny needle in a very large haystack.

Having explained to her bosses at work that she needed time off to deal with a family crisis (she did not explain the details, naturally, as she feared she would be asked too many questions she just couldn't answer, even to herself), Jane found herself free of work commitments for the first time in many years. She had asked for three months leave (unpaid, of course) and had been surprised to get it. It helped that she hadn't taken much of a break during all her years at the firm. She was always available, at short notice, to return early from her holidays as she didn't have a family to consider in her plans; all very flexible and convenient for everyone. Perhaps too flexible and too convenient, in hindsight. That would all have to change now, Jane accepted. All would be different now. She wasn't sure why she was so certain but she just knew her life as she had lived it up till then would never be the same again.

With her free time, Jane started to look at what voluntary groups were active near the location the boat had landed. Unlike countless other boats that had attempted the treacherous journey across the Mediterranean, this one had got lucky and had been intercepted before vanishing into the perilous waters. The refugees had been brought to Barcelona, after much debate. Due to the vast numbers of people seeking refuge, it was no longer so easy to bring them ashore. In fact, captains of rescue vessels were actively discouraged from doing so. One had even been arrested for such daring. Yet, somehow, this one did make it and so Jane narrowed her search to Barcelona and the surrounding area.

In her investigation, Jane discovered that there were many possibilities, many good people trying to act in solidarity with those who found themselves in challenging times; she checked out the Spanish Red Cross, *ACNUR*, the Spanish branch of the UN Refugee Agency, *Save the Children*, and many other groups that were actively providing help. She finally decided to contact one called *Proactiva Open Arms* as they rescued people directly from the sea and they were recruiting lifeguards. She nearly jumped out of her skin with excitement when she saw that on their website. All the stars were aligning for her, she felt. Mentally, she thanked her parents for enrolling her in 'little nippers' when she was a kid so she had learnt to swim at an early age and her parents never missed a session when she would be training for some competition in the local pool. Later, she did her lifeguard training and was now a fully-fledged RLSSA licence holder and was even a Level 2 Professional Ocean lifeguard. All those days spent watching others have fun on the beach were now making sense! She had found satisfaction in it all at the time, of course, but had often wished she could claim to have family commitments when the phone rang early on a summer morning and she would be asked to cover for some fellow saver whose daughter had come down with a cold or whose son had sprained an ankle at footy. Instead, she always answered the call: 'sure, I can be there in ten minutes. No. No worries. I had nothing planned. Nothing at all.'

Now she did have plans. Big plans. She packed up some essentials, headed to the airport and, with a spring in her step, boarded her flight. In three days, she was in Barcelona, having coffee with a new group of friends, acquaintances really who had taken her to the *Glaciar* to hear more about her plans and why she had travelled so far. She would have to prove her skills in due course but, for now, they were fascinated to hear all about the Aussie who had come to help, an Aussie who could speak fluent Spanish. *¡Qué cosa más divertida!* They found it all very amusing.

So it was that she found herself in *El Glaciar* when her nemesis had appeared. She couldn't believe her bad luck ... here was the very person who had caused her to completely rethink her life, the one who, she thought, was safely back in Sydney and consigned to her 'old' life, never to be thought of again. Mr Chris Nielson, cosmetic surgeon, and rudest man on earth! She couldn't believe it when she saw the difficulty he was in. It had been so satisfying to swoop in and 'save' him. The look on his face had been priceless. Yet, now, in her hotel room, she found it strangely disturbing to think that he was in the same city. It was as if her old life just wouldn't let go. Her new leaf was still attached to a tree rooted in her past and that was not how she wanted it at all.

Chapter 7

Jane woke early the following morning to the sounds of a city getting ready for a new day. The unmistakable waspish sound of *vespas* taking their riders to work, the clattering of shutters as they were opened to let in the new day, the blare of car horns as drivers made their way noisily through the city traffic. It all seemed fresh and exciting to her. She had agreed to meet up with her new friends again at 10 am. 'Friends' was probably a bit of an exaggeration since she'd only met them earlier the day before. They worked for one of the NGOs based in Barcelona that rescued migrants at sea and, when she had phoned, one of them told her they were going for lunch at the *Glacier*, if she'd care to join them. They had promised to show her the set up today and discuss where she would be best placed, should she want to join them. She hadn't mentioned her main goal: that of finding an unnamed little girl. She realised they would think her foolish and, also, they would suspect her motives. Was she using them for her own ends? Well, it would be hard to deny that she had her own motivations but did that mean she couldn't also do some good while being watchful? The ethics of a situation weren't always cut and dry. So Jane justified her actions in her own mind while remaining clear that she would not share her main reasons for being there with anyone, at least not just yet.

At 10 sharp she found herself at the Marina in Badalona, just north of Barcelona. She had caught a train from the *Plaza de Catalunya* as far as *Sant Adriá de Besos* and had walked from there. She could have got a taxi, she supposed, as it was quite a walk, but she didn't feel it was appropriate to arrive in such style. Silly, perhaps, but it felt more fitting to find her own way, even if it took more time. They had told her she couldn't miss the red and white boat that would be moored at the Marina, opposite the Palace Restaurant. If she couldn't find it, she was to text Paca, one of the girls she had had coffee with the previous day.

Jane needn't have worried for it was very easy to find the vessel. It was very distinctive and, in any case, Paca was standing outside waiting for her.

'Hello, *chica*, you found us! We knew you would. Did you have a good sleep? I expect you did though jetlag might have stopped you, I suppose. I know from experience that it is not easy to adapt to a new time zone. How long have you been here, Jane? A few days, you said, I think?' Without waiting for Jane to respond, Paca went on to tell her that she, Paca had spent some time in New York a few years back so understood all about the woes of the long-distance traveller.

'*Huy*, the nights I spent tossing and turning, *chica*. Never mind. Come. You must come on board and I will give you the tour. It is all fairly basic but we have the essentials. We are between trips just now so are restocking and cleaning up. We do plan to set out again in the next few days so you must meet the rest of the crew and we will see if you can come with us. If that is what you wish to do, naturally.' At this, Paca waved at a man who was busy inspecting some equipment on the deck. 'Jorge, here is Jane, the Australian I was telling you about earlier. You know, the one who had to rescue that man at the *Glacier*. It was all so funny. Right, Jane?' At Jane's nod, Paca continued her introductions. 'Jane, Jorge is the one who coordinates the lifeguards so you will have to impress him most of all. ¿*verdad*, Jorge?'

As Paca had been talking, she and Jane had crossed the gangplank and had boarded the *Astral*, and Jane had been trying to take it all in. She now went to greet Jorge who, instead of giving the welcome she had been expecting, brusquely nodded his head and then turned to address Paca:

'You know the rules, Paca. No visitors on refurb days! They just get in the way.'

'But, Jorge, Jane may be joining us. She's a qualified lifeguard, all the way from Sydney. She could be a big help.'

At that, Jorge stopped and looked Jane up and down in a very disconcerting way.

'Hmm! Doesn't look all that strong. Does she know what the conditions are like?'

'Why don't you ask her yourself, Jorge. She speaks excellent Spanish'

Jane was feeling very uncomfortable at being discussed in the third person so intervened:

'Yes, I do, and if you'd rather I didn't stay on board, that's fine with me. I'll be in the café over there if you or Paca wish to speak with me further.'

At that, Jane did her best impression of an offended diva and attempted to glide gracefully back across the gangplank. The effect was slightly spoiled by her toe getting caught in a rung and, if it weren't for Jorge's swift thinking and even swifter hand grabbing her by the elbow, she would have ended up in the water. Instead, she found herself staring up into two twinkling eyes. Jorge was seeing the funny side of things so it seemed impolite not to do likewise. Thanking him for his help, Jane started to laugh at her predicament with Jorge soon joining in the laughter.

Once she had composed herself a little, Jane suggested that the three of them should, indeed, head over to the café as she suddenly felt in the need of a restorative shot of caffeine. And so they did. Once settled at a small table, Jorge got straight to the point:

'So why are you here, *Señora* Jane? It seems it is long way to come to volunteer. From what I hear, you Australians have only too much opportunity to rescue people from the sea ¿*verdad?* Why come all this way to do something that you could do nearer home?'

Jane was taken aback at the directness for she hadn't given the issue much thought. She knew, of course, of the Australian government's policy of *stopping the boats*, as they called it. The idea seemed to be to discourage people-smugglers from profiting from the plight of refugees: if they couldn't promise a safe passage to Australia, then they couldn't extort money from those in dire need to leave their own countries. That, at least, was the theory. The reality was very different, with many lost at sea, all too many so desperate to take the ultimate risk in the hope, not just of a better future but of any future. Survival was the instinct that spurred them on but no one knew just how many lives had been lost in the quest. No one ever would.

Jane returned from her ponderings to see two pairs of eyes staring at her, waiting for an answer. Paca and Jorge deserved an answer and Jane found she couldn't but be honest despite her earlier decision to fudge the truth. She filled them in on her reason for being there: her search for one particular child, from one particular boat. *Could they help her?*

'Unfortunately, dear Jane, there are many such children who arrive on our shores unaccompanied. And many who do not make it. It would be very difficult to track one particular child. However, it seems to me that, if this is what you want to do, you must not spend time with us. We concentrate on sea rescues. That little girl has already found her way to land. So, you must look on land. It is logical ¿*no*?' It was Jorge who spoke.

Put that way, yes, it *was* logical. But where to begin?

'What happens to the children when they are found? Where do they go? Can you point me in some direction?'

Paca was the one to answer that crucial question.

'There are many options, Jane. That, I suppose, is the positive side of things. There are many groups who are trying to help. Never enough but people are very concerned about the situation here. NGOs and state-supported agencies who are trying to do something, even private individuals. A drop in the ocean, if you will forgive the unfortunate imagery. This little girl is one of the lucky ones. She got to dry land, alive. She was photographed. Meaning that someone saw – someone witnessed her arrival. Many children just vanish. If I were you, I would start with that photographer or the reporter who brought the story to you. Can you remember who that was?'

'I should remember as I've watched it so many times but I can't quite remember his name. The report was on our SBS channel but, I suppose I could try to track him down. It's a good place to start. What else do you think could be done?'

'Well, *Señora* Jane, as you are here, perhaps you should do some work for one of the NGOs. Volunteer and see how things work. Choose one that deals specifically with children. Who knows? You might get lucky and find your child.'

My child. Jane liked the sound of that.

'Thanks, Jorge. And you too, Paca. Good advice and sorry for wasting your time. I really didn't think things through, did I? I'm not usually so impulsive. I can't explain it but I feel I must find that girl and I also feel that time is running out. Ridiculous, perhaps, but, sometimes, we must follow our gut instincts ... sometimes they turn out to be only too right.'

With that, she took her leave of Paca and Jorge, asking them to say her goodbyes to the rest of the group she had been with in *El Glaciar*. She headed back to her hotel, not exactly sure what to do next but certain she would figure it out in due course. She would just have to.

Meanwhile, Chris Nielson was having his own crisis. His phone call to Arturo that morning had confirmed that he would be expected to spend several weeks training before being allowed onto the front line. It seemed the so called 'powers-that-be' who were to make the decision about his application, predictably, were concerned as to his motivations and, to be blunt (Arturo's words), equally concerned about his mental state. Chris was now faced with what seemed like a stark decision: go through training or give up on volunteering with the *MSF*. Maybe he could think of a third option? What that was just wasn't clear. Alone in his hotel room, Chris stared for a long time at the walls. When he found himself tempted to talk to one of those very walls (the movie *Shirley Valentine* came to mind...

hello, Wall!), he decided he should go for a walk. That would do the trick, surely. At least it would stop him talking to inanimate objects.

As he wandered without any fixed idea of where he was going, he found himself heading in the general direction of the *Plaça Reial* and *El Glaciar*, the location of his humiliation the previous day. Why on earth would he return to the 'scene of the crime'?, he asked himself. The answer he couldn't avoid was that he felt indebted. After all, *that woman* had paid for his lunch. He should, at the very least, attempt to pay her back. It was around the same time of day and perhaps she was a creature of habit; she might just be there again. And, if not, he could leave the money with that waiter. He didn't really relish the thought of meeting that particular individual again but it would give him a chance to redeem himself, to explain to the waiter that he wasn't in the habit of doing such things as trying to get a free lunch at the expense of others. Why that was important, Chris couldn't answer even to himself. It just was.

So, a few moments later, Chris found himself repeating his actions of the previous day: opening the door to *El Glaciar*, walking inside, his eyes taking a moment to adjust to the change of light before scanning the interior. He found he was holding his breath, wondering if he would spot her before she spotted him, if, indeed, she was even there. His first impression was that she was not and he felt curiously disappointed. Heading towards the counter, he started to take out his wallet (he had double checked its presence in his jacket pocket before leaving the hotel for fear of a repeat performance). As he was doing that, he heard the door open behind him and, on turning, there she was! Time seemed to stand still as they both stood looking at each other ... in other circumstances this would be a beautiful scene from a romantic movie ... he sees her, she sees him, they realise their true feelings etc. Now, however, it just felt acutely embarrassing.

Jane was the first to react.

'Well, this is a surprise, Mr Nielson! I really didn't think you'd darken this particular door for a long while'

'Ms Murphy. Actually, I was hoping to find you here. I owe you lunch. I mean, I owe you the money you paid for my lunch yesterday. I thought you might be here with your friends or that the waiter might know when you would return. I'd like to pay back my debt.'

'Very noble of you! Why don't we just have lunch ... you pay this time, of course ... and we'll call it quits.'

Jane was appalled at herself. *Why on earth had she said that? Now she'd have to spend at least an hour in the company of that odious man! That's if he accepted ... and if he didn't ... even more humiliation.*

'That sounds a lovely idea.' Chris was equally appalled. *Why had he said that? Why didn't he just hand over the money and claim to have an urgent appointment?*

Chapter 8

Against their better judgement, Jane and Chris found themselves heading for a table, sitting down, and staring at each other. Silence stretched for longer than was comfortable, gratefully broken by the arrival of the waiter, the same one who had accosted Chris the day before.

'Ah, *Señora*, how are you today? And how is your forgetful friend?' He said this with a chuckle, clearly having forgiven Chris for the previous episode.

'All good, today, *gracias*. The treatment seems to be working.' Jane avoided the glare sent in her direction. 'We'll just have the same as yesterday, if that's okay. A white wine and some *tortilla* for me and, what was it you had, Chris? Can you remember, dear?' Another chuckle greeted that question and another glare.

'Do not worry, *Señor*, I remember exactly what you had. I will bring you a *cerveza* with a *ración* of *patatas bravas*, some *pan con tomate* and another *ración* of *croquetas*, okay?' The waiter said this as if talking to a child, each syllable spoken loudly and clearly, all the better to be understood. All Chris could do was to nod in agreement, totally mortified.

When they were alone again, Jane couldn't keep her laughter under control. It took her a few moments to gather her composure and, just when she did, she looked at Chris and the expression on his face set her off again. Finally, she made a supreme effort:

'I'm so sorry! Your face! You look as if you're going to explode!' Jane wiped the tears of laughter from her eyes.

'Well, that waiter is treating me like a two-year old child... worse... like an imbecile! All I did was forget to pay and that, Ms Murphy, was all your fault. If you hadn't been there, I wouldn't have got on the wrong side of that gentleman.' Against his better judgement, Chris found his mouth begin to twitch and his eyes begin to twinkle.

'Hang on. You were the one who forgot his wallet. You'd have been in trouble anyway.'

'Fair enough. But it *is* your fault, too, that he thinks I'm memory challenged! Thanks a lot for that!'

And at that he found he could not contain his laughter and both he and Jane spent the next few minutes laughing heartily – the first time either had laughed quite so heartily in a very long time.

Finally, they managed to compose themselves when the waiter arrived with their food and drink. They munched in silence, each suddenly realising they were starving. When the edge had been taken off their hunger, they started to chat in a strangely companionable way:

'Well, Jane, if I may – again! ... Can I ask you what brings you to Barcelona?'

'I was going to ask you the very same question, Chris. It seems very strange that we both found our way here – and not just to Barcelona but to this very café, *El Glaciar*, don't you think?'

'Yes, I do. You were the last person I expected to see here, if I'm honest'

'If you're honest, I was the last person you *wanted* to see here. I'm right, aren't I?'

'Well, yes, but so was I ... I mean, the last person *you* wanted to see.'

'Too true – it was a bit of a shock. I mean, our first encounter wasn't all that enjoyable.'

'Listen, Jane, about that, I really do apologise. I don't know what came over me. Unforgiveable of me, absolutely unforgiveable and very much out of character, really!'

'Apology accepted, Chris. In fact, I should thank you.'

'Why so? Why thank me for being such a cad!'

'A cad? I haven't heard that word for years - it sounds very 'southern belle', if you don't mind my saying so!'

'Well, a rotter, then - no, that sounds like I'm straight out of a comic strip! You know what I mean, anyway. What I want to know is why you think you should thank me?'

'If it hadn't been for that - let's call it that 'episode' ok? - I probably would still be in Sydney, going about my daily business without a thought for the future, a pleasant thought anyway because I'd certainly be having some unpleasant ones. Nothing would have changed. Now, here I am on a bit of an adventure - almost a quest, if you like. So, thanks for shaking me out of the rut I was in. I knew I needed to change. I thought changing how I looked would give me the boost I needed but, instead, I got a good talking to - that certainly did the trick!'

'Look, Jane, I really should explain a bit more about that. You see - no - let me finish ....' Jane had made to interrupt. 'You see I was in a rut too, of sorts. Since Sally - that's my wife -since Sally died - well, life's been very routine. It had to revolve around the children, Sophie and Andy. They were young at the time, just teenagers, and, to be honest, they were my salvation, the only reasons I had to go on. Now, they're more or less independent - getting there at least - and don't need their old dad hanging around. Don't get me wrong, we are close but, somehow, it's not the same as being part of a couple.'

Jane nodded in agreement. She realised her predicament wasn't the same at all. She hadn't gone through the trauma of losing a partner or of having to support children financially and emotionally. Yet, she did understand, especially the loneliness of being on one's own.

Chris continued, as if, now that he had started talking, he might never stop. It had been many years since he had talked about his feelings, his worries, and his doubts. It felt good to have someone willing to listen to him for a change.

'That day, when I saw you come into the surgery, something just snapped. You see I just got tired of listening to attractive women finding fault with their looks. And being the one to nip and tuck their so-called 'faults' when, really, what I was nipping and tucking were laughter lines. Lines caused by life's experiences at the very least and that only added to the beauty of their faces. I just realised I couldn't do it anymore. Can you understand that, Jane?'

Finally, Chris looked up from the glass of beer which he had been staring at while talking. His eyes met those of Jane and, yes, there he saw amusement but, also, he realised, understanding.

'Are you laughing at me again, Jane?'

'No, Chris, not at you at all. Or maybe just a little and maybe a lot at myself. Did you really think I was one of those 'attractive women' who didn't need to fix anything about my face? Do you think these crows' feet add to *my* beauty?'

Jane touched her face with the tips of her fingers, wistfully, tracing the lines.

'Well, yes, I have to say I did. I do.'

'Why, Mr Nielson, aren't you the charmer. Why couldn't you have said something along those lines before, instead of shouting at me the way you did? We could have avoided a lot of unpleasantness! Or, on second thoughts, maybe better you didn't. Anyway, you still haven't told me how you come to be here. So, you snapped and then you decided: I'll head off to Barcelona. Surely, there's more to it than that. Why here and why not just go for a nice, long holiday. Or is that it? You're here on holiday? Are you having a nice time so far?'

'No, that's not it exactly – and now you *are* laughing at me again, Jane. That's getting to be quite a habit of yours and I'm not at all sure I like it!' Chris accompanied this with a smile which belied his words. It seemed that, in fact, he was getting to like the sound of Jane's laughter quite a bit.

'No, I didn't just decide to go on holiday, just because I shouted at you. That, probably, would have been the normal, sensible thing to do. That's what Katie advised – you know – my receptionist?'

'That kind woman who showed me in and, very quickly, showed me out again? Worth her weight in gold, I would think, putting up with you.' Jane was enjoying this banter, amazed at how easy it was to be in Chris's company and how easy it was to tease him. Who would have thought, even 24 hours ago, that she would be here, drinking her wine and teasing 'that horrid man'?

'You're right, she is, and she does! Anyway, to get back to my reasons for being here. It's a bit strange but, that night, after the 'episode' as you put it, I was looking at the news and there was a report about migrant children being rescued off the coast of Spain. There was this one child, a little girl, and there was something about her. She had the most exceptional eyes but it was her mouth that got my interest – my professional eye could see that there was something wrong – a slight disfigurement – and I got to thinking that someone should do something about that. Then, I thought, well, who would have the time? And, then, it struck me, I could be the one. I could make a difference. I could use my skills better if I returned to my original calling. You know, even if I say so myself, I used to be a darned good reconstructive surgeon, before I turned to the cosmetic stuff. I got great satisfaction fixing faces, children's faces in particular, that nature didn't quite design so well – removing birth marks, doing skin grafts, and fixing facial anomalies, for instance. That's what I think that girl has - a cleft lip, maybe even a palate though I'd need to examine her - and if that were the case, it could make it very difficult for her to eat and it might affect her chances of getting on in life. I got to thinking that that child had enough challenges. Surely she deserved some help - my help. So, here I am, looking for her, in a way - hoping that fate will be kind and lead me to her. Well, there it is. You know, that's the first time I've actually told anyone the whole story. In fact, I don't think I've spoken for so long to anyone for years...' Chris suddenly became aware that he'd been talking nonstop for a very long time and that Jane was looking at him with a strange expression. Surely she wasn't upset at him monopolising the conversation, was she?

'Why are you looking at me like that, Jane? You think I'm talking too much, right? Or that I'm really stupid to try to find that girl, right?'

Jane couldn't believe her ears. How could this be? Chris had seen the same news report as she had and had seen the same little girl - like thousands of other viewers that night, no doubt. And yet, the two of them had come to the exact same decision: to search for one little girl and try to make her life a little better. How amazing was that? How extraordinarily coincidental!

'No, Chris, I don't think you are stupid at all. Or, if you are, then so am I. No - it's your turn to hear me out - you see, I went home that night and watched the same report. I saw that little girl and she seemed to cry out directly to me. She needed someone so badly - someone to look after her. I just had to come. And so I did but, now that I'm here, I really am not having much luck.'

'But that's amazing! So we both had the same idea and we both ended up here ... not just in Barcelona but in the same café at the same time - *twice*. I have great difficulty in believing in a greater power, Jane, but something seems to be forcing us together. Do you think it might be so that we can both help that child? Together?'

'... maybe – two heads *are* supposed to be better than one, right? Perhaps if we pool our resources, work together, we might just find her.'

'Yes, we might – in fact, I think we must.'

'But, then what, Chris? That's a question I've been avoiding since I saw her that first time. Then what?'

'A very good question. But let's see if we can find her first. It may be that she doesn't need either of us – or that the next step will present itself if she does. First things first, let's just find her, okay?'

Chapter 9

The rest of the day was spent hammering out a plan. Chris brought Jane up to date about his idea of joining *MSF* and she told him about her efforts to volunteer for *Proactiva Open Arms* They laughed some more at the idea that they had both hit a brick wall due, in no small part, to each not thinking their plan through completely. Neither had ever done anything as impulsive before but neither regretted it. It was just a setback and, now, the real search could begin.

'First and foremost, we must locate that reporter, you know, the one who presented the story for SBS. If we can find out where exactly those images were taken, we'll have a starting point.' Chris had been interested to hear the advice Jane's contacts had given her.

'Yes, I've saved the link to the broadcast on the SBS internet site so it shouldn't be hard to do. Just give me a moment.'

They had gone back to Jane's hotel and were now sitting in the foyer, laptops on the table in front of them and conventional notebooks open, too, both busily making lists of possibilities as they occurred to them.

'Here it is, let's watch it again and see if we can get some clues.'

Two pairs of eyes stared at the screen for the ten minutes it took to get through the special report. It was strange to see it again and in such company – strange but also exciting.

'Look, the report just says: 'source AAP', but I recognise the journalist as Lucas Fernández. I've seen him do lots of other stories on TV but I wouldn't have a clue where he's based.'

'Well, AAP stands for the Australian Associated Press. Can you go to their webpage? They may have some contact details for him.'

'Okay. Let's see. Just a sec. No. There are no specific reports but there is a contact page. Look, there's a phone number. We could ring and see if we can get more details? It's an Australian number. What time is it there now?'

Chris looked at his watch and was surprised to see it was so late – almost midnight. They had been working side by side for hours. How time flies when you're having fun! On the bright side, that meant it was morning in Oz.

'I'll ring now and see what I can find out. I didn't realise it was so late.'

'Not late for Spain though – see – there's quite a crowd walking about outside still – almost more people about now than in the middle of the day.'

'I don't know how they do it. They'll all be up bright and early tomorrow morning, ready for work. Anyway, let's see if I can get through to that number.'

'And then what?'

Chris looked at Jane, puzzled, not understanding why she was asking him that as it seemed straightforward to him.

'Well, I ask if they can tell me more about the report. Such as what happened to the kids in the pictures?'

'And they'll tell a complete stranger about where to find defenceless children? If they are doing the jobs right, I certainly hope not!'

'Oh! I see you're point. It doesn't look good, does it? So, what do I say instead? Now that you've pointed out how suspicious I would sound, every scenario I can think of sounds dubious. Why on earth didn't I think of that before?'

'Give me the phone, Chris. I've got a hunch I might sound less suspicious.'

Chris dutifully handed over his phone, not even thinking why Jane didn't just use her own. He was getting used to doing what he was told to do by this woman.

Having entered the number, Jane pressed the dial button and waited for an answer. It wasn't long before she heard an Aussie twang at the other end. She explained that she was searching for more information on a report broadcast on - she gave the date - could they help her? The man at the other end hesitated for a moment while he looked through their database and then:

'I'll put you through to Lance. He'll know how to help you out. Hold the line a mo.'

Seconds later, another voice was talking.

'G'day. So, you're looking for info on that report on child migrants, is that right? Can I ask why, exactly?'

'Hi there. I know this is a bit of a strange request - Lance, is it? - but I'm talking from Barcelona. I wanted to contact the journalist who put the story together. I'd like to do a follow up - you know - human interest on how Spain is coping with unaccompanied minors etc... Bring some light onto the situation etc... The SBS website just credits the story to AAP but I recognised the journalist as Lucas Fernández. Would you be able to give me his phone number or email? It would really help me with my own investigation.'

'So, you're a fellow journalist then? Always happy to help out a colleague. Hang on. I'll see what I can find out - yes, you're right, here it is - the original feature was presented by Lucas Fernández - he's freelance, you know, he does all sorts of foreign reports, usually in war-torn regions. He's based in Madrid but travels around a lot, naturally.'

'That's great, Lance. So, do you have a contact for him? It would be very helpful to talk directly with him and get his input.'

'I do have a work email you can use. I don't usually give out such information but I don't suppose it can do any harm in this case. I'm sure Lucas would be only too happy to contribute to your story. He is absolutely committed to letting the world know what's going on in the Med. Here is the email – have you got a pen?'

'Yea. Shoot.' Jane scribbled down the email address as it was called out. 'Excellent. I've got that. Thanks so much, Lance. I owe you one.'

'Well, just let us know when you've completed your story. Maybe we'll take it up if it has a fresh angle. Good luck!'

'Will do – and thanks again – bye!'

Jane hung up and turned to Chris with a broad grin on her face.

'Mission accomplished. We have an email for Lucas Fernández – give me a moment and I'll dash off a message and see if we can organise a meeting with him as soon as possible'

'What are you going to put? Again, he might be a bit suspicious of our motives, mightn't he?'

'True – I suppose I could stick with the story of being a freelancer like himself. What do you think?'

'Hm. What role would I have in this story, then? Chief bag carrier?'

'I could do with one of those, right enough. No, maybe not.' Jane backtracked when she saw Chris's expression. 'Did you bring a camera with you? You know, a good one – not just one on your phone?'

'No, but I was planning on buying one when I got here – had a notion about creating a photographic diary of my time here. I thought it would be a good way to keep in touch with the kids back home.'

'Well, okay. Tomorrow you buy your camera while we wait for Lucas to get back to us, if he will. I'll say in the message that I'm travelling with a photographer who is going to provide images for my feature. Sound good to you?'

'Great idea. I'll head back to my hotel now and leave you to write that message. I have a few things to sort out, not least I should ring the kids and see if the house is still standing. Let's meet up again tomorrow around noon and see what the next step will be?

Chapter 10

At exactly 12 noon the next day, Chris arrived at Jane's hotel carrying an expensive camera case containing an equally expensive camera. He'd enjoyed his morning shopping, trying out his rusty Spanish in several specialist shops before settling on buying an Olympus OM-D E-MIX in a small, slightly pokey establishment. He had always wanted to have a good camera, having often thought photography would be a good hobby to take up and that he'd be good at it, given his keen surgical eye. It was one of the things he had planned to get better at, once he had more time on his hands. It looked like that day had come or, at least, he now had a good excuse to get the equipment. The man in the shop had assured him that this model would serve him well. He had stressed the ease of use so much that Chris began to think his photographic talent and abilities were being drawn into question. He, the shop assistant, kept emphasizing the sturdiness of the model, how easy it was to use, fool proof he had said, even a child could take stunning pictures with it. Chris's ego was somewhat bruised by the perceived slight but he didn't have the technological know-how to show off so he just paid his money and left as quickly as he could. It didn't help that the assistant looked about twelve years old. Why was that nearly always the case, lately? Why was everyone around him so young just when he had become conscious of his own age? He remembered his own parents laugh at how the first signs of old age were when the police and doctors began to seem far too young to be qualified. Well, he knew how they felt now!

Jane was waiting for him with news of her own. They sat in the hotel bar, with a coffee each in front of them, and brought one another up to date with events. Chris spent a few moments showing off his new acquisition, pointing out all the various buttons and lenses while Jane tried to look impressed: *Oh lovely, very nice. That should do the job!* All the while, she was trying to contain herself as she was just bursting to tell her own story.

Finally, after Chris had exhausted his new-found knowledge, her turn came:

'Guess what, Chris?'

'What?'

'Lucas answered my email. Almost immediately, in fact. He is very interested in meeting up. He has to leave Spain to cover another news story tomorrow and he was very anxious that his story on the migrant children wouldn't just be forgotten. He had hoped to follow up himself but has to go to where a story that would be bought up takes him. He's more than happy to share all the information he has with us. Isn't that great?'

'Yes, it is great, but does he know we're not *real* reporters? I mean, won't he feel put out when no story appears?'

'Well, I've been thinking about that. What's wrong with us actually writing a feature on whatever we find out - accompanied by your fabulous photos, of course? How hard could it be?'

'Hard enough, I'd imagine. Professional reporters find it challenging at the best of times. How are we going to put it all together? And who'd publish it?'

'We're freelance, remember. We'll find some publication willing to take it on. That guy at the AAP said they might be interested, remember, so I'm sure we'd find some outlet. Let's just give it a try and see how we go, okay? *Please, Chris?* Let's just do it.'

'Well, let's meet with Lucas first and take it from there. I suppose there's no harm in keeping up the pretence for a few days. See what doors it opens. Where is he, anyway? Does he suggest a place and time when we can get together?'

'Yes, he does. He's flying out of Madrid Airport tomorrow morning. He's heading to Syria to do a report or two on the latest developments. He says if we could meet there before his flight, he could spare us an hour. His flight leaves at 11 am so we'd have to be there by 8 am at the latest - it's an international flight so he'll have to check in by 9 am.'

'Madrid before 8 am tomorrow? Crikey, that doesn't give us much time, does it? We'd better get going. I'll head back to my hotel and pack up, check out and meet you back here in under an hour, right? We can head to the train station together.'

'Fine with me. Off you go. I'll be ready by the time you get back. I'll just finish my coffee first.'

'You seem very calm about it all, Jane. I'll dash off and, as said, meet you here in an hour or less.'

Chris was as good as his word and Jane soon saw him hauling his luggage in through the revolving doors. She was sitting in the same spot as before, looking as if she hadn't moved.

'Whew, made it! It was a bit of a scramble getting everything done. I had to ring my contact at *MSF* to let him know that I still hadn't decided what to do ... which I haven't. And then, checking out was a bit of a nightmare. Seemingly tonight is a big fiesta night ... San Joan or Bonfire night or something. And tomorrow is a public holiday so the hotel was very busy with people checking in - they were none too pleased with me checking out on such short notice, I can tell you. And we might have a bit of a problem with tickets on the train, given this is a fiesta all over. Maybe we should try to book online before we head to the station. *And* it might be difficult to get a taxi, given the crowds ...'

'Calm down, Chris - gee! I thought surgeons were cool under pressure! It's all under control. I've already booked us a flight to Madrid. I checked and it was actually cheaper than going by train, not to mention it takes just 1 ½ hours. *And* I've booked a taxi which, if I'm not wrong, has just pulled up outside so, grab your bags and follow me!'

Chris could do nothing but follow Jane meekly out the door and into the cab, thinking that he really should have been the one to solve the problems rather than the one to point them out. *Why hadn't he thought of booking a flight? Or a cab?* He wasn't making much of an impression on Jane, he felt, and why that made him feel so acutely inadequate he just couldn't say.

Chapter 11

The flight from *El Prat* airport to Madrid's *Barajas*, o *Adolfo Suárez Barajas* to give it its full name, was uneventful. Short and sweet, Jane thought. With the added bonus of earning brownie points in Chris's eyes. She still chuckled when she thought of his expression as they were getting into the taxi. Priceless!

As if to make up for his oversight, as he seemed to view it, Chris 'took charge' once they landed in Madrid. He retrieved their luggage, got them smoothly through the airport corridors to the taxi rank, into a cab, giving the address of a hotel he had Googled before take-off where, to prove his efficiency, if only to himself, he had booked two rooms. Once in possession of their keys, it was decided they would each order room service in their own rooms for dinner and have an early night. It had been a challenging few days for each of them and time to absorb everything as well as to prepare for the early start the following day would be very welcome.

The next morning, feeling somewhat refreshed after their early night and, after a very early breakfast, Chris and Jane headed back to the airport for their meeting with Lucas Fernández. As arranged, he was waiting for them in *Starbucks* café in Terminal 4. Despite the early hour, it was busy but Lucas had already commandeered a table so, once they had collected their various coffee orders, Jane and Chris sat down across from the man who would, hopefully, provide them with their next move. Lucas was not alone at the table; he was accompanied by a glamorous young woman, perhaps in her early thirties, with dark, glossy hair and dark flashing eyes and impeccably dressed in a designer 'power' suit. Attractive in an aloof kind of way, Chris thought, as the other man stood to make the introductions. Jane's thoughts were not so charitable.

'*Hola*, Ms Murphy, this is Magdalena Sánchez, *mi novia*, my girlfriend, though that is not why she is here. I will explain more about that in a moment. It is good that you are following this story, Jane ... may I call you Jane? I am very glad that it will not be forgotten, that the children will not be forgotten. As I said in my message, I would have liked to do a follow-up myself but I must now turn my attention to another war, no less or more important, and I cannot do two stories of this magnitude at the same time. Though, in any case, they are linked since it is the war that is the cause of so many refugees.' While Lucas was talking, Jane and Magdalena greeted each other with the usual *dos besos*, usually a friendlier greeting, Jane thought, than a simple shake of hands. In this case, though, Jane felt there was something frosty about the younger woman, something she just couldn't put her finger on just yet.

'*Hola*, Lucas, it's great you agreed to meet us and lucky we could meet before you fly off. This is Chris, by the way, my photographer.' The men nodded at each other, cautiously weighing each other up. Jane understood Chris's feelings of unease; he was not accustomed to deception, to his credit, but she wasn't sure why Lucas seemed equally uneasy. Or maybe the word was 'wary'.

Once all four were seated, Lucas handed over a memory stick to Jane:

'*Toma*, here is all the information I have gathered on the issue of migrant children coming into Spain. I warn you it is difficult to absorb - especially the images - but it may help you with your story.'

'*Gracias*, Lucas. You have no idea how much I - we - appreciate this. But, you know, every journalist tells a story in a different way. I am conscious that we may not tell things as you would have done. For example, I am not sure how to make any sense of the immensity of the problem. From what I've already discovered, it is a complicated matter with many different players involved.'

It had been agreed that Jane would do most, if not all, the talking so Chris was just sitting sipping his coffee, striking a photographer's pose, in his own mind. That involved an attempt to view every scene as if through a lens. For that reason, it took a few moments for him to realise that Jane had brought the conversation around to the image that had brought them to this point: the little migrant girl.

'You see, Lucas, my idea is to follow the path of just one or two of those children, trace their journey from the moment they reach Spain and show exactly what's involved.'

After a moment of hesitation, Lucas responded:

'I see. Yes, I suppose that could be a good angle. It could overcome reader fatigue. When you think of the thousands of children who arrive here, some accompanied but many on their own, it is just too immense. In the world, just imagine, there are, right now, about 30 *million* children who have had to leave their homes. According to *Save the Children*, 2,500 unaccompanied children arrived in Spain in 2017, an increase of over 60% on 2016. In 2018, our Autonomous Communities took charge of 5000 children. Can you imagine? 5000 kids with no adult to look out for them.'

'That's just it, Lucas. It's impossible to imagine. As I see it, it's our job to make it more possible – to put faces to the numbers, make them more personal, more individual. You can feel sympathy, or maybe it's empathy I mean, on a one-to-one basis but it's far more difficult if the numbers are vast. Then, you can be manipulated into thinking of them as a homogenous group, one that's just causing problems or that contains too many challenges to be solved. It becomes *them* and *us*. But, the face of a little boy or girl who needs help, well, that's a very different story. A story I want to tell.'

'I understand. But how do you focus on just one. There are so many. Just go to any of the *centros de acogimiento*, of, what's the English term? 'Welcoming centres' doesn't seem quite right...'

'Refugee centres, we call them. Well, in your report, you did manage to focus on the personal, Lucas. Do you remember the images of children who had been rescued and were disembarking? One little girl in particular stayed with me. Do you know the one I mean?'

After a sudden intake of breath, Chris was aware of being unable to exhale. How could Jane be so daring? All now depended on Lucas's reaction. Their quest could end right here, right now. What was Jane *thinking*, taking such a risk? What if Lucas grew suspicious? What if he refused to give any more information?

It wasn't Lucas who answered, however. Instead, Magdalena put a restraining hand on Lucas's arm and interrupted him before he had a chance to respond:

'The little girl you speak of is Eva. She and two others were rescued by an NGO ship that ignored warnings. As you must know, it is now strongly discouraged to pick up drowning migrants. Several of the rescuers have been arrested and accused of human trafficking. Ludicrous. In any case, Eva and her friends were extremely lucky, up to a point.'

'*EVA!*' Jane and Chris exchanged a look, both delighted to put a name to the little face that had been haunting their sleep for many nights.

'What do you mean 'lucky up to a point', though?'

'Eva, unfortunately, has vanished.'

Chris and Jane both exclaimed at the same time: 'Vanished? What do you mean, 'vanished'?'

There was a moment's silence while each tried to come to terms with this dead end. They hadn't really expected Lucas to be able to provide exact details as to Eva's whereabouts, but they had got their hopes up that he would know which organisation had taken her under its wing. The fact that she had just disappeared was very troubling.

Chris was the first to break the silence:

'But how can a little girl just disappear? Especially one who has been on TV?'

'That is just it. We think the media attention must be behind it.' Magdalena seemed a bit reticent to continue. Then, as if she had made a decision, about what exactly neither Chris nor Jane had any idea, she turned to Jane.

'Jane, may I be very honest with you?' Not waiting for Jane to agree or disagree, Magdalena took a deep breath and launched into an explanation of why she was there and what she hoped to achieve.

'You see, Jane, when Lucas told me about his meeting with you, I wondered if this would be the opportunity I have been looking for. He said you were Australian, ¿verdad? But with a name like Jane Murphy you must have some connections with Ireland, ¿no? So, I thought I would tag along because I need to find someone who can travel to Ireland and follow a lead. I thought that someone might be you?' Almost as an afterthought, Magda added: 'And you too, Chris, of course.' As she said this, she turned to a bemused Chris. Jane was no less bemused, not having been given any opportunity to reply or to ask any questions.

Lucas intervened, seeing their lack of understanding clearly written on their faces.

'Magda, perhaps you should explain a little more before asking favours, ¿verdad, querida? These people have no idea what you mean.'

'Oh! Of course. Sorry, I get so carried away I forget that I have not filled in the crucial details. Okay, you see, I, too, have been following this story for quite a while. I work in one of the centres here in Madrid that deals specifically with children.' Here, Magda mentioned the name and address but neither meant much to the two Australians given their lack of local knowledge. 'I have noticed that, every now and again, a certain number of little ones just seem to vanish. When I try to find out where they have gone, I am told nothing. In fact, I am becoming a little afraid at the reactions I get when I ask questions. No-one else seems to be worried but I cannot help but be concerned. The latest little girl to vanish is the one you have asked about. Little Eva. She came to us straight from the rescue ship. I remember her especially because, well, she had a problem with her mouth. Then, one day, I came into work to start a new shift and she was not there. That is not very unusual. Often, children are moved on to new accommodation when it becomes available. But, in this case, no-one at work could – or would – tell me where she had gone.'

'But that's terrible. Did you call the police?' Jane was horrified. *How could a little girl just vanish over night?*

'You must understand. It is not that simple. The paperwork for each child takes many months. There was, in fact, no real proof that Eva had vanished. She could simply have been moved to another centre. The strange thing is, though, that her friends did not report her missing. You remember, from that report, she came ashore with two other little ones. They were a bit older. Though they did not speak Spanish, they did speak a little English and I was able to communicate with them, but they just shrugged their shoulders when I mentioned Eva. Seemed to be saying they did not know who I meant.'

'That doesn't make any sense. Why wouldn't they say she was gone?'

'Well, they might not trust us, simply. When you think about it, why should they? They arrive in a strange country, all alone, not knowing what is going to happen to them, not sure who to trust. Then, one of them goes missing. What should they do?'

'When you put it like that, I see what you mean. But, have you any clue as to what happened to Eva? Was there any trace? I mean, why did you mention Ireland?'

'Good question, Jane.' Jane was sure she wasn't imagining the patronising tone in Magda's voice, but she let it go as the other woman continued speaking. 'Yes. After a lot of digging, I discovered that there was talk among the children of a man called Lonergan, a priest in fact. They seemed to think he was a friend. That he would help them, but they were not to say anything to anyone. You can imagine how I felt when I heard that? All the dreadful stories of past abuse by priests just came flooding back to me. Could this be what is happening? Children being kidnapped for reasons too dark to contemplate? I just cannot stand by and do nothing. I have to find out what is happening.'

'So what else have you discovered about this Lonergan guy?' Chris was interested to find out more, especially as it all seemed so vague. Why hadn't these people gone straight to the police? He still wasn't convinced that it wouldn't be the wisest course of action.

'He seems to be a shadowy figure. None of the children would expand when I asked them. They all looked very uncomfortable when they found out I knew his name. I told Lucas about him and he did a bit of investigation. Lucas?'

'I found out that he does, indeed, exist but his connection with the children is difficult to figure out. I was not able to find an address for him here in Spain, but I did find out that he was a Franciscan. He seems to be based in Ireland, which is why I had planned to travel there next. That's why Magda was hoping you'd have some connections, Jane, so she could persuade you to go instead.'

'And I was hoping to go with you. I really want to talk with that man, see what he has to say for himself and see what his set up really is.'

'That could be very dangerous, couldn't it? Not just for you but for any children he has contact with. Again, why not talk with the police? Europol could track him, surely? They're better equipped for such tasks. Or just talk with him here in Madrid. He's bound to pop up at some stage, right?'

'To be honest, I do not trust anyone. We have no specific proof so they could just alert him that we are on his trail. OR, even worse, they could be helping him.'

'Why, on earth, would you think that? Why would they - I presume by 'they' you mean the police? What would they gain from such a despicable act?'

'I do not know. I just know that we are in very dangerous territory. Make a false accusation and everything could go even deeper underground. I do know children have vanished before and I am very afraid they will again. So, will you help, Jane? Have you any Irish connections?'

'Well, that's just it. My name is very Irish, it's true. But I haven't ever been to Ireland and, though I must have some distant relatives there, my family lost track of them years ago. I wouldn't know where to start.'

That news didn't go down too well with either Magda or Lucas, both exchanging a look that seemed to say they had reached a dead end.

The silence was broken by a hesitant Chris:

'Err ... I may be able to help out. I ... um ... well, my father is actually Irish and I've been to Ireland a couple of times, to Dublin and to Cork too. I have an Aunt who lives there - in Cork I mean. My father's sister - I'm sure she wouldn't mind a visit from her favourite nephew.'

'Really, Chris! How wonderful! And you would be prepared to travel as soon as possible? And I could go with you? Oh, this is the best news!' Magda accompanied her words by embracing Chris and kissing him on each cheek, clearly delighted with his offer.

Looking back, Jane would think of this moment as the one when Magdalena's attention first rested on Chris. Right now, she was beaming in his direction, and she continued to beam, it seemed to Jane for the next few days. Not that Jane was jealous. Of course not! It was just that she wished men could be more aware of when they were being targeted. Could they not see the weaponry used by some women in the war between the sexes? Not that she really believed it was a war, exactly, but, watching Magda in action, Jane certainly wished she herself had spent time becoming better equipped. Now, she could only watch as Chris seemed to melt at the attention. He was putty in Magda's expert hands, it would appear.

'Oh, well, yes. I'll contact my Aunt and let her know the good news. She'll be delighted.'

'Wonderful! I'll look into flights etc...' Magda, then, turned to Jane.

'Should I book a flight for you too, Jane, or just for me and Chris?' Was it Jane's imagination or was there a subtle (or not so subtle) hint that it would be preferable if she stayed out of the excursion?

Before Jane could answer, Lucas stood up, saying he really had to leave to catch his flight. He still had to go through passport control, so he'd leave them to make their arrangements. All he asked was that they keep him in the loop, let him know if or when they located Eva and the dubious priest. Turning to Magda, he embraced her in such a way as to make it clear, should clarification be needed, that she was *his* girl. Jane chuckled to herself, understanding that she had not been alone in noticing the multiple layers of communication. Lucas clearly felt it necessary to establish boundaries.

Once he had left, and there were just three at the table, Chris spoke up on Jane's behalf, saying that, of course, she, Jane, would be travelling with them. He looked to Jane for confirmation. She nodded in agreement:

'Yes, of course, I will follow this story wherever it leads us but, perhaps we should hold off on flight bookings for a day or so. I would like to look into this Fr. Lonergan a little more before chasing off after him. After all, he may be an innocent man. Let's not jump to any conclusions.'

Clearly, Magda was not impressed with this plan of action but, given that Chris was nodding in thorough agreement, she had no choice but to accept their decision. As they headed out of the terminal, Chris and Magda exchanged phone numbers (Jane noted mentally that Magda did not ask for hers) and they arranged to be in contact later that day, when Chris would update her on any developments. She took her leave of them, heading for the carpark (again Jane noticed she did not offer them a lift back to their hotel), and they, Chris and Jane, took a taxi.

Chapter 12

Silence reigned as the taxi made its way slowly through the Madrid streets, allowing both Jane and Chris to take stock of the information they had gleaned from their early-morning meeting. They had plenty of time to look out the car windows at the passing landscape. This was June and the city was gearing up for the first fiesta of the summer. Soon, the weather would chase the locals south to the beaches or north to the mountains, leaving the museums and cafés free to welcome just the bedraggled, over-heated tourists. Now, however, there was the usual chaos and cacophony with cars, trucks and pedestrians juggling for space. Finally, tiring of the taxi's slow progress, Chris turned to Jane, eager to discuss the latest developments.

'Well, that was very useful, don't you think, Jane?' Chris seemed delighted at how the meeting had gone.

'Yes, very, though I'm not really sure how reliable Magda's information is. She doesn't seem all that trustworthy to me'

'Really? Maybe you're right but I thought she was being very helpful. Very credible.'

'You would! I'll grant you she was convincing but surely you noticed that you were invisible to her until she realised you might be the useful one? It was like a switch went on and she was all smiles in your direction when you mentioned your auntie. Up to that point, you might not have even been at the table.'

'Yes, I did notice. I'm not totally stupid and I did see how she changed. I'm not blind but, even so, she knew about Eva. How good is that! How great we now know the child's name? And we know where she was for a while. That's a start, anyway.'

'Yes, it certainly is. You're right about that. We should get working on that immediately. Do you think we could trace this priest she mentioned? It shouldn't be too difficult, surely.'

'No, it shouldn't. I'll start looking into that. Maybe you could look into the other disappearances, given that your Spanish is much better than mine. Magda said there had been others. You could see if there's any connection, anything those children had in common.'

'Right, I'll go through old newspaper archives and read over the information Lucas gave us ... So you weren't fooled at all by Magda's act?'

'Not for a minute – do give me some credit, Jane. What I couldn't fathom is why Lucas didn't do something. I wouldn't like to be in his shoes with a girlfriend like Magda.'

'But he did do something – didn't you see the very possessive farewell kiss he gave her? I got the distinct feeling that was mainly for your benefit – and also maybe to remind Magda where her loyalties should lie.'

'Oh really? – I totally missed that. Ah well, Lucas has nothing to worry about. She's definitely not my type.'

'Why not? She's a very attractive woman, I have to admit, or hadn't you noticed?'

'Yes, I *had* noticed but she doesn't have any of those lovely lines and wrinkles I mentioned before – you know – the ones that add to a woman's beauty – without them she's just a blank page... ouch! What was that for?' Jane, though finding Chris's words strangely consoling on one level couldn't let him get away without some punishment for his lack of tact. A jab in the ribcage had served as sweet revenge. Then, with a renewed spring in her step, she got out of the taxi that had, finally, pulled up at the hotel entrance, and headed inside. Her trip was proving to be even more energising that she had hoped when she had left home just a few days ago and, she was beginning to realise that Chris's presence had a lot to do with how she was feeling.

The rest of the day went by in research: Jane spent quite a few hours going through the material Lucas had given them while Chris did his best to trace Father Lonergan. Both had agreed to meet later in the evening for dinner so they could fill each other in on their progress.

Jane found that, as she prepared to go down to the hotel foyer, she was taking extra care with her appearance. Though chiding herself for being ridiculous, she still put on her favourite eyeshadow – the one that made her eyes sparkle that bit more – and that blue silk dress that made her feel a million dollars. She'd packed it at the last minute, just in case she'd need something nice to wear, arguing that it wouldn't take up much room. She was glad she had, now. Her hair, too, got an extra brushing, making it shine in the light as it brushed her shoulders. She felt a bounce in her steps as she headed for the lift. She just hoped Chris wouldn't get the wrong impression – or the right one, if she were honest with herself. *Stop it, now, Jane. You're far too mature to start getting such ridiculous ideas. Get a grip. You know you don't need any complications at this stage of your life.*

When Chris saw the lift doors open, he was surprised to feel his heart beat just a bit faster. Jane looked amazing! He hurried over to her and found it natural to greet her in the Spanish way: two kisses, one on each cheek. Her hair smelt delightful, her eyes sparkled and he suddenly felt himself to be a very happy man indeed. Instead of revelling in that new sensation, however, he gave himself a mental shake and a reprimand. *Stop being ridiculous, man, this is no time for such nonsense and, anyway, you're far too set in your ways to go complicating your life any more than you have already.* So, instead of telling Jane how well she looked or paying her any compliment of any kind, he just politely greeted her as if she were a mere acquaintance:

'Hello, Jane. I've booked a table in the dining room. I thought that would be a bit quieter than in the midst of the fiesta revelry.'

Jane, likewise, kept to the job at hand:

'Good idea. We can fill each other in on developments. I, for one, have a few things to report. I hope you do too. And I'm starving. I didn't take a break for lunch so I'm ready to make up for that, big time!'

They headed into the hotel restaurant which, truth be told, could have been located anywhere in the world: it had a classic layout of white-clothed tables, distributed around a central buffet which was laden with every dish known to humankind, it seemed, with starters at one end, mains in the centre and desserts at the far end, no doubt to make sure guests had some exercise before tucking into them. To one side was an area where guests could order dishes to be made especially for them: steaks, omelettes, fish, and poultry were all being expertly fried, boiled, roasted, brazed, seared, and served. When the maître d' had shown Jane and Chris to their table and had explained their choices (they could choose the buffet menu or opt for table service), they had a quick look at the wine menu before choosing a bottle of the house wine. Tonight was not a night to be extravagant, nor to over-indulge; there was work to be done, detective work, and both were determined that nothing would interfere with their quest.

Once plates were cleared and glasses emptied, they set about filling each other in on their day's activities, having spent the meal chatting about the quality of the food, the antics of the other diners and the various trials and tribulations faced by the waiting staff. Jane was first to get the ball rolling:

'Lucas has done a lot of groundwork already, you know, Chris. I went through all the files he gave us and I'm now well and truly up to date on the migrant situation here – and also right across the Med. He had a lot of information, especially about child migrants. It is astonishing how many people are on the move, all looking for somewhere safe to live. The thing that got me, from what he had put together, is that this isn't a new phenomenon: people have been moving around the planet since the dawn of time. Looking for food, shelter, safety – even the reasons haven't changed all that much, just the nationalities and their destinations vary.'

'I've often thought that people are very restless, always going or coming from somewhere, never content to stay at home – look at Australia, most of the population come from somewhere else, if you trace back through the generations. Only the Aboriginal community can claim to belong the longest – though even they must have come from somewhere sometime.'

'True, but, Chris, it's one thing to make that decision to go, quite another to be forced to leave your home against your will. What really gets me is the generation of children who have no choice. Their parents choose for reasons that seem logical, for survival, for a better future, to escape violence, but the kids just have to follow – for them, their parents are their universe. So, how awful it must be when they, the kids, find themselves alone. I was reading this article where it said some parents just have enough to pay for one of their children to travel – they give the people smugglers all they have so that one child might have a future. Can you imagine having to do that? How would you choose? And how could you trust your child to a stranger?'

'Horrific! What a decision to have to make. I couldn't imagine having to choose between Sophie and Andy. Or having to send one off into the world in those conditions. Makes my blood run cold just to think of it ... even now, thinking of them back in Sydney on their own keeps me awake at night – and they are young adults, not little kids with no knowledge of the world.'

'But, seemingly, not sending them is even a tougher choice as the dangers lurking at home are just as threatening. Hobson's choice, if ever there was one.'

'So, what did you find out about what happens when they do make it this far?'

'Well, as Magda already told us, the lucky ones are taken to a refugee centre to be processed. There are centres all over Spain so they could be sent just about anywhere. The local government authorities are supposed to process their applications for residency but that takes ages. Lucas mentioned that, for example, in Madrid, at the end of last year, there were only 10 applications in the pipeline even though there were over 400 kids in their refugee centres and it's a similar story all over – far more children waiting for applications to be lodged.'

'I guess it's the usual story of not enough resources to deal with this crisis.'

'Exactly – which means it's all too easy for a child to disappear – like Eva. It just makes my blood boil to think of it – first the smugglers taking money from the poor parents and then, just when they should be safe, someone else thinks they can prey on such vulnerable children – it's just appalling.'

'Now, Jane, don't jump to conclusions so quickly. We don't actually know what's happening. We only have Magda's suspicions.'

'Okay but what did you find out about that Fr. Lonergan? Is there any trace of him?'

Chris had been waiting for his chance to tell of his day's activities and smiled triumphantly at Jane:

'More than a trace, Jane! I actually spoke with the man himself!'

'What? You found him? What was he like? Do you think he knows anything about Eva? Does he know where she is? Come on, tell me?'

'Hey, slow down, I'll tell you all. To start with, I just Googled his name and, low and behold, an article popped up about him. I was a bit surprised at that considering how Magda said she couldn't locate him. Seemingly, he travels between the Franciscans in Ireland, in Cork specifically, as Magda mentioned, and their house here in Madrid. He is in demand as a preacher and is renowned for the novenas he leads.'

'Humph! A great cover, I'd say – he could be up to anything, travelling around like that.'

'Now, now, Jane – don't go jumping to conclusions. I had a long chat with him and, to tell the truth, I quite liked the man.'

'You would! Obviously, being a preacher, he must have some charisma, right? That doesn't mean he's trustworthy.'

'No, but I think you should wait till you meet him before passing judgement. After all, you're just basing your assumptions on what Magda said and you were the one to warn me about taking everything she says at face value.'

'Point taken. Okay, fill me in on what you talked about.'

'Well, I just rang the Franciscans here and asked for him and, incredibly, he came to the phone. If I've learnt anything from you, Jane, it's not to be too quick to tell the whole truth ...'

'Hey, I don't think I like that accusation – normally, I'm a very honest person – just lately I'm finding myself a bit out of my comfort zone!'

'Fair enough – me too – and I meant it in a good way – I'm quite enjoying the challenges of this new lifestyle. In any case, I decided to carry on our subterfuge and told Fr. Lonergan that I was a photographer working on a story about migrants in Spain and Ireland and that I'd heard that he worked with that community in both countries. I didn't mention anything about children, of course, as that might have put him on alert.'

'That was good – a good cover and best to keep the story simple. What did he say when you told him that?'

'Contrary to my expectations, he was delighted to hear from me and said he thought it was a story that needed telling – that there was a lot of hardship in that community but also a lot of good people doing everything they could to help out. He thought it would be good to throw light on the day-to-day challenges and would be very happy to help out.'

'That sounds a positive start. So, what did you say then?'

'That I'd like to organise to meet with him, that I was working with a colleague who would do the writing while I was putting together a photographic portfolio. He asked if we'd be free to meet tomorrow at one of the rescue centres he worked with – so, my dear Jane, we have an appointment for 11 am tomorrow in General Perón Avenue. He'll meet us there.'

'Isn't that where Magda works? The address sounds vaguely familiar.' Chris nodded.

'Yea. I expect we'll see her there.'

'That'll be convenient. Funny she didn't know him, though, if he's used to dropping by. Anyway, let's see what turns up tomorrow. We should each prepare a set of questions for this Fr. Lonergan. We'll have to be extra clever to catch him out.'

'IF there is anything to catch him out on. Remember, Jane, we haven't any evidence that Lonergan is anything but what he appears to be: a kind-hearted priest doing his best for those less fortunate. Let's give him the benefit of the doubt, at least for now. Okay?'

'Okay. I hear what you're saying and I promise I'll be on my best behaviour tomorrow.'

After that, the conversation fizzled out as each of them was lost in their own thoughts about how the next day's interview would play out. Finally, when they had finished their dessert (Crème caramel or, more correctly *flan* for Jane, and, for Chris, an almondy Santiago tart), they each decided to call it a night and headed back up to their rooms. They agreed to meet the next morning for breakfast when they would pool their ideas about what questions to ask the infamous Fr. Lonergan.

Chapter 13

Jane didn't sleep much that night, tossing and turning as she went through various scenarios in her mind. She understood Chris's advice to remain open minded about the priest but she'd read too much about the Catholic clergy's past not to be very wary. She also was aware that she mustn't put that priest on guard by being confrontational but she was someone who always wore her heart on her sleeve; she had never been able to disguise her true feelings about someone, for good or bad. As the new day dawned, however, Jane decided she'd have to make a supreme effort to be friendly; it would be in a good cause so she'd have to put her own feelings, overwhelming though they were, to one side.

Chris was already in the breakfast dining room when Jane arrived. He looked disgustingly refreshed and cheerful. Clearly, he had slept like a log. That immediately put Jane in a bad mood: *How could he switch off his feelings like that? Didn't he realise what that priest could have done?*

Chris, on the other hand, was in a great mood. He had, indeed, had the best night's sleep he'd had since his arrival in Spain. Jet lag had finally vanished and he had fallen into a dreamless sleep as soon as his head had hit the pillow. His good mood had also been helped by a video call he'd made to his children when he had woken up; they were doing well but had actually said they were missing him and were worrying that he wasn't taking care of himself. They'd wanted to know when he'd be home or if they could come and see him in Spain. It felt good that someone was worrying about him for a change but he hadn't been able to say when he'd be home and he wasn't settled enough for visitors so he'd have to let them know about that later on. They were disappointed but the rest of the conversation went with them filling him in on their escapades; they hadn't had such a long conversation in years. It seemed to him that the old saying was true:

absence does make the heart grow fonder.

Given their contrasting moods, breakfast went by in silence. Instead of discussing strategy, as planned, they just ate in silence. Likewise, the taxi ride to General Perón Avenue did nothing to change the atmosphere. When they arrived, Chris rang the mobile number he'd been given the previous day to let Fr. Lonergan know they were outside and, during the brief wait for the man to appear, he reminded Jane to be on her best behaviour, a reminder that did nothing but darken her mood even further as she now felt like a scolded child. *How aggravating! How patronising!*

Fr. Lonergan arrived at the doorway in a matter of seconds, an amazing feat, Jane thought, given his appearance. He was a tubby little man, almost as wide as he was tall. In fact, with a slight giggle, Jane was reminded of a perfect sphere when she saw him. He was dressed in a Franciscan brown habit, with a white cord doing an amazing job of circumnavigating his middle. His face was a joy to behold as it contained two twinkling blue eyes and a broad, open smile. He was walking, or rather rolling, towards them with his hand stretched out in greeting:

'Well, hello, hello! How lovely to meet you both! Do come in, come in, come in!'

He ushered them both through the door and into a side room, a type of office with papers strewn about in, presumably, organised chaos, and he pointed out two chairs for them to sit on.'

'A cup of tea for you both?'

Jane did her best to say no, thank you, but she was ignored, as was Chris who was also struggling to get a word in edgeways. To say that Fr. Lonergan was a force to be reckoned with was an understatement. He moved at astonishing speed, given his girth, and, in record time, had cups of tea and a plate of biscuits and *madalenas* in front of the pair of pseudo journalists.

'Well, now, I always think a cup of tea is a great start to a relationship so we can get comfortable as we sip and you can tell me all about yourselves and why you're here. Australians, you said? Haven't ye come an awful long way from home, now? It must be important work you're doing so let me know how I can help.'

Chris and Jane exchanged a look, neither sure where to begin. Finally, Jane decided she'd introduce herself and explain, in broad terms, the story they were researching: child migrants. She watched Lonergan's face like a hawk when she said those words and she thought she saw a shadow pass over it. *He's hiding something. I'm sure he is.*

Fr. Lonergan's mood did, indeed, alter when he heard that topic. He sat back in his chair and sighed deeply.

'Ah now, that's a sad, sad story you're looking into. But worthwhile for sure. There are many lost children in need and, though everyone is trying very hard to help, it sometimes seems like an endless task. One child is saved and ten more arrive – a tidal wave of children, all needing help, all very scared.'

'So, what happens when they get here? Who looks after them all?'

It was Chris who spoke this time as he had noticed Jane tense up and didn't trust her to remain calm.

'Well now, some of them come here, most are sent to the various provinces, or to be more correct, to the Autonomous communities. It's a long road they're on, a long road, and, sadly, they are often sent to several different places along that road before being settled in any particular place. Sometimes, it takes so long that the child in question turns 18 before the paperwork is done. And that, good people, is another tragedy.'

'Why so?' Jane had made a supreme effort to control her voice so that it would sound calm and dispassionate.

'Why so, you ask? Because then they enter the adult stream and that is even more complex to navigate. Many get lost along the way as they give up and just take to the streets. And I don't need to tell either of you, I'm sure, that the streets are no safe place for anyone, least of all a vulnerable teenager who speaks little or no Spanish. The possibilities of abuse are endless.'

Jane stiffened again. *He's brought up the idea of 'abuse' himself! Is he being very clever, deflecting attention from himself? It would be an astute move on his part, wouldn't it? No, not astute, very cunning, Fr. Lonergan, very cunning!*

Chris put a restraining hand on Jane's arm, guessing her thoughts, guessing her internal conflict. He himself felt more at ease with Fr. Lonergan and was willing to take his words at face value. It was clear, to Chris at least, that the priest was very disturbed at the path some children faced.

'So, Father, where do you think we should start our story?' When in doubt, Chris thought, ask a question and see where it leads.

'Well now, you could start right here. I'll show you around. I drop in every now and then when my schedule allows, just to give a bit of support. I've spoken to the management team and they're happy for you to ask any questions you like and take some photos ... not of the refugees, of course, as we must respect their privacy as much as anyone else's. So, if ye've finished that tea, follow me.'

So they did and the priest led them all around the centre, giving them free access to speak with whoever was happy to speak with them. Chris took multiple photos, mainly of the facilities. And he took one or two photos of the refugees too, men, who agreed to pose for photos in return for some cigarettes Chris had taken the trouble to stock up on. Fr. Lonergan explained that they were probably here looking for their own family members as this centre catered mainly for women and children. Jane listened intently to the stories they told, challenging stories of stormy nights at sea, friends who had not made it, hopes they had for the future, frustrations they were experiencing in the present ... all the human pieces of a very complex puzzle.

Chapter 14

Thinking about the visit to the refugee centre later in bed that night, Jane could not reconcile her previous ideas of the priest with the attitude of both staff and those who had shared their experiences of getting to Spain with her. Everywhere he went, Fr. Lonergan was greeted with warmth and enthusiasm and he, in turn, moved with ease through the centre, stopping often to chat, placing an encouraging hand on someone's arm, gently slapping someone else on the back. If you were to judge anyone by body language alone, then, Jane thought, Fr. Lonergan was an open book: kind, friendly, cheerful. Why, then, had Magda had such a poor opinion of him? And why, too, did she seem not to know him when it was clear that all the other staff at that centre were very aware of his presence? That was the question that puzzled Jane most and, if truth be told, she also felt ashamed at her willingness to condemn the priest, sight unseen. Why had she believed Magda? And why did she feel so irritated with Chris just because he had kept a more open mind? These questions and many others kept Jane awake for a second night in a row, adding to her bad mood the next day.

Once more Chris and Jane met at breakfast the following morning and, once more, Jane was grouchy and irritable while Chris was full of the joys of life.

'What has you so cheerful?' Jane grumbled when she saw him tucking hungrily into a mushroom omelette.

'Oh, I don't know, really. I just woke up feeling like we're making good progress *and* this omelette is really good! You should try one. Might do you the power of good!'

'I don't know how you can face all that food at this time of the morning. I'll just have a coffee and a piece of toast.'

'I suppose my body is still working on Sydney time – I get really hungry during the night and, anyway, we'll need some nourishment to get on with our day today.'

'Well, my body is quite aware it's morning, thank you very much, so I'll stick with a light breakfast. Why do we need special nourishment today of all days?' Jane noticed that Chris was looking particularly pleased with himself, a look that made her feel all the more uncomfortable. She was beginning to realise that it often meant he had done something she wouldn't approve of.

'Yes ... um ... you might not like it, Jane, but I've made some plans for our day.'

'Okay, out with it. What have you done?'

'I rang Magda last night after I left you. Remember, I'd said I would keep her in the loop. She wasn't at all happy that we had gone to the centre without telling her, though. Strange that! I told her I thought we'd see her there. It turns out it was her day off so she calmed down when she realised we weren't actually going behind her back.'

'Did you ask her why she didn't seem to know Fr. Lonergan when all the others working there did? Not only knew him but seemed to be on very friendly terms?'

'*I* was thinking that too. But, no, I didn't ask. I thought it might be awkward.'

'Awkward for whom? You or her?'

'Well, for me, actually, as it would sound like we were checking up on her'

'We *are*, aren't we? Or at least we should be. Don't you think it strange that she was so intent on colouring our view of a man she claimed she didn't know? Or that she just knew by hearsay? I think it's very suspicious.'

'There you go again, Jane. Leaping to conclusions. Why don't you let me finish what I was saying? Just because you're in a bad mood doesn't mean the whole world is conspiring against us.'

'I'm *not* leaping anywhere. I'm just saying it's odd. Anyway, go on! Tell me the worst. What do we have to do today?'

'Magda said that she thinks Eva might have been moved to a centre in the South ... the south East actually, to Alicante. She said a few of the other children were sent there the same day she noticed Eva was gone. It might be that her paperwork got mislaid and she got on the same bus as the others without anyone checking.'

'Really? But that would be great, wouldn't it? It would mean she was safe all along, just that her file or whatever was misplaced. So, are we going to Alicante? Is that the plan?'

'Exactly! We get the train - and yes, this time we'll go by train rather than plane as it's easier   I've checked it all out - and we'll be in Alicante in a matter of hours. Magda will meet us at the train station in two hours' time.'

'*Magda's* coming too? Oh great! Why does *she* want to tag along?'

'She's the one who provided the information, so I suppose she wants to be there to check if it's true that Eva is safe. And, of course, she's just totally taken in by my charms, right?'

Chris chuckled at Jane's reaction to that claim. She tossed her hair and all but harrumphed out of the dining room.

'I'll leave you to your delusions, Chris. I'm going to my room to pack. I'll see you in the foyer in half an hour.'

And so Jane disappeared out the door, almost toppling a waiter in her hurry, with Chris's laughter ringing in her ears.

By 10.30 am, Jane and Chris were in Madrid's *Atocha* station, having quickly checked out of their hotel. Chris had learnt from past experience and had booked their tickets online so all they had to do was find the correct platform, not an easy task as this was fiesta time and it seemed everyone in Madrid was on the move. Finally, however, they made it through the crowds to the awaiting high-speed *AVE* train and found their seats. Just a minute before the train was due to depart, Magda arrived in a flurry of bags. She was carrying two cups of coffee and stopped short when she saw Jane.

'Hola Chris ... Jane. I grabbed you a coffee, Chris, on my way but I had no idea what you would like to drink Jane. Sorry!'

She smiled as she said this and batted her eyes at Chris who had the good sense to look uncomfortable.

'Thanks, Magda, but I'm okay. I had my coffee quota at breakfast. Jane, would you like it?'

Jane thought she would choke on it so politely declined, glaring at the cup as if it contained poison. Magda just shrugged and sat herself down beside Chris, a bit too close for comfort from both Jane's and Chris's point of view.

'I did not think I would make the train. It was all such a rush. I hardly had time to put on any make-up. I must look a sight.'

Jane had to bite her tongue as she was on the point of stating the obvious: *how come you had time to buy coffee, then?* Plus, clearly, Magda had spent quite a bit of time on her appearance, which, to Jane's complete disgust, was impeccable. Clearly, too, the statement was intended to make Chris react positively but, whether by intent or through obliviousness, he didn't utter a word, just smiled enigmatically. Jane felt like cheering but thought better of it.

Since her comments hadn't elicited the desired reaction, Magda tried another tactic:

'So, Chris, please fill me in on your thoughts about Fr. Lonergan. What impression did you get? Do you think he is suspicious?'

Before Chris had time to consider his response, Jane hurried to ask her own question, the one that had been burning in her mind since it had first struck her:

'How come you haven't met him yourself, Magda? He seemed very much at home in your place of work. Surely you would have come across him at some stage?'

Magda glared at Jane who was acutely aware that Chris was also staring at her, not at all impressed by her questions but she avoided looking at him and just stared back, feigning wide-eyed innocence, at Magda.

'I have not worked there very long. I only heard his name from the children. I had no idea who he was.'

But that didn't stop you tarnishing his reputation, now did it. Luckily, Jane did not voice that thought as she knew Chris would not approve of such a direct approach to the subject. Instead, she just nodded and smiled, letting it seem that she was convinced, something that was far from the truth. Fearing that Jane might just ask for more details about Magda's lack of knowledge about the priest, Chris rushed to change the subject:

'Well, that explains that, then. Can you tell us a little about the place we're going to, Magda? Are they expecting us? Did you ring them to ask if they have Eva there?'

'No, I did not get a chance to ring, Chris, but I left a message. I am sure they will get it and we will sort this out. Of course, even if Eva is there, that does not mean Lonergan is blameless. Other children have vanished too.'

'So you say. But what proof do you have?' Jane wasn't about to let Magda get away with any more baseless innuendo.

'I know what I know, Jane,' Magda answered, sounding as if she would like to share more details but that poor little Jane just wouldn't understand.

'Yes, but *how* do you know and *what* exactly do you know?'

'We will find the evidence; I am sure of that.'

'Now, ladies, let's just leave the topic for now.' Chris had had enough of the verbal fencing and didn't relish spending another couple of hours listening to it. 'I, for one, would like to enjoy the scenery. And, maybe, Magda, I will have that coffee after all. I think it's going to be a long and challenging day.'

At that, silence descended on the little group, with only the occasional slurping of cold coffee to be heard. Each of them plugged themselves into their various phones to listen to their various choices of music, glad to tune out of any conversation for a short while and, instead, stare out the train window at the passing scenery.

It really wasn't long before the train pulled into Alicante station and the threesome found themselves heading for the taxi rank just outside. Magda had tried to take charge, suggesting they all book into a hotel she knew near *Postiguet* beach but Chris explained that he had already booked himself and Jane into a hotel near the *Ayuntamiento,* Alicante's town hall. He had been worried that there wouldn't be any vacancies, given that the fiesta of *San Juan* was in full swing so hadn't taken any chances. At Magda's suggestion that she book into the same hotel, he was quick to explain that they'd told him he had be very lucky as they were now full to capacity. He had the good grace to look supremely disappointed but promised Magda that, once they had settled in, the three of them could all meet up later for dinner. Magda shrugged and agreed, begrudgingly, that she would meet them in the *plaza* opposite the *Ayuntamiento*. There was a Galician restaurant there that had a good reputation. They could eat first and take a stroll afterwards or vice versa, depending on their appetite ... As her eyes remained on Chris the whole time she was speaking, Jane understood only too well that she was not included in Magda's plan. *No problem, Mags, I'm more than happy to fend for myself and let Chris deal with you all on his own.*

Chapter 15

Having checked into, and checked out the rooms, Chris and Jane met up again in the hotel foyer, something that was becoming almost a habit for them. Jane put it to Chris that he was free to meet up with Magda on his own. She, Jane, was feeling tired – after two sleepless nights – and would quite like to have an early night.

'No way, Jane. I know you think that Magda is some *femme fatale*, with men dropping at her feet. But I find her a little intimidating, if I'm honest. All this attention, *and* she has a boyfriend already. It's just not on!'

'Well, it's nice to know you're not fooled by her act. It is an act, you know. She's using us for some purpose I'm not clear about yet.'

'I suppose that's true. She could just have rung up the refugee centre here and asked about Eva. There was no need for her to come in person. But it might just be that she's following up on the story for Lucas, right?'

'True, he did seem keen to be kept informed, didn't he? So, you might be right. She's just keeping an eye on us which, if I'm honest, I don't like one bit. Though, she doesn't seem to be too bothered about her boyfriend's wishes in other areas. The way she keeps invading your personal space is creepy.'

'You're right there, but what really bothers me is why Lucas might have asked her to keep an eye on how we followed up. He mightn't trust us to do a good job. I mean, all he had to do to check our credentials was to *Google* us – he wouldn't have found any publications accredited to us. What kind of investigative reporter would he be if he hadn't done at least a background check on us before handing over all that information?'

'That's a point. I can see that might be why Magda doesn't like me. She thinks I'm not what I claim to be ...'

'Exactly, which is how you think about her. So each of you mistrusts the other and I'm stuck somewhere in the middle!'

'Oh, you love it, Chris - two women sparring over you.'

'If it really were over me, I might - but it isn't, is it?' Chris had meant to ask that last question as a joke but, as he said the words, he realised he really did hope that Jane might confirm her feelings. *Did she have feelings for him? Was he the only one to sense the tension? Did he really want something to happen between them? Did she?* Part of him felt like he was betraying the memory of his wife even thinking like that. But another part of him had to admit that he had been very lonely for a very long time.

Jane laughed. She was only too aware that part of her dislike of Magda stemmed from the fact that the other woman was all she wished she were: tall, with long, dark, wavy hair, and equally dark, flashing eyes, the perfect figure - *and* young - or younger than she herself was at least. The list went on and it all added up to a stunning individual who seemed to ooze sex appeal. *Would I feel the same way towards Magda if she were short and fat and fifty? Not in a million years!*

Jane became aware that the gap between Chris's question and her answer was becoming a little too long for comfort, so she did what she always did when embarrassed: she made light of the situation and then changed the subject.

'In your dreams, my dear! Well, what about we two go for lunch and figure out our plan of action? Then, later, you can take young Magda to dinner. See if she'll unburden herself to you about her reasons for following us around. And I'll have that early night I was hoping for.'

Chris shook off his disappointment and agreed half-heartedly:

'Fair enough. I'm not keen on meeting Magda without you ... though, thinking about it again, it might be a relief not to have to listen to you two sniping at each other all the time. Let's go for lunch. I'm starving and quite fancy that restaurant Magda mentioned. I believe I spotted it just outside the hotel so we wouldn't have far to go.'

After all the tension and unanswered questions, lunch turned out to be a very pleasant affair. They sat at a table inside the restaurant from where they could see lots of activity happening in the square. Clearly, Alicante was gearing up for the main event which would happen on the night of the 24th of June: the burning of the bonfires on what was known locally as *la nit del foc* or the night of fire, when the start of *la cremà* would be signalled by gigantic fireworks launched from the top of Monte Benacantil. There were people everywhere, getting on with the preparations. To Jane and Chris, it all seemed very chaotic as well as exotic. Far from the kind of bonfires they were used to seeing, the one in the square was really a work of art. It was immense, almost 20 metres high and featured a beautiful woman in the centre and surrounded by all kinds of figures, including Jane's favourite, an owl with wings outstretched which seemed on the point of taking flight.

A waiter approached them as they were lost in their discussion of how incredible it was to think that beautiful, intricate construction would, in a few short days, just vanish into flames.

'*Buenos días, Señor, Señora.* I see you are looking at our *ninot*, our bonfire to be. Have you come to Alicante to enjoy the *Festa de San Joan*?'

'Well, not exactly. We're here on business, of sorts. We had no idea that the fiesta was such an occasion. Are they really going to burn that beautiful construction there?' Jane was not at all convinced that what she had been looking at was, indeed, a planned bonfire. It was so far removed from any she had seen before; bonfires, in her world, were always made of unwanted wood, even car tyres perhaps, the odd table or chair, nothing at all like this beauty.

'Yes, on Monday night, it will all go up in smoke. It will be quite a night with bonfires blazing all around Alicante and fireworks of course. And parties all over. Will you be able to witness it?'

'We're not sure yet if we will still be here on Monday. I'd certainly like to be, though. What time does it all start?'

'That's a very good question, *Señora*. Officially this bonfire is to be lit at midnight, followed by others later in the night. But there will be various events all weekend, and the fireworks will go on all next week with a big competition over on the beach. You really must try to stay. It is very special. We are all very proud of our festivities.'

'We'll certainly try. How long does it take to get these figures together?' This time it was Chris showing his interest.

'Ah, another very good question. In fact, the designers probably have already started planning next year's versions. And, to build, it takes months in the *talleres*, you know, the workplaces. Then they move them to the sites. This one took over a week to build here. It was too big to get out of the *taller* so they had to divide it in two. It was quite the challenge.'

'But what does it represent. I mean, is there a theme or some instructions that have to be followed?'

'Not exactly, but each *ninot* – that is what we call those figures – has a theme. This one is called '*con otra mirada*'. Let me see, that is 'with other eyes', I think, in English. It features lots of eyes looking at the world in a different way – to find new solutions to the problems we have.'

'That's so interesting. But why destroy such creations and in such a destructive way?'

'It shows how beauty and creativity are fleeting. It is very emotional but also very profound. And, of course, there is lots of fun to be had during the whole fiesta much of it also has to do with food so, on that subject, I should take your order before I am fired!'

'Oh, I hope you don't get into trouble for answering our questions. It's been really good to hear. But we were so distracted by the - what did you call it? The *ninot*? - well, we forgot to look at the menu. Can you recommend something?' Jane suddenly realised that she really was hungry but, staring at the menu, she couldn't quite figure out what to choose. Chris looked equally confused.

'Why do I not just bring a selection of our dishes? I promise you will enjoy them and it will cost the same as the *menú del día*, just €30.'

'That sounds perfect. *¡Gracias!*

The waiter was as good as his word and the next half hour or so went by as Chris and Jane munched their way happily through a variety of exotic-sounding dishes: *queso de cabra con miel; calamares a la andaluza; fritura de pescado; champiñon al ajillo con jamón serrano; croquetas caseras.* All washed down by a very pleasant house wine. It took Jane all her willpower not to lick her lips like a satisfied pup when she finally pushed her plate away from her.

'That was *deelishous*! I don't think I've enjoyed a meal as much for years!'

'I know what you mean, Jane. It was all so good. Simple but very tasty. That waiter certainly did us proud. We must leave a big tip.'

'Agreed. But my problem now is that I had planned to do some reading up on the refugee situation but it's all I can do to waddle back to the hotel and collapse on the bed. I never really understood the idea of a *siesta* before but I feel in the need of one right now. How about you, Chris?'

'Ditto! Let's head back to the hotel and gather our strength for an hour. And I should check my phone messages. Magda has been sending me texts every ten minutes. It got a bit tedious so I switched off my phone - she'll be mad if I don't respond soon!' Jane just nodded, not wanting to spoil her happy mood by even thinking of her arch-rival, the younger, more sophisticated, more elegant Ms Magdalena Sánchez.

Having paid their bill, and adding an extra-large tip, they thanked their waiter profusely. Manuel, for such was his name, repeated his advice to stay in Alicante until after the bonfires were lit, something Jane and Chris both were hoping would be possible *if* they located Eva safe and sound. It was exciting to imagine that they might all watch the fires burn together, a pseudo family blending in with all the other real families that would soon gather to celebrate midsummer. Of course, that could happen if, and only if, they'd be allowed to treat the little girl to such an outing and, before that, so much needed to fall into place, not least the task of locating her.

Chapter 16

Both Chris and Jane woke up not one but two hours later feeling refreshed and happier than either had felt for quite a while. Neither could put their finger on why that was but each decided just to revel in the new-found contentment. Chris texted Jane to say that he would call her after his meeting with Magda later that night. If she were still awake, he could fill her in on any information he had been able to glean from the Spanish woman. If she were asleep, he'd do that the following morning. No worries! Jane just texted back with a line of happy-faced emojis which left Chris not quite sure if she were happy or angry at being left behind. He had never quite got the idea of emoticons and whether the lack of a message attached was a good or bad thing. He knew what she had said earlier but did she really not care about leaving him to Magda's attentions for the whole evening? He decided to ring her to make sure. After a few ring tones, she answered:

'Oh hi, Chris. What time are you meeting Magda? I was hoping we'd have a chance to chat beforehand - you know - about what to do next.'

'That's exactly why I'm ringing. If you meet me in the hotel bar, we can decide a plan of action.' So, Chris's suspicions had been justified: Jane had wanted to see him before he headed out to see Magda. The realisation that he was getting to know his travel companion's moods made him feel quite cheerful, for some reason he wasn't quite ready to admit.

A quarter of an hour later, they, Chris and Jane, were sitting comfortably in plush armchairs, sipping restorative coffee and trying to think of how to approach the next step in their adventure.

'I expect Magda will have a suggestion about when to call into the refugee centre, won't she?'

'No doubt at all, Jane. But I was hoping we could pre-empt her taking charge. I know she works for the same NGO but, as you were saying, she has been acting a little strangely. I was hoping to create a bit of distance between her and us and not just because she's such a scary lady!'

Jane chuckled at that. It was somewhat consoling to think that a person who seemed to have it all could sometimes have too much of it all! She didn't suffer from that problem at least.

'Well, we must keep you away from the 'scarey lady', now, mustn't we? I suppose we could tell her we have plans for tomorrow - you know - go to the beach etc.. Be careful, though, 'cos she might just decide to come along if you make it sound too appealing.'

'I know - why don't we say we have to go to church! It is Sunday tomorrow, after all. Something tells me Magda wouldn't be caught dead near a church.'

'Brilliant idea, Chris! That will keep her away for at least the morning. And, meanwhile, we can go to the centre without her.'

'Right. Do you think they'll let us in? Especially considering it *is* Sunday - they won't be open as such. I expect they'll have a skeleton staff, given that it's also fiesta time.'

'Exactly, they'll be less able to monitor our activities, once we get in. Okay, while you entertain Magda this evening, I'll do a bit of research into the NGO and the centre and see if I can figure out how to get us in. Do call me when you get back and we can exchange news!'

'Fair enough.' And with that, Chris headed to his meeting with Magda, looking, for all the world, as if he were heading into battle and not to spend an evening with a very beautiful woman.

Much to Jane's amusement, she never did get to hear all the details of what happened between Chris and Magda that night. All she knew was that Chris arrived back at the hotel at 10 pm, far earlier than anticipated. Instead of ringing her, he just arrived knocking at her door and, without waiting to be invited in, brushed past her when she opened it and headed for the bar fridge. He grabbed a small bottle of whiskey, opened it, and drank it without even pouring it into a glass.

'So, your evening went well, then?' Jane couldn't help being a little pleased that his mood didn't seem the best.

'Don't ask. Just don't ask. I'm saying nothing but just don't leave me alone with that woman again, alright?'

'Why? What happened?'

'I said 'don't ask', so just don't. Let's just say I'm glad I'm not Lucas. I expect loyalty from my women, at the very least.'

'Your women! How many of them are there, exactly?' Jane was really enjoying Chris's consternation. Obviously, something had happened to make him lose his cool. How she would have loved to have been a fly on the wall and have witnessed events? What a shame it looked like Chris wouldn't confide in her!

'Okay, I won't say anymore, except did you find out anything useful?'

'Not a thing. *She* just kept asking me questions, like how well I knew Ireland, whether I'd travelled a lot, if I'd been married and so on. It felt like a cross between an interrogation and a seduction. I couldn't get a word in edgeways.' Chris helped himself to another drink which he drank a little more slowly this time. Clearly, he was calming down somewhat.

'Sounds intriguing.' Seeing Chris glare at her, Jane decided she would change the subject and fill him in on what she had discovered about the refugee centre.

'Let's draw a veil over the whole thing, Chris. You sit down there at the desk and let me tell you what I've discovered – not a lot but at least we can make a plan for tomorrow.'

'Fair enough, thanks, I'll sit quietly. Fire away! What did you find out?'

Jane explained that the centre itself was located in Ramón de Campoamor Street in an area north of Alicante city. She'd read up about the work they were doing and one of the big things was that they'd opened a residential unit in San Joan, not far from the centre. They had converted an old hotel and now they could house up to 50 refugees there, of all ages. She figured that's where Eva might be though it would be a long shot. It would be worth going there tomorrow and checking it out. What did Chris think?

'Sounds like a plan. Being Sunday, it'll probably be quiet, a good time to walk around the area and see how the land lies.'

'Did you manage to persuade Magda to leave us alone for the day?'

'Actually, yes, it seems she's also got plans of her own. She didn't even ask what we were going to do. So we're free to please ourselves for the day. What if we meet at about 11? I'm going to check out the beach early in the morning, have a swim and maybe have a coffee in one of those cafes along the shore. Join me if you like but I know you'd probably prefer a bit of a lie in.'

'You are getting to know me too well, Chris. Though, to be honest, I'd normally not skip the opportunity for a swim. It would probably do me the power of good, but, on this trip so far, I can't seem to get enough sleep. I might join you for coffee and, maybe later in the day I'll go for that swim, depending on how things go. Have a good rest till then and see you tomorrow.'

Chris took his leave, giving Jane a quick peck on the cheek, and headed back to his room. He had had enough of the day and was soon snoring soundly in his bed, with not even a dream disturbing his slumbers.

Jane, on the other hand, tossed and turned. Her earlier nap had ruined her chances of dozing off. She was condemned to spend a third night wide awake, wondering what the next day would bring. Would she finally meet Eva? What then? It was all beginning to seem pointless. What did she think she could do that wasn't already being done by countless volunteers, all of whom knew the system better than she did? Not all that much, she suspected. She was searching for a little girl who might not even be lost, but she was here now and she would see her quest through to the finish. She was glad to have Chris's company at least. He was equally committed to the task in hand but, she feared, equally unsure of what lay ahead.

Chapter 17

Sunday dawned fresh and sunny. The forecast was for a high of 27 degrees. After a fairly leisurely start to her morning, Jane made her way towards the beach, passing the *ninot* as she went and she marvelled, once again, at the sheer size of it. It also seemed incredibly close to the buildings that surrounded the square. The fire fighters would have a challenging job to keep sparks at bay, that's for sure. Contrary to her expectations, it was easy to find the beach: she just followed the crowd of people carrying lilos and sun chairs, buckets and spades and all the usual paraphernalia of the beachgoer the world over. She crossed *Conde Vallellano* Avenue with the rest of the throng and turned left towards *Postiguet* beach, passing the newspaper kiosk and the old port road that led to the iconic Meliá hotel and its sister, the Spa Porta Maris. Jane would have liked to linger and take in the scenery but today wasn't the day for that. She was anxious to find Chris and get on with the task they had set themselves. She texted him once she reached the first part of the promenade and was pleased she didn't have much further to go as his response just said: *look left - in café - 1st row.*

'Well good morning, sleepy head!' Chris greeted her, looking far too refreshed for Jane's liking. *How does he do it every morning! It wasn't fair. He seems to sleep no matter what while I fall out of bed, wrecked!*

'Sorry if I'm a bit late. Didn't sleep *again*! Remind me not to have a siesta in future. Not a good idea at all. It made the jet lag worse. Anyway, you seem to be full of the joys of life this morning.'

'Yea! Sorry! I've had a great swim and now I'm having *chocolate con churros*. I feel like a teenager, having *the* unhealthiest breakfast but enjoying every morsel. Would you like some?'

'Oh yes please! Just what the doctor ordered! I'm tired of being good – a little hot chocolate sounds just the thing. I hope it's got plenty of sugar in it.'

It had! That, together with the plate of *churros* she demolished, changed Jane's mood for the better.

'Yum! That's set me up for the day, I can tell you. Though, if I stay in Spain much longer, I'm going to have to change my diet. Any more meals like this and I'll be waddling onto the plane home.'

That was the first time either of them had even contemplated the prospect of going home as, inevitably, they would have to sooner or later. A silence descended as each considered the future: *when would they be going back to Sydney? Would they be going home alone, back to their usual lives? Would this trip to Spain have no impact on those lives? Surely things would be different? Better?*

After a few moments, Chris waved at the waiter and got the bill. Once paid (Jane resisted the temptation to remind him of another bill he hadn't paid), they walked to the taxi rank on the other side of the road, near the *Plaza del mar* fountain. In less than half an hour, they were in *San Joan* and walking towards the reconverted hotel. Chris was the first to put the next challenge into words for, now that they were faced with the hotel entrance, it was none too clear how they would get any further.

'So, what do we do when we get there, Jane? Just walk in and ask for Eva?'

'Hardly. They'd think we were up to no good. Let's see what the set-up is first. Then we can see if there is a way to get in.'

'But we can't really knock on every room once we're inside. That would be ridiculous.'

'I know, but there must be some sort of reception area, right? We could ask for information about volunteering there.'

'Or why not stick with our original story, Jane. You're doing a story on unaccompanied refugee children and was there anyone you could talk to about it.'

'Oh right! That sounds better. I keep forgetting our cover story. Let's do that, then.'

As it was Sunday morning, in full fiesta season, the area was comparatively quiet in this particular neighbourhood. People were obviously recovering from the previous night's festivities and having a restful start to the day, except, of course, those involved in the *despertá* that had happened at 8 am or the children's games that were taking place in the *Rambla* around now. It would get busier as the day progressed, no doubt, as lots of activities were planned, culminating with a bonfire, one of the first, at midnight. This area of Alicante, like all other areas, would celebrate the season to the full, no holds barred. Chris was thinking, as they approached the entrance to the ex-hotel, how similar people were the world over; bonfires and fireworks, those two things were core to a good party. After all, what would Sydney's New Year's Eve be without the excitement of the midnight firework display, preceded by the children's 9 o'clock one? He could still remember his own children's faces when he and Sally would bring them into the city and watch from the Botanical gardens. Happy days!

Chris was lost in such reverie when he suddenly became aware that Jane had stopped in her tracks. She was a few paces behind him and whispering furiously:

'Chris... Chris!'

'What is it?'

'Look – in the doorway – isn't that Fr. Lonergan?'

'So it is. I wonder how he got here.'

'I imagine the same way we did. That's not the real question, though. It's *why* is he here? What's he up to?'

'Why should he be up to anything? Maybe he fancied a break to come and see the bonfires. Who knows?!'

'Maybe but it's a bit of a coincidence isn't it - seeing him right here where Eva might be?'

'He could say the same thing about you, couldn't he?'

Their argument was interrupted as the aforementioned Fr. Lonergan had spotted them and was waving furiously:

'¡Hola! ¡Hola! Well, if it isn't my new Australian friends, Jane and Chris. What has you in this neck of the woods? If I'd known you were coming down to Alicante, sure we could have travelled together.'

Chris directed a meaningful look at Jane, seeming to say: *See, no mystery here!*

Jane did her best to avoid his eyes, not wanting to be convinced quite so easily. She was the first one to react to the priest's greeting:

'Hello, Father. This is a surprise and a coincidence. Imagine bumping into you here, of all places.'

Jane's face was a picture of innocence as she avoided Chris's attempts to interrupt.

'Yes, indeed, though not such a coincidence really since I often visit the other centres when I'm in Spain. Spread myself around, I do!' At this, the priest chuckled and rubbed his large tummy, amused at the joke. 'Plenty of me to go around, I always say!'

Jane avoided the distraction, even though she could hear Chris's polite laughter and carried on her line of questioning:

'So, you know the people staying here, then? Were any of them moved from Madrid, do you happen to know, Father?'

'Ah, now Jane, I see you are hot on the trail of your story. That's good. I like a dedicated soul, someone who knows what they're about. But this is no place to be talking. Why don't we find ourselves a nice café and have a bit of a *merienda*? I could do with a nice cup of tea after my travels and, though I know my friends inside here would be more than generous, something tells me that what you want to say is better said in private. Am I right about that, Jane?' These last words were accompanied by a surprisingly steely stare as the priest held Jane's gaze.

Jane could only nod in agreement as they were led skilfully away from the door and up the road toward a small establishment with a table or two where coffee and nibbles were served around the clock.

Once they had settled at one of the tables, Fr. Lonergan opened the conversation with a surprising question:

'So, are ye ready to tell me who you really are, now?' He accompanied this with a stare that both Chris and Jane found strangely reminiscent of their school days. The same stare of a school principal who is determined to get to the bottom of some prank or other. Neither were ever able to hold that stare for long, cracking quickly under the pressure as the guilt became too much to bear. So it was in this case as they squirmed in their seats. Jane did try to delay the inevitable a little longer:

'Why do you ask that, Father? You know we're following up on a lead for our story on refugees. We told you that yesterday.'

'Ah, yes, you told me a lot of things yesterday. What you didn't tell me, though, was even more interesting. You didn't tell me why this story? Why the children? Why travel all the way from Australia? And, most of all, why you're working with Magdalena Sánchez? Don't deny it! A friend of mine at the Madrid centre said Magda mentioned you to her.' A silence followed these questions as the two Australians considered how to reply.

'Okay, Father, you're right.' Chris was the first to crack. 'We have been a bit reticent with the truth, but it isn't for any very furtive reasons. We have the best of intentions.'

'What about allowing me to be the judge of that, lad?'

Chris looked at Jane who nodded curtly. Taking that as permission, he launched into a brief explanation of why they really were in Alicante, how they had seen a news report that featured Eva and how both had made their own decision to come and find her, for reasons they couldn't quite explain even to themselves.

After a long silence, during which Fr. Lonergan sat, seemingly contemplating the ramifications of what he had just heard, he finally spoke:

'Well, now, that is all very strange. You say you didn't know each other before coming here?'

'We did meet briefly once but, no, we didn't know each other.' Jane was the one to clarify.

'Doesn't the Lord work in mysterious ways? This takes the biscuit, it really does. Now, one last question ... well, maybe the last one ... depends on how you answer. How come you know Magdalena? What are you doing with that woman?'

Since Jane could see there was nothing for it but to be completely honest, notwithstanding her own feelings regarding Fr. Lonergan, she explained about meeting with Lucas and how Magda was his girlfriend and that she had decided to stick with the story, stick with them, actually.'

'Do you mean she's here in Alicante with you?' Seeing Chris nod, Fr. Lonergan continued, almost to himself:

'Ah, that's not good, not good at all. That throws a whole new perspective on things. What to do? What to do?'

'What to do about what, Father? Is there a problem?'

'Well, Chris, yes, you could say there's a problem. But the question is, can I trust you? My instincts tell me that I can but there's so much at play. Can I be sure?'

'Look, Father, I'm very sorry for deceiving you.' This time it was Jane who had decided to fill in a few of the blanks that Chris had left out of their story. 'What Chris didn't tell you is his reasons for coming here, his particular reasons. You see, he's a world-renowned surgeon, a specialist in facial reconstruction. That's how I met him: I was consulting him about getting rid of a few of these wrinkles.' Embarrassed, Jane waved her hand in the general direction of her face before continuing. 'He's here because he saw that Eva might need his help. He saw she had some kind of disfigurement that might mean extra challenges for a kid in her position and he just wanted to help.'

Fr. Lonergan looked at Chris in amazement:

'Is that true, Chris?' As Chris nodded, the priest continued muttering to himself again: 'Well now, this is a turn up for the books. A Godsend, I would say, if only we can figure things out in time ...Well! Well! Who'd have thought it? Who indeed?'

'Look at this, Father. This will convince you, I'm sure.' Jane handed the priest her phone where she had opened the *LinkedIn* page for Dr Christopher Neilson, showing the details of his education, his employment, his publications, and his awards. 'See, he *is* famous. He's a good, kind man and could help Eva and others like her if he got the chance.'

Jane became aware that both men were looking at her. She couldn't quite fathom Chris's expression but the priest was nodding, as if convinced by her argument.

'Very well. I'm going to take a chance and trust you both. But not here. We'll go to the hotel and I'd like to introduce you to a few people there. Okay?'

Chris and Jane drained their coffees and quickly followed the man out the door and back down the street. Not for the first time, Chris couldn't help thinking that, for such a large-girthed man, he could certainly move quickly when he wanted to, as he almost had to run to keep up with him. Jane, on the other hand, could hardly keep her excitement at bay: *Are we finally going to meet little Eva?*

Chapter 18

Fr. Lonergan entered the hotel, as he called it, as if he were completely at home. It was clear that he was a welcome guest and that the residents were very used to seeing him come and go and, more importantly, that they had been expecting him that morning. It was also clear that they viewed his two companions with suspicion, their words of welcome drying quickly on their lips when they saw them.

'Now, don't be worried at all. I've brought a couple of friends with me this morning. They're going to give us a hand, though they don't know it yet!' Fr. Lonergan chuckled to himself as he said this, amused by some private joke. 'Chris, Jane, let me introduce you to my families.'

At this, the priest presented the two Australians to the group that had assembled. There were six adults though no children were to be seen, much to Jane's disappointment. There was Amal and Fadil from Syria, Nadim, Uzair and Aishia from Yemen and Paula from Venezuela. Though they listened attentively, when Chris and Jane attempted to recall any of the names later that day, it was all a blur for, what the priest had asked of them after the introductions wiped out all other memories of the occasion. The six adults and the priest had led them into a room where there was a table laid out with food and drink: plates of falafel, hummus, tahini and pickles with flat bread, olives and cheese, rice with chicken, and even *arepas*, that corn cake typical of Venezuela. Clearly, there was something of a party planned, with each of the residents having contributed their speciality. Chris and Jane felt like interlopers, the uninvited guests who spoil all the fun.

Fr. Lonergan took one of the group of residents, Uzair, to one side and had a whispered conversation during which there was lots of gesticulating (on Uzair's part) and calm assertiveness (on the priest's). Finally, Uzair approached the two intruders:

'Forgive us for our cold welcome. Fr. Lonergan has explained why he brought you. Any friend of the good Father is a friend of ours so please, will you join us for our celebration? We are fare-welling some friends who are going on a long journey. We would be very pleased to share what we have.'

'Thank you, Uzair, you are very generous. We would be honoured to join you, right, Jane?'

'Yes, thank you and sorry for arriving unannounced but Fr. Lonergan insisted and, well, it's hard to say no to that man.'

Uzair laughed aloud.

'You are right. I have never seen anyone say no to him. It is one of his great talents. Please, come, sit with us and share our meal.'

Everyone sat at the table and soon conversation was flowing in many different tongues. Jane complimented Uzair on his English. In fact, a few of the group spoke English very well, which surprised her.

'I'm wondering why you've settled here in Spain since your English is so good. Wouldn't it be better to head to an English-speaking country?'

Silence met her question and she became aware that everyone in the room was looking at her.

'What did I say? Sorry if I've asked a stupid question but it's hard to learn another language. If you already have a good level of English, it must be challenging to start again with Spanish, right?'

Father Lonergan sat down beside her and took it upon himself to respond.

'You are right, Miss Jane. It would be more logical but not all that easy. You know that most, if not all the English-speaking countries have closed their borders or have strict quotas. It's not easy for people like my friends here to move from place to place. According to the Dublin Regulation, have ye heard of that?' The priest broke off to see if the two Australians were following. As they shook their heads, never having heard of such a regulation, he continued his explanation: 'Well, as I was saying, according to that, asylum seekers must have their status registered in the first European country they land in. Whatever decision reached in that country is the final decision. They can't travel on to any other EU country until a decision is made and they are granted refugee status. So, those who arrive in Spain must stay in Spain until they find out if they are granted asylum. If not, they are returned to their country of origin. In a word, my friends here are stuck.'

At this moment, Fadil interrupted:

'Miss, you must not think that we are ungrateful. We, here, are happy to be in Spain. We each have gone through a lot of difficulty to get this far and we consider we are the lucky ones. This centre is luxury compared to what we lived in on our journey. We have food and drink, we have shelter, we have education and medical attention for our children. We feel safe, though it is difficult not to be free. And we know there are others out there who are not so lucky.'

He stopped speaking and looked at the priest. His expression was hard to read but Fr. Lonergan seemed to understand.

'Fadil is wondering if he can trust you with our secret. Fadil, my friend, I think we can speak freely. Chris, Jane, when Fadil speaks of others, he is speaking of particular people. Children mainly. You see, there are many children who arrive without an adult to look out for them. For a long time, many would just disappear, never to be seen again. We became very concerned so have set up a network to bring such vulnerable children to safety. There are people throughout Europe who are working hard to keep them well. But we run into problems, particularly with children who have extra challenges.'

Here, he broke off and looked around the room, as if seeking encouragement or, at least, reassurance that he could continue. He must have found it for he started to speak again.

'What I am going to tell you, my Australian friends, if you were to reveal it, would get me and everyone here in grave trouble. Can I ask you to think very carefully before I go on? Can you pledge an oath that you will keep our secret?'

'That is difficult to do without knowing exactly what you are going to say.' Chris responded for them both. 'But, if it has to do with the safety of children, know that we will do everything in our power to protect them. But, be warned, if that means reporting you for any abuse, we will do that too.'

'Fair enough, fair enough. We are all determined to keep the children safe. Well then, we became aware, as I said, that children were vanishing and usually it was the children who no one cared for ... the challenging ones, the sickly ones, the ones with some disability or other. Who would miss them if their parents were already gone? In some cases, those parents had drowned, some had handed over their children to others in the hope they would have a better life. Whatever their story, the children ended up alone, defenceless, easy prey. We decided we had to do something, especially as we began to suspect that someone close to our refugee base was involved. Which meant we could trust no one.'

At this point, Jane couldn't help herself and interrupted:

'Who is 'we'? You keep mentioning 'we', Father.'

'At the beginning, it was just me and one of the other volunteers at the centre in Madrid, Yasmina. She was the one who alerted me to the vanishing children when she noticed that a little one called Adhira had gone. When she made enquiries, she was told there was no record of such a child. But I remembered her. I distinctly remember her as she had a limp and I recall thinking about how difficult it must have been for her to make the journey on her own.'

'So, there are just two of you?'

'That was at the beginning. Now, there's a network, as I mentioned. I'll tell you how it works. First, Yasmina alerts me when a child arrives at the centre that may 'fit the profile', so to speak. In other words, a child with a disability or some extra challenge who has arrived alone and, so, is even more vulnerable than the rest. I get to Madrid as quickly as possible, that's if I'm not already there. Sometimes I arrive a little late, as in this present case so Yasmina took action.'

'Do you mean Eva's case?' Chris now found he had to ask the burning question. No one had mentioned Eva and he was anxious to find out about her.

'Exactly. Eva's case. Yasmina phoned me when Eva arrived at the centre, alone, so little and with her slight deformity. As you noticed, Chris, she may have a cleft lip. She was skin and bone. It was amazing she had managed, against all odds, to make it that far. Yasmina, as I said, alerted me and I set out to get there as soon as I could.'

'And what were you planning to do when you arrived?' Jane asked, trying to make her question sound innocent but, even to her ears, there was an accusation in her tone.

'Nothing sinister, I can assure you, Miss Jane. Quite the contrary.' Fr. Lonergan's denial was supported by a general hum of approving voices as the other refugees voiced their support.

Fadil rose from his seat and approached the priest, putting his hand on the man's shoulder.

'This man is a hero, Miss. He has helped us to rescue countless children from a fate we do not wish to even contemplate. He works with us, never assuming he knows what's best and, if we agree, he arranges for the children to be moved to Ireland or elsewhere, depending on the circumstances. If they go to Ireland, for a short while they stay at the friary where he lives and then they are moved on to families who care for them. In some cases, he has even reunited them with their own parents. How he has managed I do not know but I do know that everyone in this room would lay down their lives for this man.'

Again, there was a murmur of approval and agreement.

'But isn't that child smuggling?' Jane again couldn't prevent the accusation from escaping from her mouth.

'Yes, you are right, Miss Jane.' Fr. Lonergan looked sheepishly around the room as he spoke. Then, as if remembering what had led him on this road, he shook his head and continued: 'But, I fear, I am a man who believes that sometimes the end does justify the means. Or, in this case, the happiness and safety of a child justifies the bending of rules. Do you not agree?'

'I suppose.'

'I hope so, because now comes the difficult bit. I must ask you a favour.'

'A favour? Go on.'

'Well, you have told me of your interest in Eva. I wonder, would you help me to get her to Ireland? I fear she is in great danger here in Spain and we need to move her tomorrow at the latest.'

'Danger? What kind of danger? Why was she moved from Madrid? What happened?'

'I'm not sure of all the details but Yasmina felt it necessary for the girl to be moved.'

'But why?'

'She thought a certain person was showing far too much interest in Eva, and she thought it was urgent to get Eva away from Madrid and it couldn't wait until I arrived. So she, with my blessing, brought her here. She's upstairs, playing with the other children. Safe and happy – for now at least.'

Jane and Chris exchanged a look of relief. Eva was safe and within reach. With luck they would meet her very soon.

'So who was showing such interest in the child?' Chris had a terrible feeling he knew the answer to his question even before he asked it.

'Need you ask? It was your friend, Magdalena Sánchez.'

There was a stunned silence as Jane and Chris digested this new piece of information. What did it mean? Should they believe the worst of Magda, simply because Fr. Lonergan was suggesting it? And what exactly was he suggesting? That Magda was responsible for kidnapping children and worse? And, finally, the most difficult aspect to endure: if all this were true of Magda, were they the ones responsible for providing her with an excuse to come to Alicante? It certainly seemed as if they were.

Chapter 19

Once they had recovered from the shock of discovering that they may have been on the wrong side of things all along, Chris and Jane urged Father Lonergan to continue.

'So what is it you want us to do now?' Jane directed her question at the priest who had been waiting calmly for them to digest his accusation. He had also been searching their faces for anything that might suggest they were aware of Magdalena's activities. He had seen no sign of collusion so went on with his request.

'Since you have told me that Magdalena is now in Alicante, it has become even more urgent that we act. Our plan had been to move Eva along with another couple of children next week. But we now think we should bring the plan forward and go tomorrow when people are distracted by the burning of the official bonfires. Would you be willing to bring Eva to the Marina around 1:00 am early on Tuesday morning? We have a boat there which will set sail after the first bonfire has been lit and before the second lot are scheduled at 1:30. That's when there will be lots of people wandering around and you'll blend in with all the tourists. You'll look like an ordinary family out for the evening's festivities.'

'But isn't it very late for a little girl to be wandering around? Won't people notice?'

Fr. Lonergan chuckled at that thought.

'Not at all, Miss Jane. This is Spain and it's fiesta time. Whole families will be out and about. All enjoying the atmosphere, having ice creams and *churros con chocolate* and what not. I'd bring her myself but you can imagine what people would think if they saw a priest with such a young girl.

These are not good times to wear a habit. I could dress in civvies but I'm going to be busy elsewhere and my friends here are also busy.'

'Doing what? It would be good to know the whole plan before we agree to get involved.' Chris's reticence was holding him back from agreeing to the priest's request.

'Well, Chris, I think I'll keep that to myself for now. After all, if you don't want to help out, it's probably better you know as little as possible. We wouldn't want you to spill the beans, no matter how unintentionally. I've heard Magdalena can be a very persuasive woman.'

Jane couldn't help laughing at Chris's hurt expression which betrayed his dismay at the priest's lack of trust in him while also acknowledged his wariness of Ms Sánchez. Chris was none too sure of his own ability to withstand Magda's demands should she apply any undue pressure.

'So, Father, all you need us to do is collect Eva tomorrow and bring her to the Marina. Drop her off there and that's that?'

'Exactly, Jane. Nothing too complicated.'

'Can we think about it? We could let you know in the morning. I'd like to sleep on it.'

'Fair enough. Do that but, whatever you do, please don't discuss anything with anyone else.' The priest stressed the word 'anyone' but everyone in the room knew exactly who he meant: Magdalena Sánchez was clearly no one's favourite person, an opinion that Jane had no problem sharing. But did that mean she was guilty of one of the worst crimes imaginable? It seemed clear at this stage that someone was and the choice seemed to be between a priest and a social worker, both people who should surely be trustworthy and beyond reproach but, sadly, that was only in an ideal world and this world was far from being that.

Jane and Chris took their leave of the group very quickly after that. They had asked if they could meet with Eva but Fr. Lonergan explained that it wouldn't be in the child's interests. If they didn't feel they could help, it would confuse her to meet two strangers whom she wouldn't ever meet again. Time enough tomorrow if they agreed to help with the plan.

The two Australians wandered down the street for a while before hailing a cab that happened by. They went straight back to the hotel and each retired to their room to think things over. They would meet up again in the evening. That, at least, was the plan. Five minutes after parting, Chris was knocking frantically on Jane's door.

'What's wrong? Has something happened?'

'It's Magda. She's just texted me. She wants to meet. She's in the lobby. What should I do?'

'Uh-oh! That's not good. Why not ignore the text? Or text back and say you have a headache?'

'I thought of that but she's quite capable of coming up to my room.'

'Yea! She might offer to rub the pain away.'

'You're enjoying this, aren't you? It's not funny. I might say something to jeopardise Lonergan's plan.'

'No, you wouldn't. But you are right. I shouldn't laugh. This is a serious business. Okay, there's nothing for it but for both of us to go downstairs and hope my presence puts her off.'

'You'll come with me?'

Jane had to laugh at Chris's sheer relief at not having to face Magda alone.

'Of course I will. All for one and one for all! Let's just make sure we don't mention Eva or anything about where we were this morning. Keep the conversation light. Talk about koalas and kangaroos. Anything but the one thing neither of us can stop thinking about.'

'Gotcha. Will do. Koalas and kangaroos it is.'

Chapter 20

Magdalena Sánchez was waiting for Chris outside the main door of the hotel. She was standing, looking at the *ninot*, dressed in her white trouser suit, and looking a million dollars. Jane immediately felt old and dowdy, given that she hadn't had a chance to change since their excursion earlier in the day. She had been looking forward to a nice shower, and a rest; a nice siesta had never seemed such a wonderful invention even if she had resolved earlier not to give in to that particular temptation. So, today, she'd have to keep that resolution, much as she wished she could break it.

'*Hola*, Chris, *querido*. How nice to see you. Did you have a nice morning? Oh, *hola*, Jane. I didn't expect you to be up and about. You must be so tired.'

'Why ever not, Magda?' It was galling that Magda seemed to be able to see through Jane. Jane was exhausted but it didn't help for the younger woman to point it out.

'Oh, I just thought you'd like a *siesta*, given the time of day it is and it is Sunday.'

'You don't seem to want one so why should I, Magda?'

For an answer, Magda just smiled enigmatically and turned her attention to Chris.

'So, Chris, would you like me to show you around Alicante? I thought we could go up to the castle or wander down the *Explanada* or walk over to the Marina. You choose.'

Chris was just about to make their excuses when Jane jumped in:

'Oh I'd love to have a look at all the yachts in the Marina. Let's do that,

Magda.'

Chris glared at Jane but she avoided his eyes, knowing full well what he was thinking. *Why on earth would you attract attention to the very place we want Magda to ignore?* Jane, however, thought it would be useful to discover the lay of the land. If they were going to go through with the plan, it could only help if they knew where, exactly, they were going.

'Very well, if that's what you'd like to do too, Chris?' In response, Chris nodded curtly, not trusting himself to speak.

The threesome headed through the archway of the *plaza* and crossed the same road that, earlier, Chris and Jane had each crossed on their way to the beach. This time, instead of turning left toward the beach, they all headed right, skirting the sea where lines of yachts and motorboats of all sizes and dimensions were anchored. On some, people could be seen having drinks, or busy tidying up, or simply sitting and admiring the scenery. A Sunday afternoon was a good excuse to take a break from the week's normal activities and enjoy the fruits of one's labour.

Jane let the other two take the lead, with Chris asking the odd question to keep Magda talking. That allowed Jane time to look carefully at how the boats were arranged, where the entry ramps were, what security was in view. Her experience as a diver came in useful as she was very accustomed to sailing out from similar places and knew exactly what to look out for. She made several mental notes and soon felt she could find her way around the Marina with her eyes closed, or, more likely, in the dark. When she was happy she had discovered as much as she could, she spoke to Chris:

'Chris, I'm going to head back to the hotel now. I am a little tired after all.'

'I'll come too. I could do with a nap. And I need to catch up on a few emails.'

'Ay, Chris, surely you would like to join me for an ice cream, or a coffee? There is plenty of time later for a nap. You sound like an old man!' Magda looked pointedly at Jane as she said these last words, her message seemed clear: *You are too old for him! I am much more fun!*

Jane stayed quiet, allowing Chris to fight his own battle this time.

'I feel like an old man, Magda. Much too old to be wandering any more today, at least for now. Thanks for showing us around but, now, please, I just need my bed.'

'Well, you can still have your bed. I could come and give you a nice massage, ease some of that stress you are carrying on your shoulders.'

'Very kind of you to offer, Magda. But...' Chris looked amused and glanced at Jane before going on, as if weighing up what her reaction would be to his next words. 'But Jane is very good at massage. I'm sure she'll be happy to rub some liniment on my old bones.'

Jane nearly choked when she heard what he had said. She could only nod as she wiped the tears from her eyes, concentrating on catching her breath and not laughing out loud.

Chris grabbed her by the arm and led her away as he waved goodbye to Magda before either woman had the chance to argue.

A few minutes later, when Jane had finally recovered, she asked him:

'What on earth possessed you, Chris? I thought I'd suffocate. Did you see the look on Magda's face? She's furious with you.'

'I *know* but I thought the flirtation had gone on long enough. I need her to keep her distance and make it clear I'm not interested. That was the only way I could think to persuade her to leave me alone.'

'Oh, you poor man. It must be terrible to have an attractive young woman pursue you. Joking apart, do you think it was wise to alienate her quite so dramatically?'

'Yes, I do actually. How else are we going to carry out the plan? If she stuck with me like glue, we'd never get time to even discuss what we want to do, let alone get Eva to the Marina, if that's what we decide to do.'

'True. Do you think she'll back off now, though? She's a very determined lady. And, if you'll forgive me for saying so, I don't really think it's just your charms that's keeping her nearby. If we're to believe Fr. Lonergan, she's using you to get to Eva. Somehow, she's sure you'll lead her to the child. Though she must know she's at that hotel place. I'm really confused as to her intentions, to tell the truth.'

'It's a sobering thought to think that she thinks I might help her get to Eva. But she's gone for now at least so let's get that coffee and talk about what we're going to do.'

'What about getting a bite to eat instead. I know there was lots of food at the refugee place but I was so stressed by the whole situation that I didn't eat hardly anything and I, for one, could do with something.'

No sooner said than done. They picked one of the restaurants close to the Marina where, logically enough, the seafood was delicious. The conversation didn't linger long on whether or not they would do Fr. Lonergan's bidding. In fact, it almost went without saying that they would help out. Instead, they spoke of what preparations would need to be made. Should they check out of the hotel or would that alert the infamous Magda? Should they leave their belongings or pack them up, again taking the risk of making their intentions known? Once they had discussed all the preparations they could think of, they headed back to their hotel, and both fell asleep until darkness fell and the sound of distant fireworks awoke them.

Neither felt in the mood for celebrations that night so they agreed to rest up in order to be at their best the next day, a day that they foresaw would be a long one. Chris reported that there had been no further communication from Magda so, either she had got the message or was taking time to plan her next move. Chris very much feared the latter was far more likely. He was more than happy to lie low for the night rather than risk bumping into her in the highways or byways of Alicante city.

Chapter 21

The next day dawned just as bright and sunny as the previous one, not an unusual occurrence in that Mediterranean city. Jane and Chris, however, didn't feel quite so cheerful as they contemplated what lay before them. Would it really be so easy to smuggle Eva out of Spain? As neither had ever broken any law, or attracted the attention of law enforcers, except for the odd parking ticket, they did not relish the task ahead of them. Yet, when their courage faltered, they just remembered what had brought them this far: the needs of a young child who had touched their hearts.

'Well then, here we are again.' Chris stated the obvious as they stood outside the refugee accommodation. They had rung Fr. Lonergan early that morning and agreed to meet at the hotel and take things from there. They had no sooner arrived than the priest almost magically appeared and escorted them into the same room as the day before. This time, however, there was no food on the table and no party atmosphere. Instead, the feeling among those in the room was sombre.

'We're all a bit gloomy today, I'm afraid,' the priest explained. 'We've grown fond of Eva and the others and it would be so much easier for the children to stay here but there were reports of people watching the hotel last night. It just isn't safe for them to remain.'

'Do you really think they'd be snatched when so many people are looking out for them –You know, you, Yasmina and all the people here.'

'I'm afraid we are talking from experience. Other children have vanished. We did report them to the police who, though sympathetic, held little hope of finding them. I haven't given up, of course. There's always scope for a miracle. But, meanwhile, we must do all we can to prevent it happening again. Your help will be very welcome.'

'Yes, well, talking about that. What, exactly, do we do?' Jane liked to have all details sewn up whenever she was undertaking a task. It came from working in a legal firm: nothing could be left up to chance in a courtroom so all I's had to be dotted and Ts crossed beforehand.

'As I said yesterday, it's just a matter of blending in with the crowd tonight. There'll be lots of families wandering around, enjoying the spectacle of the burning of the *ninots*. The one at the townhall goes up at midnight, along with a few others. Then, there's a bit of a gap until 1:30 when another bunch are scheduled to be lit. That's the time, I think, that will be best to make for the Marina. People will be ambling around, some heading home, some heading to the next bonfire.'

'And what do we do when we get to the Marina?'

'I'll give you a letter to hand to the captain of a yacht called the *Aisling*. I say 'captain' but it is a small enough vessel, just two crew. The captain is called Johnny Fitzpatrick, a fellow Irishman. He's well used to sailing the high seas and will take Eva and the two other children direct to Cork. He knows of a few spots where he can make land. Meanwhile, I'll fly back home. There's a direct flight tomorrow that'll get me to Cork around noon or thereabouts. That will give me time to sort things out and I can meet Johnny when he arrives. It could take him anything between four and seven days, maybe a little more depending on weather and currents and so on. Anyway, he'll let me know when to collect the children and bring them back with me to the friary. We'll have everything ready there for them by then.'

'What happens after that?' Jane couldn't get her head around a group of friars risking everything to harbour refugees. Especially in the climate of suspicion that surrounded any priest seen alone with a child. How would their reputations fare if news of their activities ever got out? She could see the headlines now and they weren't pretty.

'We set about finding homes for them while we do everything in our power to find their relatives. We also set about giving them security as far as possible. We work with certain bodies in Ireland and in Europe.'

'So you're saying that Eva and others like her will be able to get a proper home.'

'That's the aim though it takes time and, sometimes, for the children, timing is critical.'

'It all seems very risky. And if the full weight of the law were used against you and the others, you'd find yourself in prison at the very least.'

'We are all very aware of the risks, Miss Jane. And, hopefully, you are too as you run the same risk if you help us. But I believe we are working on the side of the angels so I rely on divine protection. So far, it's worked. I'm still here and plan to go on until I'm stopped.'

'I don't have your faith, Fr. Lonergan, but, if you could, say a prayer that all goes well tonight.'

'You may be sure of it, indeed, I will. I expect I'll have said quite a few before this day is over.'

Chapter 22

Father Lonergan was used to projecting a calm exterior, no matter the circumstances. He had been through many difficult situations in the past and had faced personal challenges that would have floored a lesser man. He had grown up in what was now called a dysfunctional family though, when he was a young lad, he hadn't ever heard that term. All he knew was that his father used to beat up his mother whenever he had drink on him. It was only when Dad took the strap to him and his younger sister that things changed. That was what impelled his mum to look for help and she found it in the Church. The Franciscans, specifically. That's what she called them, that group of friars and priests who worked in the heart of Cork city. They provided her with options, with the basic necessities when she decided she'd had enough. Of course, in those days, priests and the like were meant to discourage the breakup of marriages at any cost. Yet, those particular men of the cloth were realists and violence towards children was always the line not to be crossed.

Father Lonergan, or rather Jimmy as he was then, grew up knowing there were two types of people in the world: those who complained about what life threw at them and those who did something about it. His father complained and drank to forget his troubles. The friars worked hard to bring some kind of happiness to those who were struggling. He decided pretty quickly that he wanted to be one of them. And they were delighted to help him with his studies and encourage him in every way. His mother, too, was happy to see he wasn't following in his father's footsteps. Not that she didn't love the man. It was the demon drink that had led him astray. And disappointments along the way that had given him more than enough reason to want to escape the daily grind, at least when he could afford a pint or two or three.

Jimmy Lonergan was proud as punch on his ordination day. It was one of the few occasions when all the family gathered and were on their best behaviour, with his mum and his sister clearly delighted at his achievement. Even his dad had dressed up in his best suit and looked as if he, too, would burst with pride. All day he went around telling anyone who'd listen: 'Well, at least I did one thing right.' It was a fine day and one that Jimmy would treasure in his memory forever. His Dad died not long after that day and Jimmy, now Fr. Lonergan, wondered if he had felt his work was done, that he could go out on a high point, perhaps. It was the first funeral that Fr. Jim (as his closest friends called him) had officiated as a priest and it took him all his strength, and that of his fellow Franciscans, to get him through. Memories kept flooding back and not all of them good ones. His father's story was now over: all the terror he had inflicted on Jimmy and his sister: the nights they had hidden in the corner of a bedroom, trying to muffle the sound of their mother's tears; the sound of the key in the door as they wondered what mood Dad would be in tonight; the spoilt holidays; the hungry days when all the money had been spent on paying Dad's bills. All that was over and all that was left was love. He had loved his father, despite everything, and knew that, beneath all the heartache, his Dad had loved him too.

Love. That's what now motivated Fr. Lonergan. Nowadays, since the crisis in the Church, it was hard to tell people that he loved children. A priest couldn't say such things without people getting the wrong end of the stick. And who could blame them? He hadn't been aware, as a young cleric, of all the horrors that would be revealed. There were rumours, of course, but he often wondered what he would have done had he come across any priest harming a child. *Thou shalt not kill.* That commandment seemed clear enough but he couldn't guarantee that he would have kept his anger in check. Even now, it took him all his self-control to work toward saving children without resorting to violence when faced with people who got in his way. He was a work in progress, that's what his confessor always told him: *Don't give up, Jim, you're a work in progress. Keep working on patience and you'll get there.* But Jim was a rebel; rules, if not made to be broken, could be bent a little (or even a lot) if the cause were just. And this cause was just. At least that's what he told himself.

Today, however, he could feel his impatience building like a volcano. He was anxious to get his plan started. Waiting around was the worst. He had to be doing something. Yet there was nothing to do but wait and think: *Was he doing the right thing? Was he putting the children at more risk?* They too were finding it difficult to wait. They were afraid of what was to come though they had been through so much already. It was their trust in him that strengthened his resolve. They would look at him with those beautiful big eyes and he would melt. Love. There it was again, the motivation for everything, for all the risks and all the hardships. Love.

So Fr. Lonergan girded his loins, double checked his plan, and went to meet his new-found friends and allies, Chris and Jane. Now there was a strange pair. If they didn't end up married at the end of this adventure, then he'd eat his hat, if he had a hat! Of course, they weren't aware that they were perfect for each other but it was as plain as the nose on his face that they were. He'd have to knock their heads together if they didn't get a move on. Love. Didn't people know that's all that mattered?

'Well, right then, Miss Jane and Mr Chris. Are you all set?'

'We're here but I don't know if you could say we're all set. We're anxious to get things started, though. This waiting around is a killer.'

'You never said a truer word, Chris. I'm not a patient man but time is its own boss. It neither hurries nor dallies for anyone. While we're waiting, though, let's go up to the children. It would be good now for you to get to know Eva a little. She's been told about you. She's a little dote. Very trusting which is amazing considering what she's been through. Too trusting, I'm afraid, for she'd likely go off with anyone who said a kind word to her.'

'I can't wait to meet her.' Both Chris and Jane said those words in unison, breaking into laughter as they realised they were feeling exactly the same mixture of trepidation and excitement at the prospect of finally meeting the little girl of their dreams.

'Follow me then. There's a lift but I prefer to walk. I need the exercise' Fr. Lonergan chuckled as he patted his ample tummy. Though, in this case, his laughter was as much at the pair of would-be rescuers who were so easy to read, at least to his well-trained eye.

Up the steps they went, following the priest who set a surprising pace. Finally, they got to a door, not unlike any hotel door the world over. Giving three taps, the priest said their names and the door swung open, revealing a surprisingly bright and cheerful playroom with toys and books strewn everywhere. Laughter could be heard and singing. It was like entering Alice's wonderland. On seeing them enter, all the games being played suddenly stopped as three children froze in their tracks. For what seemed an eternity, time stood still as children and adults assessed each other. Finally, one child broke away and approached Jane shyly.

In surprisingly good English, she said:

'Hello, Miss. My name is Eva. Fr Lonergan says you are going to mind me.'

Jane's heart melted instantly. She bent down on her hunkers and took Eva's hands in hers.

'Hello, little Eva. My name is Jane. And, yes, That's right. I am going to mind you and so is Chris.'

Jane looked up at Chris with tears of emotion in her eyes. She could see he was also close to breaking point as he bent down to Eva's level.

'That's right, little one. You will be safe with us.' As he said it, Chris knew he would lay down his life for this little girl. No one - absolutely no one - would ever harm her as long as he had breath left in him.

Chapter 23

The rest of the day was spent in fun and games. There was hide and seek, chasing, hopscotch, a little football, playing with dolls and teddy bears, not to mention marbles, with lots of tickling and giggling and general merriment thrown in for good measure. There was also nap time both for the children and the adults as it would be a long night before either group saw their beds. And, of course, there was some eating and drinking too and, soon, all too soon, surprisingly, it was time to set out. Each child was to be accompanied by two adults. They were to set out in different directions at different times. Some were to head to the bonfires of San Joan d'Alacant while others would make it to Alicante townhall plaza. All were to head for the *Aisling*, the boat that would be waiting for them at the time agreed. They were not to contact each other under any circumstances. In fact, all telephone numbers in common were to be deleted as was any information that would lead back to the hotel or to Fr. Lonergan. If anything happened to one group, it would be important that nothing was known of the other two. Strict silence would have to be maintained to ensure everyone's safety.

Chris, Jane, and Eva were the last to leave. They were to catch public transport to Alicante city centre, the number 23 bus which would take them as far as the market. From there they could blend in with the crowds and make their way on foot to the square. Hopefully, it would all be straightforward.

'Well, we've made it this far.' Chris was relieved to be getting off the bus at the designated spot and relieved that all had gone to plan so far. He had felt vulnerable trapped in the moving vehicle. It was as if all the other passengers knew what was happening, that Eva wasn't their daughter and that they all suspected him of deeds too vile to express.

'Yes, so far so good. Come on, Eva, let's have a look at that lovely lolly shop I can see across the road. Would you like to do that?'

'Lolly shop?'

'Oh, I think 'lolly' is an Australianism, Jane. Sweet shop, Eva. Do you like sweets?'

'Sweets? Sugar?'

'Yes, that's right, hun. Sugar.'

'Yes, please.'

Eva skipped along beside them, happily holding their hands and content that they were in charge, and she was going to get some treats.'

They were not alone in that plan. What seemed like hundreds of people were all milling around *Jaime II* and *Alfonso el Sabio* Avenues. Chris and Jane were planning to amble along with the rest, stopping off now and then at any shops that had remained open. Strangely enough, given the late hour, there were quite a few. The sweet shop was one, probably because the owners couldn't pass up such a good opportunity to catch the passing trade on a busy night like this. Clearly their plan had worked for it was crowded inside with lots of children spending far too long choosing their favourite treat or two. It was obvious that Eva had never seen such a display of edibles. There were bonbons and gummy bears, lemon sorbets and chocolate drops, toffees and caramels, lollipops and marshmallows, gob stoppers and strawberry jellies, liquorice, wine gums, Turkish delight, and every type of chocolate bar imaginable. Jane, herself, was quite dizzy to see such a selection so it was not surprising that poor Eva didn't know what to choose, her eyes darting in every direction as she tried to make sense of such offerings.

'Perhaps we should just buy a bit of chocolate and some jelly babies, nothing too fancy, eh Jane?' Chris suggested, seeing the confusion on Eva's face.

'Agreed, there's just too much to choose from but a bit of chocolate never goes amiss.'

Chris did as he had suggested and filled a bag with the jelly sweets for Eva and picked up a couple of chocolate bars for himself and Jane and, once he had paid, they wandered on, turning into the *Rambla Méndez Núñez* as they followed the crowds heading towards the bonfires. Eva munched happily between them, savouring the new-found power of deciding whether to eat a jelly baby headfirst or limb by limb.

The crowds became denser as they neared the turning into *Rafael Altamira* Street. It wouldn't be possible to get into the square itself as that would be blocked off. The lucky people were already crowding onto the balconies surrounding the plaza; they would get the best view of the fire. It was now close to midnight and the fire trucks were geared up to douse any stray embers that would go too close to the nearby buildings. Chris and Jane lingered as close to the action as they dared, not wanting to go too far into the crowds. In fact, Chris decided that Eva would be safer off the ground so picked her up and swung her up onto his shoulders, much to the child's delight.

'I can see good now, Mr Chris', the girl exclaimed, clapping her little hands together. Sticky hands, due to the demise of a few too many jelly babies.

The countdown had started. It was only a few more moments until the first flames would appear... *diez, nueve, ocho, siete...* Some people were counting in *Valenciano*, the language many Alicantinos spoke among family and friends: *sis, cinc, quatre, tres...* Just as everyone was getting ready to cheer, Chris became aware of a tugging on his shirt sleeve. He looked down and, to his amazement, he saw Fr. Lonergan's hand, attached to the man himself who was urgently trying to catch his attention. It wasn't Fr. Lonergan as he had come to know him, though. He was no longer wearing his brown habit but, instead, was dressed in a bizarre outfit: green trousers that were too small for him, a blue jacket that was too large, a pink shirt that had seen better days and, on top of his bald head, a peaky cap with

Sea Eagles emblazed in white on a maroon background. Chris decided to ignore the strange garb and ask the more pressing question:

'Father, what are you doing here? I thought we were to avoid all contact.'

'We were, Chris, we were. Thank heavens I found you. A miracle, given the amount of people. Come quickly. There's been a slight change of plan. We must hurry. Come on! Come on! Run!'

Chris, with Eva on his shoulders, did as he was bid, just taking a second to grab Jane and make sure she followed him. Fr. Lonergan was out ahead, running as fast as his short legs could go in tight trousers, not even looking back to see if they were following. He was clearly heading in the general direction of the Marina, so Chris, with Jane behind, followed, dodging the various groups of people whose attention was firmly focused on the bonfire. Soon, though, instead of turning right, they turned left and then into the old port road, racing past the *Meliá* and *Spa Porta Maris* hotels, past the Casino and along the *Levante* dock, Chris sprinting, with some difficulty given he had Eva on his shoulders, along the strip of land towards the ferry terminal and the Alicante light beacon. That was surprising since, originally, they were supposed to find the *Aisling* in the Marina itself. Chris had envisaged a gentle stroll before handing Eva over to those who would care for her during the sea voyage, not this mad gallop. As he tried to make sense of this new location, they arrived at the far end of the dock and could go no further. Fr. Lonergan stopped in his tracks allowing the others to reach him and catch their breath, but only for a moment. He suddenly started waving fiercely out to sea. It wasn't clear at first what he was doing and it did enter Chris's mind that the priest had lost his grip on reality but, then, as a little dinghy appeared, as if out of thin air, it became obvious that he had been signalling.

'Miss Jane, Chris, I'm afraid things have changed. The police called to the hotel just after you had left. Clearly someone betrayed us. They are looking for you both and for Eva. There's nothing for it but for you to go to Ireland. Get on board the dinghy, quickly now. There's no time for any discussion.

They are probably right behind me. I took a big gamble trying to find you without being seen. Hence the disguise.'

Jane finally managed to see the priest clearly. It had taken her a minute to understand why Chris had grabbed her arm earlier and, realising his urgency, she had run as fast as she could to keep up with him. He had blocked her vision of the disguised priest who now appeared in all his glory.

'Wow, Father! When you dress in civvies you really let it all hang out, don't you? That outfit would win medals in a fancy dress!'

'Ah now, Miss Jane, don't be mocking me. I dressed in haste and grabbed anything I could find. I couldn't venture out in my habit as I'd be far too easy to follow.'

'And you thought you'd blend in better in that outfit, did you?' Even given the circumstances, the group allowed themselves a moment to laugh at the irony of the situation.

'I suppose I needn't have bothered, since you mention it. But now, my young friends, please get into the dinghy. It will bring you out to the *Aisling*. Johnny's waiting for you just out of sight. I was able to get a message to him but I don't know if I was overheard. I don't think so but, then, we were so careful before and all was revealed. Hurry now. There's no time to waste.'

'But what about the other children, Father?'

'We can't wait for them. Don't worry. We'll get them to safety too. Just not this way. Now, please, go!'

They all hurried to the motor dinghy which was crewed by just one man. Later, when they were safely on board the *Aisling*, along with the dinghy, they would discover his name was Tadgh O'Riordan, who answered to Taddy as no-one outside of Ireland could pronounce his name correctly. One by one they stepped onto the little craft which bobbed disconcertingly in the water. This was not a safe mooring spot but was the best that could be organised, given the change of circumstances. Soon all but the priest were aboard and he waved them away from the dock, becoming quickly a small little dot as they almost flew over the surface of the water. They could just make him out as he turned away from them and headed back to Alicante. The view of the port couldn't have been more spectacular if only they had had the heart to notice: the Santa Bárbara castle lit up against the backdrop of all the other lights, the odd firework exploding here and there as people celebrated the bonfires, the stars competing in the night sky. None of that was noticed by either Jane or Chris as their minds were on the realisation that they had just become fugitives from the Spanish police. *What were they to do now? Would they find safe haven in Ireland? Would they ever be able to travel back home?* Those questions and many more were spinning around in their heads as they boarded the *Aisling* in grim silence.

Chapter 24

It is funny how the most bizarre circumstances can quickly become routine. So it was for Chris, Jane, and Eva as they settled into life on board the *Aisling*. Johnny had steered them away from the Port of Alicante as quickly as he could. Once they were clear of the 'no-wake zone', he set a reasonably brisk pace of 10 knots, not wanting to attract the attention of the coast guard by going too fast but still anxious to get out to open sea as quickly as possible. He explained to his passengers that it could take anything up to a week to reach their destination and safe harbour, maybe even longer, depending on the weather and the currents and what other obstacles they might encounter. Luckily, the *Aisling* was well equipped and well stocked, this not being the first time it had been called to such action. It was a 55' motor yacht used normally, Johnny assured them, for recreational fishing. He said he often hired it and himself out to groups of tourists who wanted to test themselves against large fish like marlin and tuna, or even the odd shark or two. It could sleep six at a push and had a powerful Yanmar twin engine. Built in 2008, it had seen better days, but it would get them to where they were going which was the important thing. If they were stopped for any reason, they were to stick to the story that they were on a fishing expedition. That was going to be Johnny's answer to awkward questions if he'd have to anchor at any port along the way, something he was hoping to avoid. He had stocked up on supplies, including fuel, so, all going well, they wouldn't have to talk to anyone for the duration.

Jane had been on worse craft when on diving excursions around the Barrier reef but that was small comfort to her as she contemplated the next few days on board. This was not part of the plan, that was for sure. Here she was, in the company of three men, only one of whom she knew a little and in charge of a little girl whom she knew not at all. She hadn't even got her belongings with her, except for a toothbrush and her passport, a change of undies and some make-up (a girl has her pride, after all, especially when spending so much time with a plastic surgeon!). Luckily, when planning their night, she and Chris had agreed that they should be ready for the unforeseen. They mightn't be able to get back to the hotel straight away so they had brought the essentials. Small comfort now since, on top of having left her favourite jacket and shoes behind her, she was on the run from the police and, if apprehended, there was little she could use in her defence. She *was* attempting to smuggle a child from one country to another. *Guilty as charged, Your Honour! And* she had absolutely no proof that the child had needed to be rescued in the first place. After all, Eva had been in the care of a perfectly respectable agency. Why take her away from them? She didn't even know for sure where she was taking her to, if it came to that. The Franciscan Friary in Cork. How ludicrous did that sound when you said it out loud? How on earth had she let herself be persuaded to get involved in such a madcap plan?

Chris, too, was contemplating their situation with equal disbelief. He had always considered himself a sensible person, not given to hair-brained schemes. Too sensible if it came to that. Always the one in the group to point out the flaw in a plan. And now, here he was, on board a boat heading to Ireland having, basically, kidnapped a child. How was he going to explain that to his own children? That is, if he would ever get to see them again before he was locked up for good. Maybe, with luck ... lots and lots of luck ... they'd all look back on this escapade in a few years and laugh. If they got away with it. But, how on earth were they going to do that? Ah well, nothing he could do about it now. He was in the hands of Johnny and Taddy who seemed to know what they were doing. Didn't they? If only he could be sure that they did.

The next few days were spent entertaining Eva as best they could, given the limited resources. Since he had expected to be in charge of three children, Johnny had stocked up on children's books and a few toys, including a very much needed teddy bear that quickly became Eva's favourite. Clearly Johnny was a resourceful man and knew a thing or two about young children and their needs. As they sailed down the coast of Spain, through the Strait of Gibraltar and headed northwards, the weather got cooler and the seas got choppier. Johnny and Taddy did the main work of crewing the vessel, clearly used to working in tandem as they barely needed to utter a word to each other. In the confines of below deck, Chris and Jane too found they had little to say to each other but for very different reasons. They had no shared history beyond the last week together and contemplation of the future was out of bounds, given the uncertainty, so their conversation topics were limited to the weather, and Eva's needs: what she could eat, what games they could play, what time she should have a nap. Strangely, though, they found comfort in the domesticity and the days flew by all too quickly. To Eva's amusement, Chris turned out not to be a very good sailor. He couldn't understand that since he had spent many happy hours on Sydney harbour but the choppiness of the waters in the Bay of Biscay proved beyond his tolerance. Eva, on the other hand, loved the unpredictability of the sea:

'Whee! Up. Up. Up. And then we go down. Bang!'

'Oh, please, Eva, don't! I think I need to lie down. Must be something I ate.

'But, Chris, you ate nothing today. Remember. I wanted to give you some of my breakfast but you said no. You do look very green, though.'

Similar conversations took place between the pair for the rest of that day with Jane laughing in the background. It was funny to see someone else tease poor Chris.

It took them a week to reach the Irish coast. The weather hadn't been too kind and Johnny had played it safe, given the precious cargo he and Taddy were carrying. Once they were close to shore, he explained to his guests that they wouldn't be sailing directly into the Port of Cork, exactly, but would use a little inlet that he knew. He was expecting Fr. Lonergan to meet them there, if all had gone to plan from his end of things. They had made relatively good time, considering the various unforeseeables and the priest would be delighted to welcome them, or so Johnny hoped.

The night of the 30ᵗʰ of June, just as the sun was setting, they edged their way into a beautiful bay with golden sands and crystal-clear waters. If the air had been warmer, they could have imagined themselves in any tropical location. However, this was an Irish June evening and, though midsummer had just been and gone, here it was a cool 12 degrees centigrade. Any warmth from the midday sun was long gone and Jane thought longingly of the cosy jacket she had left hanging in the hotel wardrobe in Alicante. What a pity she hadn't worn it that night. Would she ever see it again? She couldn't help thinking, though, that that was the least of her worries but, still, there was something comforting about having one's own possessions and something very disconcerting about losing them.

Johnny soon dropped the *Aisling's* anchor and Taddy quickly got the dinghy ready to bring the three passengers to shore.

'Give my best to the Father, won't you?,' Johnny said in a loud whisper as they pulled away from the craft. 'No doubt we'll be in touch again but, if not, good luck with it all.'

'Thanks, Johnny. And thanks for getting us here safely. It was smooth sailing all the way.'

'Strange that. I was expecting a bit more interest from the coast guard, to be honest. The priest must have said a rosary or two to clear the way for us. All the best now to the three of ye. We'll weigh anchor once Taddy gets back on board. He'll stay with you until someone comes to collect you.'

They waved back from the dinghy, Eva's face alight with excitement for she had proven herself to be a great sailor, strange given her previous experiences at sea which hadn't seemed to haunt her at all on this trip. Her favourite mode of transport, though, was the dinghy as it crashed over the breaking waves. If Chris were honest, he would have to admit to being equally joyful but his joy was at seeing dry land. Of all of them, he had suffered most on the voyage, discovering that he was definitely and happily a land lubber. He almost felt the urge to kiss the sand as he jumped ashore, followed by Jane who handed Eva to him. Taddy stayed with the dinghy but took out his phone and checked to see if there were a text.

'Great', he said as he read a message. 'They'll be here in a minute. See the car lights up there. That must be them. They say here that the coast is clear.'

'Well, that's good news, isn't it? We've got this far. Let's hope Fr. Lonergan's luck holds out just a bit longer.'

As Chris finished saying that, a car pulled up to where rocks met the sandy shore and out jumped the self-same priest, back in his normal attire and looking very pleased with himself indeed.

'Hello there! Hello there! What a sight for sore eyes, the three of you. And you too, Taddy, of course. Are you off now, then? Say hello to Johnny for me and thanks to the pair of you. We'll fix up the usual way.'

'Right you be, Father. A couple of pints in O'Donovan's will do nicely. All the best, now. We'll be seeing you.'

Taddy set off back to the *Aisling* and left the small group alone on the beach.

''Tis getting late so let's hop into the car and you can tell me all about your adventure on the high seas. Was it ok? No trouble along the way, was there?'

'No, it went as smoothly as possible … if you don't count the rough seas around the Gulf of Biscay and as we headed north of there.'

'Ah, that's to be expected. No, I meant any other trouble. No coast guards or such like?'

'No. Johnny was just saying he was surprised by that. So am I, actually, given how we left Spain. Do you think it's a good sign?'

'I don't know, lad. It's been very quiet. Maybe too quiet. But, anyway, let's worry about that tomorrow. Tonight we must get you all to some warm beds as soon as possible. My friary brothers are expecting you. You'll sleep well tonight – no rocking and swaying of the furniture or the floor.' Fr. Lonergan chuckled as he saw the relief on Chris's face. He too preferred solid ground beneath him, especially as he slept.

Chapter 25

The next day, the first day of July, started in the Friary Refectory with a big breakfast of porridge, sausages and scrambled eggs for Chris, cereal and orange juice for Jane, and soggy rice krispies for Eva. The little girl's face was a picture as she listened to her food going 'snap, crackle and pop'! So was Fr. Lonergan's as he watched her, grinning from ear to ear to see her simple joy.

'Oh it's so good you all got here safely. Now, we must set about the next stage of proceedings. You'll be glad to know, Jane and Chris, that a certain delivery arrived for you today - your belongings from the hotel.'

'No! Really? That's brilliant. How did you organise that?' Jane nearly did a dance of joy to hear that she would soon be reunited with the stuff she'd left behind.

'A few phone calls did the trick. We had to be careful, of course, that nobody in the hotel knew the address they'd be coming to so you have Yasmina to thank for most of the organisation. In any case, one of the friars will bring everything to your rooms shortly.'

'I'm so relieved. Though, I also feel a bit guilty because these last few days on the high seas have given me a small taste of what it must be like for all those poor people who set out with nothing. I mean, I was travelling in relative comfort. The *Aisling* might not have been the most luxurious vessel but it was seaworthy and we had beds and food a plenty. But I was so upset at not having all my things. What it must be like for people like little Eva, I'm just beginning to imagine.'

'True, but for Eva's sake, let's change the subject.'

Jane suddenly realised that Eva's mood had changed and the little girl was looking at her with a sad, lonely expression.

'Sorry, Eva, I forget sometimes how much you understand. You really are a clever, brave girl. Now, how about we go upstairs and I'll brush your lovely hair and we'll read a story to teddy?'

The dark clouds vanished as if by magic from Eva's face as she nodded her head furiously.

'Yes, Teddy wants a story. A story 'bout finding honey. He likes honey. And me too.'

Jane and Eva marched off on a mission, leaving Chris and Fr. Lonergan to discuss the plan for the day.

'So, Father. We're here. What's going to happen now?' Chris was not about to make small talk and wanted to get straight to the point. He didn't like his life being so out of control, his destiny in the hands of others.

'I can see you're anxious to get things sorted out, Chris. First things first. Today, we'll be getting news of the other two children who were supposed to travel with you. Due to our change of plan, they missed the boat, literally. As you know, Johnny had to leave earlier than we'd told them and I didn't manage to find them in time.'

'What happened to them? Were they able to get out of Spain?'

'Yes, and if they managed to stick with plan B, they should arrive in Ireland later in the week.'

'Plan B? You didn't tell us anything about a plan B.'

'No, because you'd have needed a guide and I wasn't able to organise for one to be available at short notice. Not one I trusted 100% anyway and trust was vital.'

'And what would the guide have done, exactly. Where are the other children now?'

'They're following a route over the Pyrenees that has been followed many times before. A circuitous route, unfortunately, but it was necessary. Maybe we could go for a walk and I'll show you something that might help me explain. Have you been to Cork before?'

'As it happens, I have, Father. Did I tell you I am half Irish? My father is from Cork and he has a sister who still lives here, my Auntie Louise. The whole family came over when I was about 12 and spent a few weeks here. We hired a camper van and toured around. Then, when I was a bit older, I toured Europe with a few friends and we visited Auntie Louise for a few days. I have great memories of both trips so it's nice to be back. Though, given the circumstances, I'm between two minds about contacting my aunt this time. I don't think she'd approve of my recent activities.'

As Chris was speaking, the two men had made their way out of the friary and onto Liberty Street. They made their way towards St Patrick's Street, Cork's main thoroughfare, via Castle Street and Daunt Square. Chris was amazed that he recognised so much since his earlier trips. True, there had been changes. St Patrick's street, or Pana as the locals called it, had been thoroughly modernised. The footpaths were much wider now and allowed space for people to wander at whatever pace that suited them. There were new lights too, reminiscent of a ship's sails, recalling the sea-faring history of the city. Recalling, too, that this city had been built on a marsh and floods were never too far from people's memories. There were plans to install flood gates or walls to protect the city but that would be for a future day once the negotiations had been done. Now, it was all Chris could do to keep pace with his companion who was clearly heading for a particular destination and not just one of the crowd 'doing pana'.

Finally, they came to the top end of St Patrick's street and turned into Merchant's Quay. There were fewer people about here, given that it was a Monday morning in summer, exactly a week since Chris and Jane, along with Eva, had set sail from Alicante. The priest slowed his pace somewhat, giving Chris time to admire the view of the River Lee. From this point, he could see up the steepest hill, imaginatively called St Patrick's Hill. His aunt had told him that, one year, a stage of the *Tour de France* had been held there. He had always thought that was odd but, seemingly, it had caused quite a stir. On the near side of St Patrick's bridge, was Fr. Mathew's Statue, known by Corkonians simply as *de stacha*, beloved meeting place for many a generation. *City centre* had rarely been put on the front of a bus heading into town. Rather, *The Statue* featured as a destination, which must have been very confusing for any foreigners trying to find their way about the city. Today, things had changed somewhat but Chris thought *de stacha* still had the best view of the city and Fr. Mathew, apostle of temperance, would have had many a story to tell if he ever deigned to share all he had seen through the decades.

Such thoughts were hopping randomly into Chris's mind as he followed Fr. Lonergan down Merchant's Quay towards the Bus Station. About halfway, the priest came to a stop at what looked like a building site. Indeed, that's what it was though what was under construction was not a new building but, rather, a bridge. Chris had often thought that bridges were very symbolic things, literally uniting people divided by such things as rivers or chasms or vast canyons. This bridge was straddling the river Lee, one of many, for Cork was not lacking in river crossings. However, this one would be just for pedestrians and cyclists, providing safe passage across the waters and away from the hazards of the many cars, trucks, buses, and vans that often clogged up Cork's streets. Still, for all that symbolism, Chris was not sure why the priest had brought him to view this particular bridge. He could have stopped on St Patrick's bridge had he just wanted to talk of bridges in general. That was one of the more beautiful examples and allowed those living on the north of the river (the Norries) to cross into the foreign territory of their southern neighbours.

Fr. Lonergan stood watching the work for a few minutes before he turned towards Chris.

'You must be wondering why we're here, Chris.' Seeing Chris nod, he continued:

'Well, we're here because of a woman called Mary Elmes. Have you ever heard of her?'

Chris had to admit that he hadn't, the name not ringing any bells for him.

'Well, she was a remarkable woman, from Cork, from Ballintemple to be exact, where she was born in 1908, the same year as Oskar Schindler. In fact, we call her the Irish Oskar Schindler - You'll have heard of him, no doubt?' Chris nodded, relieved not to be shown up as completely ignorant. Of course he knew of Schindler, the German industrialist who had saved so many Jews from extermination camps by putting them on his list of workers.

The priest continued, clearly enjoying his role as storyteller:

'Well, then, you'll know about the people Schindler saved during WWII. Mary did similar good work, saving countless children, over 400 we think, when she was working in the camps in France. But what isn't as well known is that she also volunteered during the Spanish Civil War just before that. She'd studied French and Spanish at Trinity College so her language skills were very useful during both wars. While in Spain, she started out at a feeding station in Almería. She must have witnessed such hardships there. As part of an ambulance unit, on the Republican side of things, she moved northwards as Franco's troops advanced. Do you know anything about the Spanish Civil War, Chris?'

Chris was once again relieved that he could say yes, he did, having studied it a bit during his degree. He was beginning to think very kindly of that lecturer who had forced him to read that novel for his Spanish assignment. Little had he thought how useful the knowledge gained would be, first when he was looking for a place to eat in Barcelona and now when he wanted to impress the priest. It made him regret his lack of enthusiasm as a student. *Note to self: must look her up and thank her when - if - I ever get back to Oz.* For now, he just wanted to take the opportunity to show off in front of the priest:

'Yes, actually, we read up about it at Uni. The Nationalists rose up against the Republicans who had won the elections under a banner of the Popular Front in 1936. They, the Nationalists, didn't like the liberal direction the country was taking and, under General Franco, they ousted the Republican leaders during a three-year battle that some say lasted even longer as, after 1939, Franco, who had appointed himself *Caudillo* or supreme leader, continued to crack down on any republican sympathisers.' Chris recited his knowledge as if reading it from a history book.

'Yes, that's it, lad. Well done. Well, our Mary found herself having to move camp ahead of the advancing Francoist troops, moving up northwards, from Murcia to Alicante, from there up into the mountains, eventually crossing the Pyrenees when it became impossible to stay in Spain. She got many refugees into France and to relative safety, at least until WWII broke out and some had to keep moving on. So, you see, Chris, refugees have always been with us, it's just the nationalities that keep changing but the hardship and the suffering stays the same. Here we have a Corkonian who gave up her own comforts to help strangers. She inspires me to do what little I can to do the same. When this bridge is finished, I look forward to sitting in the seats and watching Cork go by, a multicultural Cork that has welcomed many to its banks – *the banks of my own lovely Lee*, as the song goes.'

'I see. So Mary Elmes is your inspiration, Father?'

'Partly, yes. Partly I just found myself in a situation and reacted. The first child I saved, with a lot of help from my friends, was a beautiful little boy named Paulo, or at least that's the name he has now. He arrived in Madrid, having gone through the various stages – rescue at sea, his parents drowned, no papers. I saw him arrive at the centre and, next day, I called to see how he was and was met with denials: *he had never been there, I was imagining it, only girls had arrived the day before.* As I left, Yasmina stopped me and ushered me into a tiny room. There she confirmed that she too had seen Paulo but now couldn't find him. Needless to say, the one who had denied his existence was your friend, Magdalena.'

Chris took a few moments to digest this information before speaking:

'So, you're saying that you suspect she was behind his disappearance? Perhaps she just didn't see him and someone else spirited him away.'

'Perhaps, which is why I haven't gone to the Spanish police with my suspicions. I'd need a lot more proof before they'd take me seriously – proof of her involvement and proof of Paulo's previous existence. I have neither, unfortunately.'

'But what happened to the child? You said you saved him so you must have found him, right?'

'I was lucky. I discovered that a group of children had been sent to Alicante and, to make a long story short, we managed to find Paulo and get him away from danger. He's now happily living with a family here in Ireland.'

'I suspect that's a very short version of a very long story, Father. I don't know which question to ask first, to be honest. You seem to be totally unaware of the many, many laws you're breaking and, to be frank, you're doing so on the flimsiest evidence. From what I gather, paperwork often goes astray so it's quite possible Paulo and all the others just had theirs misfiled. If they all went to Alicante, surely things would get sorted out there in due course. Your interventions just made you a child kidnapper, and if you're caught – dear Lord, if *I'm* caught, the penalties will be severe and rightly so.'

'Do you really believe, Chris, that if I weren't 100% sure of the need, I'd take such risks, not just with my life but with those of my fellow friars and all the friends who have helped me along the way? I haven't told you about the children I haven't saved, the ones that haunt my dreams, or rather my nightmares. Their little faces floating in the water, buried in shallow graves, starved to death in cold, dingy rooms, crying for help and help never comes. Trusting adults who betray that very trust, taking their innocence, and for what? Oh the hours I have railed against God, my God, accusing him of allowing such suffering. It has taken me many years to make my peace with Him, to realise that this is the price, the penalty, for free will. Innocents suffer because people make choices to cause that suffering somewhere along the line. And the suffering will continue unless good people act.'

Seeing that Chris was about to interrupt him, the priest raised his hand as if to brush away all argument.

'Oh don't get me wrong, accidents happen and innocent people die due to no-one's fault. That's a different thing entirely. I'm talking about damage that's done because of an adult making a particular decision such as to download horrid images of little children being exploited, or who share those images. They think it does little or no harm. Somehow we've become inured against the reality that lies behind the computer. Just because it's virtual doesn't mean it doesn't hurt someone, somewhere.'

'So, are you saying that these children are taken so that images can be put on screen? That that is the fate of the ones who went missing? That Eva was destined for that if you – if we – hadn't intervened?'

'Now you're getting it, Chris. That's exactly what I'm saying.'

A horrified silence descended between the two men as they contemplated the truth.

'But you still haven't offered proof. I mean, do you know all this for a fact, beyond a shadow of a doubt?'

'Sadly, I do. And I'll take you to one more place which will prove that my actions are not so foolhardy. Follow me, just once more, Chris, and I promise you will be convinced.'

Chapter 26

Chris's feet were leaden as he started walking behind the priest, not at all sure he wanted to be convinced. He shook his head as he tried to rid himself of images too awful to contemplate. Of course, he had known about the use of children's images online. He had refused to allow his own children to put up their childhood photos on their social media even though they were now grown up. He'd been lucky, he supposed, as *Facebook* and the like hadn't existed when they had been babies. Now it was the norm to have pages and pages of baby photos uploaded. What easy prey we had all become for the very few who had evil intentions!

Gradually, Chris became aware that Fr. Lonergan was heading in the general direction of the City Hall. They had passed the Bus station and crossed the river Lee yet again to get to Union Quay. There, in all its glory was the City Hall but, clearly, that was not the priest's intended destination. They marched passed that, and the Anglesea Fire station too, before turning into the police station beside it. Chris stopped in his tracks:

'Are you out of your mind, Father? What are you doing bringing me here? Don't you realise I'm here illegally? They'll arrest me if they find out, and Jane too, no doubt – I'd crack under interrogation and reveal everything. I'm sure I would!'

Chris was astonished at the priest's reaction for he just let out a guffaw, a real belly laugh which took quite a few moments to abate.

'Oh, Chris', he said as he wiped the laughter tears from his eyes, 'I needed a laugh. Oh, I'm sorry but your face was just such a picture and the idea of you cracking under garda interrogation – well, it was just too much for me. It really was.'

Chris's indignation nearly caused the priest to start laughing again but, in his defence, he tried to remain straight faced.

'I think that's very unchristian of you, to say the least, Father. I've risked life and limb, just because you asked and here you are laughing at my impending incarceration. Not just laughing but facilitating it, bringing me right to the door, in fact.'

For some reason, that proved all too much for the priest again and he forgot his good intentions of remaining straight faced. Instead, he guffawed again, attracting the attention of several *gardaí* who were leaving the building and who stopped for a moment before deciding there was no need for their intervention. When he finally managed to get a grip on himself, he just took Chris's arm and led him, an unwilling victim, to the reception desk inside Garda headquarters.

'Well, hello again, Fr. Lonergan. Long time no see! Have you been away again on your travels?'

Such was the greeting that welcomed the priest and Chris into the heart of the law-enforcement headquarters. The friendly greeting did little to calm Chris's pounding heart. He had no idea what the priest was up to but it was clear he was no stranger to the police. *Was that a good or a bad development?* Chris could only stand silently by and await his uncertain fate.

'Hello to yourself, Sergeant McCarthy. Yes, I'm just back from Spain. I was hoping to see Superintendent Reilly, if he's about? How have you been yourself?'

'All good, Father. Busy of course, with the kids and all but school holidays are here now so we'll take a few weeks off and that's something to look forward to. I'll ring up and let the Super know you're here. He'll be anxious to see you, no doubt. All went ok, did it?'

'Yes, considering what might have gone wrong, all went remarkably well.' Turning to Chris, the priest set about introductions.

'Sergeant, this is my friend, Chris Nielson. He's from Australia and has been an immense help in my current undertaking. Chris, Sergeant Sheila McCarthy. Between you and me, this place would fall apart without her. Isn't that right, Sergeant? She knows just about everything about the law.'

Chris's face had turned puce with supressed anxiety. He didn't know what to say or do. And the fact that Sergeant McCarthy's name was Sheila didn't help matters – all women were *sheilas* in Aussie slang but something told Chris that this wasn't either the time or the place to share such politically incorrect cultural anecdotes. Instead, he heard himself babble some incoherent sentence about it being a pleasure to meet her. He did notice the priest and Sheila exchange a knowing glance, something that did nothing to abate his discomfort. The ensuing silence was broken by a door being opened behind them and the entry of Detective Superintendent Tom Reilly who greeted the priest as a long-lost friend, bear hug included.

The superintendent was an imposing man: tall, broad-shouldered, and rugged, hair greying around the temples. Clean shaven and dressed in uniform, he had that unmistakable air of a law enforcement officer used to giving orders that would be immediately and unquestioningly followed. Now, he invited his guests to follow him upstairs to his office where they could talk uninterrupted. As Chris followed the two friends, he couldn't help thinking that the last thing he wanted to do was spend any uninterrupted period of time with this man. He would end up confessing to crimes he hadn't even contemplated, not to mind the ones he had committed. What would Jane say when they came to arrest her and she found out that he had given her up – isn't that what the criminals called it? – and to give up your friends was the worst betrayal.

Soon, too soon, they were all seated in Reilly's office, a bright room cluttered with paperwork waiting for attention, files piled high on the desk, some on the floor, all attesting to the pressure the man worked under. If Chris had been feeling more charitable, he would have noticed the weariness of the other man as he sat down at his desk. However, Chris was more intent on projecting his own air of innocence, trying to keep his mind blank lest he betray himself. He felt so out of his depth. Give him a scalpel in his hand and a theatre to work in and he was coolness personified. Here, it was quite a different story, one he could only wish would have a happy-ever-after ending.

'Well, Father Jim, here we are again. It seems we spend more time each month trying to sort out certain matters. Since our chat on the phone last week, I've cleared it with the Minister. He's on board, so to speak.'

'Ah now, that's good to hear, very good indeed. Did it take much persuading on your part, Tom?'

'Not too much this time, Father. He's well aware of the issues.'

'What about the situation with my friend here, and the other Australian? Were you able to sort out their status?'

Chris squirmed in his chair as he waited to see what the answer would be, amazed that the garda officer seemed to know already about him and about Jane. What's more, he didn't seem in the least bit phased by the events of the last few days.

Seeing Chris's confusion, the Superintendent smiled and hastened to fill in a few of the blanks in Chris's knowledge.

'I can see you're a bit out of the loop, Mr Nielson. Father, here, telephoned me as soon as he arrived from Alicante. He filled me in on your part of the – shall we call them the proceedings? Not something we usually condone, but, given the particular circumstances, you are to be commended on getting involved.'

'Tom, here, knows that we had to intervene again, Chris. With three children at risk there was no option. We were blessed to be able to get them all to safety but, unfortunately, we still haven't got enough to act against the group. We got closer. In fact, that's why I've brought you here, Chris. I've been thinking that your friendship with Magdalena Sánchez may prove very useful.'

Following the priest's words, Chris suddenly found himself the focus of the Superintendent's attention. He tried to meet his eyes with a steady stare but found he had to quickly look away, fearing the man's piercing gaze could see right into his mind and read his thoughts.

'Well, that's very interesting, Mr Nielson. Or do you mind if I call you Chris?'

Unable to speak, Chris just nodded.

'Good. Yes, as Father Jim has said, your connection with Ms Sánchez may well prove very useful, very useful indeed.'

Chris finally found his voice. His head was buzzing with questions, the main one being:

'Are you telling me that the Irish police have been aware of what's been happening all along? That everything we were doing was legal after all, that we're not, in fact, in this country illegally?'

The superintendent and the priest looked at each other in amusement.

'Father, you haven't told the poor man. That's very naughty of you.' Turning to Chris, the policeman continued:

'Sorry about that, Chris. I told Father Jim, here, to explain things to you but, it seems, he didn't get around to it. Unforgivable of him under the circumstances, but just like him. He forgets that not everyone is as laid back about taking risks as he is. Isn't that right, Jim?'

'Jim' had the decency to look ashamed of himself, and avoided looking at either of his companions, instead, twiddling his fingers and staring at the ground as if hoping it would swallow him up.

'I suppose you'd like me to do the honours, right?' The slightest nod of the priest's head gave the superintendent the green light to go ahead with the explanation.

'First of all, to be very clear, the *Garda Síochána* do not condone moving children across jurisdictions the way you just did. However, there are some mitigating circumstances in this particular case. You see, a couple of years ago, this man here came to me with an incredible story. He believed that children were disappearing from a refugee centre in Madrid and that someone working there was responsible. He hadn't any proof as such but I've known Fr. Jim for many years so I wasn't prepared to dismiss his hunch. After all, there were children involved so if anything were amiss we were duty bound to do everything possible to find out what the situation was. I made enquiries of the Spanish police and Europol. It turned out that there were suspicions about some criminal activity but not enough proof to intervene. We agreed we'd keep a watching brief but that wasn't enough for the good Father here. He wanted a more hands-on approach so cooked up a plan to follow up on things. He arrived here a few months later with a child in tow, little Paulo as he's called now. That child was able to tell us enough to make us worry. He spoke of a woman who had taken him away from the others, who promised she would keep him safe from people who wanted to harm him. She didn't get the chance, thanks to Father Jim. He spirited him away without a by-your-leave and got the boy all the way to Ireland without anyone asking any awkward questions. I can tell you that gave us all pause for thought. Although Fr. Jim's intentions were the best, it shouldn't have been so easy for any man, or woman for that matter, to take a boy across borders without being stopped. So, since then, protocols and so on have been tightened up a lot.'

Hearing that, Chris couldn't help but intervene. After all, he had done the same thing and no-one had stopped him either. However, before he could speak, the superintendent raised a hand.

'No. I know what you're going to say. It is surprising that you weren't stopped by the Spanish Coast Guard but, in your case, we, here in Ireland and in Europol, were well aware all the way where you were and what your intentions were. In fact, give me a minute and I'll prove how close we were to you.'

The policeman lifted the phone and gave a few instructions which were closely followed by a knock on the door. After hearing the Super's order to *come in*, the door opened and, there on the threshold stood Johnny Fitzpatrick, captain supreme of the *Aisling*.

All three men were looking at Chris and enjoying his reaction of total shock and amazement. When he finally got his jaw off the floor, where it had dropped on seeing Johnny, he started to babble:

'What? ... I mean, where? I mean ... but you ... No!'

The other three men couldn't help but laugh at poor Chris's inability to speak coherently. Finally, the superintendent decided to continue with the explanations, having indicated to 'Captain' Johnny that he could go back to work.

'You see, Chris, we were beside you all the way. Sorry we had to do that covertly but, without meaning to, you and Jane got into the middle of a Europol operation targeting people smugglers, initially. When Fr. Jim brought Paulo to us, that operation expanded into child trafficking. It has become a complex case involving people on the ground and behind the scenes. I don't mind admitting that, at the start of your involvement, we considered you to be major suspects. Your initial interest in the girl called Eva aroused suspicion. In fact, Fr. Jim thought you might be behind several of the disappearances, especially when you seemed to know Ms Magdalena Sánchez rather too well.'

Chris thought it was about time he defended himself, and indeed Jane, from any accusations.

'Now, that wasn't friendship at all, Superintendent. Quite the opposite. She was just the girlfriend of a contact, the journalist behind a story we saw about kids like Eva. She glued herself to us, travelling to Alicante and so on. She even convinced us that Fr. Lonergan was the one to be suspicious of – that he was the one kidnapping children. And, to be fair, she wasn't wrong.'

At this, the priest exclaimed indignantly.

'The cheek of that woman! How dare she try to make me out to be the criminal!'

'Now, now, Father. Keep your hair on!' The superintendent tried to pacify his friend. 'No one here believes a word of it and, you have to admit, it was a clever ploy on Sánchez's part. Throw suspicion away from herself and wheedle her way into the confidence of those helping you. She's a clever piece of work, that's for sure.'

'But what evidence do you actually have against her, Superintendent?' Chris was still confused as to why, if all pointed to Magda's involvement, she was still free to carry on her evil ways. 'Why isn't she under lock and key if you all know what she's up to?'

'A very good question, Chris. Truth is we haven't enough proof yet. And we're hoping that's something you might be able to help us with.'

'How do you mean? I don't know any more than you do. In fact, clearly I know a lot less.'

'Yes, but maybe you wouldn't mind trying to find out a bit more, eh? We were thinking you might return to Spain and try to set up a meeting with the infamous Magdalena. See what she says when she sees you again. She might let something slip.'

'What about Jane? Is she to come with me?'

'No, not this time. It might cramp Sánchez's style if you travel together. No, Jane can stay here in Ireland with Eva. It would be good for the little girl not to lose contact too quickly with her rescuers. She's been through a lot.'

'So, what's the plan for her now? Is she staying in the Friary?'

'No, we'll send her to a safe house shortly, with Jane, if she's agreeable to stay with her. Then, we'll get you to contact Sánchez and see what she says. With luck, we'll have some progress to report in a few days to our Europol friends in Spain. It's about time we cracked this case wide open.'

Both Fr. Lonergan and Chris couldn't agree more with the superintendent's hopes though each man had his own reasons for such agreement.

Chapter 27

Chris couldn't wait to get back to the Friary and speak with Jane. His head was bursting with all the information he had just found out and he knew Jane too would be totally amazed by developments. *They had been involved with Europol! They hadn't really broken any laws!* He was concentrating so much on his future conversation with her that he didn't utter a word to the priest for most of the way back to the Franciscan Friary. It was only when they were approaching the church steps that he became aware that Fr. Lonergan wanted to say something to him.

'Chris. I just wanted to say sorry. I didn't think things through enough before involving you and Jane in this mess. I hope you can forgive me?'

'Forgive you? But, Father, we were involved long before we met you, you know. We both had travelled from Sydney to find Eva so, even if you hadn't appeared, we would have followed her as far as it took. Without you, it might have ended badly for the little girl. So, no, I can't forgive you since there's nothing to forgive. You got us out of Spain and away from Magda so, for that, I for one am very grateful.'

'Oh, Chris, that's such a relief to me. I've been so worried you'd hold me responsible for your present predicament. I only hope Jane will be as understanding.'

'Let's go and find out, shall we? I can't wait to tell her what's been happening. She's going to be absolutely amazed.'

The two men entered the friary by the side door and agreed they would meet in the central patio area in half an hour to give Chris time to bring Jane up to date on the story so far. And Fr. Lonergan would make enquiries about Eva's next destination as well as see if he could find out Magda's whereabouts. Exactly thirty minutes later, the three of them, Jane,

Chris, and the priest, were sitting on a bench, admiring the peace and tranquillity of the Friary's inner sanctum: a square patio garden more in keeping with a southern Italian *palazzio* rather than an inner-city residence in the very heart of Cork.

Jane was the first to break the silence, still not having got to grips with the story Chris had told her just minutes before.

'So, our mad dash across the seas was monitored all along by Europol *and* Johnny is an Irish police officer? Why on earth didn't he tell us? Surely he could have divulged his identity once we were on board?'

'Johnny, or should I say Detective Sergeant John Fitzpatrick, has learned not to give any information away unless it's on a need-to-know basis. Safer for everyone that way.'

'I s'pose. But he could have put us out of our misery. There I was thinking I was a criminal and entering Ireland's jurisdiction illegally. I was really worried I'd be arrested, you know?'

'I do know and, as I've said to Chris, I'm really, really, sorry for getting you involved in all of this.' The priest had the good sense to accompany his words with a dejected expression.

'And as I've said to you earlier, Father, we were already involved the minute we each got on a plane from Australia to Spain. So let's put all that behind us and see where we go from here.'

'Right, agreed. Well, the first thing is that Eva is going to join the other children in a safe house in Wexford. There are already a few people there who can speak her language and will look after her. We were hoping you, Jane, would go with her and help her settle in.'

Jane looked at Chris, clearly not sure whether to agree or not.

'What's Chris going to be doing, Father? I mean, can't he come with us too?'

'Ah, I see he hasn't filled you in on the big plan.'

'No, I haven't. I'm still not sure I want to go through with it. You tell her, Father.'

'We want Chris to go back to Spain and meet up with Magdalena Sánchez one more time. We think it might be helpful. She might reveal some information that would be useful in bringing the case to a close.'

'Isn't that a bit dangerous? I mean, if she's as bad as you all seem to think she is then Chris could be in a lot of danger. I should go with him.'

'No, no - Superintendent Reilly thought it would be better if Chris went alone ...'

'I don't really care what this Reilly person thinks. It strikes me that he's just using Chris as bait.'

'I wouldn't put it quite like that, exactly.'

'Well, how would you put it, exactly? Sending him off alone, into the lion's den - or in this case, the lioness's. He'd be at her mercy. No. I have to go too. She thinks we're together so it would be more suspicious if he were to turn up alone.'

'Excuse me, could you both stop speaking about me as if I weren't here, or as if I'm two years old? I haven't agreed to this plan, in any case. So, let's just think a bit more about it. What you - and the superintendent - think is that, if I speak with Magda, she's going to let slip some useful details. Well, I can tell you right now, she's not that stupid. She's not going to tell me anything at all. Her story is that you're the criminal and now that we've vanished - along with Eva - she's going to think - or pretend to think - that we're the criminals. If I go back to Spain, what's to stop her getting me arrested and locked up?'

'Europol, my dear friend. She might try but they'll get you out in no time.'

'Oh yes, Europol. But the policeman – or woman – on the street doesn't know anything about the inner workings of Europol. I could end up in a prison cell for days before they work anything out.'

'She's not going to do that to you. You're just panicking about nothing. She's more likely to quiz you about me and what you know about me and that's where you can come in very useful.'

'Ah! So now we're getting to the real truth about the plan. You don't expect Magda to tell me anything. You want me to tell her! I'm to let her know something you want her to believe. I'm to be a snitch! No, I don't like it. I don't like it at all!'

'Actually, Chris, that's not such a bad plan after all.' Jane was warming to the scheme. 'You can set up a trap. Tell her where she can get to Eva. Yes, that might just work, you know. It just might – Listen, Father, this is what we could do ...'

The next fifteen minutes were spent with Fr. Lonergan and Jane deep in conversation, their heads close together as they plotted and schemed, while Chris looked on, aware of a very unpleasant feeling that his fate was being decided by others and not by himself and there was little if anything he could do about it.

The rest of the day was spent making preparations for all that was to happen in what remained of the week. First, Eva had to be prepared for her new abode. That task was to fall to Jane as she was the one closest to the little girl. She was to join a group of her fellow nationals in Co. Wexford, in the seaside resort of Courtown, the very next day. There would be other children to play with and two couples who could share parenting duty until something more permanent could be arranged. It wasn't ideal but it was the best that could be done under the circumstances. It broke Jane's heart to think of Eva setting out on her own once more but she, Jane, was determined that Chris would not travel alone to Spain. She knew how he felt about Magda and knew he would want her support. Yet, that did not make it easier to see Eva prepare to set off without her. *How can such a young child tolerate that amount of hardship?* Still, Eva herself seemed quite excited. Everything was new to her and she clearly had an adventurous soul. She was never happier than when she made a new discovery: a chocolate drink; fish fingers; bubbles; bed linen with a teddy bear design; rice krispies. Everything was new and exciting. Some things, though, brought back sad memories and Jane would often see a shadow pass over the girl's face as she stopped to fix a thought in her head. Sometimes she would confide in Jane: 'Mama had a necklace like that one'; 'Baba liked to sing a song that sounded just like that'; 'we used to have a puppy that barked like the one I can hear now.'

Slowly an image of Eva's previous life started to form in Jane's mind. Clearly, she had had a happy start, with loving parents. Jane wasn't sure if that made things better or worse. Would it have been better if little Eva didn't remember the good things about home? Would it make it easier for her if she only remembered the bad? Surely not. Our memories are what add up to our identity and Eva would need to cling to her past so as to be able to face her uncertain future with confidence, of that there could be no doubt.

While Jane was spending time with Eva, Chris had his own preparations to carry out. He had refused point blank to head back to Spain without having a definite plan. To that end, it had been agreed that he would ring Magda from Ireland. He would have to call on the resources of the technical unit of the *Gardaí* so that the call would appear to come from within Spain; they didn't want to alert Magda to Eva's whereabouts before they were ready and it was just possible she, or her 'colleagues' would have the know-how to trace the location of Chris's mobile. He would ring, therefore, from the Anglesea Street headquarters using some special technology he didn't quite understand even though they did try to explain it to him, while Detective Superintendent Reilly listened in. Seemingly, his phone could be diverted through sophisticated monitoring equipment. His number would appear on Magda's screen but she wouldn't be able to trace his whereabouts. And they could listen in with ease so they might just learn something useful, though Chris was unconvinced: he knew that Magda was an astute woman and wouldn't reveal anything she didn't intend to reveal.

Once he had made contact, he was to arrange to meet with her in Madrid or Barcelona or wherever she suggested – in a public place, of course. From there, he'd have to follow his instincts. He wouldn't be alone, though, for he would have a garda escort. Johnny would be in the neighbourhood and, as well as that, much to Superintendent Reilly's dismay, Jane had insisted that she would go with Chris. She felt Magda would be very surprised to find her absent and, after all, she and Jane had a special relationship based on mutual dislike. That could prove just as useful, for Jane felt sure that, by being her most irritating, she could provoke her adversary into revealing some important information, a far more likely scenario than using Chris to sweet-talk the woman. Chris had been on the point of objecting when he'd heard that argument but, on consideration, he'd decided Jane was right: he was no Lothario and had no desire to be alone with the seductive Magda. He was more than happy to admit to being way out of his depth where she was concerned.

So it was arranged that the phone call would occur on Wednesday, the 3rd of July at 1pm which would be 3 pm in Spain, lunch time or thereabouts. With luck, Magda would be available to chat a while and Chris would be able to allay her doubts about him. After all, he had been supposed to contact her again in Alicante but, due to the sudden developments, had fled without telling her. He had no doubt that she knew his reasons for vanishing but he would have to play the game and provide a reasonable explanation. Depending on her reaction, he may or may not be able to take things further.

Chapter 28

So it was that, at 12:45 pm, Chris arrived at the Garda Headquarters, accompanied by Fr. Lonergan for moral support. Jane had wanted to come too but Chris had refused point blank. The fewer witnesses to this phone call the better. He had an awful feeling he was going to make a complete fool of himself. He had tried to prepare a script of sorts but it had proven impossible since he couldn't predict the direction Magda would take. He'd just have to ad lib - something he had never been good at, at the best of times. Not for the first time did he wonder why on earth he had left his cosy life back on Sydney's North Shore: it was looking so good to him right now, even if winter was at its height. Soon, he promised himself, soon I'll be back home.

Chris and Fr. Lonergan made their way once more to Superintendent Reilly's office, where they were met by Reilly and two other uniformed *gardaí*. They were the 'technical support' and would ensure that the phone call, though being made through an Irish land line would appear as if it were from Chris's own mobile, but it would be untraceable as to geographical location. Though Chris didn't really understand the details, he did understand the need for caution so he waited patiently while the equipment was set up and tested. It didn't take long and soon - all too soon in Chris's opinion - he was given the go ahead to place the call. He dialled - or, rather, pressed the preset button that linked with Magda's mobile - and waited. It rang, and rang again. Just when he thought she wouldn't answer, he heard the familiar, dulcet-toned voice:

'*¡Hola! ¿Quién es?*'

'Hello. Magda? It's me, Chris. Chris Nielson. Remember?'

There was a slight hesitation before she answered:

'Chris? Yes, of course I remember. Dear Chris. How strange your name didn't appear on my screen! No matter. You have been a naughty boy. I thought we were to meet again in Alicante but they told me in the hotel that you had left without warning. Did something happen?'

'Sorry about that, Magda. Yes, I had to rush away. You see, I heard from *MSF*, you know, the organisation I had intended joining when I first got to Spain. I'm sure I must have mentioned them, right? Well, they wanted me to come back to Barcelona to start my induction. I was so excited, I just up and left.'

'Without paying your hotel bill, Chris? That was rather bad of you, *¿verdad?*'

'I don't know where you got that idea from. I did pay it, of course I did. Whoever you spoke with at the hotel must have got the wrong end of the stick.'

'But they said you'd left all your belongings behind you. You must have been very excited to do such a thing.'

'Again, you've got things wrong there. I asked them to send them on to me here. I hadn't a lot of time to catch the plane. I've got all my stuff here with me now so all's good.'

Chris was glad he'd thought up the story of joining *MSF* so he thought he sounded fairly convincing and he was now hoping that Magda would take the bait. By repeating that he was in Barcelona, he was dangling a carrot in front of her. With luck, she would swallow it, hook, line, and sinker, if that weren't mixing metaphors too much. He waited silently, aware that Magda too was pondering her next words.

'Ah, so you are in Barcelona now? *¡Qué casualidad!* I fly there later today. Perhaps we could meet up tomorrow? I would love to hear how you are getting on with the *MSF*. It must be fascinating.'

Careful now, Chris. Careful. He could almost hear the thoughts of the superintendent and the others in the room, echoing his own. *Don't seem too eager. Don't reel her in too quickly.*

'Well, that would have been lovely, Magda, but they're keeping me fairly busy here, what with training and lectures and the like. I suppose I could escape for a quick coffee on Friday. That's if you'll still be in Barcelona?'

Magdalena's response was rapid.

'Perfect, *cariño*. Friday is good – I am sure they will allow you a *merienda*, a morning break? Tell me the name of your hotel and I will call there to pick you up.'

Chris wasn't sure if it were his own paranoia but he thought he could detect doubt in Magda's voice. He didn't want to hesitate too much as that might add to her suspicions but he hadn't foreseen the need to come up with a hotel name. Damn it! Even if he could remember where he'd stayed before, if he gave her that address, and if she were already in Barcelona, all she'd have to do would be turn up there today and she'd be told there was no such guest staying with them. *What to do? What to do?* Suddenly, a plan came to him.

'No need, Magda. In fact, I'm not staying in any hotel. My *MSF* contact invited me to stay with him and his family. Very nice people they are and it cuts down the cost and stress of having to find my own way around the city. He brings me to the various locations involved in my training, so I'm sure he won't mind dropping me off somewhere.'

Chris was aware that, as he was speaking, he was buying time in an effort to think of some neutral place to meet but his knowledge of Barcelona was sparse at best. The only place he could think of was the coffee shop where he'd bumped into Jane. He didn't really relish the thought of turning up there again with a different woman. He could just imagine the waiter's reaction. He looked around at his companions in the hope that they might provide some inspiration. He noticed Fr. Lonergan scribbling furiously on a scrap of paper which the priest then handed to him.

Tell her you'll meet at the Michael Collins Bar in the Sagrada Familia Plaza.

Without thinking too much about it, Chris just read out the directions, hoping they'd make sense to Magda. If they didn't, he wouldn't be able to clarify much. *Why on earth is there a Michael Collins Bar in Barcelona, anyway?*

'What about we meet at the *Michael Collins* Bar in the Sagrada Familia Plaza?'

'*Muy bien*, Chris, an interesting choice of venue. That is a date. We will meet at 2 pm on Friday at the *Michael Collins* Bar. I look forward to it and you can tell me all about your training.'

Again, Chris didn't think he was imagining the note of incredulity in Magda's voice. He thought he'd better bring the call to a halt quickly before she started to ask any awkward questions.

'As you say, a date. We'll talk then. Must dash now, Magda. All the best. See you!'

And with that, Chris hung up and everyone in the room released a collective sigh of relief.

'Well done, Chris. That worked out better than expected.' From the beam on the Super's face, it was clear that he approved of the direction the phone call had taken. 'Now, we'll just have to make the necessary arrangements to get you to Barcelona on time and to have Johnny ensconced in the *Michael Collins* Bar before you and Magda get there. May I ask, Father Jim, how you thought of that venue for the meeting?'

'I have happy memories of a trip to Barcelona a few years back, in 1997. The bar was just opened and a few friends brought me there to try it out. They wanted me to tell them if it was a real Irish pub. I was happy to step up to the challenge. A great night was had by all. Not that I shared that information with my superiors. I was a relatively young friar at the time so

I'm not sure they would have approved.'

'I was a bit troubled about the Irish connection, to be honest, Father. I hope Magda doesn't put two and two together.'

'Well, you did say she was wondering if you'd be prepared to travel to Ireland with her. You can reason that was why you thought of an Irish pub – to get into the mood!'

'True, a good background story, I suppose. Well, let's get back to the Friary and fill Jane in on what's happened. I wonder if she'll still want to go with me. She might prefer to stay back here out of harm's way.'

Even as he spoke, Chris knew he was talking absolute nonsense; there was no way Jane would stay in Ireland without him, and no way she'd let him face unknown perils without her.

As expected, Jane wouldn't hear of Chris travelling alone, partly through her feelings of solidarity but, if truth be known, mostly because of other feelings that she had developed for her one-time nemesis. She had grown more than fond of her companion and come to know his strengths and weaknesses. Without him saying so, she knew that he would value her presence more than he could admit. She did not believe he actually needed her there to carry out his task successfully. Rather, it was a question of being in it together.

So it was that Jane and Chris boarded the 18.45 pm Aer Lingus flight to Barcelona the next day, Thursday, the 4th of July. The irony of it being the US Independence Day was not lost on Chris as he had never before felt so dependent. He was dependent on Johnny, the Irish detective, turning up on time at the meeting place, dependent on Magda playing her part, dependent on Jane to watch his back. He'd have felt better if there were a clear plan but it all felt very hazy to him. Jane didn't seem to think so, however, so he took some consolation from her confidence. It was amazing, he thought, how much he had come to rely on Jane's presence in his life. He had fervently hoped that she would insist on coming with him, and was relieved he didn't have to explain why he wanted her with him either to her or to the other players in this dangerous game. He wasn't sure he could have done so even if he had had to. He couldn't even explain it all to himself. One of these days he might just have to do that. One of these days, when life became less complicated.

The flight went as planned, nothing out of the ordinary having occurred and Jane and Chris found themselves checking into yet another hotel on yet another night.

'This is becoming quite the habit, isn't it?' Jane seemed to find it all quite amusing. 'Do you notice the strange glances we always get when we confirm that, yes, we booked two separate rooms? It's as if no one ever wanted to have their own room.'

'Somehow I don't think that's what's causing the glances, Jane.' It was Chris's turn to be amused.

'Why? What do you mean?' Slowly the penny dropped and Chris laughed out loud to see Jane try to disguise her embarrassment.

'Didn't it ever occur to you that they would find it strange we *didn't* share a room?'

'Well, no, I didn't ... I mean ... well ... can we change the subject, please? I'm too tired right now to think of a clever answer so just stop laughing.' Jane's response did nothing to stop the laughter, however, and she had to tolerate continuous chuckles all the way to her bedroom door.

'Good night, Jane, sleep well. Hope you have nice dreams – remember, if you have a nightmare, I'm just next door! Otherwise, see you for breakfast downstairs bright and early ...' With that, Chris took himself off to his own room, chuckling all the way.

Once Jane had got over her embarrassment, she sank into her bed with a sigh of relief and, for once, she fell into a deep, untroubled sleep. Chris, on the other hand, didn't manage to shut his eyes all night. Whenever he tried, he either saw himself left to the mercy of Magdalena Sánchez or, more troubling still, he found himself imagining what it would be like not to be alone in his hotel bed but to have Jane lie there beside him. Not for the first time did he wish his life could be less complicated and he vowed that, soon, very soon, he would do something about it.

Chapter 29

Friday morning dawned sunny and warm, with a top temperature forecast of a pleasant 26 degrees for later in the day. Jane's humour was equally sunny as she literally bounced down for breakfast, having had one of the best night's sleep since leaving Australia, just a few short weeks before. Chris, on the other hand, was like a grumpy bear. Lack of sleep and the prospect of the day to come were taking their toll on him. He'd have given anything to be back home with nothing to do but hit the beach. *Chance would be a fine thing!*

Sensing his gloomy mood, Jane tried to cheer him up:

'Just think, we might have it all sorted out by evening, Chris.'

'Do you think so? I can't imagine this story ever coming to an end. We seem to be going around in circles, never really getting anywhere.'

'How can you say that? Isn't Eva safe and sound now? And here we are about to confront the mastermind behind the disappearances of several children. Surely that's progress?'

'When you put it like that, I suppose it is. But I can't help feeling we're not seeing something. I mean, would Magda really put children in harm's way? I'm finding it very difficult to believe that.' Seeing Jane's expression, he hurried to dismiss her objections. 'I know what you'll say, Jane. I know you don't like her much but, for all that, surely you can't believe she's that bad.'

'I'll admit, Chris, that it is hard to believe. In a way, I'm glad we're meeting with her today. She'll get a chance to explain things, perhaps, depending on how it all develops. Let's just agree to give her the benefit of the doubt. That's what you told me to do with Fr. Lonergan, right? Let's see how it goes and be ready to pick up on any signals she might give. You know, hesitations, facial tics and so on.'

'Aren't you the proper Miss Marple or, given your nationality, I should say Miss Fisher. You know, Miss Phryne Fisher?'

'Oooh yes, I prefer that comparison rather than to Miss Marple - much more glamorous. I'm not really into thick stockings and sensible shoes, not to mention knitting.'

'No, I can't exactly see you knitting - sewing, now that's another matter entirely or maybe a little crochet.'

For his impertinence, and completely out of character, Jane threw a spoon at him, causing him to duck to avoid it and so the utensil went clattering to the floor, attracting the attention of all their fellow diners, and causing them to stare at the two eccentric guests. More importantly, though, the silliness lightened the mood and Chris and Jane finished their breakfast in companionable silence.

As he drained the dregs of his coffee, Chris got to his feet:

'Well, we have a few hours to kill before meeting the infamous Magda. How about we play tourist and head to the *Sagrada Familia* basilica? I've never seen it but I've heard it's worth the visit. I don't much fancy just hanging around and waiting here until 2 pm and the Basilica is nice and close to the *Michael Collins*.'

'Great idea. Give me a few minutes to freshen up in my room and I'll join you in the foyer.'

Less than half an hour later, Jane and Chris were sitting comfortably in a taxi, making their way, like many hundreds of other tourists, towards the iconic building set in what some would call the epicentre of Barcelona. They happily joined the queues that had formed, glad to be able to blend in and take on the appearance of normality, at least for a few short hours. Who could have guessed the mission they were on to trap a possible child abuser? What secrets were hidden behind the other tourists who seemed so carefree? Who, indeed, would ever guess the dark side that lurked beneath everyday life?

Chapter 30

Having learnt from past experience, when Jane had had the foresight to arrange for the plane tickets to Madrid, Chris and Jane bought their tickets for entry into the Basilica online as they journeyed through the streets of Barcelona in the taxi. They decided against taking a tour, given that they only had a few hours to spare and neither felt like joining a group of happy tourists. Instead, they opted for the ticket that included an audio guide and access to the completed towers. They preferred to wander on their own, taking in the magnificence of the building. It was hard to imagine it would ever be finished and that, someday, the cranes would no longer be part of the scene. In a way, they were as iconic as the basilica itself, standing lofty above the steeples, symbolic of a link between imagined and constructed space.

They entered the building via the Nativity façade, having spent quite a while marvelling at the intricate sculpture and stonework of the exterior. The interior was equally awe-inspiring and the two wandered silently around the central nave, which was crossed by side aisles forming the shape of a Latin cross. At the top of the cross was a semi-circular apse or niche, with stained-glass windows casting coloured light on the altar. A forest of columns completed the scene, giving a sense of the unreal. This was, perhaps, the greatest accomplishment of its designer, Antoni Gaudí: to create a spiritual space in the midst of an urban metropolis, a place of sanctuary and calm, where anyone could believe that there was more to life than the mundane.

Such were the thoughts of the two travellers as they passed from module to module, from façade to façade, and from lofty heights of the towers to the depths of the crypt. It was a thought-provoking distraction from their other worries. Soon, though, time drew them back to reality and Chris was the first to suggest they leave and head for their appointment. Jane, with a heavy heart, nodded in agreement and followed him out into the bright sunlight.

'That was certainly something, wasn't it, Jane? I wouldn't mind coming back again someday when we have more time.'

'More time and less pressing engagements. So would I. Do you think that day will come?' Jane looked longingly back at the basilica, hoping that she would return very soon with a lighter heart.

'Of course it will. We'll be back before we know it. Might even have the kids with us.'

Jane smiled as she realised Chris had included her in his future plans without even realising what he was saying. She knew this wasn't the time to tease him about it, though, but the possibility of being part of his future life warmed her heart. *Once we get through this little challenge. Let's just concentrate on that for now and let the future take care of itself.*

With that thought, they arrived at the *Michael Collins* Bar. Having just travelled from Ireland, it was quite disconcerting to enter this particular spot as it was like going through a magic door that linked two geographically distant spaces, something akin to the wardrobe that led to Narnia. The interior of the pub was dark and filled with polished wood, old photographs on the walls, glass cabinets filled with treasures from past times. There were advertisements for *Lyons* tea, *Player's* cigarettes, and *Guinness* stout lining the walls along with more modern signs announcing the next football matches to be screened, not forgetting the Irish music (live on Monday nights) and the large *Céad Míle Fáilte* on a beam above their heads. For a moment, both Chris and Jane felt they had never left Ireland and that they had dreamt the last few hours but then they were brought back abruptly to their reality with the sound of a familiar voice:

'Chris! Chris! Over here!' It was Magda who had spotted them as soon as they had entered and was now waving from a table in the corner, beside a wooden dresser. 'How good to see you, *cariño.*' Then, turning to Jane, she looked her up and down before adding: 'And you too, dear Jane, so good you could make it.' Jane did her best to ignore the coolness, imagined or otherwise, and smiled back at her adversary:

'Hello, Magda. Good to see you too. Shall we sit down? Chris and I are just dying for a coffee or maybe something stronger. Right, Chris?' Jane couldn't help putting a proprietorial hand on Chris's arm. Luckily, Chris didn't seem to mind and played along, patting her hand with his own.

'Hi, Magda! I'd love an Irish coffee, actually. It's been a long morning, as you can imagine. I'll go and order for everyone. What will you both have?'

Jane said she'd have the same as him, a creamy Irish coffee, while Magda just pointed to the table where her drink was already half consumed.

'Can't I get you another, Magda?' Seeing her shake her head, Chris headed to the bar, leaving the two women alone in an uncomfortable silence. Magda was the first to speak:

'An interesting choice of location. Does Chris come here often, do you know?' Sensing that the other woman was trying to find out more than met the eye, Jane decided to be less than forthcoming.

'Actually, I'm not sure. I've not been here before. It is certainly different. You mentioned once that you had no connections with Ireland so this must be a new experience for you, Magda, right?'

Magda took a slow sip of her gin and tonic before nodding. 'Yes, it is. I am not sure it would be my first choice for lunch but the drinks seem good. Ah, here is Chris now with yours.'

Silence descended again as Jane was handed her Irish coffee and Chris sat down to join the two women.

'Well, here we all are. We must start by apologising to you, Magda, for leaving Alicante so abruptly. As I explained on the phone, I couldn't miss out on the opportunity that presented itself and I suppose I wasn't thinking too clearly in my rush to get on the next plane. My contact here did stress it was important I get here quickly.'

'Ah yes, *Médicos sin Fronteras*. How is that going?'

'Good, very good, I think. We'll see if I can start officially once the training is out of the way.'

'And you, Jane, what part have you to play in all of this? Are you joining them too?' There seemed to be an edge to Magda's tone as she asked that question, a sense that she found the situation all too incredible. Chris and Jane exchanged a glance, both aware of the thin ice they were treading. At a nod from Jane, Chris gave the answer they had rehearsed many times on the plane from Cork, trying to make it sound convincing:

'Jane is just looking into volunteering opportunities here. She's an expert diver and lifeguard, you know, so that might be useful in sea rescues.'

'Is she? I did not know that. What many talents you have, dear Jane!' Magda's words were directed at Jane but her eyes were darting around the locale, seeming to search for something, or someone. Whatever it was, she seemed to find it for her demeanour changed abruptly.

'I have enough of playing games now. I think it is time we – what is that expression in English – ah yes – we put our cards on the table, yes?'

'What cards would they be, exactly, Magda?' Chris's eyes narrowed as he attempted to assess this turn of events.

'I see you want me to put down the first card, dear Chris. For one thing, I know you are not training for *MSF*. Enquiries were made and they were unaware you were in Barcelona. The last they knew was that you were taking time to think about your options.'

'Ah. Well you have caught me out there, true enough.'

'I also know that you – and Jane – were in Ireland, in the company of Fr.

Lonergan.' Magda almost spat as she said the priest's name. 'Are you denying that fact?'

'I see you have excellent sources.' It was Jane who decided first to deny nothing but just see where Magda was heading. 'What else have they reported to you, these spies of yours?'

'Spies? Well, yes, I suppose you could call them that. Since you ask, they have also told me that you kidnapped Eva and brought her to Ireland. Is that not correct?'

'Rescued her, more like.' Chris was trying to keep the indignation out of his voice, following Jane's lead.

'Rescued her from what, exactly?' Magda's tone was icy cool.

'Well, from you, since you ask.' As she had just taken a sip of her gin, Magda almost choked at that answer. When she had recovered her breath, she replied:

'That is priceless. From *me*! And what, exactly, did you think I was going to do to the poor child? - Oh, I see. You thought *I* was going to take her, is that it. And who, exactly, told you that? Fr. Lonergan, I suppose. And you believed him? After all I told you about him? Incredible! So, you just did as he bid you to do and took the child out of this jurisdiction. Incredible, I say again. Have you any idea what trouble you are in now?'

'Look, Magda, it's no use trying to get us to believe that Fr. Lonergan is the baddie in all of this. We've seen him in action. We've seen how respected he is among the migrant community and, most of all, we've spoken to the Irish police who have verified his story over yours. In fact, they think you are - how did they put it, Jane?'

'A person of interest, wasn't it?'

'Yes, that's it. A person of interest in this whole mess.'

'ME? That really is priceless. And what has led them, and you, to this conclusion?'

'Because of your interest in Eva from the start. Because you've been sticking to us like glue and because you keep turning up out of the blue.' Jane was becoming incensed at the other woman's coolness. She didn't seem to be at all disturbed by their accusations. Rather, it all seemed highly amusing to her, not at all the reaction they had been expecting.

'Okay, I think it is time you met a colleague of mine. In fact, there are several of my colleagues present right now – if you look around, I am sure you'll notice them. They do not blend well into the background, even though they do try very hard.'

Jane and Chris looked around the bar, thinking now would be a good time to see if Johnny were at his post, but, to their horror, it was only too easy to pick out at least five men who just didn't seem to belong, dressed as they were in dark suits and pretending to be enjoying non-existent drinks. Jane noticed that they were strategically placed at all possible exits, blocking any hope they might have had of leaving. And, of course, there was no sign of Detective Sergeant John Fitzpatrick. As she, Jane, was assessing their options, Magda had signalled to the nearest man to come and join them, which he did without hesitation.

'Pedro, come and join us. This, as you know, is Chris Nielson and his friend here is Jane Murphy. I need not tell you anything else about them as you will have read the file ¿*verdad?*"

Pedro nodded both in greeting and in agreement as he settled himself into the chair beside Magda.

'File? What file would that be?' Chris didn't like the direction things were taking. He, like Jane, had noticed that they were outnumbered and didn't like their chances of leaving the *Michael Collins* bar as freely as they had entered.

'The CNI file, Mr Nielson. We, Magda and I and our other friends hereabouts, are Intelligence agents working for the *Centro Nacional de Inteligencia*, Spain's Intelligence Service. We have been following your activities with great interest, ever since you, Ms Murphy, contacted Mr Lucas Fernández with your incredible story of being Australian journalists. He, in turn, contacted Ms Sánchez who investigated your credentials. I need not tell you that they were non-existent. Or at least any proof of you being journalists. We did find out a lot about your *real* identities, however. Enough to wonder why you thought it necessary to hide them.'

Again, Jane and Chris exchanged a glance, Jane shrugging her shoulders as if to say *sorry, it seemed a good idea at the time!*

'Fair enough, we weren't completely honest with Lucas but why on earth would that attract the attention of – what was it, the CNI?'

'You were intent on tracking down a child, Mr Nielson. We take that very seriously here. And, we were right, your intentions did prove our suspicions to be correct. You kidnapped that child and removed her from Spain without permission. That, *señor*, is a serious crime, a felony, for which you will pay a high price.'

'Hang on a moment! We admit we might have looked a bit suspicious.' Ignoring Magda's harrumph of derision, Chris continued. 'As I was saying, it looks suspicious but our intentions and our actions were highly honourable. We were always acting in the interests of the safety of the child.'

'So you say. But where is she now and how are we to know she is safe, Mr Nielson?'

'Well, we need to make a phone call before we can tell you anymore.'

'So you can warn the rest of your gang, more than likely?' Magda was not in the mood to grant any requests. 'No, you tell us right here and now or you will find yourself in even more serious trouble.'

'He can't tell you what he doesn't know, Magda.' Jane decided to come to her friend's rescue, more to buy time than for any clear plan.

'I am very sorry to hear that. I do not believe he does not, at least, know some detail of her whereabouts and, to quote many a Hollywood movie, we do have means of finding out, means that neither of you will enjoy.'

Jane and Chris couldn't believe their ears. How had they found their way onto the set of a B movie? Were they really being threatened with torture by covert spies in a pseudo-Irish pub? All that was lacking was a dark alley, a foggy night and the sound of footsteps approaching.

'Now, Magda, those days are gone. Let us not frighten our guests here with such threats. We will just go to headquarters and detain them until we find further information that will help us locate the little girl. All very civilized.'

At that, Pedro made to stand up, nodding in the direction of two of his male colleagues who had been blocking the main entrance to the pub. They started to make their way towards the table, while Chris and Jane contemplated their fate. *Should we make a run for it? How far would we get? If we could just get to make a phone call...* It seemed they were both thinking the same thing for, as the two men were half-way to the table, a large group of tourists barged in through the now unblocked door. In the ensuing chaos, Chris grabbed Jane's hand and hauled her through the laughing, chattering crowd and out onto the street. Without thinking too much, they both headed straight back to the Basilica, running across *Sicilia* road, through the *Sagrada Familia* square, out onto *Sardenya* street and, in less than two minutes they were there.

'Now what?' Jane asked as she tried to catch her breath. 'Chris, what do we do now that we have the Spanish Secret Service chasing us? They can't be far behind, can they?'

'We find a quiet spot to hide where I can ring Superintendent Reilly. If I let him know what's happened, he might be able to get onto Europol and they can sort things out between them. Where the hell did Johnny get to, anyway? He was supposed to be in the pub.'

'Good question. I wish I knew the answer. Right, I guess it's plan B so make that call. Do we go back inside the Basilica again? You know, claim 'sanctuary' or something like they do in old movies and the like?'

'Something tells me that wouldn't work and, anyway, I'm not sure what phone reception I could get in there. Did you happen to notice earlier?' Jane just shook her head in response. 'No, neither did I. Damn. Maybe we can hide in plain sight, so to speak. Let's join a queue and try to blend in while I place that call. Come on, no time to lose.'

They headed for the same façade as before, the one depicting the Nativity of Christ, which was the most crowded area around the Basilica with lots of people milling around admiring the outside or waiting to get inside. As they queued, Chris placed the call to the Superintendent, praying that the man would be available. Perhaps, given the sacred ground they were standing on, that prayer was answered.

'Hello, Chris. I wasn't expecting to hear from you just yet. Have you finished with Magdalena already? That was a very short lunch.'

'That's just it. Turns out that she's an intelligence agent. They were going to arrest us for child smuggling, Tom.' In his panic, Chris didn't realise he was using the Superintendent's first name.

'An agent, you say. For which lot?'

'What do you mean, which lot? Spain, of course. Is there more than one?'

'Well, you're in Catalonia, you know. It could be theirs, though they're so secret we're not even sure they exist. So, it's Spain. Right. I'll get on to Europol and see why they haven't informed their colleagues in CNI. You stay put. The longer you stay out of reach the better. Don't want you thrown into the dungeons, now, do we? Just think of the paperwork! Any sign of Johnny?' Chris couldn't believe his ears as he heard the policeman's laughter at the other end of the phone.

'This is not funny, Tom. And no, your Johnny is nowhere to be seen.'

'No, of course it's not funny. Well, maybe just a bit. Don't worry, we'll sort something out. I'll try and locate Johnny and I'll ring you back, Okay. Lie low for now.' Chris had to be content with that though he could still hear the laughter ringing in his ear as he pressed the disconnect button.

'Well, what did he say.' Jane couldn't read Chris's expression as it wavered between annoyance, consternation but, mainly, fear. 'Did he say what we should do?'

'Yes, he said, 'Lie low.'

'Lie low? Was that it? Was that all he said?'

'Well, he seemed to find it all very funny?'

'Funny?'

'Yes, and will you stop repeating everything I say!'

'Sorry! It's just I can't understand why he'd find it funny. We're in a pickle. We can't go back to the hotel. We can't leave Barcelona - they'll be watching the airport and the trains and buses too, no doubt. Of all the agencies, why that one? They'll have eyes all over the world. Oh Chris, I thought things were bad before when we had to leave Alicante, but this is far worse.'

'I know, and I hate to break it to you but things are about to get even worse again. Look! We've been spotted.'

Chris didn't have to say any more as Jane could clearly see they were being approached from all sides by men in black suits. They had nowhere to run. For a moment, they considered sprinting into the Basilica and climbing one of the steeples or hiding out in the crypt but what would that achieve? It would merely delay the inevitable. So, with heavy hearts, they stood and meekly awaited their fate.

Chapter 31

The five agents, Pedro among them, hovered at a polite distance from where Chris and Jane stood watching, for some reason not completing their approach. A few moments later, the reason behind their hesitation was revealed as an imposing black limousine pulled up in front of Chris and Jane. In the driver's seat was the elegant Magda, not a hair out of place, Jane noted, in comparison to her own dishevelled look. *See what she'd look like if she'd raced here on foot rather than having glided up in a limo!*

'Ah, there you are. I am glad you did not get too far. And that my friends found you before you did anything very foolish.' Such was Magda's greeting. 'In your haste to leave us, you missed out on a very interesting development, my dears!'

Was it their imagination, or was Magda's voice a little warmer than usual?

'Yes, I believe you know these two gentlemen.' Magda turned around to indicate the back of the car from where two passengers were in the process of descending. Chris and Jane could only look on in astonishment as, first, Johnny appeared, closely followed by none other than Fr. Jim Lonergan himself, resplendent in his brown habit and huffing and puffing from the effort of heaving himself out of the low-lying vehicle.

'Hello there.' The priest was curiously good humoured, given the dramatic circumstances and the company he was in.

'What do you mean 'hello there'?' Jane couldn't contain herself anymore. 'What's going on? What are *you* doing here?' She looked helplessly from face to face, trying to figure out if circumstances had improved or had just got even worse than they had already been.

'It's a bit of a story, Jane, so I suggest we go with these fine folks to their base here in Barcelona and all will be revealed. Does that meet with your approval, Ms Sánchez?'

Jane couldn't believe her ears. Fr. Lonergan was being more than polite to his arch-enemy and, worse than that, he was suggesting they accompany her back into the lion's den, back to CNI headquarters. *Had he lost his mind?* Jane looked in Chris's direction and could see he was equally confused, totally taken aback by this turn of affairs.

Without giving them any time to think about things, Magda ushered them into the back of the limousine and, before they could get their bearings, they found themselves speeding down *Carrer de la Marina* and heading northwards, and, within minutes, the limo came to a smooth stop outside an unremarkable office block. Having exited the car, they entered the office block and took the lift to the top floor where they were shown into what could pass as a board room in any location on any continent. Curiously, given the circumstances, teas and coffees were provided and the atmosphere was strangely laid back and welcoming. Chris would have preferred a more austere setting as, at least then, he would have known what to expect. This pleasantness was far too disturbing.

Once they had all taken their seats around the oval conference table, Magda, taking on the role of chairperson, addressed the impromptu meeting. She looked at each of them in turn: Chris sitting to her left, Jane beside him, Fr. Lonergan on Jane's left, Pedro on Magda's right with Johnny sitting at the furthest point from her. Five pairs of eyes were all firmly focused on her.

'I can see from your puzzled expressions, dear Jane and dear Chris, that you are very confused. It seems – and I apologise most deeply for this – it seems I have misjudged you. Let me explain what has just happened. After your – let us call it your hasty departure from the *Michael Collins* – two things happened. First, as I was getting ready to follow you, Fr. Lonergan appeared in the doorway, accompanied by this nice man, Johnny, isn't it?' The said Johnny nodded his head, beaming at all in the room. 'Yes,

Johnny and Fr. Jim appeared and quickly explained that they were supposed to meet you and me but had been delayed.' So far, Chris and Jane were not finding any of Magda's supposed explanation of any help whatsoever. *Why had Johnny blown his cover? What on earth was Fr. Lonergan doing here in Barcelona? And since when did Magda call him by his first name?*

Not completely unaware of what was going on in their minds, Magda continued with her explanation:

'As you can imagine, I was very surprised to see them, especially when Johnny identified himself as a member of the *Garda Síochána*, the Irish police force. Just as I was going to ask a few pertinent questions, I got a phone call from my superiors at CNI. They had been contacted by Europol who had asked them to explain a few details to me. Can you imagine my surprise? They had not contacted CNI before about their involvement in this case as they had had some suspicions about *my* involvement. Can you imagine that? Or at least they thought someone at CNI was involved but, so far, their investigations have not uncovered any evidence. So I and my colleagues are in the clear. They could also verify that Fr. Jim, and consequently you, dear Jane and Chris, are also in the clear. Is that not good news?'

The tension in the room almost visibly dissipated. The two Australians slumped back in the seats, the relief of not being wanted by the police *again* clear to see on the faces. Everyone else was talking and laughing at the irony of both camps suspecting the other. Chris looked around the room in stunned amazement, especially when he witnessed Magda and Fr. Jim (as she now called him) laughing together at how much misunderstanding had occurred over the last few months when they had been busy trying to outwit each other. Finally, he could take no more:

'Excuse me. Relieved as I am - as we both are - aren't you all overlooking one crucial point in all of this?'

The general chatter died out as they looked at him, with one or two quick to understand his meaning.

'Yes, if Fr. Jim isn't the one behind the disappearances of children and Magda isn't either, then, we have to ask, who is?'

The atmosphere quickly turned from one of celebration to one of dismay as the realisation slowly grew that, perhaps, they were no closer to solving that mystery than they had been at the very start of the story. Fr. Lonergan was the first to attempt to bring some light to bear.

'Let's think a bit about it while we're all together. Magda, can you remember when you first suspected me of being involved? What made you think I was?'

'Ah – it was one day when I was undercover at the centre in Madrid. Someone said they thought it was strange how much time you spent there.'

'Okay, did they say anything else?'

'They did. They said it was suspicious you always came alone and how you always had sweets for the children.'

'That's true. I do always have sweets in my pockets. Not many people know that habits have pockets, deep pockets – very useful for holding lots of stuff. Anyway, I digress. That, surely, wasn't enough for you to think I would kidnap children, was it?'

'No, not really, except that I was working there because we had had an anonymous report about some irregular activity, so I was already looking out for someone suspicious. After that conversation, I kept my eyes on you and it all began to add up. You did seem too good to be true.'

'Well, thank you, Magda! Glad my good deeds didn't go unnoticed.' The priest had a distinct twinkle in his eye as he said that, taking away any sting that might have been in the words. After pondering for a few moments, he continued: 'The strange thing is that something very similar happened regarding you. I mean, I had a conversation with someone, just can't quite remember who, about you and how they didn't really think you fitted in – that there was something a bit fishy about how you turned up. Can you remember who spoke to you about me? Maybe it was the same person?'

'Let me think. It was a while ago and so much has happened.'

As the two, Magda and Fr. Lonergan, sat thinking back to events at the migrant centre in Madrid in the previous months, the rest of those at the table could only look helplessly on. Each person there realised that they had judged one or other of those two people harshly, all because of the opinions that had been shaped, mistakenly, by the words of others. No one was feeling very proud of themselves but, for now, all they could do was sit and wait to see if either could pin down their recollections.

The moments ticked by, the teas and coffees were growing steadily cold, but no one wanted to be the first to give up. It was as if everyone there realised that this meeting was the final opportunity to solve the question about who was endangering the innocent little children who had no one else to protect them. Finally, just when it seemed they would have to draw this unusual meeting to a close without success, Magda and Fr. Lonergan both jumped up from their seats and, with one voice, shouted out the name of the person who had planted suspicion in both their minds:

'Yasmina! Yes, it was Yasmina who planted the doubt.'

The table erupted into a chaotic babble of words expressing disbelief, shock, horror and, most of all, a sense of betrayal. Of all of them, Fr. Lonergan felt that betrayal the sharpest. He had believed Yasmina to be his right-hand, his main support, the one he went to for advice and encouragement. He had confided in her, relied on her and, worst of all, he had asked her to arrange to forward his Australian friends' belongings, thus giving her their exact whereabouts and, now, it looked as if he had chosen the very person who had put them all in danger. What could have been her purpose? What had she gained by acting so despicably? As he considered these questions, Magda's response was more immediate. She had grabbed her phone and was speaking furiously to whoever she had rung, giving instructions for Yasmina's immediate arrest. When she hung up, she addressed the gathering:

'Well, I have just spoken with my boss in Madrid and he will get the local police there to detain Yasmina. We do not want her to know of the involvement of the CNI, or Europol for that matter, not to mention the Irish police, at least at this stage.' As she said this, she smiled flirtatiously in Johnny's direction. Seeing Johnny's abashed response, Jane smiled to herself. It looked as if Magda had made a conquest there. Funnily enough, though it was early days, she had a sudden image of Johnny and Magda sailing the high seas together in the *Aisling*. Maybe there would be a happy ending for someone in this whole mess. As she was thinking this, she became aware of Chris beside her, looking at her and taking her hand in his.

'Looks like there's a bit of an attraction going on there between Johnny and Magda. What do you think?'

'I think you may be right, Chris. Who'd have thought sensible Johnny would be struck so suddenly by Cupid's arrow, not to mention the devastating Magda? Isn't love a strange thing. Ah well, who knows, it might just work out for them. I do hope so, don't you?'

'Well, I'm hoping they're not the only ones to get a happy ending.' And with that cryptic comment, Chris let go her hand and went to talk with the priest.

Chapter 32

The next days were filled with activity. Jane, Chris, and Fr. Lonergan headed back to Ireland while Magda and Pedro and the other four men in black suits returned to headquarters in Madrid. Interestingly, Johnny requested a few days' leave and vanished without saying goodbye. No-one knew for sure where he had gone but everyone in the Irish group had a strong suspicion that Madrid was on his agenda, even given how far inland that was and given Johnny's love of all things marine. Yasmina's whereabouts, however, remained a mystery for, when the police had arrived at the migrant centre in Madrid, she was nowhere to be found. Likewise, the home address she had provided to her employers was unoccupied.

On their return to Cork, the Irish contingent (as Fr. Lonergan had taken to calling them), were summoned to Garda headquarters to meet with Superintendent Reilly for a debriefing. They were somewhat relieved to discover that simply involved a cup of tea and biscuits while they each filled the other in on developments. Superintendent Reilly had certainly been working hard in their absence, having stirred up his contacts at Europol. They were busy putting a case against Yasmina together and attempting to follow her trail.

'I feel sure they will apprehend her very shortly. They do have excellent resources, as you can imagine.' Tom Reilly seemed very confident that the case would be put to bed, as he put it, within the next few days.

'I wish I had your confidence, Tom.' Fr. Lonergan was not happy that Yasmina had managed to evade capture for longer than expected. 'That girl must have plenty of her own resources. I feel so guilty that I didn't suspect a thing. She fooled me completely and I pride myself on being able to judge character. Serves me right – *judge not and ye shall not be judged*

– that's how the bible puts it. And I've always tried to live by those words. But, in this case, I've been judged harshly by some who thought I would harm a child and I judged others equally harshly while totally missing Yasmina's part in it all. I should have judged *her*. I should have been able to see what she was up to.'

'Now, Fr. Jim, don't be so hard on yourself. How were you to know she was up to no good?'

'Superintendent, Father Lonergan, are we sure about Yasmina? You know, we don't have any real proof against her and, well, I've learnt a bit of a lesson there myself about leaping to conclusions. You know, first I – we – thought the good Father here was the one behind the abductions and then, we were sure it was Magda. Maybe we should give Yasmina the benefit of the doubt? You know, innocent until proven guilty and all that.' All eyes turned to Jane as she voiced doubts that were in everyone's mind.

'But why, then, did she run?'

'That's a good question. And here's another one: How did she know we were on to her?'

Everyone in the room fell into a troubled silence, realising that this case was far from closed. Their ponderings were interrupted abruptly by the sound of the Superintendent's landline ringing.

'I'll have to take that. It's an internal call so, given they know I'm in a meeting, it must be important or they wouldn't ring me.' He lifted the receiver and, though at first his companions tried not to listen in, all attention was soon focused on his words:

'Hello, yes – I see – when was this? And no one saw or heard anything? Right. Get a car ready. I'll go up there myself immediately. Yes, do that.'

The Superintendent's face was grim as he replaced the receiver and looked around the room.

'Not good news, I'm afraid. It seems Eva has been abducted from her lodgings in Courtown.' Gasps of horror greeted his words, followed by a stream of questions.

'Hang on, hang on and I'll tell you the little I know. When they went to wake her for breakfast this morning, her bed was empty. Her clothes were gone. No one heard anything but the lock to the front door had been broken. They organised a search, called the local *gardaí* and so on but, so far, no sign. I've arranged for a car to drive us to Wexford as I expect there's no way I can persuade you all to stay here, is there?'

A general agreement was followed by a rush to the office door. All four charged down the stairs to the car park where a police car, together with its driver, was already primed to head up to Wexford where Eva had been placed in a refugee centre. It would be a long journey but, with sirens blazing, they would get there within a few hours.

Jane's mind was abuzz with questions. She was vaguely aware of towns and countryside flying by the car window, exotic names to her such as Carrigtohill, Youghal, Dungarvan, Waterford. Once past Gorey, the roads narrowed, and the car seemed to fly over the bumps and potholes. She clung to Chris's hand, both sharing the worry of what might be happening to Eva, wondering if they'd find her or if she'd join the countless children in the world who seemed to vanish into thin air. Surely not Eva. Not her. Jane just couldn't contemplate such an eventuality.

Chris, equally, was unable to concentrate on the journey. His mind was filled with murderous thoughts of what he would do to Yasmina if ever she were so unlucky as to cross his path. He would make sure she and her gang, for he was sure she wouldn't be acting alone, would get what they deserved, so help him God. He almost smiled as he thought that. *What would Fr. Lonergan say if he could hear him addressing God? Maybe a prayer or two wouldn't go amiss? Though asking God to help them find Yasmina so he could kill her mightn't exactly be a prayer that would meet with the good priest's approval ... Or God's for that matter.*

Curiously, Fr. Lonergan's thoughts weren't too far removed from those of Chris. He, too, was fighting his inner demons. He wanted to pray but his anger, both at Yasmina and, more so, with himself, prevented him from getting into the right frame of mind. At least, if the definition of prayer was something calm and meditative. Instead of the usual way he would talk with God, today he was shouting at Him: *How could You let this happen? Eva needs Your protection. Hasn't she suffered enough?* As they approached Courtown, however, a strange peace descended on the priest and he could almost hear a voice (inner or divine?) tell him that all would be well, all would work out fine in the end. Maybe this was just the darkest hour before the dawn.

Chapter 33

Courtown, a small village in county Wexford, on the east coast of Ireland, is described in all the tourist blurbs as a family-friendly seaside resort. They also tell how it owed its very existence to the Stopford family, specifically James George Henry Stopford, the 5th Earl of Courtown, who had the foresight to order the construction of the harbour during the Famine years, giving employment and some prosperity in the otherwise gloomy days of mid-nineteenth century Ireland. Now, it was a thriving tourist hub, with the normal population of around 1,500 more than doubling in the summer months. Looking out of the car window, Jane could see lots of people strolling around, some heading to the adventure park, some to the seal rescue centre and some to the nearby beach or the gaming arcade near the port. She envied them their carefree spirit. She wished she could join them as the car slowed down and pulled up outside the local garda station. The small bungalow that housed the station had a curious air of jolliness that belied its function. It looked more like a holiday cottage than a law enforcement centre but, as they would discover, looks could be very deceptive.

As the car came to a stop, Superintendent Reilly told the rest of the occupants to wait for him as he wouldn't be long. He got out and headed straight for the front door of the bungalow which swung open before he reached it. Clearly, the local *gardaí* had been forewarned and Reilly was expected. He vanished inside, leaving the others to gaze expectantly at the door which had been discreetly closed again. Silence reigned in the car as each of them was lost in thought, wondering if there would be any good news. Unlikely, since, had anything of note happened, surely they would have contacted the superintendent on his mobile during their journey.

A few moments later, the door opened once more and they could hear Reilly speaking to someone unseen behind him:

'Right so. We'll go to the hotel and have something to eat. Meet us there when you've finished with that and we'll all head around the corner.'

Superintendent Reilly got back into the car and told the driver to carry on down the road, turn right, and then left and pull in beside the Taravie Hotel. He explained that they would get a bite to eat while they waited to be joined by two local *gardaí*. Then, once they had arrived, they would proceed to Courtown Hotel which was just around the corner. It was from there that Eva had vanished. She was just one of the refugees who were now housed within the hotel under the Direct Provision scheme whereby food and lodgings were provided by the State via what was known as the Reception and Integration Agency. Refugees would remain housed and fed (not always in the best conditions) while their status as asylum seeker was being reviewed. It was the superintendent's plan to question the others staying there, as well as any support staff, to ascertain (his word) if anyone knew anything they hadn't shared up to this point. Surely a child couldn't just disappear into thin air in a town as small as Courtown? If it had been Dublin, or even Cork, then it wouldn't seem quite so strange. But Courtown was tiny in comparison and its year-round inhabitants knew as much about each other as it was possible to know. Reilly felt he would be able to see if anyone had any information they were keeping back. He prided himself on his hunches and his ability to see into the hearts and minds of criminals and, with such high stakes, he wasn't about to rely on anyone but himself to do the interviews.

'Right then, all out!' Reilly gave the curt instruction once the squad car had pulled in in front of the Taravie. 'We'll have a quick bite to eat while we wait for the local lads to finish their door-to-doors and then proceed with the inquiries. We can't do anything until we're brought up to date so I've left instructions for them to join us here in twenty minutes.'

Jane, Chris, Fr. Lonergan and the driver all descended quickly, glad finally to be able to stretch their limbs. There hadn't been much room in the car and, given Fr. Lonergan's girth, Chris and Jane had suffered the most in the back, while the superintendent had travelled in relative comfort in the front passenger's seat. There was quite a bit of groaning and moaning as they walked to the hotel entrance and circulation returned to numbed limbs. Reilly, meanwhile, had strode into the bar cum restaurant without a backward glance, had secured a table opposite the bar and had grabbed copies of the menu which he quickly distributed among his group as they settled down at the table.

'Right. I suggest we make do with sandwiches. That'll be the quickest. A pot of tea and I'm sorted. Is that okay with the rest of you?'

A chorus of agreement answered his question except for Jane who was feeling a bit rebellious, not liking Reilly's assumptions or his gruff behaviour. It reminded her that one of the reasons she found herself in this adventure was her decision to speak up for herself so here was an excellent opportunity.

'If it's okay with you I'd rather a coffee and I see there's a ploughman's on offer.'

'Fine, whatever you want.'

'I wouldn't mind a coffee too – I wonder would they do a flat white?' Chris made haste to get his order changed too.

'That sounds good to me too, Super.' That last order came from their driver who had taken her cue from the others.

Fr. Lonergan found he was now the focus of all eyes and couldn't help feeling he had somehow been given a casting vote. How ridiculous given the circumstances but he felt he had to side with the majority. Meekly he nodded and said he wouldn't mind a cappuccino.

Glaring at him, Reilly went off to place their order, too impatient to wait for table service.

Jane couldn't help giggling.

'That was brave of you, Father. And, if I might say, I've never seen a Franciscan drink a Capuchin before now.'

'Very funny, very funny. To be honest I rather felt like a cup of tea but I didn't want to let the side down.'

Reilly returned to find all at the table laughing at some private joke, not thinking for a moment that it might be at his expense.

'I fail to see what you lot can find so amusing. This is a very serious situation, you know.'

'You don't have to tell us that, Tom. We know but, sometimes, a laugh can diffuse tension, as well you know. Now, here come our sandwiches – and ploughman's – and, of course, our beverages so let's dig in and get ready for the next move.'

Everyone nodded in agreement at the priest's words and tucked into the food with relish, only now realising how hungry they were, not having eaten since early morning, except for the tea and biscuits provided by Superintendent Reilly at the debriefing.

As they were finishing up, the two local *gardaí* appeared, looking quite smug with themselves. They stood waiting for Reilly to drain the last dregs of his tea before 'aheming', clearly wishing to speak urgently. Reilly took the hint:

'Out with it, man, you two look like the cat who got the cream. Have you some information?'

The older of the two *gardaí*, a Sergeant Aiden Burke, consulted his notebook before starting to speak.

'As you know, Superintendent, we were just finishing our inquiries when you arrived. We were asking around to see if anyone had seen a little girl matching Eva's description.'

'Yes, yes, we know all that. Get on with it. What did you find out?'

'Well, we were checking up at the housing estate on the Gorey Road and, well, this person mentioned she'd been walking in Forest Park earlier today and noticed a bit of strange activity thereabouts.'

'What kind of activity?'

'She wasn't too specific and we didn't pay too much attention, given that it's the summer. Lots of people around, you know. But, just to be sure, I sent young Davis here up to have a nosey around. Didn't I, Davis?'

The said Davis confined himself to a nod of the head before gazing intently down at his boots, clearly not used to being the centre of attention, especially when in the company of 'top brass'.

'Go on, man!' Reilly was clearly impatient to get to the interesting bit of the story, that is if there were an interesting bit, something that he was beginning to doubt.

'Yes, Sir. Davis reported back just a few minutes ago that one of the cottages up there had all the curtains drawn and looked as if there were no one there.'

'So? Why would that be suspicious?'

'Well, because as I said, it is the height of summer and all the cottages up that ways are rented out. It would be very strange to see one so quiet – especially at this time of day. Anyway, Davis went around the back and he swears he heard noise inside. He was going to knock but, given the circumstances, he thought he should get some back-up, didn't you Davis?'

Again, the nod and the downward stare were the immediate response, this time accompanied by a slight reddening at the back of Davis's neck, his embarrassment now becoming even more acute.

'Quick thinking, Davis. You'll go far. Well, let's go. You two lead the way and we'll follow in my car. No sirens, now, mind. We don't want to alert anyone to our arrival. Right now. Off we go.'

There was a general scurry as everyone followed Reilly out of the Taravie and into the cars, both of which sped off, veering left past the Courtown hotel and right onto Harbour Court, straight on through Ballinatray lower until they reached the turning into Forest Park. There, the cars slowed down and very soon the lead car came to a halt. Garda Davis got out and walked back to speak to Reilly who lowered his window.

'The cottage is just up here. It's away from the main lot of houses and surrounded by trees which should give us cover if we were to walk from here. But Aiden was wondering if we should wait for the special unit from Wexford to arrive?' Davis gave the impression that he had been rehearsing this little speech in his head for a while as the words came tumbling out without any pause for breath. Reilly either didn't notice or had decided to be kind to the young officer as he refrained from pointing out the former's lack of formality when referring to a superior officer. The younger man had even forgotten to put his hat on.

'No time to wait, Davis. Time is critical. I'll take full responsibility. There are four of us and I do have clearance from your superiors so let's get on with it. Okay, we'll get out here and head to the house.' Turning to the three civilians in the back seat, he specified:

'When I say 'we', I mean 'we' *gardaí*. You lot stay put until further instructions. Is that clear?' Jane, for some reason, felt he was speaking directly to her and she just knew that he had been on the verge of saying 'further orders' but, having seen her mutinous expression, had thought better of it. In response, she nodded, though, as she had often done as a child, she had kept her fingers crossed behind her back. She was not about to miss out on any action, especially if there were a remote chance that Eva needed her. For now, however, she'd do as she had been told and remain in the car.

Meanwhile, the four *gardaí* headed quietly toward the cottage. It was a modern building, white-washed and tidy, with a small patch of lawn and flowers growing in the tiny front garden. The rental brochure would have told them that it was a single-storey, two-bedroom property, with a modern bathroom and kitchen, a large sitting room, wooden floors and was very close to the centre of Courtown, not to mention within easy reach of forest hikes and adventure parks. A child's dream. Hopefully not about to turn into a nightmare. Jane could feel herself tense up as she watched Reilly give instructions for two of the guards to approach the house from the rear while he and his driver strode towards the front door. Her tension turned to horror as she saw him reach a hand under his jacket and check what could only have been a holster. *Guns! They were carrying guns! No! This can't be the way things will end.*

Jane felt Chris tense up beside her as he too realised what could happen next. Fr. Lonergan was equally horrified, and was the first to break the deafening silence in the car.

'I can't just sit here and watch. I'm going in. You two stay put.'

'You must be joking, Father. I, for one, have no intention of sitting here and watching this scenario play out. Jane, you stay here and we'll report back in a minute.'

'No way! I'm coming too.' The two men hesitated just for a second before giving up. Each knew Jane well enough by now to know they would only be wasting their breath if they tried to change her mind.

'Okay, let's go but let's keep out of the way too. We don't want to make matters worse.'

'Worse? I'm not sure how much worse they can get. *Fine*, I'll stay low and out of the way.'

The threesome followed the path taken by the guards, taking care not to make any noise that might alert those within the house, if, in fact, there was anyone in there to alert.

Superintendent Reilly finally reached the front door, a wooden door, painted red, with a couple of glass panels at the top. It was a door which, in other circumstances, would have seemed quite jolly and welcoming. Now, he could only see how substantial it was and how difficult it would be to batter down, should the need arise. He gave two loud knocks on the glass, hoping his authority would cause those within to open up without a fight. The only response was silence, followed quickly by what Reilly thought might have been feet scurrying about on a wooden floor. He knocked again. Nothing. A third attempt was accompanied by a command:

'Open up. This is the police. Open the door, *now!*'

Reilly had always been a one to avoid cliché, if at all possible, so he didn't tend to say the usual clichés that he sometimes saw on television, like *come out with your hands up* or *we have you surrounded* or, even, *make my day!* All phrases that had come into his mind as his hand closed around his firearm. He hoped beyond hope that he would not have to draw said weapon this day (or any day for that matter). His way was to negotiate. He believed in the power of the word though, sometimes, just sometimes, he had been tempted to shoot first and ask questions later. It'd be quicker but, no, his way was the boring way, perhaps, but it had seen him through some tough times in the past. He very much hoped it would see him through this day.

There was a definite sound from within the house in answer to his command. Slow, unsure footsteps were approaching the front door. A lock was turning, hinges creaking and, there, standing in front of him was Yasmina, recognised only from a photo Fr. Lonergan had shown him. Time seemed to stand still though it was only a matter of a few seconds before all hell broke out. Fr. Lonergan, on seeing his colleague couldn't help himself.

'*Yasmina!*'

At the same time, the two guards who had been sent to the rear of the house burst in the back door while Reilly's driver rushed past the girl at the door, all three guards intent on securing the building and making sure nothing untoward could happen to anyone inside.

Yasmina slowly sank to the floor as if exhaustion had set in. Tears flowed down her cheeks and she was trembling, whether from fear or tiredness or cold, it was not clear. Fr. Lonergan went to her and, against his better judgement, just gathered her to his chest, rocking her like a baby and making soothing noises. He could not understand why he didn't just push her away and make his way into the house to look for the little abducted girl but something stopped him. That job fell to Jane and Chris who followed the others inside, almost stepping over the priest and his care.

Chapter 34

The scene that greeting the new arrivals on entering the house was beyond their imaginings. It was not one of violence or of horror. Or even one of fear and containment. No hostage was being held here against her will. Instead, it was the most beautiful picture. A child surrounded by four adults, all seated on the floor and playing 'picnic'. There were dolls and a teddy bear all placed on a tartan rug with toy cups and plates piled high with imaginary food. Clearly, before the interruption, there had been laughter and giggling, joking, and teasing, for this was a happy scene, a joyous reunion, a family at peace.

All the adults just stood and stared, as if frozen to the spot, no-one quite sure what they were witnessing. The child was the first to react, first with fear at all these strangers who had burst in on her playtime. Then, catching a glimpse of Jane who was standing just to the left of Reilly, her face lit up.

'Jane! It's my friend Jane. And Chris! And Fr. Longan (she never could pronounce his name correctly). Mama, Baba, it's my friends! They've come to see me. Can they stay for tea?'

Mama? Baba?

Those two words had struck all four guards and all three civilians dumb. So, this was why Eva had vanished. She had been reunited with her parents after so much time. How could this have happened? How had they got to Ireland? Or had they arrived first and she had followed in some strange twist of fate?

All Jane knew was that Eva was looking up at her in expectation, waiting for a hug, and a hug she should have without delay. She picked up the child and swung her in the air, both of them laughing and hugging. Then, Chris wanting in on the fun, took Eva from Jane's arms and twirled her around, high in the air as he had done so often before. Fr. Lonergan came into the sitting room along with Yasmina and looked about, questions that were clear on his face awaiting answers. Eventually, things settled down a little and all looked in Yasmina's direction.

'Yasmina, I think you have a lot of explaining to do.' Reilly finally realised it was time to take charge of the unexpected situation. 'Can you tell us what has happened here and why you kidnapped Eva?'

'Kidnapped? No! That is not what happened. Quite the opposite.' It was one of the men who had been sitting on the floor with Eva, sipping imaginary tea from a tiny cup and eating imaginary biscuits, who now addressed the group. He was tall, dark-haired, about forty years old, and dressed in a cream-coloured suit. He spoke perfect English with a slight British accent and had a certain self-assurance that belied his present circumstances. He raised his hands as if to reassure those who had just arrived that he meant no harm and spoke again.

'Please, you are welcome to our home. Sit and we can speak a while.' He politely indicated the various empty chairs, and, with some hesitation, the newcomers complied and sat down, still bewildered at these latest developments.

'My name is Dr Ismael Mari and I am Eva's father. Please, let me explain how, and why, we come to be here and you will see there is nothing to be worried about. I am a medical doctor but, due to circumstances too difficult to explain right now, I have had to leave my homeland.' Here, Ismael broke off and smiled across the room at a woman who smiled back, a sad smile filled with pain and understanding. Nodding, he continued his story:

'At first, I had thought we could undertake the journey in relative comfort, but I left it too late. I hesitated too long and we missed our opportunity of simply driving across the border before the bombs came and before it became impossible to buy petrol, along with other vital supplies. The foolish thing is that I had been planning this trip for years, just a vague plan forming in the back of my mind as my beloved country fell deeper and deeper into chaos and confusion. We...'. Again, he smiled at the woman across the room, before continuing. 'We had some steps to prepare, making sure, for instance, that Eva could speak English, and hiding some valuables and money in a secret place in our garden. We thought that, if we had to leave, at least Eva would be able to manage in a new country and we would have enough to start again. Yet, for all those plans, we almost left it too late and, in the end, all we could do was dig up our secret treasures and grab the few possessions we could carry.'

Here, Ismael stopped speaking again and passed a hand over his eyes, as if trying to wipe out the memory of those days and nights when they had struggled through dangerous territory, evading soldiers from every side, searching for food and water wherever they could, he, cursing his foolishness at having stayed so long. *Why had he not left years ago? Why?* The answer was simple and heart-breaking: he loved his country.

'Our original plan had been to cross the Mediterranean and get to Spain. My ancestors had travelled in the opposite direction centuries ago so I thought we might find sanctuary in the old country and, then, eventually, we would be able to settle for a while until it was safe to go home. We knew it was risky but we prayed that, in summer, the risk would be less and, together we would make it'. Again, the story was interrupted while Ismael gathered his thoughts. Looking around the room, he met the eyes of his audience and could see encouragement and sympathy, so he continued:

'The real horror began when, in the rush to get on the few dinghies provided by the men who had agreed, in exchange for an exorbitant sum of money, to bring us across the water, I got on one vessel while my wife, Hanah, was directed, forcibly, to another. When we finally landed ashore... I will spare you the details of that terrible journey... I searched along the beach for the two most important people in my life. You can imagine my panic when I discovered that Eva was not there. Hanah had thought she was with me while I had thought she was with her mother.' Again, silence descended while the full horror of that moment was contemplated by all those in the room.

'We were distraught, shouting Eva's name as loudly as we dared, hoping she was hiding in one of the other boats. But there was no sign of her and none of the other travellers had noticed her. I sat there on that beach for hours, holding Hanah's hand, gazing out to sea, waiting for my Eva, but she did not appear. Finally, we could sit and wait no longer as day was breaking and we needed to take shelter away from the coast. So, with broken hearts, we headed away from the seashore, praying as we left that, someday, a miracle would happen and we would be reunited with the joy of our lives. Since that horrendous day, we haven't stopped looking for our daughter, asking in every shelter and centre we came to. Finally, our prayers were answered, and the long-awaited miracle happened for, today, here we are, together again.' The smile that lit up Ismael's face was radiant, making clear to anyone who had any remaining doubts, that Eva was loved and cherished by this man.

How Eva came to be in that room, though, was a story that would have to wait a little while longer. Ismael knew there would be more questions but, for now, he just wanted to know who these stranger were. Some seemed to know his Eva well. At least she seemed very happy to see them and they were equally happy it would seem. Perhaps they had had a role in this miracle. If so, he would thank them but, for now, he must make sure that they did not pose a threat to his family reunion. Nothing, but *nothing* must ever part him from his child again, at least not until she was an adult herself and ready to spread her wings. Now, he would fight to the death to keep his family together and all in this room must know that.

'So, you see, my daughter was not kidnapped. Yasmina is a friend. She has found our girl and brought her to us. We are forever grateful to her.'

'Is this true, Yasmina?' Father Lonergan could contain himself no longer. 'Why did you not tell me what you were doing? Didn't you know I would have helped you?'

Yasmina looked around the room at each of the people gathered there.

Finally, she gathered her strength and spoke, her voice a mere whisper:

'Father, I did not know who I could trust. I am sorry.'

'Child, you must have felt so alone. I wish you had trusted me but I can understand. How on earth did you manage to find Eva's parents? What a wonderful thing you have done!'

'Not so quick with the praise, Father. We need to ascertain the facts first and foremost.' Superintendent Reilly was not sure what, exactly, was going on and he didn't like that sensation of being out of the loop. 'I think we all need to debrief. I'd like to fill in a few details. You can't just take a child out of care and vanish into the night without explanation. So, first and foremost, Davis, plug in the kettle and make a pot of tea. It's going to be a long night.'

Chapter 35

Once mugs of tea had been distributed among the adults and everyone was seated again, some on the leather sofa, some around the kitchen table, Superintendent Reilly cleared his throat and began proceedings.

'Now I must advise you all that this is an official police investigation and Davis here will be taking notes that will form the bulk of your statements in due course. By rights we should take you all down to the station and take formal statements there but, before doing that, I think it would be helpful if we got the facts sorted out first. Yasmina, you seem to be best suited to get the ball rolling. Can you tell us how you come to be here? Your last known whereabouts were Madrid, if my sources are to be believed. And can you tell us exactly who these people are?' Reilly nodded in the direction of the four adults who had been in the house before he had arrived. Yasmina did as she was bidden and made the introductions, formally introducing Eva's parents, Ismael and Hanah, to the others, the other couple she presented as friends from Ireland, a couple who had already been given asylum and were now living in Co. Meath. They were part of a sponsorship programme that had been established in 2016 whereby a community group signs up to support a family. So far, Yasmina explained, in Ireland alone, over two and a half thousand people had been sponsored, including over fifty unaccompanied children.

'Yes, yes, that's all very well. But what are they doing *here*? What is their relationship with Eva and her parents, that's what I'd like to know?' Reilly's impatience was beginning to boil over so Yasmina took a deep breath and began to tell her story.

'It all started when I had been working at the refugee centre in Madrid for almost a year, if I remember correctly. I noticed that some children would arrive without their parents and some of those would vanish into thin air.

I asked my superiors about one or two of them and, though they answered my questions to a certain extent, I never felt that I had been told the whole story. I started to suspect that there were dark forces at play and that was when I got to know you, Father Lonergan. You turned up out of the blue one day and I wondered if I could trust you. At first I did for you seemed a ... a *buena persona*, a good person, and I had been brought up to trust a priest. But then the children still vanished and one boy in particular disappeared, do you remember him, Father?'

Father Lonergan nodded, the image of the boy now known as Paulo coming into his mind. Yasmina smiled as she too remembered.

'I heard you, Father, asking questions about him at the centre and getting similar answers to those I had been given – no one remembered him, he had never been there and so on. So I decided to speak with you and I told you that I *did* remember him, that he *had* been there and, together, we traced him and found him and today he is safe.'

'So, given that we worked together for Paulo, when did you decide not to trust me, Yasmina?' The priest couldn't keep the hurt from his voice as he asked that question.

'I am not sure, exactly. Little doubts started to creep into my mind. You seemed too friendly, too willing to help the children. And then, of course, Magda came on the scene.'

'Ah, yes, Magdalena Sánchez. Have you got that, Davis?' Reilly was making certain that the garda was getting everything down clearly in his notes. Davis nodded, relieved that he had read the case file and was familiar with the name.

'Yes, Magda volunteered at the centre and became someone I could rely on, at least at first. Gradually, she became indispensable but she also began to say little things against Fr. Lonergan.'

'Such as?' Reilly wanted to get as clear a picture as he could of the atmosphere at the centre.

'Oh, just that she could not understand why a man like him would be in Madrid so much. Or why didn't he spend more time helping Irish kids. Or had I heard the latest scandal about priests and kids. That sort of thing. Sorry, Father, but I began to wonder if she was right. At the same time, I wondered about her motives too, especially as Fr. Lonergan started asking questions about *her*, about *her* reasons for being there. It became all too much and I did not know where to turn. Then, Eva arrived and she fit the usual profile – no parents, no siblings, unwanted it would seem.'

Ismael could not listen without interrupting when he heard that.

'She was wanted, very wanted, very beloved. Is that not right, my Eva?' The child in question, who was now sitting on her daddy's knee, simply put her arms around his neck and hugged him. She was in no doubt of her ranking in that room, and she was content to be with the people she loved, all her nightmares over.

'I know that *now* but *then* all I could think of is that Eva was easy prey. I did not know how to protect her. Then Chris and Jane appeared and everything got even more complicated.' On saying those words, Yasmina gave a slight, apologetic smile in the Australians' direction before continuing:

'As I said, I did not know what to do. Then, one evening, as I was leaving the centre, a man and woman approached me. They asked me to follow them. I was a bit nervous to do so but they led me to a crowded *plaza*. We sat on a bench there and they asked me if I were trustworthy. Of course I said I was. They, then, said that they had been watching me and watching how concerned I was about the children. I said again that of course I was. They said I need not be, that the children were safe. That, since the boy now known as Paulo had been rescued, they had put in place a system to save all vulnerable children who arrived unaccompanied at the centre. They had a network, made up mainly of refugees who had 'made it' and who wanted to give back something, to help those who were still struggling.

One of the jobs they were undertaking was to try to reunite separated families. Oh yes, that happens far more than it should, children losing their parents on the road, siblings separated from each other. Heart-breaking for those who have already lost so much.'

As Yasmina's words were heard around the room, the silence became heavy with emotion. Each adult could place themselves in the terrifying position of the lost child or the panicked parent. Who could not feel their pain?

'They told me not to worry about Eva, that her parents had made it to Spain and had been informed of her location. They asked me if I could do them one favour, to make sure Eva got on the bus to Alicante. From there, all that needed to happen was for her parents to get to Alicante and they would take her from the centre there. But, Father, you intervened.'

The priest looked about in amazement, floundering for words.

'But ... but ... I thought she needed rescuing. Magda was closing in – the people in the centre were sure of it – *they* asked for my help.'

'Yes, they thought Magda was a threat too and did ask for your help but, had you stuck to the original plan and not shipped Eva off an hour before she was due to go, her parents would have arrived and all would have been well.'

This time it was the unidentified man who had spoken.

'Yes, our contacts in Spain were the ones to approach Yasmina. They were concerned at the amount of interest being shown in Eva. First, the journalist who broadcast her photograph, then Father Lonergan, then Magdalena Sánchez, then two Australians, all asking questions and attracting attention to a defenceless girl. We knew the risks and our hope was to reunite her with her parents but that could only happen if she remained where we could watch over her. So, it was arranged for Eva to get to Alicante. But, then, when Yasmina informed them that Eva was in

Ireland – she knew the address as the Father had told her to send on clothes to him in Cork, they contacted us and they arranged for Hanah and Ismael to get here, once they had been found. Not so difficult as they were frantically searching for Eva and causing quite a stir among the other refugees. News travels fast among our people. So, it was decided that Yasmina would come with them and, then, she managed to follow Eva from Cork to this place. And here we are.' The man cast a glance around the room and smiled.

'So, just let me get this straight.' Superintendent Reilly was not at all sure who were the goodies or the baddies in this story. Indeed, he wasn't even sure there were any baddies, but, just in case, he needed to see who, if anyone, had kidnapped a young girl. 'You're telling me that your group, or whatever it is, was going to take Eva out of the centre, or whatever it was, in Alicante where she was safe but Father Lonergan beat you to it?'

'Exactly.'

'Well, don't that beat all. Father, you seem to be the culprit here. Should I arrest you, do you think?' Reilly accompanied his words with a chuckle, amused at the expression of absolute outrage on the priest's face.

'I don't see how this is remotely funny, Tom. I've just discovered that I've gone to great trouble just to cause a whole lot more trouble. I do apologise to you all.'

'O come now, Father Jim, isn't it just a tiny bit amusing? I can see the headlines now: 'Priest guilty of doing no good! Now helping the police with their enquiries!! Ha! Ha! - Don't write that down, Davis - this bit is 'off the record'.' Another chuckle that found echoes around the room.

'But are we now saying that the voyage Jane and I undertook from Alicante – with your undercover cop, I might add, at the helm, was all in vain?' Chris was floundering as much as the priest and couldn't quite grasp the fact that the last few weeks of his life need not have taken the direction they had.

'I would not say that, exactly, sir.' It was Eva's father who spoke now. 'We were very grateful that you took care of Eva. From what she has told us, she felt very safe with you and Miss Jane. We also were not certain of the role played in all of this by Miss Magdalena, the other lady who, Yasmina said, worked at the rescue centre in Madrid. We, like you, suspected she had dark motives. Is that not the case? Have you found out why she was so interested in my daughter?'

'We have. Seems she was working for the Spanish secret service. She was convinced there was a case of child trafficking to investigate. Eva may not have been a target in this particular occasion but, to be honest, Mr Mari, we still believe there may be some such activity of that nature unless your group is responsible for all the missing children?'

'Not my group as I am just a grateful parent. My friend here may have some more information for you on that subject.' Ismael turned to the other man to see if he could answer the policeman's question more fully.'

'Sadly, sir, I believe you are right. We have reunited about four children with their parents, Eva here included. Another three we have taken to new families so, in all, we are responsible for the 'disappearance' of seven children. A very small number, unfortunately. The number of children who have vanished, without, shall we say, our intervention, in Spain alone, or on their way there, cannot be known with any great certainty. Some have drowned, some have taken to the streets, but many were never counted, never noticed and of those I can only surmise their fate.'

Reilly didn't quite know what to say to this. On the one hand, this self-appointed group were working illegally, snatching children from the authorities who were the legal guardians. Yet, on the other hand, their motives were honourable, as was not the case of others. Could he turn a blind eye to such activities? Should he? No. He'd have to let the courts make such a decision. His duty was to uphold the law, not become judge and jury. However, he'd leave any action for another day. Today was for celebrating the safety of Eva and the others. He'd worry about everything else tomorrow.

Again, a heavy silence fell on all in the room, with even Eva aware of the mood. She looked around at all of them and, suddenly, as if a thought occurred to her out of the blue, she spoke.

'Are you talking about when children go away at night? About the people who take them?'

All the adults looked at her and then at each other, not sure if they were hearing correctly. Reilly bent down in front of the young girl as she sat on her father's knee.

'Eva, what do you know of such people? Did someone try to take you out at night?'

Eva giggled and squirmed deeper into her father's arms.

'Nooo! Not really. Well, Yasmina did but *she* is nice *and* she brought me to my mama and baba.'

'Yes, that's ok, honey. But were there any other people who tried?'

'Not here, but we all knew in Spain that we must always stay together. We children I mean 'cos there was a man there who would bring sweets and say he had a puppy in his car and would we like to go see it.' At this, Eva looked up at her daddy with a frown.

'Baba, I really wanted to see that puppy but one of the other boys in the centre said I mustn't. That there wasn't a puppy at all. Do you think that man *lied?*' Eva said that final word with amazement, as if she couldn't believe an adult would ever lie, especially about the existence of a little dog.

'My little Eva, I am afraid he did. But you were very good not to go to see the puppy, even though you wanted to so much. You remembered what your mama always said to you, didn't you?'

'Yes, I did – ask before you leave the house and never, ever, go away with a stranger. I did right, didn't I, Mama?' Saying this, Eva reached out her arms towards her mother who had been sitting silently and listening to all that was going on. In fact, her silence had been irritating Jane quite a bit, causing her to think of the woman as downtrodden in some way. Nothing could have been further from the truth though and, now, she lifted her daughter from her father's lap to her own and spoke for the first time.

'My darling girl, yes, you did right. You have been a brave girl, braver than I have been and we are very glad to have you here with us.' Hanah's voice began to break as she spoke and, to avoid tears, she spoke again to her daughter.

'Now, Eva, you must tell this policeman everything you know about that man. Can you remember what he looked like? Did he work at the centre? How did he get to talk with you and the other children? Anything you can remember will be very helpful, darling.'

Eva took a deep breath and squeezed her eyes tightly shut, as if trying to conjure up an image of the man.

'He was tall, with a beard and he was Spanish.'

'Very good, Eva. Are you getting this down, Davis?' Reilly was eager that not a word would be missed in Davis's notes. 'Anything else you remember, Eva?'

'Well, he liked to take photos of the children.'

There was a general gasp in the room.

'What kind of photos? Did he take any of you, Eva?'

'Oh yes, he took lots. He said I would be on TV.' Another gasp followed her words as the adults considered the implications of the little girl's words.

'When did he take the photos, darling?' Hanah needed to find out the worst as quickly as possible.

'When I first got off the boat, he took my photo then.'

'You mean on the beach? When you were with the other children?'

Eva nodded and then shyly asked:

'Do you want to know his name?'

'You know his name, the name of the man who had sweets and a puppy?'

'Yes, of course, I wouldn't let just anyone take my photo, Mama. I remember you said I shouldn't and I'm not *stupid*. But *he* said he'd help me find *you*. So I let him. I stared at his camera and made a wish. I wished very hard that I would find you. And I *did!*'

Hanah couldn't help but smile at her daughter's triumphant statement. She knew too well the dangers to be faced by a child alone in the world and recalled the many times she had warned her daughter not to trust strangers. Her daughter's reaction had always been to say: *Mama, I'm not stupid. I know all about strangers.* She had hated that Eva's innocent faith in human nature had been spoilt but it had been necessary to put her on guard, given the dangers of their homeland and, later, given the journey they were about to undertake. She was very glad now that she had put her daughter on guard.

'That's true. So, darling, tell us what was his name?'

Everyone in the room waited with bated breath for her to name the man behind all the dark activities, to say a name that some in the room thought they already knew, the name of the man who had taken that photograph that had sent two of them racing across the globe to save a little girl that, in the end, hadn't needed saving at all.

'His name was Luke. That's what he said, or we could also call him Lucas.'

Chapter 36

To say that all hell broke out next would be an understatement. Everyone in the room started talking at the same time, everyone eager to share what they knew of Lucas, it seemed. Finally, when the din got too much for Superintendent Reilly, he clapped his hands together and shouted, to make himself heard above the racket.

'All right, now, all right. Let's all calm down. Settle down, people. The sooner we calm down, the sooner we can get this whole thing sorted out. Quiet. *Quiet I said!*'

Finally, silence descended and Reilly was able to talk at a normal level.

'Right, that's better. Now, I take it some of you know who this Lucas guy is?'

Again, people started talking all together to the policeman's annoyance.

'One at a time. One at a time or we'll get nowhere. Right, so Jane, you look like you'll burst if you don't get to speak. Out with it. Who is Lucas?'

Jane stood up to speak as she felt more able to address the whole room that way.

'That's Lucas Fernández, the reporter who took that photograph that we - I mean Chris and I - saw on TV in Australia. The image that made us both pack up and head for Spain. I mean it was a powerful image of little Eva here and she looked so vulnerable, so defenceless.'

'Lucas Fernández. Right, got that, Davis? So, from what Eva's says, he turned up on several occasions at the centre in Madrid. Is that right, Eva?'

The little girl just nodded, happy now to play with her mother's necklace and leave the adults get on with whatever adults did. She was getting sleepy and had no more interest in the adult world. Soon, she would fall into a world of dreams and sleep away the hours, hours when that adult world would be filled with activity, all focused on tracking down a man who enticed children with sweets and lies.

'Okay, so this Lucas, how would he have gained access to the centre, that's what I'd like to know?'

Chris and Father Lonergan both started to speak at once before Chris politely indicated that the priest should explain.

'Lucas is, from what Chris and Jane have told me, Magda's boyfriend. He could easily call to the centre with the excuse of meeting his *novia* there. No-one would think that strange. Though I never came across him when I was there, which, now I think about it, is a bit odd, almost like he was staying out of my way.'

'Magda's boyfriend, you say! So are we back to thinking that woman is implicated? Did she know what her boyfriend was up to?'

'Surely not. I mean what woman would allow such a thing?'

'Plenty have. Well, maybe not plenty, but there have been some cases, even cases where the woman just tries to ignore her own suspicions even if she's not prepared to aid and abet.'

'But Magda is not that kind of woman. If she suspected such a thing, she would take action, she wouldn't sit idly by.' Jane found, to her own surprise, that she needed to defend her arch-rival, a rival no more it was true but, still, she could not believe that the Magda they had seen last in Barcelona would be capable of such awful actions and certainly not capable of inaction when a child's welfare was at stake.

'No, I agree, but, just to be sure, I think we should let the Spanish authorities know about Lucas without delay and also ask them to bring Ms Magdalena Sánchez in for further questioning.'

Just as Reilly prepared to head out the door to go back to the police station with Davis, leaving Sergeant Burke behind with the driver, a sleepy little voice piped up.

'Oh, I forgot – Lucas was here last night, just before Yasmina came for me. I saw him outside my window.' And, with that, Eva fell back asleep, content that her part in this story was now complete.

...

In comparison to the din that had followed her previous words, this time, Eva's intervention caused a stunned silence. It took long moments before the significance of what she had said sank in. *Lucas was in Ireland. He had been outside Eva's lodgings. What would have happened if Yasmina hadn't arrived when she did? Where was he now? What did he plan to do now? And, most of all, why had he followed one little girl all the way to Ireland?*

Finally, Superintendent Reilly shook himself out of his thoughts.

'Well, that puts a completely different complexion on things, doesn't it? Davis, Burke, we need to get that man to a police interview ASAP. Get his description out and get him brought here. No, not here, obviously. I mean get him to the station. Move it, move it. He's probably still in the vicinity. Let's hope he hasn't seen us arrive here. Yasmina, do you think he might have followed you last night from the hotel? Does he know Eva's here in this house, do you think?'

Yasmina gave Reilly's words some thought before answering.

'I'm not sure. Eva said he was at the hotel before I arrived so he mustn't have followed me there. But I can't be sure if he followed me from there to here. He might have. Oh no! He could be right outside, couldn't he?'

'He could, he certainly could but that's as far as he's going to get. Burke, you stay here and make sure the premises is secure when I leave. Davis, you come with me, and Cronin, you stay here with Burke. He could do with back-up, just in case.'

Given the seriousness of the situation, the sound of Jane's giggling seemed quite out of place. Chris gave her a nudge, whispering urgently at her:

'What's got into you, Jane? What on earth can you find remotely amusing about all this?'

'Yes, I'd like to know that too?'

Jane felt all eyes upon her, increasing her embarrassment. She couldn't think of anything to say but the truth.

'Well, sorry, superintendent, I know it's entirely inappropriate. I expect it's due to the tension of the last few hours but I just found it funny that, given that we've driven all the way from Cork with your driver, this is the first time we've heard you use her name. She's been all but invisible till now - long suffering I expect, too!' Jane and the said Cronin exchanged a knowing look, two fellow sufferers of bosses who expect much and give back very little.

At her words, Chris and Fr. Lonergan choked back their laughter while Reilly had the decency to look a bit abashed.

'Cronin here knows me well enough to know she's anything but invisible. Her married name's Reilly, if you must know. Everyone, meet my daughter-in-law - and I don't know about long-suffering - I'm the best superintendent she's ever had!'

The said Cronin was now grinning from ear to ear, enjoying her father-in-law's discomfort.

'Lovely to meet you all. And yes, he's the best Super I've had but that's just because he's the only one I've had. I've only just come out of Templemore and this is my first real assignment. I don't usually get to drive the big wigs around, of course. I'm usually just out on the beat but there was a problem today back in Cork - not enough *gardaí* to go around - or maybe no-one fancied being stuck for hours in a car with himself – ya, that might have been it!'

Everyone nodded as if that explained everything and it was almost as if they had forgotten the immediate problem, until the Super 'himself' reminded them that they had more urgent matters to see about than discuss his family and/or staffing issues.

With that, he left the house with as much dignity as he could muster in the company of Davis, with Burke locking the front door behind them. Cronin (whose first name turned out to be Isabel) took the precaution of making sure the back door was equally secure before returning to the kitchen and asking if anyone would like another cup of tea.

'How about something a bit stronger?'

'*Father*! I didn't think you were a drinking man?' Chris was quite surprised at the priest's request.

'No, I didn't mean that. I meant we could get a bit of dinner on. I'm quite peckish, if anyone's interested. Is there any food in the house?'

Yasmina confirmed that she had stocked the house in preparation for its guests. There were all the ingredients to prepare a solid meal so, with the help of a few of the others and Chris who volunteered to be chief chopper, she set about the task of getting things prepared. The rest of the group searched for serving dishes and utensils and set the table for the banquet that was to ensue. It would prove to be a very multicultural affair with dishes from different parts of the world sharing counter space. Fr. Lonergan's offering had been the best roast potatoes anyone there had ever tasted while they were accompanied by Tabouli salad, kebabs, Spanish omelette all followed by a desert of apple pie and custard, and washed down with copious cups of tea and coffee. Conversation was equally enjoyable, for, while Eva slept on the sofa (no-one felt it advisable to put her into one of the bedrooms on her own), tales were told of bygone days and childhood adventures when the world had seemed a safer, smaller place, before they had all grown up.

Chapter 37

Once the dishes were cleared away and hunger had been satisfied by their very eclectic meal, the adults turned their attention to their next move. Each was wondering how long they would have to wait before news would come, freeing them to leave the house. The main question in their minds was whether it would take hours or days before Lucas Fernández was apprehended. Surely it wouldn't be too difficult to locate him. Surely he couldn't escape. Conversation had flagged along with their spirits when, suddenly, Jane's mobile phone rang, causing all to jump with fright. She went to answer it and, looking at the screen where the name of the caller was identified, she stopped dead:

'It's Magda!', she said, horrified. 'What do I do? What do I tell her? I didn't even think she had my number.'

'Well, she is secret service. They're good at finding out such things. Anyway, play it cool, Jane, just let her do the talking.' Chris tried to sound reassuring but, deep down, he was glad it was Jane's phone that had rung and not his, glad, if not a little surprised. He wouldn't know how to react any more than Jane did.

'Right, here goes. *Hola*, Magda. How are things?'

'Jane, I am so glad to hear your voice. I do not know what to do. Have you heard the awful news?'

'What news, exactly?'

'About Lucas. I cannot believe it is true.'

'What have you heard, exactly?'

'*Bien*, that he is wanted by the police, that they are searching for him in

Ireland, that he has something to do with kidnapping children. *Ay* Jane, can it be true? I cannot bear to think he used me to get close to the children in the refuge. How could I have been so blind?'

Jane could hear real pain in Magda's voice and felt her heart soften at the other woman's anguish. She could only imagine what she was going through.

'Magda, at this stage I don't really know what part Lucas has in all of this. Do you know where he is? The best thing would be for him to talk with the police here. Maybe it's all a big mistake.'

'Do you really think so? Oh Jane, I do hope so. The only problem is that Lucas won't answer my calls or messages. We were meant to meet up in Madrid when he got back from his latest assignment but I have tried to contact him. I do know he is in Ireland or, at least, his mobile is. I have one of those tracer apps, you know. In the early days of our relationship, we thought it romantic to be able to see where we each were. *Dios*, Jane, how could I have got it so wrong about that man? Anyway, it seems he is in Ireland. That is suspicious ¿*verdad?* Why would he be in Ireland? He never said anything to me, though, to be honest I have been a bit distracted over the last few days.'

Was it Jane's imagination or was there a lightness to Magda's voice that contrasted with the gravity of the present circumstances? Jane decided to confirm Lucas's whereabouts, given that Magda already seemed to know most of what had been going on.

'Yes, he's been spotted here in Wexford, near where Eva was staying so we suspect she is the reason he's here.' Hearing Magda gasp, Jane quickly assured her that Eva was safe.

'I'm with her now as is Chris and Father Lonergan. There have been a few other developments but, the most important thing now is for Lucas to be found. He must turn himself in. It really would be best so can you keep trying to speak with him? Get him to hand himself in, if you can. That would be the best outcome.'

'Yes, of course. I will try. I will call you back if I succeed. *Hasta pronto*, Jane. We will talk very soon, I hope.'

With that, the line went dead and Jane became aware that everyone in the room had been trying to listen to every word that had been said. They had got the main gist: that Lucas could not be reached. If even his girlfriend couldn't locate him, what hope was there that he would see sense?

'Well, Magda is going to keep trying to find him. She'll let us know if – when – she speaks with him. Till then, I guess we should try to get some rest. It's getting late and I, for one, wouldn't mind having a bit of a nap.'

'Good idea, Miss Jane.' Father Lonergan looked exhausted. 'There are two bedrooms not to mention that very comfortable-looking sofa here. Let's all try to get forty winks.'

Garda Cronin and Sergeant Burke agreed that it was a good idea for the civilians to head for the bedrooms while they stayed on guard. Neither could face the consequences of being found asleep on duty should Superintendent Reilly suddenly decide to call in with an update. Truth be told, the other adults were quite relieved to think there would be trained police watching over them as they slept and so Ismael, Hanah and their two companions headed for one bedroom, with Ismael carrying his sleeping daughter, while the other four stood wondering if they should all go to the second bedroom.

'You and Fr. Lonergan should take the room, Chris. Fr. Lonergan, you look done in and Yasmina and I can curl up quite happily on that sofa there.'

'I wouldn't hear of it, Ms Jane! You two take the bed and I'll take the sofa.'

'And what about Chris, then?'

'Well, I know I am a man of God and there are certain standards I should enforce in my presence but, I think Chris here is a gentleman. He can share the bedroom with you without anything untoward happening, isn't that right, Mr Chris?'

'Well, I'm glad you two got around to asking me my opinion – finally! Let's all share the bedroom, shall we, since, if you two had taken the trouble to investigate the accommodation, you'd have seen that there are bunk beds and a double. Jane, you and Yasmina can share the double while the Father and myself will return to our childhood and fight over who gets top bunk. Any arguments?'

There were none as Jane, Yasmina and Fr. Jim meekly followed Chris out of the room, down the corridor and into the bedroom, leaving the two *gardaí* grinning behind them.

Chapter 38

Silence descended on the bungalow as everyone settled down for the night. Exhaustion had taken its toll and it wasn't long before Burke and Cronin could hear gentle snoring coming from both bedrooms

'Well, this has turned out to be quite a day, hasn't it, Garda Cronin? I bet you didn't expect to be pulling an all nighter when you set out from Cork this morning, did you?'

'No, I certainly did not. I didn't even think to bring a toothbrush! Ah well, let's hope things get sorted sooner rather than later. Is it usually this exciting hereabouts, Sarge?'

'We do get our fair share of the action, unfortunately. Being so close to Dublin and Rosslare, of course, attracts a colourful assortment of individuals. Anything that can be smuggled, large or small, we've seen them try, that's for sure. Would you believe we even found an elephant on board a freighter one time?! *An elephant!* How they thought we wouldn't see it, I really don't know?'

'You're joking! What excuse did they come up with for that?'

'Ha! They said it must have run away from a circus and found its own way on board. Can you imagine - The proverbial Nelly, packing her bag but running away *from* the circus.'

'Good one! So, what happened to the elephant? Nothing bad, I hope.'

'No, she's up in Dublin Zoo now, munching her weight of hay, no doubt, and telling the other elephants all about her adventures. Speaking about munching, I wouldn't mind another helping of that apple pie. Pity the custard is all gone. What about you, Cronin?'

'A cuppa wouldn't go astray, now you mention it. Shall I plug the kettle in?'

'Nah. I'll do it. You must be tired from all the driving. Put your feet up while you can. I'll have that tea ready in a jiffy.'

Burke was as good as his word, busying himself in the kitchen, humming a tune under his breath as he got things ready. *Nelly the elephant da da da ...*

He suddenly broke off his singing and, in a low voice, he called over to Cronin.

'Hey, Cronin. Could you come over here quick like?'

'What's up. Can't you find the tea ...?' Seeing his face, Cronin stopped in her tracks.

'What is it?'

'Look out the window, to the right, near the tree. Do you see anything?'

'To the right, you say, no ... oh wait, is that ... is that a cigarette glowing?'

'Act normal now, as if we haven't seen anything. I'll ring the station. You stay here as if you're making the tea and keep your eyes peeled. No sudden movements or we'll scare him away, or worse. Lucky we're not wearing our hats or he'd know we're *gardaí*. Hopefully, he'll just think we're civilians'

'Right, Sarge. Call it in and we just might get a proper night's sleep after all.'

Sergeant Burke did as he was bidden and contacted the station. It was a sleepy Davis who answered the phone. He didn't take long to wake up, though, at Burke's news and said he would inform Reilly immediately and get back-up to the cottage within minutes. Some bigwigs had arrived from Wexford and extra *gardaí* had been drafted in to help with the search. They might now be needed in a different capacity if what Burke said proved to be true, that their target was within metres of the cottage and probably had been for quite some time. Burke hung up after reminding Davis that no sirens should be used on approach. *No need to lose the element of surprise!*

'Right, that's all taken care of. They'll be here within minutes. Meanwhile, we'd best keep an eye out.' Burke looked sadly at the slice of apple pie he had been preparing. No time now to enjoy it. Maybe later, if all worked out well.

'Do you think he'll put up any resistance? I mean, do you think he's armed?' Cronin's voice betrayed her anxiety.

'Well, he might be armed but sure we're used to dealing with all kinds here so don't worry. We'll have him arrested before you know it.' Burke did his best to allay her fears, remembering his own first assignment that had involved guns. No matter how well trained you were, when faced with a gun for the first time, it took it out of you. For the first time and every time, for that matter. He too hoped the man outside was unarmed. Unarmed and compliant, that would be best.

Cronin could see that the older policeman was trying to help and she was grateful for his efforts. She hoped that, whatever happened, she'd acquit herself well. She wished that things were more along the lines of her training. She'd never imagined she'd be the one inside a building with the suspect outside, watching. Instead, she'd visualised herself talking down a hostage-taker, or someone who had barricaded themselves inside. Her sense of being trapped was growing steadily in this scenario. It was the silence that was the worst thing. It seemed oppressive – no sound of traffic, of distant sirens, of airplanes flying overhead, of people shouting and laughing or arguing. All the usual sounds of city living. Here, the countryside seemed frozen in silence, the sound of every twig breaking amplified in the night air, every owl hooting, a ghostly sound of another world.

'What was that?'

'What?'

'I thought I heard something, a rustling?'

'Probably a fox or a cat.'

'Are you sure?'

'No.'

'Can you see anything outside now?'

'No.'

'No cigarette?'

'No.'

'Do you think that's a good sign or a bad sign?'

'No idea. Probably he's just run out of cigarettes.'

'Right.'

Another few moments went by in silence.

'Did you hear that?'

'Cronin, would you get a grip! You're giving me heart attacks here.'

'Sorry, Sarge. I thought I heard something for sure that time.'

'You city folk. You can't survive two minutes here in the country without freaking out. It's the sound of nature, that's all it is - foxes, badgers, cats, dogs, owls - they make a hell of a racket if you listen.'

'Sure. If you say so.'

'I do - now back-up will be here soon. Don't know what's keeping them to be honest. Should have been here by now, I'd have thought.'

'Maybe you could ring Davis again – see what's keeping them.'

'Good idea. You keep looking out that window.'

Burke made to pick up his phone that he'd left on the kitchen table when they both heard a rustling this time. Before either could react, the sound of little footsteps made themselves heard and, suddenly, there before them appeared Eva, looking sleepy and confused.

'Hello'

'Hello, Eva. What are you doing out of bed?' Cronin went over to where the little girl was standing.

'I was thirsty. Mama and Baba are asleep. Can I have a drink of water, please?'

'Of course, little one.' Burke headed toward the sink and filled a glass from the tap. Just as he was turning back to bring the drink over to Eva, though, the back door burst open. And, there, standing in the doorframe, was the very man for whom half, if not all, of the Wexford police force were searching: Lucas Fernández himself. To say the least, he was not looking his best. His hair was dirty and unkempt, as was his beard, his clothes were torn, his face smudged with what looked like oil, and, most disturbing of all, in his right hand, he held a gun, a Glock 17 semi-automatic pistol, to be precise. Cronin had come top of her class in weaponry and recognised it immediately, not that that was of any consolation to her now for it only served to confirm that the weapon pointing in her direction was one of the most reliable on the market.

In the seconds following Lucas's entrance, it seemed that time stood still, each character frozen in position: Eva standing waiting for her drink; Cronin within an arm's reach of the little girl, Burke's left hand resting on the cold tap, his right holding the glass, mid-turn, and Lucas trying to decide who to aim at. Cronin was the first to react, stretching out her arms to grab Eva and ensure she was as far away from Lucas as possible. On seeing Lucas reach for them both, Burke flung himself at the intruder, pushing him against the wall. In the mêlée, they both lost their balance and went crashing to the floor. Burke found he was struggling with a madman. Lucas, crazed at having his actions thwarted, lashed out at the older man, punching and kicking, trying to get the gun between them so he could pull the trigger. Cronin, desperate to help, was trying to extricate herself from Eva's arms, the child clinging to her in fright. It looked as if Lucas would soon get his way, as Burke would not be able to hold the younger man at bay for much longer.

Out of the corner of her eye, Cronin thought she saw movement in the garden. *Back up?* Now would be a good time for them to arrive. Instead, to her horror, two men she'd never seen before appeared at the back door also holding guns, the same type as Lucas's.

'What's all this? We told you to wait for instructions, Fernández. What on earth possessed you to try to take them down on your own? Now, missy, stand over there. You too, sir. Lucas, take the girl outside to the van.' Seeing Lucas hesitate, the man shouted: '*Now!*'

Lucas came towards Cronin who still had Eva in her arms and he tried to drag the child away. Cronin held on for dear life. *No way was that man leaving this house with Eva. No way!*

Burke, still lying on the floor, seeing the situation grow steadily worse, shouted to her.

'Do as the man says. You'll be no use to anyone dead.'

'But I can't ... you can't expect me to ...' Cronin felt Eva's arms loosen and let go.

'It's okay. I'll go with Mr Lucas. Maybe he really does have a puppy this time.' Eva's face betrayed her real feelings. She knew there wouldn't be any puppy but, somewhere in her very young heart, she also knew that to struggle would mean her new friends would get hurt.

Cronin's eyes filled with tears as she realised the child was trying to protect *her*. Surely it should be the other way around. This couldn't be happening. All she could do was let Eva go and hope... vow... there would be another chance to put things right. Very soon.

Once the child had left the house with Lucas, the other two men secured the back door and indicated to Burke and Cronin to sit on the kitchen chairs. One man bound their feet and hands while the other went to check the bedrooms. On his return, he verified that everyone else in the house was still fast asleep. *How on earth hadn't they heard the commotion?* It just proved how exhausted they all were and how, once they believed, falsely it had turned out, that they were now safe, that all was in the safe hands of the police, they had fallen into the deepest sleep any of them had managed for many days, if not weeks.

'That's a piece of luck at least. I don't know what possessed Fernández to burst in like that. He knew he'd be outnumbered.'

'He's lost it completely. These last days have sent him over the edge. Hasn't the mental capacity. I told you, Boss, we should never have got involved with him.'

'No, but he did have some good contacts. He did prove useful, but something tells me his days are numbered.' At that, the two men had a chuckle at Lucas's expense.

Listening to the conversation, Burke and Cronin exchanged a glance, not sure what the next move would be. Both had tried to loosen their hands but to no avail. They were firmly stuck.

'Right, what'll we do with these two, Boss?'

'Well, my motto is to leave no loose ends. These two look like they could prove to be annoying.'

'Ya! Very! Let me deal with them, Boss. A bullet to the head, that'll do the trick. Quick and clean.'

'Do you want to wake the rest of the house?'

'Nah.'

'Well, we need to deal with everyone in one go. I think a bit of an explosion might do the trick. That oven looks like it's gas. Switch it on there and we just have to wait a few seconds, then a match flicked from the back door and Bob's your uncle. We hop it to the van, speed off and no-one's the wiser.'

'Great plan, Boss.'

'Yip. *And* we finally get the girl. It'll take forever for them to figure out she wasn't here when the 'accident' happened. Nice and clean – no forensics.'

Burke and Cronin looked at each other in horror. This was not looking good. Cronin decided she'd make one more attempt to change the direction of events by engaging the 'boss' in conversation. It was worth a try at least.

'Before you finish up here, can I ask one question?' Before waiting for an answer, she continued: 'why so much interest in one little girl? You seem to have a very organised set up (*flattery can't hurt!*). Why put it all in jeopardy over one child? You must have dozens who could take her place.'

The 'boss' stopped in his tracks, weighing up whether to answer or not. In the end, the flattery had its effect.

'Since you ask, and since you're not in any position to tell anyone, I'll consider your question your dying request.' The other man was heard to snigger at that, finding his boss's words always very amusing.

'You're right. This set up is very lucrative. And the girl is just one of many. But, sadly for her, she got a look at my face one day in Madrid. She didn't know who I was but I wasn't taking any risks. She saw me with Lucas, arguing when he decided he wanted to back out of his part of the deal. She saw me swing a punch, knock him down. So, I couldn't let that go. Had to send Lucas here to get her and make sure she wouldn't be able to point the finger.' As he said this, the 'boss' dragged a finger across his own throat, making his meaning crystal clear. He continued: '... but I didn't really trust him to do the job once he got here. He's become a bit of a liability. Now, if you'll forgive me, I've got a match to light.'

All Cronin and Burke could do was sit and await their fate and the 'boss' turned away and addressed his side-kick:

'Just in case the explosion doesn't do the trick properly, see those papers over there. Scatter them outside the bedrooms and light them. The smoke will keep everyone inside.'

The boss's words were carried out to the letter, papers scattered, set alight, smoke slowly making its way under doors, around corners. Very quickly, too quickly, the two *gardaí* could feel their eyes begin to sting and they struggled all the more to try to free themselves.

'Now, now. Let's have none of that.' The boss's words were accompanied by two firm whacks, and both Burke and Cronin fell unconscious, their last vision being that of the barrel of a gun hitting each firmly on the head.

'Right, that's them taken care of. Now, switch on the gas. I've got the matches.'

A hissing sound was soon followed by the striking of a match and the so-called boss flicked the flame into the house from his vantage point outside the back door. As the two men ran in the direction of their van, their ears were deafened by a loud explosion, quickly followed by smaller popping sounds. Within seconds, flames could be seen inside the windows and it seemed clear there could be no hope for anyone inside.

Chapter 39

Courtown garda station had not seen this level of action in many years. The local police were used to busy nights, of course, but this was above and beyond the usual activities. First of all, all leave had been cancelled and there were guards drafted from what seemed all four corners of the island of Ireland. On top of that, the phones never stopped ringing with instructions coming from Interpol, Europol, the Spanish police, their secret police, Garda headquarters in Dublin and in Cork. In the middle of this maelstrom, Superintendent Reilly was trying to keep order, manfully aided and abetted by Garda Davis who was proving to be a goldmine of local information.

When Burke's phone call had alerted them to the possibility that their target, *Señor* Lucas Fernández, was in the vicinity, specifically lurking outside the cottage, the tension and activity had hit crisis levels. Orders were barked in all directions and, with what seemed the speed of light, squad cars and unmarked vehicles were speeding in the direction of said cottage. As per instructions, no sirens were engaged so as not to alert the suspect to their arrival. All going well, within minutes this case would be 'put to bed', or such, at least, was Reilly's greatest hope. He was in the lead vehicle with Davis driving like he had never driven before.

Just as they neared the turn-off for the side road where the cottage was located, Davis slammed on the brakes. Had he not done so, they would have careered headlong into a fallen tree that was lying across the road, blocking it completely.

'Right, well done, Davis. Out of the car and let's see if we can move this baby out of the way.'

Reilly and Davis headed for the obstacle but, just as they were about to grab a bit of the trunk, Davis shouted.

'*Stop!*

'Good grief, man, what's up?'

'Electricity wires... sir.'

'Oh, I see what you mean. Good call. Right, we can't move this thing manually. Can we get around it?'

At this stage, Reilly and Davis had been joined by the occupants of the other cars that had been following them. There was quite a crowd gathered around the tree but no-one had a solution. They couldn't climb over it or go around it as it had fallen in such a way that the wires were blocking every route.

'If you ask me, this is too much of a coincidence. This tree did not fall unaided.' Davis shook his head, knowingly and pointing at where it seemed the trunk was too smoothly cut for it to be an act of nature.

'You could be right there, young Davis. But do you really see Fernández felling a tree, just like that.'

'Not on his own, Sir. This is a two-man ...eh ...a two-person ... job at least.'

The gravity of Davis's words took a moment to sink in.

'Do you mean he's had help? That he's not working alone here?' Reilly rubbed his chin with his thumb, absent-mindedly feeling the stubble, not liking the idea that this case had now become even more complicated.

'So, he's got help and, more worrisome, he's expecting us. Why else block the road? Davis, is there another way to get in?'

'Not without going right around the forest and that'll take time. Maybe ten minutes.'

'Ten minutes you say. That'll have to do.' Reilly gave some orders to the group standing around, telling some to remain with the tree, while two were to try to make their way on foot to the cottage and the rest were to follow him.

'Well, let's go, full speed now and put on the sirens. It seems we've lost our element of surprise.'

Ten minutes later they were pulling up in front of a scene of complete devastation. The cottage was fully alight, flames leaping high, windows shattered, smoke billowing from every crevice. Horrified, Davis and Reilly jumped from the car and ran, full speed, towards the house, not really sure what they could do but willing to try anything to gain access. Before they reached the front door, however, they were stopped in their tracks for, gathered at a safe distance from the burning building was a group of people, some of whom they recognised, others who were complete strangers to them. While everything seemed, at first, frozen in time, the two policemen quickly realised that one of those individuals was holding a gun, something that caused Reilly to reach for his and caused Davis to wish he had a weapon, any weapon, with which to defend himself. Gradually, they started to make out more detail in the scene before them though that didn't help to clarify exactly what was going on.

Before them, two people were lying face down on the ground, with one person standing over them. That was the person holding the firearm and that person was female. There was another group leaning against a van that was illegally parked, half blocking the laneway. Reilly and Davis quickly identified Jane, Chris, Yasmina and Fr. Lonergan among that group, along with Eva's parents and the other couple they had met earlier. In the midst of the chaos, Reilly couldn't help smiling at the priest's appearance for he was standing in his vest and long johns, his brown habit nowhere to be seen.

Reilly and Davis quickly scanned the group again, failing to find their colleagues. *Where were Burke and Cronin? Isabel, for God's sake, where have you got to?* As the *gardaí* hesitated, not sure what action to take, a dark shadow was seen to emerge from behind the van. Both Reilly and

Davis stiffened, ready to do whatever needed to be done. Just as Reilly cocked the trigger of his firearm, a familiar voice came out of the darkness.

'Super, is that anyway to greet one of your own? I expected a bit more of a welcome than that, considering.'

Davis looked at the older policeman, a puzzled expression on his face, not sure if this was a welcome development to proceedings. He needn't have worried for Reilly's face changed from consternation to delight as he recognised both the voice and the outline of the man approaching them.

'Well, if it isn't Detective Sergeant John Fitzpatrick. What on earth are you doing here and who is that pointing a weapon at those people over there? Should we be worried, Johnny?'

'All under control, Sir. All under control. Though I don't mind telling you it was touch and go there for a while. What kept you, by the way? We heard you were bringing back-up hours ago?'

'Never mind all that, just fill me in on what's happened. First of all, where are Burke and Cronin and I don't see Eva? And you haven't told me who's the one with the gun?'

'Right, Super, come this way and all will be revealed.'

Davis followed Reilly as they approached the person standing and aiming the weapon at the two individuals on the ground.

'Let me introduce you to Magdalena Sánchez. I believe you know she's a special agent from Spain. Magda, this is my Superintendent, Tom Reilly.'

'Pleased to meet you at last, Superintendent Reilly. Sorry I cannot chat just now. My hands are full keeping these two in line.'

Both Superintendent Reilly and Garda Davis had total shock written all over their faces, so much so that, later, looking back on events of the night, Johnny Fitzpatrick deeply regretted not having had the foresight to take some photos. He could have dined out for years on the threat of uploading them on social media. Professional was not the word to describe the dropped jaws and the wide eyes that greeted his introductions. Sadly, he had too much else on his mind that night and so missed the opportunity of a lifetime.

All Reilly could manage to say, after a long pause, was a feeble: 'Pleased to meet you too, Ms Sánchez.' Davis just meekly nodded and, as was his habit, stared at his boots.

'Now, to answer your other question, Burke and Cronin. Well, they're a little the worse for wear, I'm afraid. We've called an ambulance.' Seeing Reilly's face drain of blood, Johnny hurried to explain.

'No. They're okay. They've just had a knock on the head and inhaled some smoke. They'll live.'

Relief all around.

'Where are they?'

'Just over there, behind the van. Resting.'

'And that guy, Fernández. Please tell me you've got him.'

'In the van, Sir.'

'And Eva? Where's she?'

'Why don't you go look for yourself?' Johnny pointed in the direction of the van and Reilly, having indicated to Davis to go over and give Magda a hand, strode purposefully to where he found his colleagues sitting, both with white bandages on their heads and both being skilfully attended to by little Eva herself. It seemed there was a doctor in the making for she seemed very much in charge and had her two patients meekly following all her orders. On seeing Reilly, three pairs of eyes filled with relief and the two *gardaí* tried to stand up to greet their superior. Eva, however, was having none of it.

'No. You must stay still, Isabel, Aiden. You have had a nasty bump on the head, Baba said so. And Baba always tells his patients not to run around after one of those. *And* he left *me* in charge so you have to do what I say.'

Both *gardaí* sank back on the ground, two weak smiles acknowledging the child's words.

'Well, I see you are both in good hands. Can you tell me what happened here? Burke? Fill me in.'

Sergeant Burke, his head in his hands, and breathing with difficulty, brought Reilly up to date insofar as he could. He told him about Fernández breaking into the house, followed by two other men, how one of those men had ordered Fernández to take Eva outside and how they had heard the plans to burn down the cottage with everyone else inside. They, Cronin and himself, had been tied up and the last thing he could remember was a sharp blow to the head where the man who seemed to be the boss of the operation had struck him with his weapon. After that, he wasn't sure what had happened. He had come to here on the grass beside this van, with Cronin by his side and a whopper of a headache. He was very sorry to have failed in his duty to protect.

'We'll have none of that now, Burke. You just concentrate on that head of yours. The ambulance will be here shortly, I'm sure. Isabel, how are you feeling?' Isabel, surprised to hear Reilly use her first name on duty, managed a grin which quickly turned to a grimace as she pointed to her head.

'Fine, Tom, just trying to get my bearings. Like Burke, I'm not sure how I got out of the house but I'm very grateful I did. And, from what Fitzpatrick has told us, everyone else got out safe too. I can hardly believe we're all alive.'

'No, we've been very lucky.' Burke nodded in agreement, a slight nod as moving his head was not a pleasant experience.

'Right, I'd better get back over there and see what I can find out. If I'm not mistaken, those sirens I can hear mean that they've finally got the road clear and the ambulance is on the point of arriving and, hopefully, the fire brigade won't be very far behind. That fire needs attention to stop it spreading, even allowing for the amount of rain we've had this summer. Geez, I'm not looking forward to the paperwork for this but it could have been a lot worse. Eva, you take care of the patients, won't you? You tell me if they cause you any trouble.'

Eva grinned up at him, and nodded furiously.

Chapter 40

Dawn was breaking by the time they got back to Courtown Garda Station. It had been a long night and many details were still hazy. What was clear was that everyone at the cottage had had a very narrow escape. Sergeant Aiden Burke and Garda Isabel Cronin had been kept overnight in Wexford General Hospital, more to make sure they hadn't suffered concussion than due to smoke inhalation. Lucas Fernández and his fellow criminals had been transported to Wexford too but they had spent the night at Garda Regional Headquarters where they were still being questioned. Reilly had been relieved to hand them over to his colleagues at the Wexford division, at least for a while, so he could get the sequence of events straight in his mind. He'd asked Davis to keep everyone at bay for an hour during which he'd grabbed himself a cup of tea, retired to a room at the back, sat in a reasonably comfy armchair, put his feet up and fell into a deep sleep for all of forty minutes. Then, somewhat refreshed, he attempted to tidy himself up as best he could but, try as he might, Reilly couldn't rid himself of the memory of the shock he had had when seeing the cottage alight. Thoughts had flashed through his mind, none of them good. Top of the pile was *how was he going to break it to his son that Isabel had been injured, or worse, while under his command?* How lucky they had all been that his call to his son had only been to tell him that his wife was recovering from a slight bump on the head. Isabel wouldn't thank him for saying 'slight' but he had been trying to lighten the mood. His son was now heading at full speed to Wexford and Reilly wasn't looking forward to their next conversation. But it could have been a lot worse. Mentally shaking himself, Reilly gave himself one last glance in the mirror to make sure that, at least, he looked the part of 'officer-in-control' even if he felt far from it and headed out to find Johnny Fitzpatrick.

While Superintendent Reilly had been sleeping, the rest of the group had been trying to sort out the sequence of events in their heads. Since most of them had been asleep when they'd become aware of the fire, or rather of smoke invading their rooms, they were understandably confused as to the cause. The first thing that had awoken them had been a male voice outside the window and the sound of breaking glass. Those sounds, combined with the smoke, had made them leap into action, Chris being the first to react, quickly followed by Fr. Lonergan, Yasmina and Jane. The voice outside the window had shouted to them to break the rest of the glass and jump outside. As they clambered out, they could hear the same voice issue similar instructions to those in the next bedroom. Soon, all eight adults were standing at the back of the house, watching as flames engulfed the roof. The initial seconds of silence were quickly followed by shouting and screaming as Eva's parents realised that, once again, their daughter was not among them. Both struggled to get back into the house while the others attempted to restrain them. The scene was one of chaos and panic, despair, and anguish, with Ismael and Hanah finally dropping to their knees, arms entwined, as they realised they were unable to get back into the house for the roof was collapsing in a pile of embers and sparks.

At that moment, the group became aware of a stranger among them, a man dressed in khaki camouflage, his face blackened, the owner of the voice that had alerted them and who was now trying to get their attention. It took a few moments to process what he had been saying:

'Hey, it's ok. It's ok. It's me ... Chris, Jane, don't you recognise me? Johnny ... Johnny Fitzpatrick! It's ok. Eva's fine. She's safe. Do you hear me? She's safe.'

'Johnny?'

'Johnny?'

The two Australians said the name together, both not able to believe their eyes. *It was Johnny, their sea-faring captain, here?*

'You say Eva's safe?' As usual, Fr. Lonergan got straight to the point. 'Ismael, Hanah, listen. Eva's safe. Your daughter's safe. This man is a friend and he says she's fine.'

Slowly, the message began to get through to Eva's parents. Hope. They looked up tearfully at this stranger who was bringing them hope and they scrambled to their feet, pleading with him to take them to her. Without saying a word, Johnny led the motley group around to the front of the cottage, or what was left of it, flames still leaping through the windows but, clearly, the fire had done its worst.

The vision that greeted the group would have been funny if they hadn't been so traumatised. In fact, days later, when recalling their first sight of the scene, they laughed heartedly at the incredible spectacle that had greeted them but, now, it just made them stop in their tracks in total disbelief.

First, lying face down on the small piece of grass that served as a front garden lay two men. They were wearing handcuffs and, standing over them, holding a gun, was Magdalena Sánchez. Seeing she was the centre of attention of the new arrivals, Magda waved and smiled.

'Hi all, cannot talk just now. Am a bit busy.' She smiled and turned her attention back to her task, clearly enjoying it.

Next, the group followed Fitzpatrick over to a van that was parked on the road. It was white with a two-seater cabin and an enclosed back. Reilly opened the rear door and, sitting uncomfortably on the floor was Lucas, also handcuffed and nursing what looked like a gash on the head. He just stared at the group, seemingly not really aware of where he was or who they were. He was muttering under his breath: *No sé, no sé, no entiendo nada.*

Chris looked at Jane and asked:

'What's he saying?'

'Nothing much. He just keeps saying he doesn't know, or he doesn't understand anything. I guess that knock on the head has left him confused.

I wonder how he got it.'

'Well, I can clear that mystery up. It was Magda. She has a hell of a left hook.' Fitzpatrick's voice sounded quite boastful and proud as he rubbed his own chin, as if imagining the impact. 'Yea, she hit him with her left fist and he went flying down. Banged his head on a rock. Knocked him out cold.'

'But, sir, please, where is Eva? You said she was safe.' Hanah could contain herself no longer.

'Sorry, yes, she's right here. Look.' Fitzpatrick pointed to the other side of the van. There was Eva, tending her two patients, Burke and Cronin, each nursing a sore head and each being soothed by their four-year old nurse. Her parents' joy was uncontainable as they swooped on her and lifted her into their arms, the relief at seeing her safe and well, palpable.

'Oh Eva, Eva, little Eva, we thought we had lost you again.'

'Oh Mama, Baba, I'm fine. It's these two who are not too good. Those bad men hit them on the head but I'm making them better. Isn't that right?'

Burke and Cronin nodded tentatively, their heads not up to much movement at all. They were glad to witness the family reunion and only too aware of what might have been. They still couldn't quite understand how the tables had been turned so dramatically on their assailants. One minute they remembered being hit on the head and the next they were being tended so well by a very competent Eva, with the three criminals in handcuffs and two other people guarding them. It was all too much to take in.

Burke made to stand up though found he was a bit dizzy. Eva frowned and in a perfect copy of a stern matron commanded:

'You must stay still, Aiden. You have confushen. That's the word, isn't it, Baba, confushen?'

Her father smiled and nodded:

'Almost, it's 'concussion' and you are right, Eva, Aiden must stay still.' He smiled gratefully at Aiden and Isabel.

'Thank you. I do not know what part you both have played in all of this but I can see you have been injured trying to defend my daughter. I can only thank you on my behalf and on that of my wife.'

Burke and Cronin just accepted the thanks, not clear themselves on the part they had played.

Fr. Lonergan turned to Johnny who had been standing to one side, enjoying the spectacle.

'Johnny, I have to ask you the million-dollar question. How on earth did you turn up here and what happened?'

'That's two questions, Father, and I'll fill you all in in a few moments. First, if I'm not mistaken, there's my Super arriving. I'd better have a word with him before all else.'

Turning on his heel, Johnny went off to meet his boss, knowing he had quite a few questions to answer before the night was over.

Chapter 41

Reilly searched the office for Detective Sergeant John Fitzpatrick but could see him nowhere. He walked over to Davis who was busy typing up a report and asked him if he had seen his colleague.

'Yes, Super, he asked me to give you this. He said it would explain everything.'

Davis handed Reilly an envelope inside of which was a report form, duly filled out and signed, plus a brief note. Shaking his head in disbelief, Reilly unfolded the note.

Dear Super,

I thought it would save us all time and energy if I wrote down everything. I know you'll find it a surprise to see the report form completed but I guess you could say I've turned over a new leaf. I have a certain person to thank for that, as you'll see. If you need me when you've done with the reading, I'll be on the boat in the harbour. Talk soon, no doubt, Johnny.

'Well, if that don't beat all.' Reilly said to no one in particular. 'Johnny's filled in a report without me having to chase him for weeks. If that's the effect that new woman in his life is having, I'm all for it.'

Davis looked up from his typing to see if a response was required of him but just saw the Superintendent disappear back into the room where he had had his nap, shaking his head as he went.

Once more, Reilly settled back in the comfy armchair, this time to read the surprisingly completed report, not sure he wanted to know all the details but curious, nonetheless. He bypassed the first page or two which just contained the usual technical details - name, rank, dates etc - and turned to the juicy bits starting where Johnny had disappeared from

Barcelona.

Report into events leading to the capture of three suspects in the attempted abduction of a minor, Ms Eva Mari, daughter of Ismael and Hanah Mari.

[...] My orders were to go to the aforementioned public house and watch developments in the meeting between Christopher Nielson, Jane Murphy and Magdalena Sánchez, the latter suspected of being involved in child trafficking and, specifically, the attempted kidnapping of the said Eva Mari at an earlier date (see above).

On my way to said establishment, unforeseen circumstances delayed me in that the vehicle I had hired developed a puncture. By the time it was repaired and I arrived at destination, the meeting had taken place and, from what I discovered later, Mr Nielson and Ms Murphy had made their escape on foot, having been accused themselves of the kidnap of a minor. I was in time to see several male individuals run through a nearby park and the said Ms Sánchez jump into a black limousine, licence plate CME 7373. I concluded that they were in pursuit of someone and, given that I had lost trace of my targets, I quickly decided to follow on foot. The limo skirted the park opposite the bar and, given the traffic direction, I decided they were heading for the Basilica (Sagrada Familia). I cut across the park and arrived at said basilica before them. As they pulled up to the footpath, I ascertained that Ms Sánchez was in the driving seat. Behind her, in the rear passenger seat, was Fr. Jim Lonergan. I found that surprising but had no time to process this development as the said priest was waving at me, attempting to get my attention. I walked over to the car and Fr. Lonergan told me to get in, that he would explain inside. Though not sure if that were a wise move, I could see no better option so I stepped into the car. Inside, Ms Sánchez introduced herself to me and identified herself as a member of the Intelligence Service, the CNI. Fr. Lonergan confirmed that to be the case and said that he had been informed by Superintendent Tom Reilly via a text message and, further to that, had been sent to intercept me, Mr Nielson, and Ms Murphy since it had been decided that he would follow them to Barcelona in case further back-up were needed.

Furthermore, Superintendent Reilly had attempted to contact me but had failed to do so. At that stage, I checked my phone and noticed there were several missed calls which, regrettably, I had failed to notice when I was attempting to sort out my car problems. I had no choice but to believe the Reverend Father and, given that we were all on the same side, I asked why the two missing individuals were nowhere to be seen. Fr. Lonergan told me that they had panicked and run out of the bar in the direction of the basilica. They thought that they were going to be arrested for child trafficking. Of course, Ms Sánchez had just now been informed (by Fr. Lonergan as well as via a phone call from her superiors in Madrid) that they were working for the Irish police and that it had all been a misunderstanding. The members of the CNI were attempting to locate them to let them know that there was no need to run and that, perhaps, if they pooled resources, they could get to the bottom of who was actually behind the criminal activities.

Reilly couldn't help chuckling when he thought of the set of bizarre circumstances that had brought all these characters together. Chris and Jane must have thought their goose was truly cooked. He could just imagine their faces when they saw Johnny and Fr. Lonergan getting out of that limousine, along with Magda Sánchez. How he wished he could have been a fly on that wall! Ha! He must ask Fr. Jim to describe it all in vivid detail next time he saw him. Anyway, back to the report. There were other more crucial details to get clear.

It was not long before Mr Nielson and Ms Murphy were discovered and the circumstances were explained to them. It was then decided we would all regroup in the Barcelona headquarters of the CNI where we would try to make sense of developments. It was during this meeting that the name of Yasmina (surname unknown at this stage) came to our attention as a possible perpetrator. After several phone calls, it was discovered that the said Yasmina had vanished. She was not at her workplace nor at her home address. The police in Madrid were informed and asked to apprehend her as soon as possible.

Following the meeting, I requested a few days leave as I had some personal issues to attend to. Given that these personal issues have had an impact on this case, I will give a brief account of them.

As I left the meeting, I shared the lift to the ground floor with Ms Sánchez. She invited me to have a coffee in a nearby café as she wanted to ask more about how we had spirited Eva out of Spain. At least that is what she said. I, of course, did not intend to reveal any operational details and, as it turned out, we did not discuss the case at all. We had coffee, which then became dinner and discovered we had a lot in common including a love of sailing. I invited her to see my boat which was anchored in Alicante Marina. Taddy, my crewman, had sailed it back there as we were planning our next intervention from that location. I invited Ms Sánchez to travel with me back to Ireland, a voyage which would take several days. She agreed and so we flew to Madrid to collect some of her personal belongings, and then on down to Alicante. I met up with Taddy who decided, in the circumstances, to remain in Alicante and take a few days to enjoy the Spanish sunshine. We, that is Ms Sánchez and myself, were just off the coast of Ireland when she got a strange phone call from Mr Lucas Fernández. Of course I knew that Mr Fernández had been Magda's partner but she had assured me that their relationship was over. He had become too possessive and quite irrational, she said. She found this latest phone call very disturbing. Mr Fernández kept asking her where she was and if there had been any developments. He wouldn't say about what exactly. Ms Sánchez said he sounded crazy, drunk perhaps, certainly not his usual self. Ms Sánchez also got a phone call from her boss in Madrid, saying that Mr Fernández was now a chief suspect and that she too needed to present herself for questioning. That is when she decided to ring Ms Murphy and was told that Mr Fernández had been seen in the vicinity of Eva's lodgings. Ms Sánchez had been tracking Mr Fernández's phone with a tracker app so she knew he was in Ireland but she hadn't realised he was following Eva. The implications were devastating. Ms Sánchez begged me to sail as quickly as possible to the harbour nearest that location, which, as luck would have it, wasn't that far and, within a few hours, we were mooring at Courtown. Once there, she rang Lucas again but he didn't answer. However, due to the miracles of modern technology, we were able to pinpoint his location and we arrived just in time to see him exit the cottage with Eva in tow. Using the element of surprise, Ms Sánchez approached him and, without giving him time to react, she hit him on the jaw, causing him to fall backwards and hit his head on a rock. While he was unconscious, we handcuffed him and locked him in the rear of a van we found parked on the roadside. We told Eva to hide in the bushes until we returned and then we both headed for the front door. As we were on the point of entering, two other men exited from the rear and before we could do anything, one of them threw a lit match through the back door, causing the building to explode. There must have been some propellant involved, given the intensity of the ensuing flames. The men admired their handiwork for a moment and then, oblivious to our presence, turned to run towards the van. We drew our weapons, shouted at them to disarm, identified ourselves as police and invited them to lie face down on the ground. At first, they resisted. One tried to make a break for it but was tripped up by Magda and fell sprawling on the ground. The other was more amenable then and lay down without the need for further encouragement. We handcuffed both and I ran to the front doorway and managed to get as far as the kitchen where I found two gardaí (I recognised Garda Cronin from the Cork Station and the other was Sergeant Burke from Courtown as I was informed later) tied to chairs and unconscious. I untied them and, using one of the chairs as defence against the flames, I managed to drag each to the front door and, with Ms Sánchez's help, we got them out of the building. One of them came around for a few moments and kept repeating that we had to get the others out. I tried to return to the building but could not enter due to the flames that were now engulfing the whole of the front of the house. I ran to the back while Ms Sánchez stayed with the two gardaí and the two detainees. I couldn't enter via the doorway at the back either but I threw a rock through two rear windows, attracting the attention of the people inside. Following my instructions, they broke the rest of the glass (in each of two windows) and made their escape. No one was harmed but the house was destroyed. Once their initial panic subsided, I led them to *the front of the house where Eva was reunited with her parents. It was at about that time that Superintendent Reilly appeared on the scene [...]*

The said Superintendent sat back in the armchair, rubbing the back of his neck. That, certainly, answered some of the questions he'd had in mind to ask Johnny. So, he and Magdalena Sánchez were an item. Didn't that beat all! For as long as he'd known Johnny, he'd never even heard him mention any woman, any detail of his personal life, in fact. And now, in an official report, he'd bared all. It must be serious. Well, Reilly wished him well. But it seemed a rather complicated relationship – a garda and an intelligence officer from different jurisdictions. Reilly was glad he didn't have to work out the logistics of that though he hoped it wouldn't mean he'd lose one of his best detectives. He gave himself a mental shake as he stood up. That was a worry for another day. Today had enough to keep him occupied. He went out to the main office to find Davis still hard at it, typing furiously.

'Davis, have you been here all night?'

'Yes, sir.'

'Well, I suggest you head home for a few hours and get some sleep. Have a shave and such. You look like you've been dragged through a hedge!'

Davis smiled thinking 'pot, kettle' but didn't dare voice his thoughts.

'Yes, sir! Thank you, sir! Do you need anything before I go?'

'No, I think I'll just head to the hospital. Did anyone bring my car here, by any chance?'

'Yes, I drove it back once the ambulances had left. I got one of the other guys to bring the station's squad car. Your keys are on the counter.'

'You know, Davis, if ever you put in for a transfer to Cork, I'd be happy to have you on the team.'

'Excellent, sir, I might just do that one of these days. For now, I'm happy where I am.'

'Good. I'll be off then.'

'Bye, Sir, and would you give Burke my best if you see him. He's a tough old nut but he must be a bit shook given the circumstances.'

'I'll do that. Off you go now. Let one of the others look after the station for a bit.'

The two men exited together, each heading in opposite directions, glad that the night was finally over and that a beautiful golden dawn was breaking, heralding a day of sunshine to come.

Chapter 42

When Reilly arrived at Wexford General Hospital, he was amazed to find so many familiar faces gathered around Isabel's bed. Fr. Lonergan, now more suitably dressed in his habit which had curiously survived the fire intact, was doing most of the talking, with Jane Murphy and Chris Nielson standing on one side of the bed, listening attentively. Yasmina was there too, her attention focused on the priest as he spoke. Surprisingly, Reilly's daughter-in-law looked none the worse for wear and was sitting up, sipping tea, and also listening intently as Fr. Lonergan entertained them all with his own, unique version of events.

'So, there I was, in my long johns, flames everywhere and, next thing I see is Magda pointing a gun at the intruders who were lying on the grass. I couldn't believe my eyes. I mean, where had the woman come from? And, then, there was Johnny, appearing out of nowhere.' Lonergan was enjoying embellishing the story, trying to take the sting out of it for Isabel who, he realised, had had a hard time before being knocked unconscious.

Also being entertained by this version of events was Reilly's son, Mike, who had arrived from Cork overnight, looking as if he hadn't slept for days. Like his father, he had dark circles under his eyes, his hair was dishevelled and his complexion pale. In fact, now that the two men were in the same room, all the other occupants couldn't help noticing the strong family resemblance.

'Wow, look at you two! No one would doubt you're related.' It was Jane who voiced what everyone was thinking. 'Isabel, it must be strange to be looking at your husband's future image every day. It's remarkable how alike they are.'

'I *know*. They are alike in behaviour too which is even worse. Can you imagine when my 'boss' says something like 'hurry along and get me a cuppa', I have to bite my tongue or I could end up telling him what to do with that cuppa as I do when Mike here tries that on.'

Everyone laughed, imagining her frustration.

'I've *never* told you to get me a cuppa! Or, at least, to hurry up about it. I wouldn't dare risk it!' Reilly's attempts to defend himself just brought on another bout of laughter.

'Okay, daddy-in-law, I'm out of uniform now so it's all right. Sit down before you fall down and tell us what the latest news is. None of us is very clear on what happened last night. These guys have told me that three men were arrested and that Johnny was responsible for rescuing myself and Sergeant Burke. How did Johnny come to be on the scene? Last I heard, he was on leave.'

At that question, there was a general hum of voices all agreeing that it was strange he was there, and very lucky. Reilly had to hold up his hands to get their attention. Looking around the group and seeing their expectant faces, he said:

'I've read Johnny's report and it seems he and Magda (yes, I know, I know... let me finish...) he and Magda were sailing in Irish waters and to cut a long story short, they landed in Courtown just in time to intervene. You'll get the details later but, for now, I suggest we see if Isabel can leave the hospital - and Burke too of course - and we Corkonians should head back to Cork and leave the Wexford lot to sort out the paperwork at their end. The three suspects, one of whom is Lucas Fernández, are in custody and we'll get a copy of their statements in due course. For now, I would very much like to head for home. Did you all make statements last night?'

There was a general nodding of heads as everyone confirmed they had told Davis and his colleagues all that they could remember, though a lot of it was still hazy.

'Good. I'll get copies of those sent on. I don't suppose there'll be anything much to follow up there.'

'Just one small detail that has been bothering me.' Fr. Lonergan scratched his head as if pondering whether to speak up or not.

'Go on.'

'Well, I've been trying to think where I'd seen those two thugs before and it's suddenly come to me. They were the two men who called to the hotel in Alicante where Eva and the other children were staying. They said they were police. They had I.D and everything.'

'So that explains why Johnny wasn't stopped by the coast guard. The police in Alicante weren't aware of any problems at the migrant centre and the men who called there were imposters so there wasn't any arrest warrant issued for two strange Australians and a Franciscan.'

'Right! That's been bothering me. Johnny shouldn't have been able to get out of the Spanish jurisdiction quite so easily, especially if the police were already alerted. As they weren't, that explains it, to some extent at least. And another thing, it means that, if we hadn't spirited Eva out of Spain when we did, she might very well have fallen into their clutches. I don't want to sound like I'm justifying my existence but it would seem I, and my friends here', the priest nodded in the direction of Jane and Chris, 'acted in the nick of time after all.'

'So it would seem. I'll admit it looks like you were right all the time, Jim, and, yes, there's going to be a lot of increased surveillance around the EU periphery from now on, that's for sure. This case has alerted us all to some worrying gaps in our network. Ah well, we'll leave that particular worry for another day. For now, let's find out when Isabel can leave so we can get on the road.'

A general nodding of heads followed his words and Reilly and his son headed out of the room in search of an update on the likely time of Isabel's discharge from the ward, leaving everyone to discuss the fact that Johnny and Magda were together. Amazing! On their way, father and son looked in on Burke who was fast asleep. His altercation last night had taken it out of him and he would take a little longer to bounce back than the younger garda Cronin. So, the two men left him to sleep.

As they walked along the corridor to the nurses' station, the younger Reilly put his hand on his father's shoulder.

'Dad, you look all done in. A bad night, was it?'

'You could say that, son. Listen, I'm sorry Isabel got caught up in all of this. If I'd thought there was any danger, I wouldn't...'

'Let me stop you there, Dad. Isabel wouldn't thank you - or me, for that matter. You know how she feels. No special treatment when on duty. And you've seen her. She's as right as rain, not a bother on her.'

'Yea, she's a good 'un, that girl. You chose well there, son. Your mother would have approved.'

'Yes, I think she would have.' Both men fell silent as they thought of the older Mrs Reilly who had died just a year before, leaving an enormous gap in both their lives. Lost in their thoughts, they didn't see the man with a gun until it was too late.

A shot rang out, a man dropped to the ground, commotion and shouting and confusion followed. Another shot!

'Dad! Dad! Are you hurt? Are you okay? Talk to me, Dad!'

Reilly could hear a voice in the distance. He couldn't understand why it sounded so far away. Where had all the bright lights gone? It was so dark, so black ... so cold. Why was he so cold? He couldn't hear the voice now. Where had everyone gone? Why was he so alone? Cold and alone ...

Chapter 43

It didn't take too long before a clear picture emerged as to what had led to the events that had occurred that morning in Wexford General Hospital. Headlines in all the newspapers, both local and national, referred to a lone gunman who had fired at random and ranged from the factual (Gunman opens fire) to the garish (Death on the Wards). The facts were less colourful. The lone gunman was quickly identified as Lucas Fernández who had been brought to the hospital the night before as he had seemed to be suffering from some trauma exacerbated by concussion, it was thought. Later, an autopsy revealed that he had an extremely high blood/alcohol level, coupled with a dangerous amount of cocaine in his system. In short, he had been out of his mind, suffering paranoia and hallucinations. He had managed to overpower the armed garda accompanying him and take the weapon. That gun was the one that had been fired first, seriously wounding Superintendent Tom Reilly. The second shot came from Detective Sergeant John Fitzpatrick's weapon and had stopped the gunman in his tracks.

The witnesses to the events were in agreement that there had been no option but to shoot though that was small comfort to Johnny. He had never before had reason to fire his gun in the line of duty, let alone kill another human being. He had been trained to shoot accurately, precisely but no training could prepare him for taking a life. Yet, he was commended by his superiors, congratulated by his friends, and held in awe by his colleagues. Only Magda was to see the anguish he went through in the following weeks, and she could only watch and wait until time healed his soul a little. He could never come to terms with whether it had been the best of luck he had decided to pay his colleague, Isabel, a visit, or the worst of it. Had he been a minute or two later, would he have been too late to intervene? If he had arrived earlier, would he have prevented the shooting entirely? He would never know.

Time would also be needed for Superintendent Reilly. His wounds were more physical. The bullet had nicked his spinal cord, damaged his liver but had bypassed all other major organs. Medical staff were in agreement that he had been a very lucky man indeed. If he had been anywhere else, things might have turned out very differently. However, he had been in a hospital, with medical help just metres away. Even so, it took him many months to see things from their point of view and count his blessings. First came months of rehabilitation, learning to walk again, taking fistfuls of tablets to take away pain, to help him sleep, to wake him up again. Through it all, Fr. Lonergan, Fr. Jim, was his most frequent visitor. The priest would never forget that fateful day when he'd heard those two shots. He, along with the others at Isabel's bedside, had rushed out to the corridor. The sight he had seen was preserved forever in his memory: Groups of strangers standing frozen in various poses, their actions halted by the unfamiliar sound, Johnny at the far end of the corridor, gun in hand, nurses and doctors leaning over two inert bodies lying in pools of blood, Mike, Tom's son, kneeling on the ground, his head in his hands, sobbing. *Where's Reilly?* Fr. Lonergan remembered thinking how stupid of Tom to have left his son when he was so upset. He thought he must have stepped out for some reason.

Slowly, however, realisation dawned and Fr. Lonergan almost galloped down the corridor to see for sure. Yes, there on the floor lay his friend. He remembered pushing his way through a wall of white coats until he too became part of the scene: a priest holding the hand of a man, a dying man? He didn't know but he muttered the words of the prayer he had said so many times before at the bedside, on the roadway, in the kitchen of too many of those who were leaving this world. Sometimes, it seemed to him that the world was emptying, so many people needed his last prayers, what used to be known as the Last Rites. Now, it was referred to among his peers as the *viaticum* but the term hadn't caught on among the grass roots. To them, a priest gave the Last Rites and that was that. In this case, he just said the prayers since Tom was unconscious and he also whispered words in his ear (just in case). *Tom, hang on! You're not alone! We'll get you back.*

You just hang on! He never found out if Tom had heard him but they had been lucky. He did hang on and they did get him back from the brink.

Isabel had followed the others out onto the corridor, moving more slowly since her head was still fragile. By the time she realised what had happened, Tom, her father-in-law, was being rushed on a trolley to the nearest theatre. She was just in time to see him wheeled by and her husband, now on his feet, following behind, with Fr. Jim supporting him. It could have been a comical sight, the taller man leaning on the little chubby priest, but no one who noticed would have had the heart to think so.

'Mike, Oh Mike. What's happened?' Isabel reached out to stop her husband and he turned to collapse into her arms.

'He's been shot, Izzy. That creep has shot him. They say it's serious. They'll do what they can. Izzy, he might not make it.' Isabel had never seen such fear in her husband's eyes. She could only hold him and pray that his worst fears would not come true.

Chris and Jane didn't know what to do. They felt they were intruding on private family grief though they felt the pain acutely too. They could not provide any great comfort for the Reilly family, not at this private moment of anxiety, so they turned their attention to Johnny who was standing silently near the body of Lucas Fernández. He had kicked the latter's weapon away and had let the trauma team check for life signs. When they had found none, they had turned all their attention to Tom Reilly. Chris went over to the policeman who looked as if he were on the point of collapse. He gently guided him towards a seat near the nurse's station and sat him down. Jane went to a machine nearby and got a coffee, one of those instant jobs that would taste of nothing much but, at least, it would be hot. Without a word, she handed it to Johnny who took it gratefully, his hands trembling so much he spilt some of the liquid on his trousers but he didn't even notice. Then, Jane left the two men and walked over to the body. She grabbed a sheet and, just as she was going to drape it over him, another person arrived on the scene. Magda ran in and was stopped in her tracks, not sure how to interpret the scene that appeared before her eyes. She looked at Jane, comprehension slowly dawning. Jane nodded, confirming her worst suspicions.

'Sorry, Magda. Lucas is dead.' Magda gasped and slowly approached the body of the man with whom she had once shared a large part of her life. She knelt down and took his hand.

'You know, he just was not himself since he covered the Iraqi war. He saw things there that changed him. He started taking drugs. I begged him to stop but he just could not cope. I knew he was suffering but I had no idea he had sunk so low. I mean *children*! How could he do it, Jane? How *could* he? And how could I not see?'

Jane took hold of Magda's shoulders and helped her to stand up.

'He's at rest now, Magda. All his fears are over. He can do no more harm.'

'Yes, you are right. It is all over now.' Magda walked over to Johnny who stood to embrace her, stronger now that they were together.

Chapter 44

It was the end of August when most of the group met up again. Isabel and Mike had invited them all to dinner to celebrate Tom's release from hospital. He had spent a week in Wexford before being transferred to Cork University Hospital. He still had to report for physio on a regular basis and see the specialist once a month but, physically, he was almost his old self, a bit wobbly but definitely on the mend. Mentally, though, he felt old, older than his years, and he was seriously considering taking early retirement. Life was short, shorter than he had considered before. Even when he'd lost his wife, he hadn't felt that time was rushing by so much, and he still had things he wanted to do. A trip to Australia might even be on the cards. Chris had issued an open invitation which he wouldn't mind taking up. Who knows - one of these days - he might just get himself on a plane?

Looking around the table, he found it remarkable how close he now felt to all of these people. Jane was sitting to his right, Mike beside her, the two deep in conversation. On Reilly's left was Chris, Isabel beside him and Johnny to her left. At the far end of the table was Fr. Lonergan. Missing from the group were Yasmina, Ismael, Hanah and Eva as well as the two mysterious individuals who had been at that cottage in Courtown, the two individuals who were members of a secret group intent on rescuing children by any means they could, legal or otherwise. By the time Reilly had recovered enough to care, they had vanished into the ether. Ismael had told him that they were not refugees like him but people who had gained European citizenship, and so were free to travel to wherever they were needed in their quest to protect the children. Reilly wasn't interested in pursuing them nor were any of the other law enforcers on the case. It would have taken too many resources and what would have been gained? Fewer children rescued and a stack of paperwork that would never lead to any arrests. The rewards just weren't worth it, Reilly had suggested when asked.

Yasmina, too, had been cleared of any wrongdoing, given that her only role had been to try to save Eva from a terrible fate. Perhaps she should have gone about that in a different way but, again, it was agreed that no further action was needed. She had returned to her post in Madrid, relieved and determined to continue to make a difference in the lives of her charges. Magda was also absent from this gathering, having returned to help tie up loose ends in Madrid. Johnny was quite lost without her but said, cryptically, that they were making plans to meet up again in the not-too-distant future. A happy ending might well be in store if Fr. Lonergan's prayers were to be answered.

Happy endings were also on the cards for Ismael and Hanah who had been granted a place on the Irish Refugee programme, along with Eva, and were settling nicely into village life in the west of Ireland. Again, their luck had held for they had avoided staying long-term in the controversial Direct Provision scheme while waiting for their status to be processed. They were eligible for a special scheme where migrants were resettled in a rural location since they met the criteria. Their joy on receiving a key to their own front door was tangible to those who witnessed the occasion. Yet, though relieved to be starting a new chapter in their lives, on stormy nights, when the waves crashed onto the rocks near their new home, they were reminded of what might have been had their dinghies not made it to shore or had Eva been lost to them forever. On those nights, they would hold each other close and try to banish those particular ghosts that would forever haunt them. They knew they were among the very few lucky ones and vowed to make their lives count by bringing as much happiness as they could to those they met along their way. Of course, there would be dark days when they would meet with obstacles such as a lack of understanding and suspicion, but, with luck, those days would be relatively few and would gradually fade away as they became part of the collective landscape.

Jane had been sad to say goodbye to the little family, especially to Eva. To make it a little easier, Chris had suggested they all had a day out together in Courtown before they headed back to Cork. It would help chase away the memories of the last days and give them a chance to have some fun before they had to leave. Ismael and Hanah said that it might be good if just Eva went with them, with Chris and Jane. They could see that she was very attached to them and were very grateful for the care and, yes, the love, they had lavished on her. The two Australians were aware of the generosity of the gesture; it couldn't have been easy for her parents to let the child out of their sight but Eva squealed with delight when she learned of the plan.

'Oh yes, please, let's go on a picnic. I can bring Teddy too. Okay?'

'Of course, that's a great plan.' Jane could only echo the little girl's excitement, her own heart fit to burst.

So, one fine morning, the day after the incident at the hospital, in fact, they, Chris and Jane, collected Eva from Courtown Hotel where she had been staying with her parents until more permanent accommodation would be found. The sun was sparkling on the harbour, as if it knew just how important this day would be. Not a cloud spoiled the blue sky, not a puff of breeze disturbed the smoothness of the sea. A perfect picnicking day!

The long sandy beach was occupied by several families but there was plenty of room for one more. Jane imagined that they looked quite typical, Chris, tall and distinguished, hair greying at the temples, she, shorter, brown hair also showing the first signs of grey and, Eva, chatting and skipping along. She probably looked more like their granddaughter than a daughter, a thought that saddened Jane just a little. She'd had a dream of rescuing the child, perhaps caring for her when no one else would. That dream was gone now but, happily, only because the child had many to care for her along the way. She, Jane, had played her part and now the time had come to let her go.

Chris suggested they have a swim before the picnic. He had borrowed some board shorts from Garda Davis - they were a similar size, though, perhaps Davis was slimmer around the waist. Eva had her swimsuit on under her sundress and didn't need any encouragement to jump into the water. Jane, however, though the best swimmer of the three, after putting one toe in to test the waters, declined and said she'd rather stay warm and dry. If she'd had her diving suit with her, it would have been a different story but *the water was freezing! How could so many of the Irish brave such iciness in the name of fun!* Chris could not disappoint the girl so dived straight in, risking heart-attack-inducing and breath-stopping coldness. Soon, though, all that was forgotten as the pair jumped and laughed over the rippling waves. Chris pretended to be a shark, snapping at Eva's ankles, she kicking in glee, confident that her Chris would never harm her; even when her face went under the water, she knew he'd be there to pluck her out again.

After a good half-hour, if not longer, their thoughts turned to food and, reluctantly, they emerged from the water and raced in Jane's direction, glad to see that she had found a nice, sheltered spot near the rocks and had been busy setting everything out on a tartan blanket. There were sandwiches, cut into triangles, potato salad and coleslaw, little tubs of jelly, some chocolate cake and a choice of orange or apple juice to drink with a flask of coffee for the grown-ups. Eva sat herself down on the rug beside her beloved Teddy Bear after Jane had helped her to dry off and had wrapped her in a big fluffy towel to keep her warm. This was no Australian beach so there was no need to worry about sunburn, today at least, for, though still summer, there was a distinct chill in the air. The food was demolished in record time and soon Eva was wondering what they could do next. Chris had forgotten just how much energy little ones had. His own two kids had been the same, no time to rest on your laurels when they were younger. No sooner was one task finished than they were on to the next. So, off they set to explore the beach – the rocky part revealed small crabs and lichen and lots of shells had to be inspected to see if their owners were still at home. Seaweed too had to be picked up and smelled. *Ugh*, it smelt of storms and shipwrecks. Jane tried to persuade Eva that it was more the smell of mermaids and seahorses but she would have none of that!

Soon, it was time to head back to the town but Chris had one more surprise in store before the day was done. *What about seeing some baby seals?*

Eva's reaction was to squeal with delight. In her mind, there could be nothing more beautiful than a baby seal. She had seen some pictures in a book. But to see one in real life. *Could they? Would they? O yes, pleeese!!!*

And so, they headed for the Courtown Seal Sanctuary, also known as Seal Rescue Ireland. Eva could hardly contain her excitement as they entered through the gate and into the shop. She was briefly distracted by the soft toys (seals of all shapes and sizes among them) but when she was taken outside to the place where the seals were being treated and rehabilitated, she just hopped from one leg to the other in silence. She listened quietly as the girl giving the tour explained all about seal pups and how they were sometimes abandoned by their mums or storms knocked them about and they had to be rescued from the sea. Her eyes filled with tears when she saw Moss and Frangipani, Snapdragon and Eucalyptus. She couldn't believe such babies had no mama. When she went to the bigger pool and heard about the seals there that were getting ready to be sent home, she clapped her hands in delight but still she said nothing. Jane was getting a little worried since she'd expected Eva to ask all sorts of questions. 'Why?' was her favourite word of all but, no, Eva asked nothing at all, just stood silently gazing into the eyes of the seals, communing with them at a level adults could not possibly understand. As they were leaving, though, Eva let go of Jane's hand and ran over to the girl who had explained everything. She looked up at her and said in a very small voice:

'Thank you for looking after the baby seals!' Then, she turned on her heel and ran back to take Jane's hand again. They had left the premises and were almost back at the hotel before Eva spoke again.

'I was like those seals, you know. But now I'm back in my ocean with my mama and baba. I think the seals will find their mummies and daddies too, don't you?'

The two adults could only nod, too moved to trust themselves to speak. This was not a time for tears but for rejoicing. Eva was home and their quest was over. Almost.

When Eva had been handed back, reluctantly, to her parents, Chris finally broached a topic that he had meant to discuss for quite a while. In their joy at finding Eva, her parents had never mentioned that she had a slight disfigurement and it had seemed wrong, somehow, to draw attention to it. Now, however, Chris was on the point of leaving for good and he hadn't made the offer that had brought him half-way across the world. It was time to step up. As he and Jane stood awkwardly at the doorway of the hotel with Ismael, Eva having scampered up to her room with her mother, Chris cleared his throat and spoke.

'Ismael, forgive me for mentioning it but your daughter has a problem with her mouth, doesn't she?'

Ismael hung his head, a shadow clouding his eyes. A few moments passed before he could answer.

'To me, my daughter is perfect, Mr Chris. But I am aware that she has difficulties. I worry for her future.'

'I can imagine, Ismael. But, please, I bring up the subject not to cause you pain. I don't think I've mentioned it to you, but my job is one that may be able to help you. I am a surgeon. I specialised in children's surgery, specifically fixing problems like the one your daughter has. From what I've observed, she has what's called a unilateral cleft lip. It doesn't seem to affect her too much. She speaks well, her hearing is fine and she seems to be able to eat without too much difficulty. All she needs is an operation to improve the appearance of the lip. I would be very willing to offer my services if we can sort out the paperwork or to organise for someone here to do the operation. It is a relatively simple procedure, a night or two in the hospital, some follow up for the next few years. Would you be willing for me to do that, to arrange things for you?'

'Willing? Mr Chris, you are an answer to prayer. In my homeland, I had planned to do something, but life was always too unsettled to risk bringing

Eva to a hospital. I would appreciated any help to put things right here. Thank you.'

'Very well. I'll look into the details and we'll arrange it. Now, I guess Jane and I must take our leave. We head back to Cork in the morning so we won't see you for a while. I understand you are heading west?'

'Yes, that is correct. They have offered us a place where we can be a family again. It is wonderful news. It is all so wonderful.'

'We'll find out your address from Fr. Lonergan once you're settled.' This time it was Jane who spoke and, as she did so, she took Ismael's hand. 'Please know we will never forget you and Hanah and Eva. We will be in touch.'

'God's blessing on you both, Ms Jane and Mr Chris, and a very safe journey home.'

Home.

How good that word was sounding to both the Australian travellers. It was time for them to turn their thoughts to home, to heading back to Sydney and resuming their own lives. What an adventure it had been! What memories they had made together! Both were wondering, though, if that was all it was. Memories, a briefly shared past. But, what of a shared future? Now, that was a million-dollar question.

Chapter 45

The conversation at the dinner table at Isabel and Mike's Cork home revolved around the simple things of life: *nice weather, considering, mmm isn't this food delicious and what a lovely vino tinto*, the latter kindly provided by Fr. Lonergan. As he said, there were some advantages to travelling back and forth to Spain on a regular basis. When inviting the group, Isabel had decided to do a 'Christmas in July' type meal in honour of the Aussies at the table as well as to celebrate her father-in-law's recovery. She'd heard that that was a thing Down Under. True, it was now August but she didn't think that anyone would really care about that slight miss-timing. The occasion was proving to be surprisingly jolly with all the guests happy to be reunited and to be tucking in to such a delicious, if out of season, meal. There was turkey and gravy, stuffing and more gravy, brussels sprouts, peas, cranberry sauce, roast potatoes, gravy, and pumpkin followed by mince pies or trifle. A typical Irish spread (except perhaps for the pumpkin which Isabel had added, it being her favourite veggie). When everyone had eaten all they could (and then some), and had retired to the various sofas and armchairs in the living room, the topic came around to the question Jane had been both expecting and dreading.

'Well, you two, when do you head back to Australia?' Isabel's question was accompanied by various heads nodding and with muttered agreement. Everyone wanted to know their plans. Not really knowing what to say, Jane automatically looked to Chris who seemed equally at a quandary. Seeing that he wasn't answering, she tried to deflect by giving a vague response: 'I haven't given it much thought.' She hoped the lie wasn't too obvious. The truth was she hadn't been able to think of much else since they had returned to Cork. She knew she couldn't go on living in a monastery, no matter how welcoming Fr. Lonergan and the other friars had been. But neither did she relish returning to her empty unit in Sydney. It was bound to seem even emptier now that she had got used to so much company. The friars were a cheerful lot and always made her feel included in the fun. Who knew that a group of devout men had such a joyful take on the world? They witnessed the worst of human nature in the course of their work. They lived surrounded by poverty, abuse, neglect, gloom but that seemed to make them more determined to emphasise the best in people, their kindness, their stoicism, and their joy in the face of adversity. She had learnt a lot from them about patience, calmness, and the need to find joy in whatever you do. It would be hard to leave. But, if she were honest, that was not the main reason she had put off booking her flight back. And that reason was now sitting beside her on the sofa in Isabel's and Mike's living room. Chris!

Aware that silence had descended after her brusque answer, Jane found she needed to babble on with some kind of explanation.

'I've been so busy – well, not exactly busy – just so preoccupied – well, just trying to figure things out – you know how it is ...'

General laughter followed her words which confused her even more. Why were her friends, for that is what each person in this room was now, why were they laughing at her?

Fr. Lonergan, being the oldest there (he was a mere six months older that Tom Reilly but the younger man always rubbed it in!) felt he had to voice what everyone else was thinking – he was never a one to resist putting his foot in it – stepping in where angels fear to tread.

'What Isabel is asking is when you *and Chris* are flying home? You know, *together?*' More laughter rippled around the room, in recognition that the priest's question was exactly what everyone there wanted to know.

For the first time in many years, Jane felt herself blush. She couldn't bring herself to look at Chris but could feel him shifting uncomfortably on the sofa beside her. *Why doesn't he answer? Why can't he think of something clever to say? More to the point, why can't I?*

Again, laughter followed the question and Jane's reaction. She was beginning to feel angry at being the centre of such embarrassing attention.

'Sorry, Jane, I guess I shouldn't have been so blunt but you two really need a bit of a push. It's plain for all of us to see that you belong together – I've never seen a couple so much in tune. And none of us is prepared to see you off on your way to Sydney without making sure you do something about it. And, just to be clear, I *am* most definitely offering my services for the wedding.'

Both Jane and Chris froze on the spot, neither one willing to be the first to turn their head to look at the other. *How insensitive! How embarrassing! How very observant!*

Jane became aware that Chris had taken her hand in his, squeezing it with affection or, perhaps, he was attempting to hold her back in case she was planning to attack the kindly priest. Clearing his throat, Chris finally spoke:

'Now, Fr. Lonergan, you know I have the greatest respect for you. After all we've been through, I count you as one of my dearest friends. I would trust you with my life. So you'll take this in the spirit it is intended. *Mind your own business!*

More laughter as the message was received, loud and clear.

'Very well. I've done my best, lad. It's up to you now. Don't say you haven't been warned. If you let this fine woman escape, you only have yourself to blame.'

And with that, the party returned to relatively safer ground. There was a brief discussion of the investigation into the events in Courtown. Isabel was able to give them the good news that a trafficking ring had been broken up due to the arrests of the two individuals who had set fire to the cottage. The boss's accomplice had proven to be a mine of information and had given up the names and whereabouts of at least a dozen individuals (men and women) involved in the criminal network. A good job done with commendations in the pipeline for Tom, Isabel, Aiden, young Davis and, of course, Johnny too. The latter just shrugged his shoulders when the group tried to congratulate him – he didn't feel he deserved it. 'Just doing my job', was all they got out of him. Jane, having recovered somewhat from the previous unwanted attention, voiced one question that everyone at the table had been pondering since the events in Courtown:

'What I want to know is how a man like Lucas, a man who outwardly seemed so respectable, so aware of the horrors in the world, could get involved in such a despicable business?'

Her question was greeted with general nodding and agreement. Superintendent Reilly had a little more information to share on that score.

'From what we can gather, Lucas was suffering from PTSD due to his job as war correspondent, you know, post-traumatic stress. He had had a few narrow escapes plus had witnessed some horrific violence. His way of coping led him to a dependence on drugs and alcohol, first prescription drugs but, gradually, he started on harder stuff, street heroin, cocaine, anything he could get in the end. His income couldn't keep up with his addiction so he got involved with some unsavoury types and, once they get their hands on you, well, it's a life-time commitment. They started to put pressure on him to do things he, otherwise, would never have done and, unfortunately, providing them with access to children was one of those things.'

'Still, it seems an incredible leap. I mean what man *could* do such a thing and live with himself?'

'You're right, Jane. It's a terrible business, terrible.' Fr. Lonergan shook his head as if trying to rid himself of the horrors that had led Lucas to such a life of crime. 'It's beyond me to comprehend but, from what Magda was telling me, he hadn't been himself for quite a while. She knew there was something wrong, but she couldn't get him to talk about it. He shut her out. Couldn't admit, perhaps even to himself, how far he had sunk, I suppose. All very sad. I pray he's at rest now, for I do think he suffered a lot in the end.'

Silence met his words, the group divided in their thoughts of Lucas, some not quite as forgiving as the priest.

Within the hour, though still relatively early for an Irish party, people started to take their leave, aware of certain tensions in the air but promising to meet up again soon, hugging their goodbyes. Within minutes, Chris and Jane found themselves sharing a taxi back to St Francis Friary with Fr. Lonergan. To say the silence was awkward would be an understatement. Even the priest seemed, for once, to be at a loss for words though the smile on his face betrayed the fact that he was quite enjoying the others' discomfort. He was the first to alight when the taxi pulled up at its destination. However, as he turned to wait for the other two to join him on the footpath, he heard Chris give instructions to the driver.

'Driver, could you take us to a beach? Any one that's not too far outside of Cork will do. Jane, do you mind? I have a longing to get some sand between my toes and it's still fairly early in the evening.'

'No problem, I'd like that - must have been the Christmas cheer. I suddenly feel the need to see the ocean too.'

Fr. Lonergan could only watch in amusement from the pavement as the taxi pulled off again, its two passengers on a journey into the unknown.

Chapter 46

'The driver chose well.' Jane looked around her at Inchydoney beach, with its hotel in the background and the Celtic Sea in front of them, sending its waves crashing onto the sandy shore. It had taken them just thirty minutes to get there, time that had been spent in light conversation, talking about the scenery as town slowly transformed into countryside and the sun slowly descending in the summer sky, giving everything a twilight glow. Even though it was gone 11:00 pm, there was still a tiny bit of daylight left, enough to make out the shapes of houses in the countryside, the shop fronts as they passed through the small town of Clonakiltey, or Clon as it was affectionately known to its inhabitants. Now, they were both standing on the requested sand, facing the water, looking out towards a fading horizon, lights from passing ships flashing like starlight.

'Yes, he did. He certainly earned his tip.' Chris seemed a bit preoccupied as he stared into the distance. Jane tried to gauge his mood but, for once, he was giving very little away. She tried again to get his attention.

'Want to go for a paddle, Chris?'

'Sure.'

Both sat down to remove their sandals and then raced towards the shoreline, stopping in their tracks as the cold water lapped over their toes.

'Oh! Brr – My feet will never get used to this icy water! It's a shock to the system, that's for sure.'

'Bracing, yes, it is. Let's walk a bit, that might bring the circulation back to my big toes.'

Jane laughed but started walking, taking Chris's arm as if they had always walked together on the sand and glad that the cold water had seemed to do the trick as Chris seemed to have shaken himself out of his reverie.

After a few moments, Chris broke the silence, clearing his throat, Jane noted, as was his habit when he had something important to say.

'Jane?'

'Yes, Chris?'

'Jane. We've known each other just a few months now. Can you believe that?' Jane just shook her head.

'It's the end of August and we met in late May ...'

'Let's not go back there, Chris. Our first meeting should be erased from memory.'

'True, let's say we met in June – in Barcelona. Come to think of it, maybe we could erase that second meeting from memory too. What do you think?'

'No way. That was fun!'

'Maybe for you. But I bet I'm still on that waiter's watch list. He's probably telling people right now about that crazy man who tried to avoid paying his bill and had to have his carer rescue him.'

Jane's laughter could be heard over the sound of the waves lapping over their feet.

'Anyway, the point is, we really haven't known each other very long and yet it feels like an eternity.'

'I'm trying to take that in a good way, Chris – are you saying every moment you spend with me is looong?' Jane couldn't help adding to Chris's discomfort. Actually, she knew what he meant. She couldn't believe they had only been together for such a short time. He had become a big part of her life. She trusted him. She even found his jokes funny. She was comfortable in his presence and she knew, no matter what, he had her back.

'You know very well what I mean. I know you do. And that's just it, Jane. I know what you're thinking and you know what I'm trying to say before I even say it. We're good together. Much as I hate to admit it, Fr. Lonergan is right *again*. We just can't go our separate ways after sharing so much.'

'So what exactly are you saying, Chris. I know you say I know what you mean before you say it but, sometimes, a girl likes to hear the words.'

'Well, right then ... Here goes ... I'm asking if you will share the rest of my life with me? Will you, Jane? Will you marry me?'

Silence filled with the sound of waves. Then, the words he had been waiting for ...

'Yes, Chris, I will.'

Their kiss was gentle, warm, and tender. At first. The passion rose slowly, echoed by the crashing of waves. Two lost souls had finally found each other, and all the clichés suddenly made sense: love conquers all, time stands still, violins play the music of love... For some reason, Jane could hear the lyrics of Cher's song echo in her mind: *if you want to know...* If there had been any lingering doubts, they were now erased. This was meant to be and both knew they were loved.

They started to walk again, this time back towards the carpark and the hotel.

'I guess we'd better get back. The driver must be tired of waiting and the meter is running. It'll be an expensive night with such extravagance.'

'Ah, yes, about that, Jane. I took the decision to send him back to Cork earlier.'

'Oh, you did, did you? That was a little presumptuous of you. What if I'd said no!'

'Well, we'd just have had to wait for another taxi - or two. Awkward!'

'Ha! So, what are we to do now, then? I don't fancy waiting, even if we do get to share the cab. And, to be honest, I'm not in the mood for a night at the Friary ...'

'Me neither! But, as luck would have it, there's a hotel right over there. See!'

'Right. So there is.'

'What if we checked in?'

'I'm surprised you haven't booked a room already.'

'Ha! You know I'm not that organised.'

'True. But sometimes you do surprise me. Chris, dear Chris. Let's go and check in.'

'But, first, what about another kiss - just to make sure.'

...

'Any doubts?'

'Hmm - none whatsoever - come on, the future Mrs Nielson ...'

'I know one man who's going to be very happy about that.'

Both looked at each other and laughed, saying the name together.

'FATHER LONERGAN!'

Chapter 47

If the staff at Inchydoney Island Lodge and Spa were surprised to see two middle-aged lovebirds approach their reception desk with not a toothbrush between them, they didn't show it, being far too professional even to raise an eyebrow. To her dismay, Jane found herself blushing for the second time that night, so she was happy to let Chris take care of the paperwork. The room assigned to them had the most beautiful view but neither of them had any mind to notice. It was morning before they looked outside as the sun rose gently and light returned to bring warmth and colour to the landscape.

Tonight, though, was for discovery of a more intimate nature. They knew each other well as friends but now they would explore new sensations and feelings as lovers. Chris had thought love was gone when his wife had died. He had reconciled himself to a life of work and child-rearing. Jane had left love pass her by, absorbed in her job but never really fulfilled by it. Second chances. They were given this second chance and both were ready to grab it with both arms, to love, with all that meant. It was scary, exhilarating, totally absorbing, a rollercoaster of emotion. Neither was in the first flush of youth, both aware their bodies had seen better days. But love is blind and neither even noticed any flaws in the other and, miracle of miracles, the thought of their own flaws didn't really cross their minds for long. True, for a moment, Jane did wonder if Chris's professional eye would be distracted by her crows' feet, her wrinkles, the signs of her life lived.

'Chris?'

'Yes, Jane?'

'Does it bother you I'm old?'

'Old? What do you mean?'

'You know ... old ... I mean, you are a plastic surgeon, used to fixing faces and things. Are you thinking you should have agreed to fix mine?'

'Jane, I don't mean to be insensitive at a time like this but you can be really stupid sometimes.'

'Stupid? You'd best explain yourself...'

'Yes, stupid - I love every line and wrinkle, every nook and cranny, every bump and lump...'

'Hey! That's enough of that. I'm not exactly over the hill, anyway! Or no further over it than you are! So, forget I asked!'

'I will, now where were we? ... mmm ... let's see... I think I need to kiss that frown away...'

The night passed quickly, too quickly, and soon it was time to think of heading back to Cork. Breakfast had been enjoyed on the balcony. News of the two lovebirds must have travelled somehow for their room service breakfast had been accompanied by a bottle of champagne, complements of the house. They sat and ate and took in the views with not a care in the world. There was little need for words as both were lost in their thoughts. Finally, Chris put down his coffee cup with determination

'Right then, I guess we'd best organise a taxi to take us back to stern reality.'

'I suppose so - Oh Chris, I've just had a thought. How are we going to face all those Franciscans? And Fr. Lonergan?'

'Ah, yes, now there is a thought to be considered. You know, I suddenly feel like a teenager who has stayed out all night. We're in big trouble, aren't we?'

Jane giggled.

'Yes, sir, I believe we are. He's going to know everything when he sees your big grin.'

'*My* big grin. Have you seen your face in the mirror? You've a smile as big as the Cheshire cat's.'

'I *know*. I just can't help it. It comes from being happy.'

'Me too.' Chris smiled back at her. 'Well, we'll just have to face the music together. I don't suppose he'll mind too much, given his offer to perform the wedding ceremony. Now, there's something we haven't discussed. When do you think we should have it - and where?'

'Do you think Fr. Lonergan would travel to Sydney? I'd like to have it there - maybe in the summer. What about a Christmas wedding?'

'Great idea. We could invite all the gang - I'm sure Tom would be well enough to travel by then, and Isabel and Mike could come. And maybe we could persuade Johnny and Magda too. What do you think?'

'I don't think they'd take too much persuading. Oh, I'm getting quite excited now. It's a pity Ismael and Hanah couldn't bring Eva but I don't suppose they would have passports by then. Oh - I've just had another thought. What about your children? What will they think of their dad marrying someone else? Oh, Chris, they mightn't like it at all. What if they don't like *me*?'

'Jane, don't worry. They're good kids, they'll love you, I'm sure of it. Now, before I call a taxi, there's one thing I think we need to do.'

'What's that?'

'Come inside and find out.'

As Jane stood up to go inside, she found herself wrapped in Chris's arms He picked her up and carried her to the bed where love found them again and the sound of the waves provided the backing melody.

Chapter 48

When they arrived back at the Franciscan Friary, as luck would have it, the first person they met was the Reverend Father himself. Fr. Lonergan was coming out of the friary, just as the taxi pulled up, almost as if he had been standing there since the night before, awaiting their return.

'Well, look at you two. Is it now you're coming back? I can see from the grins on your faces that - well, how can I put it delicately - there have been developments?'

Chris laughed and nodded.

'You don't miss much, Father. And, since you bring up the subject, may we, that is Jane and I, may we book your services for December.'

'You mean - you mean you've gone and popped the question - and she said 'yes'? Wonderful news! Good man, good man. I was wondering if you'd ever get around to it.' The priest wiped a tear from his eye and then hugged both of them, clearly overjoyed at the news. 'And December you say, well, that gives me a bit of time to prepare. Where do you want to have the ceremony? I imagine it won't be here in Cork.'

'No, we'd like to invite you and the others to come and join us for a summery Christmas in Sydney. Do you think you'd get away? I know it's a busy time for the Church.'

'Wild horses wouldn't keep me away. I'll talk to the Prior. I'm sure he'll see sense - after all, if I didn't push you - gently now mind - you might never have got around to it. So, in a way, I'm responsible for making honest people out of you. That's bound to have some weight with the Prior. How can he refuse! And you say you're going to ask the others too. Well, won't that be some party. I can't wait. Now, come along in and have a cuppa with me. I was on my way into town for a few messages but I think that can wait. We can sort out a detail or two – I nearly said you can tell me all about it but, maybe, that's going a step too far. I know when to mind my own business – well, sometimes I do.'

The next few days where a whirl of preparations and celebrations. Isabel insisted on throwing a hen party for Jane while Mike and Tom sorted out a stag do of sorts for Chris. It all went a little pear shaped when both groups ended up in the same bar in town but great fun was had by all, including Fr. Lonergan who appeared in civvies (so as not to let the side down, he explained). Chris also had to face his long-neglected Aunty Louise. He hadn't contacted her in all the time he'd been in Cork as things had been so hectic. Now, he had time and inclination but he wasn't sure how she'd feel to find out he had been nearby and hadn't stayed with her. To soften the blow, he brought Jane with him. That, and the news of the impending wedding, won her over and soon she was talking and laughing with them both and planning her trip to Sydney at Christmas, having quite forgiven their previous neglect if not forgotten it entirely.

Added to all the merriment, the Aussies had to organise their flight home. Chris was eager to see his children. He had spoken with them of his plans but he couldn't really tell how they were feeling about it all over the video link. They had seemed quiet, pensive perhaps, but he hoped they would come around by the time he and Jane landed in Sydney.

All too soon, the day of departure arrived. Mike insisted on driving them to Cork Airport. From there, they would fly to Heathrow, then on to Singapore and, after a short stop of a couple of hours, they would be heading to Sydney. So many hours in a plane were never something to look forward to but, after the excitement of the last few days, they were both eager to sit still for a while. It would give them time to regroup.

There was quite a crowd to see them off at the airport. Unbeknownst to them, Fr. Lonergan had told Ismael and, along with Tom Reilly, they had organised to bring the whole family to Cork just to say goodbye. Jane couldn't believe her eyes when, as she turned away from the check-in desk, she saw the little girl coming bounding towards her.

'Jane, Jane. I'm here! We came to see you fly off home. And the big news is I'm to have an operation. They're going to fix my face. Baba says that Chris organised it all.'

Eva beamed up at Chris who nodded.

'Well, I made a few phone calls. I offered to do the operation but, when they heard in the hospital here that it was for such a special little girl as you, all the surgical team decided to give their time for free. So, you're in the best hands, little Eva. Be sure to send us a photo of your new smile, okay?'

Eva nodded excitedly and Jane thought that her new smile could never be any better than the one that was lighting up her face right now. She was exuding love and happiness, a testament to resilience.

'Thank you so much, Eva, for coming to see us. It means such a lot to hear your news. You must keep in touch with us and let us know all about your new life. Will you do that?'

'I will! I will! Baba says he can call you on a video thing so we can see each other lots too. Isn't that right, Baba? *And* Baba says that you and Chris are getting *married!*' Eva squealed with delight as she said that last word. '*Married!* She said it again as if savouring the very idea. 'I want lots of pictures, okay?' Ismael answered as he could see Jane's composure was beginning to crack.

'Yes, my love, we will keep in touch with our good friends and I am sure they will send you lots of photographs of their big day.'

Turning to those friends, he continued.

'You can be sure we will always keep you in our hearts. And, God willing, we will meet again.' At that he nodded and backed away, allowing room for the other excited well-wishers to take their leave. Isabel, Mike, and

Tom all hugged the travellers, followed by Hanah who, with tears in her eyes, kissed Jane's hand and whispered, '*Thank you again, my friend!*' That just left Fr. Lonergan who seemed quite overcome. He was dabbing his face with an over-sized handkerchief, wiping away the copious tears that he was struggling to hide. Jane gave him a big hug and kissed him on both cheeks.

'Father Lonergan, don't take on so! We'll be meeting again in a few months, you know.'

'Yes, I *know*. I don't know what's come over me. I'm quite overcome. I think the events of the last couple of months are catching up with me – that or old age.'

'Now, Jim, you never age a day, for as long as I've known you. You're still the same as you were back in the day – must be all that travelling you do!' Tom was amused at his friend's emotional outburst, amused though not surprised for Fr. Jim was never one to be understated. Everyone laughed, including Fr. Jim, his tears turning quickly to ones of merriment.

'Well, everyone, it's time we headed through security. We hope we'll see most of you at the wedding. And we certainly will send those photos to you, Eva, you can count on it.' Chris started to head upstairs to the departure lounge, steering Jane who was trying to get one last look at all her friends, as if she were etching each face in her mind. She would never forget any one of them, though there was an extra special place in her heart for little Eva.

There was a last little scurry of farewells, waving and wishes for a safe trip and, finally, Chris and Jane were alone. There was little to report about the journey itself. All went to plan with no delays, no setbacks, no last-minute hurdles to overcome. All was routine, long, tedious, mind-numbing routine that faded into oblivion once the lights of Sydney came into view and the end of the journey was in sight. Without a word, the two travellers gathered their belongings and followed the other passengers off the plane, into the brightly lit corridors and passageways of Kingsford Smith airport, both remembering their separate journeys in the opposite direction just a few short months before. They ignored the duty-free shops that were open for custom and headed straight to the automated passport control machines and then to the carrousel to collect their luggage, Chris stopping to get a trolley along the way. *Thank heavens they changed the system and you didn't need a coin anymore. It was always a struggle to find one at this end. Good old Aussies, sense usually prevails in the end.* Chris was busy feeling very patriotic, a warm feeling of coming home washing over him.

Jane's feelings, however, were a lot less mundane and she was the first to break the silence, voicing fears that were growing now that they were so close to the end of the trip.

'Chris?'

Chris was still distracted, lost in his own home-coming thoughts and busy watching for their bags, finding it hard to concentrate given how tired out he felt from so many hours of inertia, so he didn't really notice that worried expression on her face.

'Chris!'

'Hmm? What? Do you recognise a bag?'

'No, not yet. That's not the problem.'

'Problem? Is there a problem?' Chris's dazed expression was really beginning to irritate his fellow traveller.

'Oh Chris! Would you stop looking at the carrousel for one minute? The bags haven't even started coming out yet. It takes ages, you know.'

'Oh, right. Sorry. What's wrong?'

'Well, I'm just wondering what we do now?'

'What do you mean?'

'You *know* what I mean – what do we *do*?'

'Well, I for one am going home, having a nice, hot shower and a nap.'

'Oh, right!'

From her tone, Chris realised he had said something wrong, and it took a few moments for him to realise what that might be.

'Oh, I see. I meant a nap – with you! A shower too if you fancy it though my energy levels are a bit low.'

Jane punched him in the ribs, her exasperation finally boiling over.

'You are incorrigible. That's not what I meant – well, not exactly. I mean the nap would be nice though you can forget the shower. I'm tired too. No, what I meant is – will your kids be outside to meet you? I know you told them our news but you didn't really tell me how they took it. They might not want to meet me straight away, you know.'

Chris thought a bit about that.

'Well, let's play it by ear. I'm not sure they'll be meeting me. I did tell them the flight number and that but we didn't make any real arrangements. I figure it's a bit early in the day for Andy. He likes a bit of a lie in and he only sees 6 am from the other side... you know, if he's been out partying. Sophie, on the other hand, is a lark but even she might have difficulty making it to the airport at this hour. So, all in all, the likelihood is they'll wait for me at home. I'll send a message when we get through customs, tell them to expect us both, right?'

'Maybe it would be best if I went home to my own place for now. Let you have your own homecoming with the kids alone. Then, maybe later today, or better, tomorrow, we can arrange a meeting. What do you think?'

'If you feel that's best, we'll do that. Maybe you're right. It'll give them time to get used to the idea.'

'Exactly. Right, that's settled then. Oh, look, I think that's my bag hurtling along the conveyor belt now. I'll grab that while you grab that other one that looks like it's yours.'

A few minutes later they had got through customs, helped by the fact that they had nothing to declare. They headed out through the doors separating travellers from those waiting for their arrival. Despite the early hour, there was quite a crowd, all in high excitement, with balloons and signs being waved in all directions. Chris had quite a task to negotiate a way through with the trolley and almost crashed into his own son before he realised that it was Andy. And, there, just behind him, was Sophie.

'Dad! Dad! You're here! We missed you, Dad. It's so good to have you back home.'

The pair were bestowing hugs and kisses on their father in a way they hadn't done since they were little.

'I should go away more often if this is the welcome I get. Great to see you too. I swear, Andy, you've grown another bit. You're taller than me now. How did that happen? And, Sophie, wow, you are the spitting image of your mother. So beautiful.'

They were an entanglement of affection and love, so much so that Jane, a few steps behind Chris, was not sure what to do. She considered slipping quietly by, in the hope that her presence wouldn't be noticed, not wanting to intrude, and also embarrassed and feeling very shy. *What if they don't like me?*

As she hesitated, trying to make up her mind how to escape, and wondering if she could take her bag from the trolley without being seen, she became aware that three pairs of eyes were watching her in amusement, her indecision plain to see. Andy was the first to break away from the family group.

'Jane? You must be Jane, Dad sent us a photo. Hello.'

'Hello, Andy, isn't it? He showed me photos of you too, lots of photos. He's very proud of you both.'

Sophie approached next, her eyes dancing with excitement.

'Hello from me too. Do you mind if I hug you?' She didn't wait for an answer, throwing herself at Jane with Andy quickly joining in.

'Can I join you lot?' Chris launched himself into the group hug and, then, when it was mutually decided that there had been enough hugging, just for now, the foursome headed out to the carpark.

'Oh Dad, there's just one think we have to explain before you get home...'

'Uh oh! What have you done, Andy? Have you scratched the car? Bumped the side panels? Burnt down the house? What? Tell me the worst.'

'No, it's nothing like that. Well, you see, we missed having you around and Sophie met this vet who works at the practice in Avalon. You tell him, Sophie.'

Everyone turned to look at Sophie who was throwing murderous glances at her brother.

'Go on, Sophie. I'm getting worried now. Tell me what's happened.'

'Andy, you're dead! Dad, it's not that bad, not really. You see, as Andy was saying, I met this woman, a vet. Her name's Ana and she's a friend of a friend of mine who does some volunteering at the Zoo. You remember Jackie, Dad?' Seeing her father was getting even more impatient, Sophie decided to cut to the chase. 'Anyway, that's not important, what *is* important is that, well, Ana does some volunteer work at an animal rescue centre, and they were looking for people to adopt some puppies a few weeks back. Well, not exactly puppies. They were two- years old and no one wanted them. You see, they were greyhounds and, well, they weren't the fastest on the track so they were going to be put down. Can you believe that, Dad?' Not waiting for an answer, she went on. 'Well, she asked everyone she knew if they knew anyone who would adopt one. So Jackie asked me and, well, I said yes, that we'd look after one until you came home. I didn't say we'd keep her but we will, won't we, Dad? Jane, you tell him. We'll all look after the poor thing. She'll be no problem at all.'

With that, they had arrived at the car. Chris remained silent as they stowed the luggage and he got into the driving seat. Finally, aware of three pairs of eyes staring at him, trying to gauge his thoughts, he spoke:

'Well, let's just get home. I'm too tired to make any decisions right now. I'm sure Jane feels the same. Are you both okay if she stays with us for a while?'

Sophie and Andy nodded in response, slightly disappointed at their father's lack of enthusiasm for what they had already begun to consider a member of their family. They crossed their fingers that the dog would cast a spell on him as she had done on them.

Finally, they arrived outside their home and Sophie ran to open the front door. Lying patiently just inside was the leggiest bundle of joy Jane had ever seen, fast asleep on the floor. It was love at first sight. At least between Jane and Cassie, for that was the name of the dog who, on opening its sleepy eyes, gave a wide yawn, stood up, wagged her tail, and bounded straight into Jane's arms, or tried to, given she was no longer a puppy but a leggy bundle of fun.

'Wow, she really likes you, Jane.' Andy's smile couldn't have got any wider. 'See, Dad, she's got good taste. You can't say no, now.'

Chris looked around at the three most important people in his life and knew he was well and truly outnumbered.

'Clearly, I have no vote. Yes, she can stay but only if Jane can too. What do you say?'

Nothing needed to be said for Andy and Sophie just nodded and grinned their agreement. As for Jane, she was busy getting her face licked by the newest member of the Nielson family and, had she had a tail as long as Cassie's, it would have been wagging just as hard.

Chapter 49

The day of the wedding promised to be a scorcher. 40 degrees centigrade was the estimated high to be reached in Western Sydney. Here on the Beaches, it would be a relatively cool top of 35. Blue skies, sparkling sea, a light breeze. A perfect December day with no sign of the smoke that had been lingering over the city recently, a sign of the bush fires that were raging throughout Australia this summer. The talk of all Sydneysiders these days was of the threat to properties, to stock and wildlife and how the Firies, as the fire fighters were affectionately called, were doing it tough. Every now and then, you could see people looking upwards to the skies, clearly wondering whether it would rain in the next few days or weeks. They were not to know that the worst fire season on record was in store for them in the coming months, when many lives, human and animal, would be lost to the scorching flames.

In the Nielson household, however, no one was the slightest bit aware of the outside world today. It was disorganised chaos and had been for weeks now. Jane had all but moved in and was in the process of selling up her old home on the other side of the city. Cassie, the greyhound, had been busy making her mark all over the house, literally and figuratively but, for all his grumbling, Chris had become very fond of the dog. He'd never admit it aloud but his actions spoke louder than words. He was the one who fed her and took her for long walks along the seashore. Jane would go with them in the evening and, sometimes, even the kids would volunteer. To be fair, Sophie had taken on board cleaning duties and she was chief poo collector while Andy did bath time. Visits to the vet had become a regular occurrence, given that the dog was filled with curiosity about every new thing in her world and had no great sense of fear. Ana, the vet, and Jane had become quite good friends, given the circumstances.

Today, though, Cassie was on her best behaviour, proudly sporting a red bow in honour of the occasion. The other girls in the family, Sophie and Jane, were busy upstairs, beautifying themselves for the ceremony that would take place in the afternoon. Downstairs, the menfolk were pretending it was just another day, or at least trying to. In that group were Chris, of course, along with Mike and Tom Reilly who had flown in the previous day, and Johnny Fitzpatrick who had arrived a few weeks before. He had taken extended leave from the *Gardaí Síochana*, and he and Magda were sailing around the world. The *Aisling* was presently moored at Newport while they decided where to head next. There was some disagreement as to whether to head north towards Queensland or across the Tasman Sea to Tasmania. No doubt they would make a decision in due course. For now, Johnny and Magda were content to be with their friends in Sydney and attend what they had named the wedding of the century. Magda and Isabel were out shopping for last minute items. They had insisted that Jane keep the tradition of *Something old, something new, something borrowed and something blue,* so were scouring the local shops for anything that would fit the bill.

Fr. Lonergan, too, had arrived the previous day, having flown in with the others. He was looking around the local church to get what he called the lay of the land. The religious ceremony was to be held there, a blessing, followed by a reception back at the house though 'reception' was a bit of a glamorous term for what was planned. They had thought to have a simple barbecue, as neither Jane nor Chris felt in the mood for anything very elaborate. Keep life simple. That's what they planned to do from now on. In any case, they were so happy at how things had turned out just now, they didn't want to be extravagant in case they attracted the attention of the gods or the universe or whoever or whatever was in charge. They feared that this new happiness might have been a mistake, some fortunate glitch in the universal plan. Not that either said that aloud but both knew how the other felt. However, given the total fire ban, a barbecue was now out of the question. Food would have to be prepared in the house and brought outside. And, in any case, many of the guests would bring extra edible contributions of the usual sort: salads, pavlovas, lamingtons, trifles and sponge cakes and all kinds of meat dishes, not to mention drinks, both alcoholic and juices. There would be no scarcity along those lines.

As the hour approached to head to the church, Jane was beginning to feel butterflies gather in great numbers in her tummy. It wasn't that she was having second thoughts but, rather, that she felt things had moved at an extraordinarily fast pace. She wasn't sure that the children had had time to assimilate all the changes. To that end, alone in the bedroom with Sophie, she decided it was time to have a talk with the younger girl, to make sure there was no lingering resentment. In the time since landing back in Sydney and this December day, she had grown very fond of her future stepdaughter and she thought the feeling was mutual but they had never had a proper, grown-up chat.

'Sophie, could you come and sit here beside me for a moment?'

'I'm just ironing this handkerchief for Dad ...'

'That can wait just a moment. I wanted to talk with you, Sophie.' As the girl sat down on the bed, Jane continued:

'I wanted to thank you for being so welcoming since I arrived with your father. It can't have been easy. I'm very conscious how much you loved your mother – of how much your father loved her – and loves her still. I just want you to know that I don't expect to take her place or expect you ever to forget her, even for a day. She is always with you, in your heart, and you need never be afraid to talk about her or speak her name.'

There were tears in Sophie's eyes as she looked at Jane but there was also a smile on her face.

'Oh, dear Jane, you're right. Mum is definitely here today and I think she's happy. Happy that Dad is happy again at last. You don't know what he was like in the years after she died. He was so involved in his work, grumpy nearly all the time. He never seemed to listen when we tried to talk to him. Oh, don't get me wrong. He did his best to be a good dad – took me and

Andy away for day trips and the like, made sure we had everything we needed but we both knew he was lonely and sad. It was hard to get close to him. It was like he kept pushing us both away. It's just so great to see him now. He's always laughing, telling jokes, talking about his time in Spain and Ireland. Anyone can see that he is content and – well – he's in love again.'

'And you don't mind?'

'Mind? I'm absolutely delighted! It's so great he's got you. You're good for him, Jane. You keep him from getting too arrogant – you know how surgeons are, they sometimes think they're gods – or at least divinely inspired. You don't let him get away with that. Mum was the same – and he needs that grounding. He likes it though he'd never admit it. You know something, Jane? I think Mum sent you to save him. Yes, I do. And Andy feels the same. We've talked about it a lot – serendipity, that's what got you two together and, without you, there's no way we'd have got to keep Cassie, or, if we did, he wouldn't have got so involved with her – so, all in all, things couldn't be better.'

'Whew, that's so kind of you, Sophie. I feel much better now. And, as I said, I don't want to take your mum's place in any way but, maybe we could be friends. If you ever need anyone to talk to, I'm here.'

At that, Jane leaned over and gave her new daughter a hug, thinking how strange life was. She'd left Australia in search of a little girl, thinking that she might need a substitute mum and here she was sitting with a young woman who was just starting her adult life and who might, in time, consider her a mum of sorts. How wonderful life could be! How very unpredictable!

Meanwhile, in the garden, preparations were well underway to host the guests on their return from church. The lawn had been mown to within an inch of its life, the pool was decorated with floating lights, jasmine plants lined the fence, and garlands were hanging on every available tree branch. Tables had been set up all around with white cloths and napkins, silver cutlery, crystal wine glasses and porcelain plates. It might be a simple indoor/outdoor barbie, of sorts, but that didn't mean a little luxury wasn't permitted. Andy was overseeing everything, or, at least, that was the plan. Right now, he was standing alone in the middle of the garden, lost in thought. His father, entertaining some of the early guests in the living room, spotted his son and, making his excuses, went out to speak to him.

'Hey there, Andy. A penny for your thoughts?'

'I was just remembering all the cool barbecues we used to have on that old thing over there.' Andy pointed to a rusty old barbecue that was stashed in one corner of the garden. It had certainly seen better days.

'We certainly did have good times, you, your sister, Mum and me.'

'Well, yes. But I was thinking that sometime soon, we've got to invest in one of those new shiny barbecues, Dad. You know the ones - they have loads of them in *Bunnings*.'

'Yea, you're right. I've just never got around to it - I bought that one with your mum years back, before you were even born, if I remember rightly. Never really felt like throwing it out.'

'Well, Dad, maybe the time has come. You should put it out in the next council clear up - the barbecue and maybe a few other bits and pieces. You know, make some room for Jane's things. It can't be easy for her moving into your house. She needs to put her own stamp on things.'

'Andy, when did you become so wise? It seems only the other day you were wobbling around here on your little tricycle, afraid you'd fall off. Now, look at you, giving your old dad some very sound advice.'

Andy grinned at his father.

' 'Bout time you noticed, Dad. I'm all grown up. And talking about that, I've been thinking I could go on my own adventure this summer. How'd you feel if me and the guys went on a bit of a road trip? Just around the red centre for a few weeks before Uni starts.'

'Uni - you mean university? Are you telling me you plan to go back to studying?'

'Yea, Dad. I've done a lot of thinking and I'm a bit fed up of doing casual work, hopping from job to job. I've enjoyed the freedom but, now, I think I'd like to study political science - learn a bit about international law, conflict resolution, that sort of thing. After your experiences in Spain and what you've told me about Eva and her family, I'd really like to be part of the solution. And, while you were away, I sent in my application. I should hear shortly if I've been accepted.'

'Wow, Andy. You never cease to surprise me. You know, your mother would be so proud of you. And so am I, so very proud.' The two men hugged before turning their attention back to the job at hand, the wedding.

'Well, son, I think my work is done here. I'd better go get changed. You too - who's going to watch the food that's cooking in the kitchen while we're in the church, by the way? We can't let it here without supervision. The house might burn down! Not to mention what Cassie might get up to.'

'I *know*, Dad. I've asked my friend, Kieran, to stay behind. He'll keep an eye on things. He won't let Cassie rob any of the steaks or sausages.'

'Great. I shouldn't have even asked. Now, let's get going. I don't want to be late for my own wedding.'

Epilogue

When Jane arrived at the church, her breath was taken away by the sea of friendly faces she glimpsed in the congregation. She was wearing a simple white, knee-length dress with primroses embroidered along the floating hem. What was commonly known as a fascinator that kept with the primrose theme adorned her head and her bouquet was a mixture of wildflowers. Magda and Isabel had come back from their shopping with the iconic blue garter which Magda said, with a mysterious smile hovering on her lips, she could have on loan. Perhaps, she implied, the said garter could well be needed again in the not-too-distant future. So that covered both the something blue and the something borrowed. For new, Chris had given her a beautiful opal necklace and the old was covered by a lace handkerchief that Jane's own mother had given her, a beloved possession embroidered many years ago in Spain by Jane's great-grandmother who had gifted it to her daughter the night before her trip to Australia.

Tom Reilly had been asked to step in to 'give the bride away' since Jane's own father had died so long ago. Tom had been practising his walking for weeks. The request had been just the incentive he needed to throw himself into physio so that, now, four months after the shooting, there was not the slightest trace of his previous instability caused by that bullet that had threatened his life.

As well as her friends from Spain and Ireland – Magda and Johnny, Isabel and Mike, and even Yasmina who had brought along her new boyfriend, Max – all her friends from her previous work had turned out in their finest. On her return, she had informed her employers that she was giving up the job for good. She and Chris had big plans involving travel overseas and children in rescue centres. *MSF* had contacted Chris asking if, rather than working in the Mediterranean, he'd be willing to visit various different locations where his surgical skills could be put to good use. He'd remain based in Sydney but would be 'on call', so to speak, to head to any crisis location when he was needed. After consulting with Jane, he had wholeheartedly agreed. Jane, too, was planning on a change of career. She was going to turn her attention to the migrant crisis in Australia and find a place where she could put her skills to work; her vast legal knowledge, plus her linguistic skills, would come in very useful in the task ahead. Jorge's words still echoed in her head: *Why come all this way to do something that you could do nearer home?* Why indeed! Their lives, as they had hoped that day in May, had changed forever but not in the way they had thought. While they were right back where they had started, Eva, the little girl they had first seen on the News, had given them the best gift of all: In their quest to find her, they had found each other. There would be challenges ahead but, for now, though, Jane was determined she would enjoy every moment of this day and celebrate with all the people who were important to her, some who had been in her life for so many years, others whom she had only met a few short months ago. Besides her old friends and colleagues, she could see her newest friend, Ana, Cassie's vet, was also in the church, along with her husband, Jaime, her two brothers, Peter and Joe, and her parents, Rose and Alex who happened to be in Sydney for the Christmas holidays. Near the front were Chris's parents, down from the country. The old Doc looked quite bemused by all the fuss whilst, sitting beside him, Chris's mother kept wiping away a tear, happy and sad at the same time as she remembered the last time she had seen her second son get married. The two parents were surrounded by their other children, Chris's two brothers and two sisters, with their partners and children making up the rest of the Nielson clan. And, finally, completing that clan was Chris's elderly Aunty Louise who was sitting proudly in the second pew beside her husband and grown-up daughters, all feeling the heat but excited at this turn of events that had given them the excuse to escape the cold winter back home in Cork, at least for a week or two.

Jane's mother, too, was in the church, sitting across the aisle from the older Nielsons. She looked proud and happy and, Jane couldn't help thinking, relieved that her daughter was finally getting married. She had given up all hope long ago, and now she had, to her great joy, gained not just a son-in-law but two grandchildren as well. Sally's parents had also been invited but had declined, wishing Chris well but too elderly now to make the trip to Sydney. Chris had promised that they would all visit them in the New Year. Last but not least, there was one more person without whom the wedding party could not be complete and that was Katie, the woman who had helped to unruffle Jane's feathers just a few short months before and had stood by Chris for so many years, his receptionist-cum-right-hand woman without whom he could not have coped in the years following Sally's death. She, Katie, was resplendent in her new outfit, purchased specifically for the occasion: a lavender jacket plus matching dress, matching shoes and a hat that would have won a prize on Ladies' day at the Melbourne Cup. She was as proud as punch as she sat waiting for the ceremony to begin, glad that 'her' Chris had found happiness again and that she had been there at the first meeting of the bride and groom. She liked to think that what had seemed an inauspicious beginning had, in fact, been filled with sparks and that she had *known* they were meant to be. A true romantic at heart was Katie!

Jane looked around at all her friends, both new and old, and felt a wave of contentment wash over her. That contentment grew to utmost joy when she looked ahead towards the altar and saw Fr. Lonergan standing there waiting for her, a broad smile adorning his chubby face. And, to his left, Chris, her Chris, her future husband. Beside him was his son Andy, bursting with pride at being his father's best man. Jane looked to her own right, to where Tom was waiting for her to give the signal. Seeing her smile, he nodded to Sophie, serious today in her role as bridesmaid, who, on cue, started to walk slowly up toward her father, following the bride and her stand-in father-figure. Jane's thoughts, as she walked in time with the music that played gently in the background, turned to Sally, Chris's first wife and, with a feeling of gratitude and affection toward the woman she had never met, she said in a whisper:

Thank you, Sally, I promise I will take very good care of them for you.

Whether it was her imagination or just the wedding music playing in the background, Jane was certain that, in response, she heard the distinct sound of an angel singing.

A. L. Walsh, Cork, 2023

http://www.annelwalsh.com